Critical Acclaim and Appreciation for

THE ORIGINAL FRANKENSTEIN

"Charles Robinson, more finely tuned to the authorship of *Frankenstein* than any scholar living or dead, has produced two versions of Mary Shelley's prepublication manuscript: as she first wrote it, then as it was marked with Percy's additions and alterations. With as much certainty and in as much detail as superhumanly possible, Robinson reanimates the beginnings of this vibrant novel in an authoritative, smartly accomplished, reader-friendly edition that will delight its fans no less than it will stimulate its students. An original work of imagination itself, *The Original Frankenstein*, by illuminating the genesis of this novel, is now an invaluable part of its intriguing editorial history."

—Susan J. Wolfson, Professor of English, Princeton University; President, Association of Literary Scholars and Critics

"Mary Shelley's *Frankenstein* was famously inspired by telling ghost stories with Percy Bysshe Shelley and Lord Byron during a cold, wet summer in the Swiss Alps. It continues to serve as shorthand for the dangers of reckless scientific advance, yet literary historians have never been able to agree on its origins. Could Mary Shelley, an unpublished 18-year-old, really have written the novel? Or was Frankenstein's monster her future husband's creation? . . . Charles E. Robinson presents a convincing case for crediting the novel to 'Mary (with Percy) Shelley,' revealing the major changes PBS made to Mary's first draft. . . . The novel the Shelleys wrote together represents a remarkable act of literary homage and collaboration and Charles E. Robinson's revealing new edition allows modern readers to be there at its creation."

—*The Independent* (London)

"The novel's textual instability is explored in the impressive introduction to Charles Robinson's new edition. His honourable aim is not to give us another text of the novel we know—or think we know—but to strip away nearly two centuries of revision and appropriation in order to return to what he describes as the 'original' *Frankenstein*. . . . The value of Charles Robinson's edition lies in the confirmation of Mary Shelley's assertion . . . that 'Every thing must have a beginning'—and that beginnings matter—and in its affirmation of community, cooperation and collaboration as fundamental to literary production."

—*The Times Literary Supplement* (London)

"Thanks to the dogged textual work of Charles E. Robinson . . . readers will now be able to see for themselves what Mary wrote before she turned it over to Percy's editorial ministrations. . . . [This] version of the novel . . . probably comes as close as it's possible to get to the draft that Mary first handed Percy to read." —*The Chronicle of Higher Education*

THE ORIGINAL FRANKENSTEIN

Edited by Charles E. Robinson

Charles E. Robinson is a professor of English at the University of Delaware. He has published and lectured extensively on the English Romantic writers, especially Byron and the Shelleys. His books include *Shelley and Byron: The Snake and Eagle Wreathed in Fight*; *Mary Shelley: Collected Tales and Stories*; *Mary Shelley's Proserpine and Midas*; and *The Frankenstein Notebooks*.

Mary Shelley was born in 1797, the daughter of political philosopher William Godwin and feminist Mary Wollstonecraft. At sixteen Mary began a romance with poet Percy Bysshe Shelley (1792–1822), marrying him in 1816 after the suicide of Percy Shelley's first wife, Harriet. *Frankenstein: or, The Modern Prometheus*, Mary Shelley's most famous work, was first published in 1818. In 1822, Percy drowned in a sailing accident off the coast of Italy. Mary published a number of other novels in addition to short stories, biographies, and travel writings and also devoted herself to editing and promoting the works of her husband. She died at the age of fifty-three in 1851.

FRANKENSTEIN

or

THE MODERN PROMETHEUS

Frankenstein

Chapter 7th

It was on a dreary night of November that I beheld ~~the frame on whic~~ my man compleated, ~~and~~ with an anxiety that almost amounted to agony I collected instruments of life around me ~~and endeavoured to~~ that I might infuse a spark of being into the lifeless thing that lay at my feet. It was already one in the morning, the rain pattered dismally against the window panes & my candle was nearly burnt out, when by the glimmer of the half extinguished light I saw the dull yellow eye of the creature open. It breathed hard, and a convulsive motion agitated its limbs.

~~But how~~ How can I describe my emotion at this catastrophe, or how deliniate the wretch whom with such infinite pains and care I had endeavoured to form. His limbs were in proportion and I had selected his features ~~&~~ as ~~handsome~~ ~~handsome~~ beautiful. ~~Handsome~~ Beautiful; Great God! His ~~dun~~ yellow skin scarcely covered the work of muscles and arteries beneath; his hair was of a lustrous black & flowing and his teeth of a pearly whiteness but ~~these~~ luxuriances only ~~formed~~ formed a more horrid contrast with his watry eyes ~~that~~ that seemed almost of the same colour as the dun white sockets in which they were set,

FRANKENSTEIN

or

THE MODERN PROMETHEUS

The Original Two-Volume Novel of 1816–1817
from the Bodleian Library Manuscripts

by

Mary Wollstonecraft Shelley

(with Percy Bysshe Shelley)

edited by
CHARLES E. ROBINSON

VINTAGE CLASSICS
Vintage Books
A Division of Random House, Inc.
New York

FIRST VINTAGE CLASSICS EDITION, SEPTEMBER 2009

Originally published in hardcover in the United Kingdom by the Bodleian Library, Broad Street, Oxford OX1 3BG, in 2008.

Following a period of loan-deposit, the *Frankenstein* manuscripts were purchased by the Bodleian Library in 2004 as part of the Abinger collection, with the generous support of the National Heritage Memorial Fund and of other institutional and private donors.

Illustration shelfmarks: frontispiece, [Abinger] Dep. c. 477/1, fol. 21r; p. 38, [Abinger] Dep. c. 534/1, fol. 94r; p. 254, [Abinger] Dep. c. 477/1, fol. 20v; pp. 430–31, Arch. AA e.167/1.

The Cataloging-in-Publication Data is on file at the Library of Congress.

Vintage ISBN: 978-0-307-47442-1

www.vintagebooks.com

Printed in the United States of America

For Nanette

Contents

Acknowledgements

In 1996 I published the two-volume Garland edition of *The Frankenstein Notebooks*, which reproduced and transcribed the Bodleian manuscripts of Mary Shelley's novel for a scholarly audience interested in the minutiae of the Draft and Fair Copy of *Frankenstein*. In the acknowledgements to that edition, I used the final two paragraphs to thank Dr Bruce C. Barker-Benfield, Senior Assistant Librarian at the Department of Special Collections and Western Manuscripts at the Bodleian Library, for his invaluable assistance. Here, in these first two paragraphs, I state that neither the 1996 edition nor this new 2008 text of the novel would have been possible without his extraordinary assistance. He was responsible for the Bodleian inviting me to undertake this new edition, and he selflessly sacrificed hours, indeed days, to advise me on every thing from the title page to the formatting of this new and 'original' two-volume version of *Frankenstein*.

Once again, Barker-Benfield and I consulted in person and by email and phone to determine which letters and words and cancel lines in the Draft manuscript were penned by Mary or by Percy Shelley. Those who have worked with the original Shelley manuscripts know that there is a different 'ductus' and shape to the words and letters penned by the two Shelleys; consequently, their hands for the most part can be separately identified—especially in any place where one or the other wrote multiple words in a phrase or sentence. But some single letters or single words (such as 'in' or 'it') or short cancel lines are difficult to identify as by Mary's or Percy's hand. Nevertheless, I am confident that this edition, which distinguishes Percy's words from Mary's by a different font, properly indicates which Shelley penned which parts of the manuscript Draft. (Carefully studying once again the shape of each of approximately 70,000 words in the manuscript Draft—and further attending to evidence of ink shade and density, of pen nib, and of offset ink blots—has enabled us to refine and in some cases change a few of the attributions presented in *The Frankenstein Notebooks.*) Although advised by Barker-Benfield, I am the one who takes responsibility for the attributions in this edition.

I am also greatly indebted to my wife Nanette, who not only supported my undertaking this edition but also tirelessly read typescripts of both novels (what are denominated *1816-1817 MWS/PBS* and *1816-1817 MWS*) against images of the Draft manuscript. Reading aloud word for word and comma for comma, we were able to discover new things about the manuscript. Indeed, Nanette is the one responsible for identifying Mary Shelley's neologism 'unrable' (see note 57).

Two other Mary Shelley scholars need particular mention here: Nora Crook, who was always willing to answer a question or to counsel me about the Introduction to this edition; and Betty T. Bennett, whose monumental work on Mary Shelley has so benefited contemporary scholarship. I was pleased to tell Betty about the possibility of this new edition a few days before she died in August 2006—and she was pleased for me. I honour her memory here.

I must also mention the influence of Donald H. Reiman, who as general editor of *The Bodleian Shelley Manuscripts* has made so many Percy and Mary Shelley manuscripts available for scholarly research. Other Mary Shelley and *Frankenstein* scholars and editors whose work has benefited this edition are named below in the two lists of Abbreviations and Bibliography. Unnamed are the countless undergraduate and graduate students to whom I have taught *Frankenstein* since 1965—and from whom I have learned so much about the subtleties of the novel.

Shelley studies of course owe a great debt to the staff of the Bodleian Library at Oxford University, especially Mr Hodges and others who oversee Duke Humfrey's Library, where the numerous manuscripts of Mary and Percy Shelley and their circles are housed. The Frankenstein Notebooks have been especially preserved and made available for future consultation by Robert Minte and Charlotte McKillop-Mash.

Closer to home, I wish to thank the English Department, the Center for International Studies, and the Commission on the Status of Women—all at the University of Delaware—for financially supporting my travel to Oxford in order to consult the manuscripts once again. As always, I am indebted to the University of Delaware Library for its extraordinary collection of primary and secondary materials—and electronic databases—that make my research on Mary Shelley and the Romantics possible.

I finally wish to express my gratitude to Samuel Fanous, the Publisher at the Bodleian Library, for his faith in me and in this edition, which he initiated by an 'out of the blue' email back in July 2006. Thanks are also due to those others who work for Bodleian Publications, especially Deborah Susman (Project Manager), Dot Little (Graphic Designer), Oana Romocea (Communications Officer) and Lucy Morton of illuminati, who have imaginatively produced this edition. I also thank the Bodleian's rights agents, Ros Edwards and Helenka Fuglewicz, for their enthusiastic support of this project.

To assemble the parts of this new edition of *Frankenstein*, Fanous, Susman, Little, Edwards, Fuglewicz, Barker-Benfield and I met in September 2007 in the Clarendon Building at Oxford University—in a building that already had many associations with Mary Shelley and her novel. Barker-Benfield and I had worked there in his private office in 1995 and 1996 as we attempted to put the Frankenstein Notebooks back together. Working there was all the more meaningful because Mary and Percy Shelley apparently visited the same Clarendon Building in August/September 1815 during their excursion from Windsor to Oxford; moreover, even Victor Frankenstein and Henry Clerval had visited the same building during their short stay in Oxford in April 17[95].† Here, in one building (which also housed a library when Mary and Percy and when Victor and Henry visited), the historical and the fictional pasts were intertwined. Here, by inspecting each leaf of the manuscript and by attending to torn edges, glue residue, ink blots, pin holes, watermarks, and other minutiae, Barker-Benfield and I reconstructed the disbound pages of Mary Shelley's Notebooks and discovered the process by which she created her novel. Here, in the Clarendon Building, the library became a laboratory, and the 'hideous progeny' of Mary Shelley's *Frankenstein* once again came to life.

Charles E. Robinson
University of Delaware

† For the Shelleys' visit in 1815, see *The Clairmont Correspondence: Letters of Claire Clairmont, Charles Clairmont, and Fanny Imlay Godwin*, ed. Marion Kingston Stocking (Baltimore: Johns Hopkins University Press, 1995), I, 14; for Victor and Clerval's visit in 17[95], see Volume II, Chapter 11, below. The year of that fictional visit may be determined by working out the chronology in *Frankenstein*—see 'Other Numbers and Dates in The *Frankenstein* Notebooks' in *1816-1817 Facsimile*, pp. lxv–lxvi; *1818 Crook*, I, 51n, 121n; Anne K. Mellor, *Mary Shelley: Her Life, Her Fiction, Her Monsters* (New York: Methuen, 1988), pp. 54–5, 237–8; and *1818 Wolf-1*, pp. 340–42.

Abbreviations

The following abbreviations, arranged chronologically and used in the textual commentary in this edition, provide a convenient shorthand by which to distinguish various editions of *Frankenstein* from each other: the significant versions are dated and designated *1816–1817*, *1817*, *1818*, *1823*, *1831*; and the initials MWS and PBS stand for Mary Wollstonecraft Shelley and Percy Bysshe Shelley. For a list of other primary and secondary works relating to *Frankenstein* and cited in this edition, consult the Bibliography at the end of this volume.

1816–1817 Draft — Draft of *Frankenstein* (a novel in 2 volumes): as it survives in Notebooks A and B in [Abinger] Bodleian Dep. c. 477/1 and c. 534/1.

1816–1817 Facsimile — Robinson, Charles E., *The Frankenstein Notebooks: A Facsimile Edition of Mary Shelley's Manuscript Novel, 1816–17 (with Alterations in the Hand of Percy Bysshe Shelley) as it Survives in Draft and Fair Copy Deposited by Lord Abinger in the Bodleian Library, Oxford (Dep. c. 477/1 and Dep. c. 534/1-2)*, Parts One and Two, The Manuscripts of the Younger Romantics, Volume IX (New York: Garland, 1996).

1816–1817 MWS — '*Frankenstein* [by] Mary Shelley': as printed in Charles E. Robinson (ed.), *Frankenstein or The Modern Prometheus: The Original Two-Volume Novel of 1816–1817 from the Bodleian Library Manuscripts, by Mary Wollstonecraft Shelley (with Percy Bysshe Shelley)* (Oxford: Bodleian Library, University of Oxford, 2008; and New York: Vintage Books, 2009), 255–429.

1816–1817 MWS/PBS — '*Frankenstein* [by] Mary (with Percy) Shelley': as printed in Charles E. Robinson (ed.), *Frankenstein or The*

Modern Prometheus: The Original Two-Volume Novel of 1816–1817 from the Bodleian Library Manuscripts, by Mary Wollstonecraft Shelley (with Percy Bysshe Shelley) (Oxford: Bodleian Library, University of Oxford, 2008; and New York: Vintage Books, 2009), 39–245.

1817 Fair Copy — Fair Copy of *Frankenstein* (a novel in 3 volumes): as it survives in Notebooks C1 and C2 in [Abinger] Bodleian Dep. c. 534/2.

1818 — *Frankenstein; or, The Modern Prometheus*, 3 vols (London: Lackington, Hughes, Harding, Mavor, & Jones, 1818).

1818 Butler — Shelley, Mary Wollstonecraft, *Frankenstein or The Modern Prometheus: The 1818 Text*, ed. Marilyn Butler (London: William Pickering, 1993). [Reprinted in paperback as part of 'The World's Classics' series (London: Oxford University Press, 1994). Both the original and the reprint have an appendix in which Butler prints 'The Third Edition (1831): Substantive Changes' together with 'Collation of the Texts of 1818 and 1831'.]

1818 Crook — Shelley, Mary, *Frankenstein or The Modern Prometheus*, ed. Nora Crook, Volume 1 of Nora Crook (ed.), *The Novels and Selected Works of Mary Shelley*, 8 vols, with an introduction by Betty T. Bennett (London: William Pickering, 1996). [Crook provides four valuable glosses to her text: 'Endnotes: Textual Variants' (pp. 182–227), in which she prints MWS's autograph corrections in *1818 Thomas* and the substantive variants in *1823* and *1831*; 'A Note on Spelling Variants in *1818*, *1823* and *1831*' (p. 228); 'Unauthorized Variants' (p. 229), in which she indicates that *1831 Joseph* introduced six textual errors and that then *1818 Macdonald* incorrectly listed these six errors as *1831* variants of the *1818* text; and 'Silent Corrections' (pp. 230–31).]

1818 Hunter — Shelley, Mary, *Frankenstein: The 1818 Text, Contexts, Nineteenth-Century Responses, Modern Criticism*, A Norton Critical Edition, ed. J. Paul Hunter (New

York: W. W. Norton, 1996). [Among the other texts that Hunter reprints are: 'The Composition of *Frankenstein*' from *1831 Joseph*; Anne K. Mellor, 'Choosing a Text of *Frankenstein* to Teach'; PBS's 1832 *Athenæum* review of *Frankenstein*; and partial texts of the 1818 reviews in *Quarterly Review*, *Edinburgh Magazine* (confused with *Blackwood's Edinburgh Magazine* and the review misattributed to Scott) and *Gentleman's Magazine*, and of the 1824 review in *Knight's Quarterly*. The text of the novel, as edited by Hunter, is also reprinted as a separate 'Norton Anthology Edition', with an introduction by Jack Stillinger.]

1818 Macdonald Shelley, Mary Wollstonecraft, *Frankenstein; or, The Modern Prometheus (The 1818 Version)*, A Broadview Literary Text, ed. D. L. Macdonald and Kathleen Scherf (Peterborough, Ontario: Broadview Press, 1994; 2nd edn, 1999). [Among the other texts that Macdonald and Scherf reprint are: passages from the works by Volney, Goethe, Plutarch and Milton that the monster read; and partial texts of the 1818 reviews of *Frankenstein* in *Blackwood's Edinburgh Magazine*, *Edinburgh Magazine* and *Quarterly Review*. Omissions in Macdonald and Scherf's 1994 'Appendix F: Substantive Variants in the 1831 Edition' (pp. 317–59) are noted by David Ketterer, 'The Corrected *Frankenstein*: Twelve Preferred Readings in the Last Draft', *English Language Notes*, 33/1 (September 1995), 34; 'unauthorized variants' in this same Appendix (apparently traceable to errors in *1831 Joseph*) are listed in *1818 Crook*, p. 229.]

1818 Moser Shelley, Mary, *Frankenstein; or, The Modern Prometheus. The 1818 Text in Three Volumes*, illustrated by Barry Moser and with essays by Ruth Mortimer, Emily Sunstein, Joyce Carol Oates and William St Clair (West Hatfield: Pennyroyal, 1983). [Reprinted in paperback, but without the Mortimer, Sunstein and St Clair essays (Berkeley: University of California Press, 1984).]

1818 Rieger — Shelley, Mary Wollstonecraft, *Frankenstein or The Modern Prometheus: The 1818 Text (with Variant Readings, an Introduction, and Notes)*, ed. James Rieger (Chicago: University of Chicago Press (Phoenix Edition), 1982). [This important edition (initially published in the Library of Literature, Indianapolis: Bobbs–Merrill, 1974) was the first to print a 'Collation of the Texts of 1818 and 1831' and the first to record the autograph variants in *1818 Thomas* (which Rieger incorporated into the *1818* text). The 1974 edition was reprinted (with different pagination and lineation) by New York: Pocket Books, 1976. The 1982 Chicago reprint, however, is to be preferred because it corrects 'minor errors in the introduction and apparatus' and lists 'some additional 1818/1831 variants at the end of the volume'—the 'Collation' is printed on pp. 230–59 and 288.]

1818 Thomas — The copy of the first edition of *1818* (Pierpont Morgan Library, STC 16799) that MWS corrected, annotated and presented to Mrs Thomas in Genoa in [?July] 1823.

1818 Wolf-1 — *The Annotated Frankenstein* (*Frankenstein* by Mary Shelley; Introduction and Notes by Leonard Wolf); with Maps, Drawings, and Photographs (New York: Clarkson N. Potter, 1977). [This edition prints a photo-facsimile of *1818*, but the copy chosen for microfilming (together with a flawed photo-offset process) led to a number of errors in the text, most resulting from severe cropping when the pages were rearranged. For the fourteen places where *1818 Wolf-1* misrepresents the *1818* text and/or introduces new errors, see the notes on pp. 2, 79, 105, 163, 253, 449, 479, 519, 587 (and 715), 633 (and 757) in *1816–1817 Facsimile*.]

1818 Wolf-2 — *The Essential Frankenstein*, Written and Edited by Leonard Wolf, Including the Complete Novel by Mary Shelley, [with] Illustrations by Christopher Bing

(New York: Penguin Books (a Plume Book), 1993). [This edition, a resetting of the text of the *1818* photo-facsimile in *1818 Wolf–1*, also carries over the errors from that earlier edition.]

1818 Wolfson — *Mary Wollstonecraft Shelley's Frankenstein; or, The Modern Prometheus*, A Longman Cultural Edition, ed. Susan J. Wolfson (New York: Longman, 2003). [In addition to printing selections from early reviews of *Frankenstein* and from texts quoted in or alluded to in the novel, Wolfson in this expanded second edition highlights differences between *1818* and *1831* and usefully reprints Richard Brinsley Peake's 1823 dramatic adaptation of the novel.]

1823 — Shelley, Mary Wollstonecraft, *Frankenstein: or, The Modern Prometheus*, A New Edition, 2 vols (London: G. and W. B. Whittaker, 1823). [A photo-facsimile of this edition was published by Oxford: Woodstock Books, 1993.]

[*1826*] — [Most likely a Henry Colburn reissue of remaining copies of *1823* without even a new title page.]

1831 — The Author of The Last Man, Perkin Warbeck, &c. &c., *Frankenstein: or, The Modern Prometheus*, Revised, Corrected, and Illustrated with a New Introduction, by the Author (London: Henry Colburn and Richard Bentley; Edinburgh: Bell and Bradfute; and Dublin: Cumming, 1831). [The title page is preceded by an engraved title page: Mary W. Shelley, *Frankenstein* (London: Colburn and Bentley, 1831). A photo-facsimile of this engraved title page may be seen in *1818 Crook*, p. 173.]

1831 Hindle — Shelley, Mary, *Frankenstein or The Modern Prometheus*, ed. Maurice Hindle (London: Penguin Books, 1992; rev. edn, 2003). [This hybrid edition, an expansion of Hindle's Penguin edition of 1985, prints *1831* but divides it by means of the volumes and chapters of *1818*; it also includes 'Appendix A: Select Collation of the Texts of 1831 and 1818', in which Hindle also prints 'a selection of significant revisions made by Percy Shelley at MS stage, which Mary Shelley adopted', but the reader is reminded that not all of Hindle's identifications of PBS's hand are correct.]

1831 Joseph — Shelley, Mary Wollstonecraft, *Frankenstein or The Modern Prometheus* (Oxford: Oxford University Press, 1969). [Reprinted in paperback as part of 'The World's Classics' series (London: Oxford University Press, 1980). Joseph in an appendix was one of the first to address 'The Composition of *Frankenstein*'. See *1818 Crook* above for Joseph introducing errors into the *1831* text.]

1831 Smith — Shelley, Mary, *Frankenstein: Complete, Authoritative Text with Biographical and Historical Contexts, Critical History, and Essays from Five Contemporary Critical Perspectives*, Case Studies in Contemporary Criticism, ed. Johanna M. Smith (Boston: Bedford Books of St Martin's Press, 1992; 2nd edn, 2000).

Introduction

This new edition of *Frankenstein* takes us back as far as possible to the 'original' novel that Mary Shelley first drafted during that famous and rainy summer of 1816 in Geneva. Sadly, the 'transcript of the grim terrors of [her] waking dream' that Mary Shelley wrote the very next day after the 'spectre ... had haunted [her] midnight pillow' does not survive.[1] Nor do we have any of the discarded 'foul papers' or early drafts of the novel that she continued to write during July and August 1816. We know, however, that by the middle or end of August she had written a version of her story that then became the basis for the first complete Draft of her novel. Most of that Draft survives and is now preserved, together with a portion of the Fair Copy, in the Bodleian Library at the University of Oxford.[2] And that surviving Draft is here edited for the first time in order to produce two new texts of *Frankenstein*: *1816-1817 MWS/PBS*, a corrected reading text of the Draft that makes visually evident Percy Bysshe Shelley's considerable 'hand' in his wife's novel as she drafted it (with his involvement) between August/September 1816 and April 1817; and *1816–1817 MWS* (distinguished later in this volume by tinted paper), an uncorrected representation of that same Draft that removes as nearly as possible all of Percy's editorial interventions in the novel. This uncorrected text attempts to reproduce what Mary originally wrote before giving the Draft manuscript to her husband for his pen and pencil alterations and editorial advice. These two texts, each based on the *1816-1817 Draft*, illuminate each other and confirm what has always been acknowledged: that Mary Shelley's *Frankenstein* is a very 'fluid' text, one that exists in a number of incarnations.[3]

The first edition of *Frankenstein*, which obscures the original construction of the surviving Draft of Mary Shelley's novel, was a three-volume novel published in London (in 500 copies) on New Year's Day in 1818. The next significant version of the novel was a corrected copy of *1818* that Mary Shelley presented to a Mrs Thomas in Genoa in 1823. This copy, now housed in the Pierpont Morgan Library in New York City, contains a significant number of alterations that Mary Shelley had written in the margins of the three volumes of her novel.[4] Also in 1823, just before Mary Shelley returned to England from Italy in August, her father William Godwin published a 'New Edition' of the novel in two volumes in which he (or, possibly, a printer) made 123 word changes (no more than 250 or 500 copies of that edition were published). On Halloween of 1831, Mary Shelley published yet another edition of her novel, a one-volume 'revised [and] corrected' edition of the novel (in 4,020 stereotyped copies) that incorporated most of the changes that had been introduced in 1823 and that contained many other revisions to the text that Mary Shelley herself made, including an additional chapter. Not only do the texts of these three published editions (*1818* in three volumes; *1823* in two volumes; and *1831* in one volume) differ from each other, but they differ substantially from the two new texts that are printed here. Based on the Draft, these two new texts present *Frankenstein* for the first time as a two-volume novel with a different chapter configuration.

Of the three standard editions, the *1831* 'revised' one-volume text was the one most often reprinted through the rest of the nineteenth century and through most of the twentieth century. For the past thirty years, however, there has been considerable interest in and a preference for the *1818* or three-volume text of *Frankenstein*, as is witnessed in the list of short titles offered at the beginning of this volume. Many who have judged that *1818* was superior to *1831* may prefer to read the text we privilege in this edition, namely the corrected *1816–1817 MWS/PBS* version that is based immediately on the Draft. And we also hope that many will also read or at least consult the uncorrected *1816–1817 MWS* version at the back of this volume, for it teaches a great deal about the origins of *Frankenstein*.

The 'text' of *Frankenstein*, made fluid or different by its three different versions of *1818*, *1823* and *1831*, by the changes made in *1818 Thomas*, and now by these two new versions of *1816–1817*, has been altered in other ways as a result of its phenomenal cultural success. The novel was published in a French translation in Paris in July 1821, and it first appeared on the stage in London in July 1823.[5] In such versions of the novel, Mary Shelley's original voice was often modified or lost. For nearly two centuries, hundreds of other redactions or digests or scripts of the novel continued to compromise or mute the voice behind the text as originally crafted in 1816–17: consider, for example, the shortened versions for children in the illustrated Ladybird or Classics Illustrated publications of the story; or listen to James Mason reading an 'abridged' version of the novel on an audio cassette;[6] or watch and listen to the many film or television versions of the novel that introduce new characters, change names of other characters, and rewrite Mary Shelley's text;[7] or consult not one but two very different and 'reimagined' versions of *Frankenstein*, one a screenplay and the other a novel,[8] associated with the making of Kenneth Branagh's 1994 film, *Mary Shelley's Frankenstein*.

In these incarnations or 'reimaginings' of the novel, readers or viewers frequently encounter texts far removed from the novel of 1816–17. Many of these adaptations, for example, give the name of 'Frankenstein' to the monster, even though Mary Shelley purposefully gave him no name, forcing her readers to reveal their biases by denominating him 'monster', 'creature', 'creation', 'wretch', or 'dæmon'. Indeed, the name 'Frankenstein' in popular culture brings to mind the Boris Karloff image of the monster rather than any image of Victor Frankenstein, the scientist who brought the monster to life. But the confusion of creator and creation did not have to wait for the 1931 James Whale film that made Boris Karloff a star. One may find the same kind of confusion in mid-nineteenth-century cartoons—or at a much earlier masked ball that concluded the Grand Musical Festival in Liverpool on 3 October 1823, when among the 1,475 guests a 'Mr. Harris, of Preston, personated (we are told) Frankenstein, or the Modern Prometheus. His appearance was most singular. His dress was of variegated colors, one half dark, the other light. His face was of different hues, the colors running insensibly into each other, and producing an effect at once singular and curious.'[9] Even as early as July 1819, it was suggested, in a parody of Byron's *Don Juan*, that Frankenstein was the name of 'the wretched abhorred'.[10]

The name of Byron recalls us to the origins of the tale of *Frankenstein* during that very famous summer of 1816 (the coldest on record[11]), for it was the 28-year-old poet George Gordon, Lord Byron (1788–1824) who suggested to a group of his new friends in Geneva that they amuse themselves during the cold and rainy evenings by telling ghost stories, one of which would be published as *Frankenstein* a year and a half later. Those who assembled with Byron that summer included the 18-year-old Mary Wollstonecraft Godwin (1797–1851); her husband-to-be, the 23-year-old poet Percy Bysshe Shelley (1792–1822); her stepsister, the 18-year-old Clara Mary Jane ('Claire') Clairmont (1798–1879), pregnant with Byron's child; and the 21-year-old John William Polidori (1795–1821), Byron's doctor.

The circumstances that led up to the gathering of these wonderfully 'romantic' individuals offers a plot as engaging as that of *Frankenstein* itself. Mary Shelley was the daughter of two famous fiction writers and political scientists: William Godwin, who had published *Enquiry Concerning Political Justice* in 1793; and Mary Wollstonecraft, who had published *Vindication of the Rights of Woman* in 1792. Because her natural mother died eleven days after she was born, Mary Shelley was raised by her stepmother Mary Jane Godwin and lived as one of five children of the Godwins, no two of whom had the same set of parents. When Mary was 16, she fell in love with the already married poet Percy Bysshe Shelley. They 'eloped' to the Continent on 28 July 1814 for a six-week tour to celebrate their love. They were accompanied by Mary's younger stepsister, Claire Clairmont; Percy left behind his pregnant wife Harriet and their 2-year-old daughter Ianthe. Seven months later, in February 1815, Mary gave birth to a premature daughter, who died on 6 March 1815. A month later, still unmarried but living with Percy, she again became pregnant, successfully delivering her son William on 24 January 1816. He would be nearly five months old in Geneva when his mother began to write *Frankenstein*—but later died in Italy in June 1819.

The Geneva storytellers came together as a result of circumstances involving the infamous Lord Byron and Claire Clairmont. Byron had married Annabella Milbanke in January 1815, welcomed the birth of their daughter Augusta Ada in December 1815, but was separated from his wife under the shadow of various disgraces in January 1816. A few months later, he received a seductive letter from Claire Clairmont, and by April 1816 she was pregnant with Byron's child. By this time Byron had met and was delighted by Mary Shelley, and on 24 April he left England for ever. Claire was the one who manoeuvred the Shelleys to journey to Geneva, where the two poets Byron and Shelley met for the first time on 27 May 1816.

The Shelley party rented the Maison Chappuis that summer and frequently walked to Lord Byron's residence, the Villa Diodati on Lake Geneva. They entertained themselves during the chilly damp evenings by reading from a collection of ghost stories that had been translated from German into French.[12] In the middle of June, as Mary Shelley explained in her 1831 Introduction to the novel, Byron proposed that each of them should also write a ghost story. Both Byron and Polidori wrote and eventually published fragmentary tales about vampires,[13] Percy Shelley began but did not finish or publish a story about 'his early life', and Claire Clairmont apparently did not contribute a story. Mary Shelley, the last of the storytellers, 'busied myself *to think of a story* [Mary's italics]' that would 'make the reader dread to look round, to curdle the blood, and quicken the beatings of the heart'. Finally, one evening, after hearing Byron and Percy Shelley discuss the principle of life and the possibility of reanimation, she retired to bed after the 'witching hour' and, unable to sleep,

> saw—with shut eyes, but acute mental vision … the pale student of unhallowed arts kneeling beside the thing he had put together. I saw the hideous phantasm of a man stretched out, and then, on the working of some powerful engine, show signs of life, and stir with an uneasy, half vital motion. Frightful must it be; for supremely frightful would be the effect of any human endeavour to mock the stupendous mechanism of the Creator of the world. His success would terrify the artist; he would rush away from his odious handywork, horror-stricken. He would hope that, left to itself, the slight spark of life which he had communicated would fade; that this thing, which had received such imperfect animation, would subside into dead matter; and he might sleep in the belief that the silence of the grave would quench for ever thc transient existence of the hideous corpse which he had looked upon as the cradle of life. He sleeps; but he is awakened; he opens his eyes; behold the horrid thing stands at his bedside, opening his curtains, and looking on him with yellow, watery, but speculative eyes. [*see Appendix C*]

That waking dream appears to have dominated the rest of Mary Shelley's summer. The very next morning she announced to the

Geneva storytellers that she had conceived her tale, which she began with the words, 'It was on a dreary night of November' (what eventually became the beginning of Chapter 7 of the Draft manuscript). At first she thought of producing only 'a few pages', but was urged by Percy Shelley to develop the story 'at greater length' [*see Appendix C*]. That she seems to have done, as evidenced by the many entries of 'Write' and 'Write my story' in her extant journal from the months of July and August 1816. In fact, it is quite possible that, before the Shelley party departed Geneva on 29 August to return to England, she had finished a short or novella-length version of her tale, which became the basis for the Draft manuscript. She recorded in her journal on 21 August that 'Shelley & I talk about my story.' By or not too long after that date, Mary had settled on a plan to expand the tale into a novel, most likely by adding to its beginning, its middle and its end. Textual evidence in the Draft suggests that this is exactly what she did do, adding the outermost or frame tale of the Arctic explorer Robert Walton recounting the story of Victor Frankenstein to his sister Margaret—as well as the innermost story of Safie, whose language instruction provided the monster an opportunity to learn to read and speak.[14]

As the outermost tale of *Frankenstein*, Robert Walton's letters to his sister occupy exactly 276 days—drawing our attention to the nine-month gestation period for a tale about the creation of a monster. Walton first writes to his married sister Margaret Walton Saville (her initials recalling the 'MWS' of Mary Wollstonecraft Shelley) on 11 December 17—, and he concludes his narrative on 12 September the following year. We do not know exactly when Mary Shelley began writing the extant Draft of the full novel, but the evidence from her letters and journals and from the extant manuscripts of her novel suggests that she began the Draft manuscript just before she left Geneva at the end of August or just after she returned to England and relocated to Bath on 10

September 1816. Her journal again shows that she began to 'write' on 16 September. By the end of March or early April 1817, she finished that Draft. She then corrected and added to it between 9 and 17 April. On 18 April, she began to transcribe or 'fair-copy' the Draft, and by 13 May 1817 she finished the Fair Copy that eventually became printer's copy for the first edition of *1818*. Eleven months had passed since she first conceived the story in June 1816, and it was approximately nine months since she had begun to copy and expand her novel from the earlier but now lost versions of her story. Surely Mary Shelley recognized the appropriateness of such a 'gestation' period for the production of the Draft of her own novel: not only did her writing experience parallel Walton's nine months, but her 1831 Introduction makes clear how she came 'to dilate upon, so very hideous an idea', how her novel was 'the offspring' of happier days, and how she bade her novel as a 'hideous progeny [to] go forth and prosper' [*see Appendix C*].

The gestation and birthing of *Frankenstein*, this monstrous and hideous progeny of a novel, were not without complications, for Mary Shelley drafted it during a particularly difficult time in her life. In Bath in September 1816, she cared for her eight-month-old son and assisted her stepsister Claire, who lived nearby and was five months pregnant. In October, Mary's half-sister, Fanny Imlay, committed suicide; in mid-December, Percy was informed that his first wife Harriet had committed suicide the preceding month; on 30 December, he and Mary married; from mid-December until mid-March, the Shelleys waited to hear if Ianthe and Charles, Percy's children by Harriet, would join their family. The new year continued to be traumatic: by January 1817, Mary Shelley was pregnant with another child; on 12 January, Claire and Byron's daughter Allegra was born in Bath; on 24 January, the Chancery Court trial brought by Harriet's father began, and the Chancellor Lord Eldon ruled on 17 March that Ianthe and Charles Shelley would be awarded to Harriet's parents rather than to Percy Shelley.

The very next day, Mary and Percy moved their household to Marlow, where they finished the final pages of the Draft and wrote out the Fair Copy, which was completed by 13 May.[15]

Percy Shelley then undertook to find a publisher for his pregnant wife's novel, which he represented as having been written by a young friend. Publishers that he approached included Byron's famous publisher, John Murray, who rejected the novel in late May or early June; and Percy Shelley's own publisher, Charles Ollier, who rejected it in August. By late August or early September, the publishing firm of Lackington, Hughes, Harding, Mavor, & Jones agreed to accept the novel; Percy negotiated the contract at the same time that Mary Shelley entered her 'confinement' for the birth of her daughter Clara on 2 September 1817.[16] Two creative acts were brought to fruition at the same time, and the future looked very bright for the Shelleys. From mid-September through to early November they read and corrected proofs for *Frankenstein*, and on 6 November their collaborative series of letters on their 1814 elopement and on their 1816 excursion to Switzerland were published as *History of a Six Weeks' Tour*.

Collaboration seems to have been the hallmark of the Shelleys' literary relationship: for example, Mary Shelley often transcribed Percy Shelley's poems; Percy contributed lyrics to Mary's mythological dramas for adolescents, *Proserpine* and *Midas*; and each encouraged the other to write a drama about Beatrice Cenci. At the least significant, the two engaged in such games as *bouts-rimés*, where Mary provided the rhyming words and Percy supplied the rest of the text for each line;[17] at the most significant, they collaborated on Mary Shelley's *Frankenstein*. The nature of that collaboration is evidenced by this edition: a comparison of the two versions printed below shows that Percy deleted many words in the extant Draft and that he also added nearly 3,000 words to the text of the novel. When we add to these interventions the changes that Percy most certainly made in the two missing sections of the Draft,[18] the changes he made at the end of the Fair Copy, and the one extended passage he likely made in the proofs, we may conclude that he contributed at least 4,000 to 5,000 words to this 72,000-word novel. Despite the number of Percy's words, the novel was conceived and mainly written by Mary Shelley, as attested not only by others in their circle (e.g. Byron, Godwin, Claire and Charles Clairmont, Leigh Hunt) but by the nature of the manuscript evidence in the surviving pages of the Draft.[19]

These surviving pages were once bound into two large, hardcover notebooks, the covers and spines of which have long since disappeared. These two notebooks (Notebook A in continental laid paper with a light-blue tint, and Notebook B in British laid paper in cream colour) now consist of 152 separate leaves (with text on 301 pages), supplemented by three insert leaves and two insert slips (with text on eight pages). These separate leaves make it clear that the novel was drafted while the pages were still bound in the notebooks—as evidenced by words that were written across the gutter from one verso page to the facing recto before the pages were cut from the notebooks, by ink lines from words that extend beyond the right edge of a recto that show on the fore-edge of the reassembled sheets, and by offset ink blots made when both Percy and Mary turned the pages or closed the notebook before the ink had dried. The manuscript evidence actually enables us to imagine the ways in which the Shelleys passed the notebooks back and forth between August/September 1816 and mid-April 1817, by which time Mary had finished the Draft. Mary appears to have sought Percy's editorial advice after she completed individual chapters or sections of her novel, and his corrections seem to have been made chapter by chapter (although ink evidence suggests that he may have read and corrected all or most of Chapters 1–7 of Volume I at one sitting). If Mary submitted chapters to Percy as she completed them, then it follows that she would have learned from his editorial changes and advice as she continued to draft her novel. The curious reader who compares the text in these two versions printed below will notice in the early chapters how often Percy cancelled the words 'And' or 'But' that Mary used to begin her sentences (and sometimes paragraphs), and how often he changed the word 'that' to 'which' to introduce relative clauses. Mary apparently learned from both editorial changes, for in later chapters she seems to adopt the new principles or to make the changes herself at the very moment that she reverted to her old writing habits.

Most but not all of Percy Shelley's changes to Mary Shelley's text in the Draft are for the better. Many of his interventions are minor—addressing such accidentals as punctuation, capitalization and spelling. Other corrections, however, do improve Mary's sentences: he occasionally supplied a noun after her vague 'this'; he sometimes introduced subordination and more complex relationships between sentences that she had merely coordinated with frequent use of 'and' and 'but'; he reduced her wordiness, sometimes cancelling words, sometimes rewriting a phrase; and he at times improved her parallel constructions. Although Mary's youthful voice is still apparent after these revisions, Percy did sometimes alter that voice by removing the colloquial tone of her prose—prose that might have been more in keeping with the character speaking. Consider the following alterations that Percy made in the Draft manuscript: Mary's phrase that Victor 'should go to the university' was changed to 'should *become a student at* the university'; entering a sick chamber before 'it was safe' was changed to entering a sick chamber before '*the danger of infection was past*'; Victor's 'I had plenty of leisure' was changed to 'I had *sufficient* leisure'; the monster's 'a great deal of wood' became 'a great *quantity* of wood'; De Lacey's 'my children are out' was changed to 'my children are *from home*'; Walton's remark that Victor's dream reveries were 'peculiarly interresting' became '*almost as imposing & interesting as truth*'; and Victor's lament that 'the brightness of a loved eye can have faded' was changed to 'the brightness of a loved eye can have *been extinguished*', further emphasizing the finality of death. Similar instances of Percy's preference for more Latinate words and constructions may be found by comparing the two versions of the novel in this edition (the running foots in *1816–1817 MWS* will direct the reader to parallel passages in *1816–1817 MWS/PBS*).

The italics used for Percy Shelley's words in *1816–1817 MWS/PBS* make readily visible his single-word or short revisions. Consider, for example, the sequence of the following sentence that begins Volume I, Chapter 2, of the Draft: Mary Shelley initially wrote 'Those events which materially influence our future destinies are often caused by slight or trivial occurences' (see *1816–1817 MWS*); Percy revised it in the Draft manuscript to become 'Those events which materially influence our future destinies ~~are~~ often ~~caused by slight or~~ *derive thier origin from a* trivial occurences' (see the photo-facsimile and transcription in *1816–1817 Facsimile*, pp. 16–17); and the sentence is finally printed and correctly spelled in the reading text of *1816–1817 MWS/PBS* as 'Those events which materially influence our future destinies often *derive their origin from a* trivial occurrence.' It is worth remarking that this important sentence, which disappeared from the novel either in the Fair Copy or in the proofs, does not appear in the text of any of the *1818* editions.

These italics used for Percy Shelley's words make even more visible the half-dozen or so places where in his own voice he made substantial additions to the Draft of *Frankenstein*. Some of these additions deepen our understanding of the domestic, scientific and political issues in Volume I of the novel: for example, in Chapter 1, Percy's additions emphasize the 'harmony in [the] dissimilitude' between Victor and Elizabeth; in Chapter 4, Percy expanded Professor Waldman's (and therefore Victor's) appreciation of Agrippa's and Paracelsus' influences on modern scientists; in Chapter 8, Percy added to Elizabeth's letter a long passage on Geneva being more republican and egalitarian than France or

England. Percy was also responsible for Mary making a major change in Volume II, Chapter 10, when he questioned Victor's motivation. In an earlier state of the Draft, Victor's father proposed that Victor accompany Clerval to England. Percy in the margin addressed Mary as follows: 'I think the journey to England ought to be Victor's proposal.—that he ought to go for the purpose of collecting knowledge, for the formation of a female. He ought to lead his father to this in the conversations—the conversation commences right enough.' Mary Shelley complied, and, just before she fair-copied the novel in mid-April 1817, she inserted an important passage about Victor's initial delay in 'obtaining [his] father's consent to visit England', cancelled two-and-a-half pages of the Draft, and then drafted four-and-a-quarter substitute pages in which Victor eventually and earnestly entreated his father for permission to visit England. Thus, at Percy's suggestion, Victor became the one to determine his own destiny. Such alterations to the text of *1816–1817 MWS* that resulted from Percy's direct advice in the margins of the Draft are indicated in the endnotes to *1816–1817 MWS/PBS* in this edition.

Most of Percy Shelley's changes to Mary Shelley's novel were retained when she fair-copied the Draft for publication, and those already familiar with *Frankenstein* will encounter in the corrected *1816–1817 MWS/PBS* a text quite similar (although not identical) to what they have read in the *1818* edition. To witness fully the stages of the creative process that led from Mary's 'original' Draft to *1818*, we would need at least six parallel texts (side by side) to show the stemma or genealogy of the novel: the reconstructed and uncorrected text of *1816–1817 MWS*→the *1816–1817 Draft*→ the *1817 Fair Copy*→the proofs→the revises→*1818*. If the proofs and the revises were extant, they would have shown two major additions (in what had been Volume II, Chapters 10 and 11, of the Draft) that were made to the novel in late October 1817, just two months before it was published. Only 12 per cent of the Fair Copy (which became Printer's Copy) is extant, and therefore it does not offer us a copy-text for this new Bodleian edition; had it done so, it would have erased all of the visible changes that Percy made to the Draft manuscript. However, approximately 87 per cent of the *1816–1817 Draft* is extant, and so it does provide us a copy-text for this edition—and also an opportunity to experience the novel much closer to its origins, a novel that does differ in some significant ways from *1818*, *1823* and *1831*.

As we move from the extant *1816–1817 Draft* to the first edition of *1818*, we note the following differences: minor changes that Mary Shelley made to the Draft when she fair-copied it; some substantial changes that Percy Shelley made to the Draft when he wrote out the last twelve-and-three-quarter pages of the Fair Copy;[20] the two major changes to Volume II of the Draft that were made in the proofs; and a radical restructuring of the novel. The two versions printed here respect the original structure of *Frankenstein* as a two-volume novel, with fifteen chapters in Volume I and eighteen chapters in Volume II, the second volume beginning dramatically with the monster's narrative, as he and Frankenstein sit before the fire that symbolizes Promethean knowledge. When Mary finished the Draft and started to fair-copy it, she and/or Percy decided to rearrange the chapters of the two-volume novel and turn *Frankenstein* into a three-volume novel, the rearrangements outlined on page 30 below.

This Bodleian edition offers the first opportunity to read *Frankenstein* as it was originally drafted in thirty-three chapters (rather than as it was published in twenty-three chapters in the first edition of *1818*) and to discover new things about the narrative. For example, the version here, with more chapters, reads much more quickly (the shorter chapters giving a differently paced and faster reading experience). Moreover, the beginnings and endings of ten additional chapters gave Mary Shelley more places to emphasize major points in her plot and theme. Note, for example, the end of

1816–1817 DRAFT	1818 FIRST EDITION
Volume I	*Volume I*
Introductory Letters I–IV[21]	Introductory Letters I–IV
Chapters 1–2	Chapter 1
Chapters 3–4	Chapter 2
Chapters 5–6	Chapter 3
Chapters 7–part of 8	Chapter 4
Chapters part of 8–9	Chapter 5
Chapters 10, 11 and part of 12	Chapter 6
Chapters part of 12–13	Chapter 7
	Volume II
Chapter 14	Chapter 1
Chapter 15	Chapter 2
Volume II	
Chapters 1–part of 2	Chapter 3
Chapters part of 2–3[22]	Chapter 4
Chapter 4	Chapter 5
Chapter 5	Chapter 6
Chapters 6–part of 7	Chapter 7
Chapters part of 7–8	Chapter 8
Chapter 9	Chapter 9
	Volume III
Chapter 10	Chapter 1
Chapters 11–part of 12	Chapter 2
Chapters part of 12–13	Chapter 3
Chapters 14–part of 15	Chapter 4
Chapters part of 15–16	Chapter 5
Chapter 17	Chapter 6
Chapter 18	Chapter 7

Volume II, Chapter 12, which ends with the monster's threat, 'I shall be with you on your marriage night', a threat that was buried within a chapter in the *1818* text. That *1818* text seems at times to have arbitrary chapter divisions, resulting from one or both of the Shelleys not only combining two chapters into one but sometimes dividing chapters down the middle.[23]

Regardless of the arrangement of the chapters, the theme remains essentially the same in each incarnation of *Frankenstein*. The name of Safie (suggesting Sophia or 'Wisdom') at the very centre of the narrative reminds us that this novel is about the dangerous consequences of the pursuit and the expression of knowledge. To that end, Mary Shelley subsumed and conflated the three basic Western myths about those dangerous consequences: the narrative of Adam and Eve (and God and Satan), as emphasized by the monster's reading of Milton's *Paradise Lost*, which focuses on the Tree of Knowledge and the sin of pride; the Prometheus tale of hubris as introduced by the novel's subtitle, 'The Modern Prometheus', and by the many references in the novel to fire and lightning and sparks (recalling the fire of knowledge that Prometheus stole from Zeus to give to primal man); and Aristophanes' story in Plato's *Symposium*, where love is defined in terms of the desire to reunite with one's second self after primal and globular man (four arms and four legs) was cut in half as a punishment for presuming to scale the heights of heaven to challenge the gods. All three myths speak the same lesson, a lesson that is echoed by *Frankenstein*, which has attained the same kind of mythic status in today's culture. Myth is no more or less than a symbolic language to express an essential truth, and *Frankenstein* takes its mythic place as a cautionary tale about pride. As Victor Frankenstein warns Walton early in this narrative, 'Learn from me, if not by my precepts at least by my example, how dangerous is the acquirement of knowledge and how much happier that man is who believes his native town the world, than he who aspires to become greater than his nature will allow.' The creation uses the same words as his creator when he addresses Victor later in the novel: 'I cannot describe to you the agony that these reflections inflicted upon me; I tried to dispel them, but sorrow only increased with knowledge. Oh, that I had for ever remained in my native wood, nor known or felt beyond the sensations of hunger, thirst, and heat!' Both creator and creation left their 'native' or Edenic environs (Geneva and the woods) to pursue 'knowledge' (at the University of Ingolstadt and at the De Laceys' cottage), and both fell from grace and goodness as a consequence of their pursuits.

The book of Genesis and various religious traditions have taught that man is made in the image of God—Mary Shelley, by paralleling the expression of Victor and his creation, is merely telling us that the monster is made in the image of Victor, his creator. That mirroring or doubling is emphasized in *Frankenstein* by Victor's awareness of his relation to the monster: 'I considered the *being* whom I had cast in among mankind *and endowed with the will and the power to effect* purposes of *horror, such as the deed which he had now done*, nearly in the light of my vampire, my own spirit let loose from the grave and forced to destroy all who were dear to me' (PBS words in italics). Mary Shelley, consciously working within the doppelgänger tradition, shows that Victor's relations with the monster—as well as with other characters—serve to externalize his internal conflicts. For example, the scientists Walton and Victor mirror each other in their pursuits of knowledge and fame, and in their willingness to sacrifice the lives of others in that pursuit; the social scientist Henry Clerval also mirrors but tempers the ambition of Victor, who remarks that 'in Clerval I saw the image of my former self; he was inquisitive and anxious to gain experience and instruction.'

By the time Mary Shelley revised the *1831* edition, she further emphasized these doubling relationships. In the framing Letter IV to his sister Margaret, Robert Walton reports his own heartless ambitions and Victor's reaction: ' "Unhappy man! Do you share my madness? Have you drunk also of the intoxicating draught? Hear me,—let me reveal my tale, and you will dash the cup from your lips!" ' Although Victor at that moment sees the worst of himself in Walton's selfish disregard for life, within the space of three more paragraphs Victor explains that he sees the best of himself in Clerval's selflessness. Alluding to Aristophanes' myth of the circular man, Victor explains to Walton: '"I agree with you, ... we are unfashioned creatures, but half made up, if one wiser, better, dearer than ourselves—such a friend ought to be—do not lend his aid to perfectionate our weak and faulty natures. I once had a friend [Clerval], the most noble of human creatures"' (*1831*, pp. 15, 16).[24] Clearly, Victor saw Clerval as his better self, a complement whom he needed for fulfilment and wholeness, but a complement he abandoned, together with the loving Elizabeth, when he went to university to pursue knowledge. One of the Shelleys (probably Percy) again stressed Clerval's symbolic position as a noble creature by adding an important passage in the proofs just before the novel was published: 'Clerval! beloved friend! ... He was a being formed in the "very poetry of nature." His wild and enthusiastic imagination was chastened by the sensibility of his heart' (*1818*, vol. III, ch. 1, pp. 17–18). The heart of Clerval had balanced the unchastened head of Victor. The following diagram helps to demonstrate the symbolic relations among all of the major characters as they externalize Victor Frankenstein's internal conflict:

HEAD	Robert Walton	Victor Frankenstein	The Monster
HEART	Margaret Walton Saville	Elizabeth and Clerval	The Female Monster

The dynamics of this diagram control the plotting of the novel. For example, when Walton and Victor separate themselves from the 'heart' (as represented by Margaret and by Elizabeth and Clerval) to pursue science, they begin their fall into division and alienation; or when Victor further isolates the monster by destroying his unfinished female complement, the monster reciprocates and further isolates Victor by killing both Elizabeth and Clerval. Reading this narrative as a doppelgänger novel that externalizes psychological conflict, I suggest that the action of the novel itself concludes the night of the creation of the monster: for two years Victor had severed ties with hearth and home, he was unable to love Nature, and he abhorred the very work upon which he was engaged—in effect, he thrust a dagger into his heart. That is, by destroying his capacity to love, he committed psychic suicide; the rest of the novel externalizes and literalizes the psychomachia we witness in Victor. Victor in the form of the monster kills Clerval and Elizabeth, the two loving characters who represent the better part of himself.

To reduce the novel to this simple plot is not to belittle or demean it—rather, it is to clarify its fable-like attraction to so many readers: Paradise has been lost in the microcosm of the Frankenstein world. Invoking the concluding words of *Paradise Lost* ('The World was all before them', as Adam and Eve 'with wand'ring steps and slow/ Through Eden took their solitary way' [XII.646]), the monster declares that 'with the world before me, whither should I bend my steps?' These words immediately follow the monster's destruction of the De Lacey cottage. With Promethean fury and Satanic glee, the monster 'lighted a dry branch of tree' with which he 'fired the straw and hay' that had been gathered from 'the fields of Paradise': 'the cottage was quickly enveloped by the flames which clung to it and licked it with their forked *and destroying* tongues' (PBS words in italics). That fiery branch of the Tree of Knowledge exiled the De Laceys from their cottage and their 'garden'. The family of De Lacey and Felix and Agatha and Safie, though cast once again into an alien world, still had each other, making all the more painful the monster's lament in his only reference to Eve in the entire novel: 'No Eve soothed my sorrows or shared my thoughts. I was alone.'

Of course, *Frankenstein* is more than just a retelling of *Paradise Lost*: it is a cautionary tale that uses the monster to stand for any and all human constructs. The monster can stand for science gone wrong, the French Revolution gone wrong, or even a novel gone wrong. Whether the creator is a scientist, a political scientist, or a creative writer, the attempt, as Victor Frankenstein remarked, will be disastrous to anyone who 'aspires to become greater than his nature will allow'. Knowledge can be constructive, but it too often leads to the fiery destruction of self and others. That message is Mary Wollstonecraft Shelley's warning to her husband, to us, and possibly to herself—although she seems to heed that warning and survives in the margins of the novel in the person of Margaret Walton Saville. That fictional MWS living in the novel surely represents the historical MWS who lives on because of her novel, living on in literary history with and by means of her 'hideous progeny'.

NOTES

1 See MWS's Introduction to *1831*, reprinted in Appendix C below.
2 [Abinger] Dep. c. 477/1 and Dep. c. 534/1 for the Draft; [Abinger] Dep. c. 534/2 for the Fair Copy.
3 See John Bryant, *The Fluid Text: A Theory of Revision and Editing for Book and Screen* (Ann Arbor: University of Michigan Press, 2002).
4 For a transcription of MWS's revisions and suggestions in *1818 Thomas*, see *1818 Rieger* and *1818 Crook*. (Readers are urged to consult the list of abbreviations that identifies the citations for these specialized editions.) See especially MWS's assessment of her own work in a note at the end of Volume I, Chapter 2, of *1818 Thomas*: 'If there were ever to be another edition of this book, I should re-write these two first chapters. The incidents are tame and ill arranged—the language sometimes childish.—They are unworthy of the rest of the narration.'
5 For early and foreign editions of *Frankenstein* and of its stage productions, see W. H. Lyles, *Mary Shelley: An Annotated Bibliography*, Garland Reference Library of the Humanities, Vol. 22 (New York: Garland, 1975); Donald F. Glut, *The Frankenstein Catalog: Being a Comprehensive Listing of Novels, Translations, Adaptations, Stories, Critical Works, Popular Articles, Series, Fumetti, Verse, Stage Plays, Films, Cartoons, Puppetry, Radio & Television Programs, Comics, Satire & Humor, Spoken & Musical Recordings, Tapes, and Sheet Music Featuring Frankenstein's Monster and/or Descended from Mary Shelley's Novel* (Jefferson, NC: McFarland & Company, 1984); Steven Earl Forry, *Hideous Progenies: Dramatizations of Frankenstein from Mary Shelley to the Present* (Philadelphia: University of Pennsylvania Press, 1990); and the electronic database *WorldCat*, the OCLC union catalog.

6 *Frankenstein*, retold in simple language by Raymond Sibley, illustrated by Jon Davis (Loughborough: Ladybird Books, 1984); *Frankenstein*, Classics Illustrated Study Guides (originally published as Classics Illustrated, No. 26), with an essay by Debra Doyle, PhD (New York: Acclaim Books, 1997); *Frankenstein* (Abridged), read by James Mason (New York: Caedmon Cassette, 1979).

7 For comprehensive lists of titles, see Glut, *The Frankenstein Catalog*; Stephen Jones, *The Frankenstein Scrapbook: The Complete Movie Guide to the World's Most Famous Monster* (New York: Citadel Press, 1995); Caroline Joan ('Kay') S. Picart, Frank Smoot and Jayne Blodgett, *The Frankenstein Film Sourcebook*, with a foreword by Noël Carroll, Bibliographies and Indexes in Popular Culture, No. 8 (Westport, CT: Greenwood Press, 2001). For the most recent and authoritative study of the various incarnations of *Frankenstein*, see Susan Tyler Hitchcock, *Frankenstein: A Cultural History* (New York: W. W. Norton, 2007). For an informative website on the cultural Frankenstein, consult http://frankensteinia.blogspot.com.

8 The very titles of these works suggest they differ from the novel published by MWS: Kenneth Branagh, *Mary Shelley's Frankenstein: The Classic Tale of Terror Reborn on Film; With the Screenplay by Steph Lady and Frank Darabont*, ed. Diana Landau, photographs by David Appleby, afterword and notes by Leonard Wolf (New York: Newmarket Press, 1994); and Leonore Fleischer, *Mary Shelley's Frankenstein: Based on a Screenplay by Steph Lady and Frank Darabont from Mary Shelley's Novel*, with an afterword by Kenneth Branagh (New York: Signet Books, 1994).

9 From the *Liverpool Courier* of 8 October 1823, as quoted in the *New York Spectator*, 28 November 1823.

10 The stanzas from the William Hone parody are quoted and briefly discussed in *1816–1817 Facsimile*, p. xcviii.

11 See John Clubbe, 'The Tempest-Toss'd Summer of 1816: Mary Shelley's *Frankenstein*', *The Byron Journal*, 19 (1991), 26–40; and Jeffery Vail, ' "The Bright Sun Was Extinguis'd": The Bologna Prophecy and Byron's "Darkness" ', *The Wordsworth Circle*, 28 (1997), 183–92.

12 See *Fantasmagoriana, ou recueil d'histoires d'apparitions de spectres, revenans, fantômes, etc., Traduit de l'allemand, par un amateur* [Jean Baptiste Benoît Eyriès], 2 vols (Paris: Lenormant et Schoell, 1812), a translation into French of two volumes of the five-volume German *Der Gespensterbuch*. For an English translation of these stories, see Sarah Elizabeth Brown Utterson, *Tales of the Dead* (London: White, Cochrane, & Co., 1813); for a modern reprint of this translation, see Terry Hale (ed.), *Tales of the Dead: The Ghost Stories of the Villa Diodati* (Chislehurst: Gothic Society at the Gargoyle's Head Press, 1992).

13 These 'vampire' texts may be found together in Appendix C ('The Ghost-Story Contest') in *1818 Rieger*, pp. 260–87.

14 See *The Journals of Mary Shelley*, ed. Paula R. Feldman and Diana Scott-Kilvert (Oxford: Clarendon Press, 1987), pp. 112–32, for MWS's references to her writing during this period. For these and additional references to the writing and publication of *Frankenstein* (with ample quotations from primary sources), see the '*Frankenstein* Chronology' in *1816–1817 Facsimile*, pp. lxxvi–cx. For manuscript evidence of the two 'traumas' in the Draft that suggest MWS added to a shorter version of the novel, see 'Hypothetically Reconstructing an Ur-Text of *Frankenstein*' in *1816–1817 Facsimile*, pp. lx–lxii.

15 For more specifics on these events, see MWS *Journal*; *The Letters of Mary Wollstonecraft Shelley*, 3 vols, ed. Betty T. Bennett (Baltimore: Johns Hopkins University Press, 1980–88); and the '*Frankenstein* Chronology' in *1816–1817 Facsimile*.

16 See MWS *Journal*, p. 179, for her being 'confined' on that date—and compare Victor Frankenstein's entering his 'confinement' (vol. I, ch. 6) as he brought his creation to life.
17 See B. C. Barker-Benfield, *Shelley's Guitar: An Exhibition of Manuscripts, First Editions and Relics, to Mark the Bicentenary of the Birth of Percy Bysshe Shelley, 1792/1992* (Oxford: Bodleian Library, 1992), pp. 128–9.
18 As indicated in this edition, the extant Draft manuscript lacks two sections: in Volume I, the four introductory letters from Walton to his sister, together with a part of Chapter 1 (totalling nearly 6,000 words); and in Volume II, some of the Safie episode (part of Chapter 3 and all of Chapter 4, totalling nearly 3,000 words). It is possible that PBS's hand was more in evidence in these missing sections.
19 These attestations and the manuscript evidence provide ample proof to counter the claims that MWS merely acted as PBS's amanuensis, as has been alleged by Selwyn Jones, John Lauritsen and Phyllis Zimmerman, each of whom maintains that PBS actually authored *Frankenstein* as well as other works ascribed to MWS. For these claims, see the listings for these authors in the Bibliography at the end of this edition.
20 The extant Fair Copy, although existing for only 12 per cent of the novel, suggests MWS's and PBS's different methods in fair-copying the Draft. When MWS fair-copied, she followed the Draft very closely; and the many similarities between *1816–1817 Draft* and *1818* (together with the evidence from MWS *Journal*) suggest that MWS was the one who fair-copied most of the Draft. But when PBS fair-copied the concluding section of the Draft, he took it upon himself to embellish MWS's text, for example turning the Draft text of '& the flame that consumes my body will give *enjoyment or tranquillity* to my mind' (PBS words in italics) into the Fair Copy text of '& exult in the agony of the torturing flames. The light of that conflagration will fade away. My ashes will be swept into the sea by the winds. My spirit will sleep in peace; or if it thinks will surely not think thus. Adieu.' (For a full comparison of these last pages of the *1816–1817 Draft* and PBS's portion of the *1817 Fair Copy*, see *1816–1817 Facsimile*, pp. 810–17.)
21 As noted above, the four introductory letters from Walton to his sister Margaret (together with a portion of Chapter 1) are missing from the Draft.
22 As noted above, the concluding Draft pages for Chapter 3 are missing, as are the Draft pages for Chapter 4 (what eventually became Chapter V in *1818*)—the 'trauma' in the text at this point concerns the intersections of Notebook A (continental blue paper) and Notebook B (English cream paper).
23 That MWS herself determined (or approved) at least some if not all of these restructurings is suggested by a marginal note in her own hand ('Finish Chap. 2 here'—see *1816–1817 Facsimile*, p. 472), one-third of the way through Chapter 12 in Volume II of the Draft, at the point where in Volume III of the *1818* text (and therefore in the Fair Copy, which is missing at this point) Chapter 2 does in fact end. Both MWS and PBS did sums in various places in the Draft in order to determine how to transform the two-volume into a three-volume novel—see 'Hypothetically Reconstructing the Fair Copy of *Frankenstein*' in *1816–1817 Facsimile*, pp. lxii–lxv.
24 MWS may not have known or recalled Aristophanes' mythic story when she was drafting her text in 1816–17; not until July 1818 did she transcribe PBS's translation of Plato's *Symposium* (see MWS *Journal*, pp. 217–22).

If a desire for revenge remained to you in death it would be better satisfied in my life than in my destruction – But it was not so. You wished for my extinction that I might not cause greater wretchedness to others & now you will not desire my life for my own misery. Blasted as you were my agony is superior to yours for remorse is the bitter sting that rankles in my wounds & tortures me to madness.

But soon, he cried clasping his hands I shall die and what I now feel will no longer be felt – soon these burning miseries will be extinct – I shall ascend my pile triumphantly & the flame that consumes my body will give enjoyment to my mind.

He sprung from the cabin window as he said this upon an ice raft that lay close to the vessel & pushing himself off he was carried away by the waves and I soon lost sight of him in the darkness & distance.

Mary (with Percy) Shelley

NOTE ON THE TEXT

The following version of *Frankenstein*, which is based on the *1816–1817 Draft*, presents a new reading text of the novel. In addition to respecting the original two-volume and thirty-three-chapter divisions in the manuscript of the *1816–1817 Draft*, this new text of *Frankenstein* enables the reader to determine at a glance PBS's specific contributions to his wife's novel (his words represented by italic type).

In this new text, here denominated *1816–1817 MWS/PBS*, all spellings have been made consistent after having been checked against nineteenth-century usage in the *Oxford English Dictionary* and against the spellings in *1818*. Misspellings in the Draft have been silently corrected; superscripted letters have been lowered; ampersands have been printed as 'and'; capitalization has been standardized and made consistent; a few letters or words mistakenly omitted in the Draft have been supplied (by reference to the Fair Copy or to *1818*); and words mistakenly repeated or left uncancelled during revision have been deleted. The punctuation of the Draft was frequently misplaced or missing or redundant, the Shelleys evidently expecting the printers to point or punctuate even their Fair Copy. Consequently, punctuation has been standardized in accordance with acceptable principles manifest in the Draft and in *1818*: specifically, commas are used in a series of three or more (and a comma is used before the 'and' preceding the last word in the series—this being the convention in *1818*); a semicolon is normally used between two independent clauses if one of those clauses demands an internal comma; commas are not employed between compound words or phrases or verbals if they are sufficiently parallel in structure; commas are used to set off non-restrictive clauses, but they are not used for restrictive clauses (whether introduced by 'that' or 'which', the latter PBS's preference); the many dashes at the end of independent clauses in the Draft are often changed to periods or semicolons; other dashes are occasionally introduced, singly or in pairs, to clarify complex syntactical passages that otherwise might be misunderstood; and periods and commas are placed within closing quotation marks (the convention in *1818*).

The italics in this *1816–1817 MWS/PBS* text represent PBS's interventions in the Draft of the novel: his added sentences, clauses, phrases, words, and portions of words. If PBS overwrote MWS words or if he cancelled MWS words and then wrote the same words in the identical grammatical or syntactical space, the rewritten words are represented as MWS's. If, on the other hand, PBS cancelled and moved a MWS word or phrase into another grammatical or syntactical space, then that word or phrase is represented as PBS's; if PBS added letters to a MWS word in order to change tense, add a capital, or correct spelling, then those letters are represented as PBS's. Those interested in the original text prompting all of PBS's alterations may consult *1816–1817 Facsimile*, or consult the representation of MWS's text in *1816–1817 MWS*, the second text of *Frankenstein* printed in this volume.

In the reading text of *1816–1817 MWS/PBS* printed immediately below, two sections missing from the Draft are supplied from the text of *1818*: from Volume I, the four introductory letters from Walton to his sister Margaret and the first part of Chapter 1 (see pp. 44–62); and from Volume II, almost half of Chapter 3 and all of Chapter 4 (see pp. 139–47). These two sections are signalled by notes and running foots. Unless otherwise indicated in the notes, the spelling and punctuation in these two sections are printed exactly as they appear in *1818*, although italics used for titles and for words as words in *1818* are changed to underlines (in order to prevent any confusion with the use of italics for PBS interventions in this reading text). The bulk of the notes for *1816–1817 MWS/PBS* explain circumstances of the Draft that bear on the meaning of the novel as well as gloss historical persons and works and events mentioned in the text.

Those interested in experiencing the Draft manuscript in its 'purer' or more uncorrected state may consult *The Frankenstein Notebooks* (photo-facsimiles of each extant page faced by a transcription and notes) published by Garland Press in 1996 (see *1816–1817 Facsimile*). Or, more conveniently, readers may consult *1816–1817 MWS* below (pp. 255–429) for an additional text of MWS's *Frankenstein* that attempts to remove all evidence of PBS's intervention and, at the same time, to represent diplomatically all of the misspellings, ampersands, irregular capitals, incomplete phrasings, repeated words, and inconsistent and often missing punctuation in the Draft that the Shelleys prepared.

[illegible] ON THE [illegible] ON THE TEXT

The notes [illegible] MS [illegible] represent PBS's intervention in the [illegible] of [illegible] words, clauses, phrases, words and portions of words. If PBS [illegible] MWS's words [illegible] he cancelled MWS's words and then [illegible] to the [illegible] the [illegible] space, the [illegible] MWS [illegible] PBS [illegible] MWS word [illegible] word or phrase [illegible]. If PBS had added letters to a MWS word [illegible] to change tense, add a capital, or correct spelling, then those letters are represented in PBS's [illegible] in the original text [illegible] all of PBS's alterations [illegible] consult the [illegible] MWS [illegible] the second text of [illegible] of this volume.

In the reading text of [illegible] The printed [illegible] Volume I [illegible] from Walton to his sister [illegible] and the first part of Chapter [illegible] and from Volume III [illegible] of Chapter [illegible]. These two sections [illegible] the spelling and punctuation in these two sections are printed exactly as they appear in [illegible] in italics are changed to underlining in order to prevent any confusion with [illegible] PBS's interventions in this reading text. The bulk of the notes [illegible] explain [illegible] of the Draft that bear on the meaning of the novel as well as give [illegible] persons and books and events mentioned in the text.

Those interested in [illegible] the Draft [illegible] may consult [illegible] where the [illegible] transcription and notes [illegible] by Garland [illegible] MWS [illegible] to [illegible] PBS's [illegible] the same time to [illegible] of the [illegible] lines, [illegible] words, and [illegible] in the Draft [illegible].

Frankenstein

or

The Modern Prometheus

VOLUME I

LETTER 1.†

To Mrs. SAVILLE, England.[2]

St. Petersburgh, Dec. 11th, 17—.

You will rejoice to hear that no disaster has accompanied the commencement of an enterprise which you have regarded with such evil forebodings. I arrived here yesterday; and my first task is to assure my dear sister of my welfare, and increasing confidence in the success of my undertaking.

I am already far north of London; and as I walk in the streets of Petersburgh, I feel a cold northern breeze play upon my cheeks, which braces my nerves, and fills me with delight. Do you understand this feeling? This breeze, which has travelled from the regions towards which I am advancing, gives me a foretaste of those icy climes. Inspirited by this wind of promise, my day dreams become more fervent and vivid. I try in vain to be persuaded that the pole is the seat of frost and desolation; it ever presents itself to my imagination as the region of beauty and delight. There, Margaret, the sun is for ever visible; its broad disk just skirting the horizon, and diffusing a perpetual splendour. There—for with your leave, my sister, I will put some trust in preceding navigators—there snow and frost are banished; and, sailing over a calm sea, we may be wafted to a land surpassing in wonders and in beauty every region hitherto discovered on the habitable globe. Its productions and features may be without example, as the phænomena of the heavenly bodies undoubtedly are in those undiscovered solitudes. What may not be expected in a country of eternal light? I may there

† Manuscript missing until word 'servants' on p. 62: text supplied from *1818* edition.[1]

discover the wondrous power which attracts the needle; and may regulate a thousand celestial observations, that require only this voyage to render their seeming eccentricities consistent for ever. I shall satiate my ardent curiosity with the sight of a part of the world never before visited, and may tread a land never before imprinted by the foot of man. These are my enticements, and they are sufficient to conquer all fear of danger or death, and to induce me to commence this laborious voyage with the joy a child feels when he embarks in a little boat, with his holiday mates, on an expedition of discovery up his native river. But, supposing all these conjectures to be false, you cannot contest the inestimable benefit which I shall confer on all mankind to the last generation, by discovering a passage near the pole to those countries, to reach which at present so many months are requisite; or by ascertaining the secret of the magnet, which, if at all possible, can only be effected by an undertaking such as mine.

These reflections have dispelled the agitation with which I began my letter, and I feel my heart glow with an enthusiasm which elevates me to heaven; for nothing contributes so much to tranquillize the mind as a steady purpose,—a point on which the soul may fix its intellectual eye. This expedition has been the favourite dream of my early years. I have read with ardour the accounts of the various voyages which have been made in the prospect of arriving at the North Pacific Ocean through the seas which surround the pole. You may remember, that a history of all the voyages made for purposes of discovery composed the whole of our good uncle Thomas's library. My education was neglected, yet I was passionately fond of reading. These volumes were my study day and night, and my familiarity with them increased that regret which I had felt, as a child, on learning that my father's dying injunction had forbidden my uncle to allow me to embark in a sea-faring life.

These visions faded when I perused, for the first time, those poets whose effusions entranced my soul, and lifted it to heaven.

I also became a poet, and for one year lived in a Paradise of my own creation; I imagined that I also might obtain a niche in the temple where the names of Homer and Shakespeare are consecrated. You are well acquainted with my failure, and how heavily I bore the disappointment. But just at that time I inherited the fortune of my cousin, and my thoughts were turned into the channel of their earlier bent.

Six years have passed since I resolved on my present undertaking. I can, even now, remember the hour from which I dedicated myself to this great enterprise. I commenced by inuring my body to hardship. I accompanied the whale-fishers on several expeditions to the North Sea; I voluntarily endured cold, famine, thirst, and want of sleep; I often worked harder than the common sailors during the day, and devoted my nights to the study of mathematics, the theory of medicine, and those branches of physical science from which a naval adventurer might derive the greatest practical advantage. Twice I actually hired myself as an under-mate in a Greenland whaler, and acquitted myself to admiration. I must own I felt a little proud, when my captain offered me the second dignity in the vessel, and entreated me to remain with the greatest earnestness; so valuable did he consider my services.

And now, dear Margaret, do I not deserve to accomplish some great purpose. My life might have been passed in ease and luxury; but I preferred glory to every enticement that wealth placed in my path. Oh, that some encouraging voice would answer in the affirmative! My courage and my resolution is firm; but my hopes fluctuate, and my spirits are often depressed. I am about to proceed on a long and difficult voyage; the emergencies of which will demand all my fortitude: I am required not only to raise the spirits of others, but sometimes to sustain my own, when their's are failing.

This is the most favourable period for travelling in Russia. They fly quickly over the snow in their sledges; the motion is pleasant, and, in my opinion, far more agreeable than that of an English stage-coach. The cold is not excessive, if you are wrapt in furs, a dress which I have already adopted; for there is a great difference between walking the deck and remaining seated motionless for hours, when no exercise prevents the blood from actually freezing in your veins. I have no ambition to lose my life on the post-road between St. Petersburgh and Archangel.

I shall depart for the latter town in a fortnight or three weeks; and my intention is to hire a ship there, which can easily be done by paying the insurance for the owner, and to engage as many sailors as I think necessary among those who are accustomed to the whale-fishing. I do not intend to sail until the month of June: and when shall I return? Ah, dear sister, how can I answer this question? If I succeed, many, many months, perhaps years, will pass before you and I may meet. If I fail, you will see me again soon, or never.

Farewell, my dear, excellent, Margaret. Heaven shower down blessings on you, and save me, that I may again and again testify my gratitude for all your love and kindness.

Your affectionate brother,

R. WALTON.

LETTER II.

To Mrs. SAVILLE, England.

Archangel, 28th March, 17—.

How slowly the time passes here, encompassed as I am by frost and snow; yet a second step is taken towards my enterprise. I have hired a vessel, and am occupied in collecting my sailors; those whom I have already engaged appear to be men on whom I can depend, and are certainly possessed of dauntless courage.

But I have one want which I have never yet been able to satisfy; and the absence of the object of which I now feel as a most severe evil. I have no friend, Margaret: when I am glowing with the enthusiasm of success, there will be none to participate my joy; if I am assailed by disappointment, no one will endeavour to sustain me in dejection. I shall commit my thoughts to paper, it is true; but that is a poor medium for the communication of feeling. I desire the company of a man who could sympathize with me; whose eyes would reply to mine. You may deem me romantic, my dear sister, but I bitterly feel the want of a friend. I have no one near me, gentle yet courageous, possessed of a cultivated as well as of a capacious mind, whose tastes are like my own, to approve or amend my plans. How would such a friend repair the faults of your poor brother! I am too ardent in execution, and too impatient of difficulties. But it is a still greater evil to me that I am self-educated: for the first fourteen years of my life I ran wild on a common, and read nothing but our uncle Thomas's books of voyages. At that age I became acquainted with the celebrated poets of our own country; but it was only when it had ceased to be in my power to derive its most important benefits from such a conviction, that I perceived the necessity of becoming acquainted with more languages than that of my native country. Now I am twenty-eight, and am in reality more illiterate than many school-boys of fifteen. It is true that I have thought more, and that my day dreams are more extended and magnificent; but they want (as the painters call it) keeping;[3] and I greatly need a friend who would have sense enough not to despise me as romantic, and affection enough for me to endeavour to regulate my mind.

Well, these are useless complaints; I shall certainly find no friend on the wide ocean, nor even here in Archangel, among merchants and seamen. Yet some feelings, unallied to the dross of human nature, beat even in these rugged bosoms. My lieutenant, for instance, is a man of wonderful courage and enterprise; he is madly desirous of glory. He is an Englishman, and in the midst of national and professional prejudices, unsoftened by cultivation, retains some of the noblest endowments of humanity. I first became acquainted with him on board a whale vessel: finding that he was unemployed in this city, I easily engaged him to assist in my enterprise.

The master is a person of an excellent disposition, and is remarkable in the ship for his gentleness, and the mildness of his discipline. He is, indeed, of so amiable a nature, that he will not hunt (a favourite, and almost the only amusement here), because he cannot endure to spill blood. He is, moreover, heroically generous. Some years ago he loved a young Russian lady, of moderate fortune; and having amassed a considerable sum in prize-money, the father of the girl consented to the match. He saw his mistress once before the destined ceremony; but she was bathed in tears, and, throwing herself at his feet, entreated him to spare her, confessing at the same time that she loved another, but that he was poor, and that her father would never consent to the union. My generous friend reassured the suppliant, and on being informed of the name of her lover instantly abandoned his pursuit. He had already bought a farm with his money, on which he had designed to pass the remainder of his life; but he bestowed the whole on his rival, together with the remains of his prize-money to purchase stock, and then himself solicited the young woman's father to consent to her marriage with her lover. But the old man decidedly refused, thinking himself bound in honour to my friend; who, when he found the father inexorable, quitted his country, nor returned until he heard that his former mistress was married according to her inclinations. "What a noble fellow!" you will exclaim. He is so; but then he has passed all his life on board a vessel, and has scarcely an idea beyond the rope and the shroud.

But do not suppose that, because I complain a little, or because I can conceive a consolation for my toils which I may never know, that I am wavering in my resolutions. Those are as fixed as fate; and my voyage is only now delayed until the weather shall permit my embarkation. The winter has been dreadfully severe; but the spring promises well, and it is considered as a remarkably early season; so that, perhaps, I may sail sooner than I expected. I shall do nothing rashly; you know me sufficiently to confide in my prudence and considerateness whenever the safety of others is committed to my care.

I cannot describe to you my sensations on the near prospect of my undertaking. It is impossible to communicate to you a conception of the trembling sensation, half pleasurable and half fearful, with which I am preparing to depart. I am going to unexplored regions, to "the land of mist and snow;" but I shall kill no albatross, therefore do not be alarmed for my safety.[4]

Shall I meet you again, after having traversed immense seas, and returned by the most southern cape of Africa or America? I dare not expect such success, yet I cannot bear to look on the reverse of the picture. Continue to write to me by every opportunity: I may receive your letters (though the chance is very doubtful) on some occasions when I need them most to support my spirits. I love you very tenderly. Remember me with affection, should you never hear from me again.

Your affectionate brother,

ROBERT WALTON.

LETTER III.

To Mrs. SAVILLE, England.

July 7th, 17—.

MY DEAR SISTER,

I write a few lines in haste, to say that I am safe, and well advanced on my voyage. This letter will reach England by a merchant-man now on its homeward voyage from Archangel; more fortunate than I, who may not see my native land, perhaps, for many years. I am, however, in good spirits: my men are bold, and apparently firm of purpose; nor do the floating sheets of ice that continually pass us, indicating the dangers of the region towards which we are advancing, appear to dismay them. We have already reached a very high latitude; but it is the height of summer, and although not so warm as in England, the southern gales, which blow us speedily towards those shores which I so ardently desire to attain, breathe a degree of renovating warmth which I had not expected.

No incidents have hitherto befallen us, that would make a figure in a letter. One or two stiff gales, and the breaking of a mast, are accidents which experienced navigators scarcely remember to record; and I shall be well content, if nothing worse happen to us during our voyage.

Adieu, my dear Margaret. Be assured, that for my own sake, as well as your's, I will not rashly encounter danger. I will be cool, persevering, and prudent.

Remember me to all my English friends.

Most affectionately yours,

R. W.

LETTER IV.

To Mrs. SAVILLE, England.

August 5th, 17—.

So strange an accident has happened to us, that I cannot forbear recording it, although it is very probable that you will see me before these papers can come into your possession.

Last Monday (July 31st), we were nearly surrounded by ice, which closed in the ship on all sides, scarcely leaving her the sea room in which she floated. Our situation was somewhat dangerous, especially as we were compassed round by a very thick fog. We accordingly lay to, hoping that some change would take place in the atmosphere and weather.

About two o'clock the mist cleared away, and we beheld, stretched out in every direction, vast and irregular plains of ice, which seemed to have no end. Some of my comrades groaned, and my own mind began to grow watchful with anxious thoughts, when a strange sight suddenly attracted our attention, and diverted our solicitude from our own situation. We perceived a low carriage, fixed on a sledge and drawn by dogs, pass on towards the north, at the distance of half a mile: a being which had the shape of a man, but apparently of gigantic stature, sat in the sledge, and guided the dogs. We watched the rapid progress of the traveller with our telescopes, until he was lost among the distant inequalities of the ice.

This appearance excited our unqualified wonder. We were, as we believed, many hundred miles from any land; but this apparition seemed to denote that it was not, in reality, so distant as we had supposed. Shut in, however, by ice, it was impossible to follow his track, which we had observed with the greatest attention.

About two hours after this occurrence, we heard the ground-sea; and before night the ice broke, and freed our ship. We, however, lay to until the morning, fearing to encounter in the dark those large loose masses which float about after the breaking up of the ice. I profited of this time to rest for a few hours.

In the morning, however, as soon as it was light, I went upon deck, and found all the sailors busy on one side of the vessel, apparently talking to some one in the sea. It was, in fact, a sledge, like that we had seen before, which had drifted towards us in the night, on a large fragment of ice. Only one dog remained alive; but there was a human being within it, whom the sailors were persuading to enter the vessel. He was not, as the other traveller seemed to be, a savage inhabitant of some undiscovered island, but an European. When I appeared on deck, the master said, "Here is our captain, and he will not allow you to perish on the open sea."

On perceiving me, the stranger addressed me in English, although with a foreign accent. "Before I come on board your vessel," said he, "will you have the kindness to inform me whither you are bound?"

You may conceive my astonishment on hearing such a question addressed to me from a man on the brink of destruction, and to whom I should have supposed that my vessel would have been a resource which he would not have exchanged for the most precious wealth the earth can afford. I replied, however, that we were on a voyage of discovery towards the northern pole.

Upon hearing this he appeared satisfied, and consented to come on board. Good God! Margaret, if you had seen the man who thus capitulated for his safety, your surprise would have been boundless. His limbs were nearly frozen, and his body dreadfully emaciated by fatigue and suffering. I never saw a man in so wretched a condition. We attempted to carry him into the cabin; but as soon as he had quitted the fresh air, he fainted. We accordingly brought him back to the deck, and restored him to animation by rubbing him with brandy, and forcing him to swallow a small quantity. As soon as he shewed signs of life, we wrapped him up in blankets, and placed him near the chimney of the kitchen-stove. By slow degrees he recovered, and ate a little soup, which restored him wonderfully.

Two days passed in this manner before he was able to speak; and I often feared that his sufferings had deprived him of understanding. When he had in some measure recovered, I removed him to my own cabin, and attended on him as much as my duty would permit. I never saw a more interesting creature: his eyes have generally an expression of wildness, and even madness; but there are moments when, if any one performs an act of kindness towards him, or does him any the most trifling service, his whole countenance is lighted up, as it were, with a beam of benevolence and sweetness that I never saw equalled. But he is generally melancholy and despairing; and sometimes he gnashes his teeth, as if impatient of the weight of woes that oppresses him.

When my guest was a little recovered, I had great trouble to keep off the men, who wished to ask him a thousand questions; but I would not allow him to be tormented by their idle curiosity, in a state of body and mind whose restoration evidently depended upon entire repose. Once, however, the lieutenant asked, Why he had come so far upon the ice in so strange a vehicle?

His countenance instantly assumed an aspect of the deepest gloom; and he replied, "To seek one who fled from me."

"And did the man whom you pursued travel in the same fashion?"

"Yes."

"Then I fancy we have seen him; for, the day before we picked you up, we saw some dogs drawing a sledge, with a man in it, across the ice."

This aroused the stranger's attention; and he asked a multitude of questions concerning the route which the dæmon, as he called him, had pursued. Soon after, when he was alone with me, he said, "I have, doubtless, excited your curiosity, as well as that of these good people; but you are too considerate to make inquiries."

"Certainly; it would indeed be very impertinent and inhuman in me to trouble you with any inquisitiveness of mine."

"And yet you rescued me from a strange and perilous situation; you have benevolently restored me to life."

Soon after this he inquired, if I thought that the breaking up of the ice had destroyed the other sledge? I replied, that I could not answer with any degree of certainty; for the ice had not broken until near midnight, and the traveller might have arrived at a place of safety before that time; but of this I could not judge.

From this time the stranger seemed very eager to be upon deck, to watch for the sledge which had before appeared; but I have persuaded him to remain in the cabin, for he is far too weak to sustain the rawness of the atmosphere. But I have promised that some one should watch for him, and give him instant notice if any new object should appear in sight.

Such is my journal of what relates to this strange occurrence up to the present day. The stranger has gradually improved in health, but is very silent, and appears uneasy when any one except myself enters his cabin. Yet his manners are so conciliating and gentle, that the sailors are all interested in him, although they have had very little communication with him. For my own part, I begin to love him as a brother; and his constant and deep grief fills me with sympathy and compassion. He must have been a noble creature in his better days, being even now in wreck so attractive and amiable.

I said in one of my letters, my dear Margaret, that I should find no friend on the wide ocean; yet I have found a man who, before his spirit had been broken by misery, I should have been happy to have possessed as the brother of my heart.

I shall continue my journal concerning the stranger at intervals, should I have any fresh incidents to record.

August 13th, 17—.

My affection for my guest increases every day. He excites at once my admiration and my pity to an astonishing degree. How can I see so noble a creature destroyed by misery without feeling the most poignant grief? He is so gentle, yet so wise; his mind is so cultivated; and when he speaks, although his words are culled with the choicest art, yet they flow with rapidity and unparalleled eloquence.

He is now much recovered from his illness, and is continually on the deck, apparently watching for the sledge that preceded his own. Yet, although unhappy, he is not so utterly occupied by his own misery, but that he interests himself deeply in the employments of others. He has asked me many questions concerning my design; and I have related my little history frankly to him. He appeared pleased with the confidence, and suggested several alterations in my plan, which I shall find exceedingly useful. There is no pedantry in his manner; but all he does appears to spring solely from the interest he instinctively takes in the welfare of those who surround him. He is often overcome by gloom, and then he sits by himself, and tries to overcome all that is sullen or unsocial in his humour. These paroxysms pass from him like a cloud from before the sun, though his dejection never leaves him. I have endeavoured to win his confidence; and I trust that I have succeeded. One day I mentioned to him the desire I had always felt of finding a friend who might sympathize with me, and direct me by his counsel. I said, I did not belong to that class of men who are offended by advice. "I am self-educated, and perhaps I hardly rely sufficiently upon my own powers. I wish therefore that my companion should be wiser and more experienced than myself, to confirm and support me; nor have I believed it impossible to find a true friend."

"I agree with you," replied the stranger, "in believing that friendship is not only a desirable, but a possible acquisition. I once had a friend, the most noble of human creatures, and am entitled, therefore, to judge respecting friendship. You have hope, and the world before you, and have no cause for despair. But I——I have lost every thing, and cannot begin life anew."

As he said this, his countenance became expressive of a calm settled grief, that touched me to the heart. But he was silent, and presently retired to his cabin.

Even broken in spirit as he is, no one can feel more deeply than he does the beauties of nature. The starry sky, the sea, and every sight afforded by these wonderful regions, seem still to have the power of elevating his soul from earth. Such a man has a double existence: he may suffer misery, and be overwhelmed by disappointments; yet when he has retired into himself, he will be like a celestial spirit, that has a halo around him, within whose circle no grief or folly ventures.

Will you laugh at the enthusiasm I express concerning this divine wanderer? If you do, you must have certainly lost that simplicity which was once your characteristic charm. Yet, if you will, smile at the warmth of my expressions, while I find every day new causes for repeating them.

August 19th, 17—.

Yesterday the stranger said to me, "You may easily perceive, Captain Walton, that I have suffered great and unparalleled misfortunes. I had determined, once, that the memory of these evils should die with me; but you have won me to alter my determination. You seek for knowledge and wisdom, as I once did; and I ardently hope that the gratification of your wishes may not be a serpent to sting you, as mine has been. I do not know that the relation of my misfortunes will be useful to you, yet, if you are inclined, listen to my tale. I believe that the strange incidents connected with it will afford a view of nature, which may enlarge your faculties and understanding. You will hear of powers and occurrences, such as you have been accustomed to believe impossible: but I do not doubt that my tale conveys in its series internal evidence of the truth of the events of which it is composed."

You may easily conceive that I was much gratified by the offered communication; yet I could not endure that he should renew his grief by a recital of his misfortunes. I felt the greatest eagerness to hear the promised narrative, partly from curiosity, and partly from a strong desire to ameliorate his fate, if it were in my power. I expressed these feelings in my answer.

"I thank you," he replied, "for your sympathy, but it is useless; my fate is nearly fulfilled. I wait but for one event, and then I shall repose in peace. I understand your feeling," continued he, perceiving that I wished to interrupt him; "but you are mistaken, my friend, if thus you will allow me to name you; nothing can alter my destiny: listen to my history, and you will perceive how irrevocably it is determined."[5]

He then told me, that he would commence his narrative the next day when I should be at leisure. This promise drew from me the warmest thanks. I have resolved every night, when I am not engaged, to record, as nearly as possible in his own words, what he has related during the day. If I should be engaged, I will at least make notes. This manuscript will doubtless afford you the greatest pleasure: but to me, who know him, and who hear it from his own lips, with what interest and sympathy shall I read it in some future day!

Chapter 1

I am by birth a Genevese; and my family is one of the most distinguished of that republic.[6] My ancestors had been for many years counsellors and syndics; and my father had filled several public situations with honour and reputation. He was respected by all who knew him for his integrity and indefatigable attention to public business. He passed his younger days perpetually occupied by the affairs of his country; and it was not until the decline of life that he thought of marrying, and bestowing on the state sons who might carry his virtues and his name down to posterity.

As the circumstances of his marriage illustrate his character, I cannot refrain from relating them. One of his most intimate friends was a merchant, who, from a flourishing state, fell, through numerous mischances, into poverty. This man, whose name was Beaufort, was of a proud and unbending disposition, and could not bear to live in poverty and oblivion in the same country where he had formerly been distinguished for his rank and magnificence. Having paid his debts, therefore, in the most honourable manner, he retreated with his daughter to the town of Lucerne, where he lived unknown and in wretchedness. My father loved Beaufort with the truest friendship, and was deeply grieved by his retreat in these unfortunate circumstances. He grieved also for the loss of his society, and resolved to seek him out and endeavour to persuade him to begin the world again through his credit and assistance.

Beaufort had taken effectual measures to conceal himself; and it was ten months before my father discovered his abode. Overjoyed at this discovery, he hastened to the house, which was situated in a mean street, near the Reuss. But when he entered, misery and despair alone welcomed him. Beaufort had saved but a very small sum of money from the wreck of his fortunes; but it was sufficient to provide him with sustenance for some months, and in the mean time he hoped to procure some respectable employment in a merchant's house. The interval was consequently spent in inaction; his grief only became more deep and rankling, when he had leisure for reflection; and at length it took so fast hold of his mind, that at the end of three months he lay on a bed of sickness, incapable of any exertion.

His daughter attended him with the greatest tenderness; but she saw with despair that their little fund was rapidly decreasing, and that there was no other prospect of support. But Caroline Beaufort possessed a mind of an uncommon mould; and her courage rose to support her in her adversity. She procured plain work; she plaited straw; and by various means contrived to earn a pittance scarcely sufficient to support life.

Several months passed in this manner. Her father grew worse; her time was more entirely occupied in attending him; her means of subsistence decreased; and in the tenth month her father died in her arms, leaving her an orphan and a beggar. This last blow overcame her; and she knelt by Beaufort's coffin, weeping bitterly, when my father entered the chamber. He came like a protecting spirit to the poor girl, who committed herself to his care, and after the interment of his friend he conducted her to Geneva, and placed her under the protection of a relation. Two years after this event Caroline became his wife.

When my father became a husband and a parent, he found his time so occupied by the duties of his new situation, that he relinquished many of his public employments, and devoted himself to the education of his children. Of these I was the eldest, and the destined successor to all his labours and utility. No creature could have more tender parents than mine. My improvement and health were their constant care, especially as I remained for several years their only child. But before I continue my narrative, I must record an incident which took place when I was four years of age.

My father had a sister, whom he tenderly loved, and who had married early in life an Italian gentleman. Soon after her marriage, she had accompanied her husband into his[7] native country, and for some years my father had very little communication with her. About the time I mentioned she died; and a few months afterwards he received a letter from her husband, acquainting him with his intention of marrying an Italian lady, and requesting my father to take charge of the infant Elizabeth, the only child of his deceased sister. "It is my wish," he said, "that you should consider her as your own daughter, and educate her thus. Her mother's fortune is secured to her, the documents of which I will commit to your keeping. Reflect upon this proposition; and decide whether you would prefer educating your niece yourself to her being brought up by a stepmother."

My father did not hesitate, and immediately went to Italy, that he might accompany the little Elizabeth to her future home. I have often heard my mother say, that she was at that time the most beautiful child she had ever seen, and shewed signs even then of a gentle and affectionate disposition. These indications, and a desire to bind as closely as possible the ties of domestic love, determined my mother to consider Elizabeth as my future wife; a design which she never found reason to repent.

From this time Elizabeth Lavenza became my playfellow, and, as we grew older, my friend. She was docile and good tempered, yet gay and playful as a summer insect. Although she was lively and animated, her feelings were strong and deep, and her disposition uncommonly affectionate. No one could better enjoy liberty, yet no one could submit with more grace than she did to constraint and caprice. Her imagination was luxuriant, yet her capability of application was great. Her person was the image of her mind; her hazel eyes, although as lively as a bird's, possessed an attractive softness. Her figure was light and airy; and, though capable of enduring great fatigue, she appeared the most fragile creature in the world. While I admired her understanding and fancy, I loved to tend on her, as I should on a favourite animal; and I never saw so much grace both of person and mind united to so little pretension.

Every one adored Elizabeth. If the servants[8] had any request to make, it was always through her intercession. *We were strangers to any species of disunion or dispute. For, although* there was a great dissimilitude in our characters, *yet there was an harmony in that very dissimilitude.* I was more calm and philosophical than my companion. Yet I was not so mild or yielding. My application was of longer endurance, but it was not so severe whil*st* it *endured. I delighted in investigating the facts relating to the actual world—she busied herself in following the aerial creations of the poets. The world was to me a secret which I desired to discover—to her it was a vacancy which she sought to people with imaginations of her own.*

My brothers were considerably younger than myself, but I had a friend in one of my schoolfellows who compensated for this *deficiency.* Henry Clerval[9] was the son of a merchant of Geneva, an intimate friend of my father. He was a boy of singular talent and fancy. I remember when he was only nine years old he wrote a fairy tale which was the delight and amazement of all his companions. His favourite study *consisted in* books of chivalry and romance; and, *when very young, I can remember that* we used to act plays composed by him out of *these* books, the principal characters of which were Orlando, Robin Hood, Amadis, and St. George. No youth could be more happy than mine. My parents were indulgent, and my companions amiable. Our studies were never forced, and by some means we always had an end placed in view which excited us to ardour *in the prosecution of them.* It was by this *method*, not by emulation, that we were urged. Elizabeth was not told to apply herself to drawing *that* her companions *might not* outstrip her, but *by the desire of* pleas*ing* her aunt by *the representation* of some favourite scene done by her own hand.

We learned Latin and English *that we might* read the writ*ings in* those languages; and, so far from study being rendered odious to us through punishment, we loved application, and our amusements *would have been* the labours of other children. Perhaps we did not read so many books or learn languages so quickly as *those who are disciplined according to the ordinary method*, but what we learned was impressed *the more deeply* on our memory. In th*e* description of our domestic circle I include Henry Clerval, for he was constantly with us. He went to school with me and generally passed the afternoon at our house; for being an only child, and destitute of companions at home, his father was pleased that he should find associates at our house; and we were never completely happy when Clerval was absent.

Chapter 2

Those events which materially influence our future destinies often *derive their origin from a* trivial occurrence. Natural philosophy is the genius that has regulated my fate; I *desire* therefore in this account of my early years to state those facts which led to my predilection for that science. When I was eleven years old[10] we all went on a party of pleasure to the baths near Thonon. *T*he inclemency of the weather obliged us to remain a day confined to the inn. In this house I chanced to find a volume of the works of Cornelius Agrippa.[11] I opened it with apathy; the theory that he attempted to demonstrate and the wonderful facts that he relates soon changed this feeling into enthusiasm. A new light dawned upon my mind; and, bounding with joy, I communicated my discovery to my father. I cannot help here remarking the many opportunities instructors *possess* of directing the attention of their pupils to useful knowledge, which they utterly neglect. My father looked carelessly at the title page of my book and said, "Ah! Cornelius Agrippa! My dear Victor, do not waste your time upon this; it is sad trash." If instead of this remark, or rather exclamation, my father had taken the pains to explain to me that the principles of Agrippa had been entirely exploded and that a modern system of science had been introduced which possessed much greater power than the ancient, because the powers of the ancient were pretended and chimerical, while those of the moderns are real and practical—under such circumstances I should certainly have thrown Agrippa aside and, with my imagination warmed as it was, should probably have applied myself to the more rational theory of chemistry which has *resulted from modern discoveries. It is even possible that the train of my ideas might never have received that fatal impulse which led me to my ruin*. But the cursory glance my father had taken of my volume by no means assured me that he was acquainted with its contents; and I continued to read with the greatest avidity.

When I returned home, my first care was to procure the *whole* works of this author and afterwards those of Paracelsus and Albertus Magnus.[12] I read and studied the wild fancies of the*se* authors with delight; they appeared to me treasures known to few besides myself; and, although I often wished to *communicate* these secret stores of knowledge to my father, yet his definite[13] censure of my favourite Agrippa always withheld me. I disclosed my secret to Elizabeth, therefore, under a strict promise of secrecy; but she did not interest herself in *the subject*, and I was left by her to pursue my studies alone.

It may appear very strange that a disciple of Albertus Magnus should arise in the eighteenth century; but our family was not scientifical, and I *had* not attend*ed* any of the lectures given at Geneva. My dreams were therefore undisturbed by reality, and I entered with the greatest diligence into the search of the philosopher's stone and the *elixir of life*. But the latter obtained my most undivided attention; wealth was an inferior object, but what would be the glory of the discovery if I could banish disease from the human frame and render man invulnerable to any but *a* violent death.

Nor were these my only visions; the raising of ghosts or devils *was a promise liberally accorded by my favourite authors, the fulfilment of which I most eagerly sought*; and *if my incantations were always unsuccessful*, I attributed *the failure* rather to my own inexperience and mistake, than *to a* want of skill *or fidelity* in my instructors.

The natural phænomena that take place every day before our eyes did not escape my exa*min*ations. Distillation,[14] of which my favourite authors were utterly ignorant, excited my astonishment, but my utmost wonder was *engaged by some experiments on* an air pump which I saw *employed* by a gentleman whom we were in the habit of visiting.

The ignorance of my philosophers on these and several other points served to decrease *their* credit with me—but I could not entirely throw them aside before *some* other system *should* occupy their place *in my mind*.

When I was about fourteen years old,[15] we were at our house near Belrive when we witnessed a violent *and* terrible thunder storm. It advanced from behind Jura, and the thunder burst at once with frightful loudness from various quarters of the heavens. I remained while *the storm* lasted, watching its progress with curiosity and delight. *As I stood at the door, on a sudden* I beheld *a stream of* fire issue from an old and beautiful oak about twenty yards from our house; and *so soon as* the dazzling light vanished, the oak had disappeared, *and* nothing remained but a blasted stump. When we visited it the next morning, we found the tree shattered in a singular manner. It was not splintered by the shock, but entirely reduced to thin ribbands of wood. I never saw any thing so utterly destroyed. The catastrophe of the tree excited my extreme astonishment.

Among other questions suggested by natural objects, I eagerly enquired of my father *the nature and the origin of* thunder and lightning. He replied, "electricity," describing at the same time the effect of that power. He *constructed* a small electrical machine and exhibited a few experiments and made a kite with a wire *and* string *which* drew down that fluid from the clouds.

This last stroke completed the overthrow of Cornelius Agrippa, Albertus Magnus, and Paracelsus, who had so long reigned the lords of my imagination. But by some fatality I did not feel inclined to commence any modern system, and this *dis*inclination was influenced by the following circumstance.

My father expressed a wish that I should attend a course of lectures upon natural philosophy, to which I *cheerfully* consented. *Some accident prevented my attending these lectures until it was nearly finished. The lecture which I attended, being thus almost* the last in his course, *was entirely incomprehensible to me.* The professor talked with the greatest fluency of potassium and boron, of sulphates and oxides, *terms* to which I could affix *no* idea: I was disgusted with a science that appeared to me to contain only words.

From this time until I went to college I entirely neglected my formerly adored study of the science of *natural philosophy,* although I still read with delight Pliny and Buffon,[16] authors in my estimation *of nearly equal interest and utility.*

My occupations at this age were principally the mathematics, and most of the branches of study appertaining to that science. I was also busily employed in learning languages; Latin was *already* familiar to me, and I began to read without the help of the *lexicon* some of the easiest Greek authors. I also understood English and German perfectly. This is a list of my accomplishments at *the age of* seventeen;[17] and you may conceive that my hours were fully employed in acquiring and maintaining a knowledge of this various literature.

Another task also devolved upon me when I became the instructor of my brothers. Ernest was five[18] years younger than myself and was my principal pupil. He had been afflicted with ill health from his infancy, *through which* Elizabeth and I had been his constant nurses: his disposition was gentle, but he was incapable of any severe application. William, the younge*st* of our family, was quite a child and the most beautiful little fellow in the world; his lively blue eyes, dimpled cheeks, and endearing manners inspired the tenderest affection. Such was our domestic circle from which care and pain seemed for ever banished. My father directed our studies, and my mother partook of our enjoyments. Neither of us possessed an envied pre-eminence over the other, the voice of command was never heard among us, but mutual affection engaged us all to comply with and *to* obey the slightest desire of each other.

Chapter 3

When I had attained the age of seventeen, my parents resolved that I should *become a student at* the University of Ingolstadt.[19] I had hitherto attended the schools of Geneva, but my father thought it necessary for the completion of my education that I should be *made* acquainted with other customs *than* those of my native country. My departure was therefore fixed at an early date. But before the day resolved upon could arrive, the first misfortune of my life occurred: an omen, *as it were*, of my future misery.

Elizabeth had caught the scarlet fever; but her illness was not severe, and she quickly recovered. During her confinement, many arguments had been urged to persuade my mother *to refrain from* attending upon her. She had yielded *to our entreaties*; but, when she heard that her favourite was recovering, she *c*ould no longer debar herself from her society and entered her sick chamber long before *the danger of infection was past*. The consequences of this imprudence were fatal: on the third day my mother sickened. Her fever was malignant, and the looks of her attendants prognosticated the worst evil. On her death-bed the fortitude and benignity of *this admirable woman* did not desert her. She joined the hands of Elizabeth and myself. "My children," said she, "it was on your union that my firmest hopes of future happiness were placed. It will now be the consolation of your father. Elizabeth, my love, supply my place to your young cousins. Alas! I regret *that I am* taken from you; and, happy and beloved as I am, is it not hard to quit you all? But these are not thoughts befitting me; I will endeavour to resign myself cheerfully to death and will indulge a hope of meeting you in another world."

She died calmly, and her features expressed affection even in death. I need not describe the feelings of those whose dearest ties are rent by that most irreparable evil, the void that every where presents itself to the soul, and the despair that is exhibited on the countenance. It is so long before the mind can persuade itself that she, whom they saw every day, and whose very existence appeared a part of theirs, can have departed for ever: that the brightness of a loved eye can have *been extinguished*, and the sound of a voice so familiar and dear to the ear can be hushed, never more to be heard. These are the reflections of the first days. But when the lapse of time proves the reality of the evil, then the bitterness of grief commences. *Yet, from whom* has not that rude hand *rent away some dear connection*, and why *should* I describe a sorrow which all have felt, and must feel? *T*he time at length arrives when grief is rather an indulgence than a necessity; and the smile that plays on the lips, although it is deemed sacrilege, is not banished. My mother was dead, but we had still duties which we ought to perform; we must continue our course with the rest *and learn to think ourselves fortunate, whilst one remains whom the spoiler has not seized.*

My journey to Ingolstadt, which had been deferred by these events, was now again determined upon. I obtain*ed* from my father *a* respite of some weeks. This time was spent sadly. My mother's death and my speedy departure depressed our spirits, but Elizabeth endeavoured to *renew the spirit*[20] of cheerfulness in our little society. Since the death of her aunt, her mind had acquired new firmness and vigour. She determined to fulfil her duties with the greatest exactitude, and *she felt that the* most imperious duty *of* render*ing* her uncle and cousins happy *had devolved on her*. She consoled me, amused her uncle, instructed my brothers; and I never beheld her so enchanting as at this time when she was continually endeavouring to contribute to the happiness of others, entirely forgetful of herself.

The day of my departure at length arrived. I had taken leave of all my friends excepting Clerval, who spent the last evening with us. He bitterly lamented that he was *unable* to accompany me. But his father could not *be persuaded* to part with him, intend*ing that he should* become a partner with him in his business, and *in compliance with his favourite theory that learning was superfluous in the commerce of ordinary life*. Henry had a refined mind, he *had no desire* to be idle and was well pleased to become his father's partner, but he believed that a man might be a very good trader and yet *possess* a cultivated understanding.

We sat late, listening to his complaints and making many little arrangements for the future. The next morning early I departed. Tears gushed from the eyes of Elizabeth; they proceeded partly from sorrow at my departure, and partly because she reflected that the same journey was to have taken place three months before when a mother's blessing would have accompanied me.

I threw myself into the chaise that was to convey me away and indulged in the most melancholy reflections. I, who had ever been surrounded by amiable companions, continually engaged in endeavouring to give mutual pleasure; I was now alone. In the university whither I was going, I must form my own friends and be my own *protector*. My life had hitherto been remarkably retired and domestic, and this had given me an invincible repugnance to new countenances. I loved my brothers, Elizabeth, and Clerval; these were "old familiar faces";[21] but I believed myself totally unfitted for the company of strangers. Such were my reflections as I commenced my journey. But as I proceeded, my spirits and hopes rose. I ardently desired knowledge. *I had* often, when at home, thought *it* hard to remain during my youth cooped up in one place, and *had* longed to enter into the world and take my station among other human beings. Now my desires were complied with, and it would indeed *have* be*en* folly to repent.

I had *sufficient* leisure for these and many other reflections during my journey to Ingolstadt, which was long and fatiguing. At length the steeples of the town met my eyes. I alighted and was conducted to my solitary apartment to spend the evening as I pleased.

Chapter 4

The next morning I delivered my letters of introduction and paid a visit to some of the principal professors and, among others, to M. Krempe, professor of natural philosophy. He received me with politeness and asked me several questions concerning my progress in the different branches of science appertaining to natural philosophy. I mentioned, it is true with fear and trembling, the only authors I had ever read upon those subjects. The professor stared. "Have you really," said he, "spent your time in studying such nonsense?" I replied in the affirmative.

"Every minute," continued M. Krempe with warmth, "every instant that you have wasted upon those books is utterly and entirely lost. You have burdened your memory with exploded systems and useless names. Good God! in what desert land have you lived where no one was kind enough to inform you that these fancies which you have so greedily imbibed are a thousand years old and as musty as they are ancient. I little expected in this enlightened and scientific age to find a disciple of Albertus Magnus and Paracelsus. My dear Sir, you must begin your studies entirely anew." So saying, he ste*pp*ed aside and wrote down a list of several books upon natural philosophy which he desired me to procure, and dismissed me after mentioning that in the beginning of the next week he intended to commence a course of lectures upon natural philosophy *in its general relations*; and that M. Waldman,[22] a fellow-professor, would lecture upon chemistry the alternate days which he missed.

I returned home not disappointed, for I had long considered the authors useless which the professor had so strongly reprobated—but I did not feel very much inclined to study those books which at his recommendation I had procured. M. Krempe was a little squat man with a gruff voice and repulsive countenance, and the teacher did not prepossess me in favour of his *doctrine*. Besides, I had a contempt for the uses of modern natural philosophy. It was very different when the masters of the science sought immortality and *power*: such views, although futile, were grand. But now *the scene* was changed: *the ambition of the enquirer seemed to limit itself to the annihilation of those visions on which my interest in science was chiefly founded. I was required to exchange chimeras of boundless grandeur, for realities of little worth.*

Such were my reflections during two or three days spent almost in solitude: but, as the ensuing week commenced, I thought of the information M. Krempe had given me concerning the lectures. And although I could not consent to go and hear that little conceited fellow deliver sentences out of a pulpit, I recollected what he had said of M. Waldman, whom I had never seen as he had been hitherto out of town.

Partly from curiosity and partly from idleness, I went into the lecturing room which M. Waldman entered shortly after. This professor was a very different man from his colleague. He was about fifty but with aspect expressive of the greatest benevolence;

a few grey hairs covered his temples, but those at the back of his head were nearly black. He was short in person but remarkably erect, and his voice the sweetest I had ever heard. He began his lecture *by a recapitulation of the* history of chemistry and the various improvements made by various men of learning, pronouncing with fervour the names of the greatest discoverers. He then took a cursory view of the present state of *the science* and explained many of its terms. *After making* a few preparatory experiments, *he* concluded with a panegyric upon modern chemistry, the words of which I shall never forget.

"The ancient teachers of this science," said he, "promised impossibilities and performed nothing. The modern masters promise very little. They know that metals cannot be transmuted and that the elixir of life is a chimera. But these philosophers, whose hands appear only made to dabble in dirt and their eyes to pore over the microscope or crucible, have indeed performed miracles. They penetrate into the recesses of nature and shew how she works in her hiding-places. They ascend into the heavens; they have discovered how the blood circulates and the nature of the air we breathe. The*y* have acquired new and almost unlimited powers: they can command the thunders of heaven, mimick the earthquake, and even mock the invisible world with its own shadows."

I departed highly pleased with the professor and his lecture and paid him a visit the same evening. His manners in private were even more mild and attractive than in public. For there was a certain dignity in his manner during his lectures which was replaced by the greatest affability and kindness in his own house. He heard my little narration concerning my studies with attention and smiled at the names of Cornelius Agrippa and Paracelsus, but without the contempt that M. Krempe had exhibited. *He said that* "*these were men to whose indefatigable zeal modern philosophers*[23] *were indebted for most of the foundations of their knowledge. They* had *left to us*, *as an easier task*, *to give new names and arrange in connected classifications the facts which they to a great degree had been the instruments of bringing to light. The labours of men of genius, however erroneously directed, scarcely ever failed in ultimately turning to the solid advantage of mankind.*" I listened to his statement, which was delivered without any presumption, and then added[24] that his lecture had removed my prejudice against modern chemists; and I requested at the same time his advice concerning the books I ought to procure.

"I am happy," said M. Waldman, "to have gained a disciple; and if your application equals your ability, I have no doubt of your success. Chemistry is that branch of natural philosophy in which the greatest improvements have *been* and may be made. It is on that account that I chose it for my peculiar study. But at the same time I did not neglect the other sciences. A man would make a very sorry chemist if he attended to that department alone. If your wish is really to become a man of science and not merely a pretty[25] experimentalist, I should advise you to apply to every branch of natural philosophy, *including* mathematics."

He then took me into his laboratory and explained to me *the use of* his various machines, *instructing me as to* what I ought to procure and promising me the use of his *own* when I should have advanced far enough in the study not to derange their mechanism. He also gave me the list of books which I had requested, and I took my leave.

Thus ended a day memorable to me, for it decided my destiny.

Chapter 5

From this day natural philosophy and particularly chemistry became nearly my sole study. I read with ardour those books so full of genius and discrimination *which modern enquirers* have written on these subjects. I attended the lectures and cultivated the acquaintance of the men of science of the university; and I found even in M. Krempe a great deal of sound sense and real information—combined, it is true, with a repulsive physiognomy and manners, but not on that account the less valuable. In M. Waldman I found a true friend. His gentleness was never tinged by dogmatism, and his instructions were given with an air of frankness and good nature that banished every idea of pedantry. It was perhaps the amiable character of this man that inclined me more to the study of that branch of natural philosophy which he professed than an intrinsic love for the science itself. But this *state of mind had place* only in the first steps towards knowledge; *the more fully* I entered into *science*, the more I *pursued* it for its own sake. That application, which at first had been a matter of duty *and resolution*, now became so ardent and eager that the stars often disappeared *in the light of morning* while I was yet *engaged* in my laboratory.

As I applied so closely, it may be easily conceived that I improved rapidly. My ardour was indeed the astonishment of the students, and my proficiency that of the master. Professor Krempe often asked me with a sly smile how Cornelius Agrippa went on, *while M. Waldman expressed the most heartfelt exultation in my progress*. Two years passed in this manner during which I paid no visit to Geneva, but was engaged heart and soul in the pursuit of some discoveries which I hoped to make. None but those who have experienced it can conceive of the enticements of science. In other studies you go as far as others have gone before you, and there is nothing more to *know*; but in a scientific pursuit there is continual food for discovery and wonder. A mind of moderate capacity who closely pursues one study must infallibly arrive at great proficiency in that study. And I, who continually *sought the attainment of* one *object* and *was* wrapt up in this *sole pursuit*, improved so rapidly that at the end of the two years I made *some* discoveries in the improvement of some chemical *instruments*, which procured me great esteem and admiration at the university. When I arrived at this point *and had learned all the professors at Ingolstadt were qualified to teach*, my residence *there being* no longer conducive to my improvement, I thought of returning to my friends and to my native town, when an incident happened that protracted my stay.

One of those phænomena which had peculiarly attracted my attention was the structure of the human frame and, indeed, that of any animal endued with life. Whence, I often asked myself, did this principle of life proceed? It was a bold question and one *which* has ever been considered as a mystery. Yet how many things are we on the brink of becoming acquainted with, if cowardice or carelessness did not restrain *our enquiries*? I revolved these circumstances in my mind and determined from thenceforth to apply myself more particularly to th*ose* branch*es* of natural philosophy which *relate to* physiology. Unless I had been animated by an almost supernatural enthusiasm, my application to this study would have been irksome and almost intolerable. To examine the causes of life, we must first have recourse to death. I became acquainted with the science of anatomy, but this was not sufficient. I must also observe the natural decay and corruption of the human body. In my education my father had taken the greatest precautions that my mind should be impressed by *no* supernatural horrors. I do not ever remember having trembled at a *tale of superstition* or to have feared the apparition of *a* spirit. Darkness had no effect upon my fancy; and a churchyard was to me merely *as* the receptacle of bodies deprived of life and *which*, from being the seat of beauty and strength, *became* food for the worm. Now I was *led* to examine the cause and progress of this decay and forced to spend days and nights in vaults and charnel houses. My attention was fixed upon every *object the most insupportable to the delicacy of* the human feelings. I saw how the fine form of man was degraded and wasted; I beheld the corruption of death succeed to the blooming cheek of life; *I saw* how the worm *inherited* the wonders of the eye and brain. I paused, examin*ing* and analyz*ing all the minutiæ of causation as exemplified in the change from life to death*, *and death to life*, until from the midst of this darkness a sudden light broke in upon me. A light so brilliant and wondrous yet so simple that, while *I became dizzy with the immensity of the prospect which it illustrated*, I was surprised that I—among so many men of genius who had applied to the same science—that I alone should discover this astonishing secret.

Remember, I am not recording the vision of a madman. The sun does not more certainly shine in the heavens than that wh*ich* I now *affirm* is true. Some miracle might have produced it. But the stages of discovery were distinct and probable. After days and nights of incredible *labour* and fatigue, I succeeded in discovering the cause of generation and life. Nay more, I *became* myself capable of bestowing animation upon lifeless matter.

The surprise *which* I at first experienced on this discovery soon gave place to delight and rapture. After so much time spent in painful labour, to arrive at once at the summit of my desires was the most gratifying circumstance that could have occurred. But this discovery was so great and overwhelming that all the steps *by which I had been* progressively led to it were obliterated, and I beheld only the result. What had been the study and desire of the wisest men since the creation of the world was now *within* my grasp—not that, like a magic scene, it all opened upon me at once. The information I had obtained was *of a nature* rather *to* direct my endeavours *so soon as I should point them towards the object of my search*, *than to exhibit that object already accomplished*. I was like the Arabian who had been buried with the dead and found a passage to life, aided only by one glimmering and seemingly ineffectual light.[26]

I see by your eagerness and the wonder and hope which your eyes express, my friend, that you expect to be informed of the secret with which I am acquainted—*that cannot be*. Listen patiently to the end of my story, and you will easily perceive why I am reserved upon that subject. I will not lead you on, unguarded and ardent as I then was, to your destruction and infallible misery. Learn from me, if not by my precepts at least by my example, how dangerous is the acquirement of knowledge and how much happier that man is who believes his native town the world, than he who aspires to become greater than his nature will allow.

Chapter 6

When I found *so* astonishing *a* power placed *within* my hands, I hesitated a long time concerning the *manner in which* I should *employ* it. Although I possessed the capacity of bestowing animation, yet to prepare a *frame* for the reception of it with all its intricacies of fibres, muscles, and veins *still remained* a work of inconceivable difficulty and labour.[27] I doubted at first whether I should attempt the creation of a being like myself or one of simpler organization; but my imagination was too much exalted by my first success to permit me to doubt of my ability to *give life to* an animal as complex and wonderful as man. *The materials at present within my command* hardly appeared adequate to so arduous an undertaking, but I *doubted not that I should ultimately succeed. I prepared myself for a multitude of reverses*; *my operations might be baffled incessantly, and at last my work be but imperfect*; *yet, when I considered* the improvement *which* every day takes place in science and mechanics, *I was encouraged to hope* my *present* attempts would *at least lay the foundations of future success. Nor could I consider* the magnitude and *complexity* of my plan as any argument of its impracticability. *I*t was with these feelings *that* I began the creation of a human being. As the *minuteness* of the parts *formed* a great hindrance to my speed, I resolved, contrary to my first intention, to make *the being* of a gigantic stature; that is to say, about seven or eight feet in height, and proportionably large. After having formed this determination and having spent some months in *successfully* collecting *and arranging* my materials, I began.

No one can conceive the variety of feelings which pressed upon me during this time. When success raised me to enthusiasm, life and death appeared to me ideal bounds, which I should first break *through*, and pour a torrent of light into our dark world. A new *existence* would bless me as its creator and source; many happy and excellent *natures* would owe their *being* to me. No father could claim the gratitude of his child *so completely as I should deserve theirs*. Pursuing *these* reflections, I thought that if I could bestow animation upon lifeless matter I might in process of time (although I now found it impossible) renew life where death had apparently devoted the body to corruption.

These thoughts supported my spirits while I pursued my undertaking with unremitting ardour. My cheek *had grown* pale with study; and my person, *become* emaciated by confinement. Sometimes on the very brink of certainty I failed, yet I still clung to the hope which the next day or the next hour might realize. One secret which I alone possessed was the hope to which I clung; and the moon gazed on my midnight labours while, with unrelaxed and breathless eagerness, I pursued nature to her most secret hiding-places. Who shall *conceive the horrors of* my secret *toil* as I dabbled among the unhallowed damps of the grave or tortured the living animal to animate *the* lifeless clay? My limbs *now* tremble, and my eyes swim with the remembrance; but then a resistless and almost frantic *impulse* urged me *forward*; I seemed to have lost all soul or sensation but for one pursuit. It was indeed a passing trance that only made me feel with renewed acuteness *so soon as*, the unnatural stimulus ceas*ing* to operate, I had returned to my old habits. I collected bones from charnel houses and with profane fingers meddled with the secrets of the human frame. In a solitary chamber—or rather cell at the top of the house and separated from all other apartments by a gallery and staircase—I kept my workshop of filthy creation; my eyeballs were starting from their sockets in attending to the minutiæ of my employment. The dissecting room and the slaughter house furnished many of my materials, and often did my human nature turn from my occupation *whilst*, still urged on by an eagerness which *perpetually* encreased, *I brought* my work near *to* a conclusion.

The summer months passed while I was thus *engaged*, heart and soul, in one pursuit. It was a most beautiful season: never did the fields bestow a more plentiful harvest, or the vines yield a more luxuriant vintage. But my eyes were *insensible* to the charms of nature, and the same feelings which made me neglect the scenes around me caused me also to forget those friends who were so many miles absent and whom I had not seen for so long a time. I knew that my silence disquieted them, and I well remembered the words of my father: "I know that while you are pleased with yourself, you will think of us with affection, and we shall hear regularly from you. And you must pardon me if I regard any interruption in your correspondence as a proof that your other *duties* are equally neglected." I knew well therefore what would be *his feelings*; but I could not tear my thoughts from my occupation, loathsome in itself, but which had taken a*n irresistible* hold of my imagination. I wished as it were to procrastinate *all that related to* my feelings of affection, until the great object *which swallowed up every habit of my nature should be* completed.

I then thought that my father would be unjust if he ascribed my neglect to vice or faultiness on my part; but I am now convinced that he was in the right in conceiving that I should not be altogether free from blame. A human being in perfection ought always to preserve a calm and peaceful mind and never to allow passion or a transitory desire to disturb his tranquillity. I do not think that the pursuit of knowledge is any exception to this rule. If the study to which you apply yourself has a tendency to weaken your affections and to destroy your taste for those simple pleasures in which no alloy can possibly mix, then that study is certainly unlawful, that is to say, not befitting the human mind. If this rule *were* always observed—if no man allowed any pursuit whatsoever to interfere with his tranquillity and *his* domestic affections—Greece had never been enslaved, Cæsar would have spared his country, America would have been discovered more gradually, and the Empires of Mexico and Peru had not been destroyed.

But I forget that I am moralizing in the most interesting part of my tale; and your looks remind me to proceed.

My father made no reproach in his letters, and only took notice of my silence by enquiring more particularly than before what my occupations were. Winter, spring, and summer passed away during my labours, but I did not watch the blossom or the expanding leaves—sights which before had always yielded me supreme delight—so *deeply* was I *engrossed in* my occupation. The leaves of that year were withered before my work drew near a close. And now every day shewed me more plainly how well I had succeeded. But my enthusiasm was checked by my anxiety, and I appeared rather like one doomed by slavery to toil in the mines, or any other unwholesome trade, than an artist occupied in his favourite employment. Every night a slow fever oppressed me, and I became nervous to a most painful degree—a disease I regretted *the* more because I had hitherto enjoyed excellent health and had always boasted of *the* firm*ness of my* nerves. But I believed that exercise and amusement would soon drive away *such* symptoms, and I promised myself both of these when my creation should be complete.

Chapter 7

It was on a dreary night of November that I beheld my man completed; with an anxiety that almost amounted to agony, I collected instruments of life around me that I might infuse a spark of being into the lifeless thing that lay at my feet. It was already one in the morning, the rain pattered dismally against the window panes, and my candle was nearly burnt out, when by the glimmer of the half-extinguished light I saw the dull yellow eye of the creature open. It breathed hard, and a convulsive motion agitated its limbs.

How can I describe my emotion at this catastrophe, or how delineate the wretch whom with such infinite pains and care I had endeavoured to form? His limbs were in proportion, and I had selected his features as *beautiful*. *Beautiful*!—Great God! His yellow skin scarcely covered the work of muscles and arteries beneath; his hair was *of a lustrous black and* flowing; and his teeth of a pearly whiteness; but these luxuriances only formed a more horrid contrast with his watery eyes, that seemed almost of the same colour as the dun white sockets in which they were set, his shrivelled complexion, and straight black lips.

The different accidents of life are not so changeable as the feelings of human nature. I had worked hard for nearly two years for the sole purpose of infusing life into an inanimate body. For this I had deprived myself of rest and health. I had desired it with an ardour that far exceed*ed* moderation; but, now that I had succeeded, these dreams vanished, and breathless horror and disgust filled my heart. Unable to endure the aspect of the *being* I had created, I rushed out of the room and *continued* a long time traversing my bed chamber, unable to compose my mind to sleep. At length, lassitude succeeded to the tumult I had before endured, and I threw myself on my bed in my clothes, endeavouring to seek a few moments of forgetfulness. But it was in vain; I slept indeed, but I was disturbed by the wildest dreams. I saw Elizabeth in the bloom of health walking in the streets of Ingolstadt; delighted and surprised, I embraced her; but as I imprinted the first kiss on her lips, they became lurid with the hue of death; her features appeared to change, and I thought that I held the corpse of my dead mother in my arms; a shroud enveloped her form, and I saw the grave worms crawling in the folds of the flannel. I started from my sleep with horror, a cold dew covered my forehead, my teeth chattered, and every limb *became* convulsed, when, by the dim and yellow light of the moon as it forced its way through the window shutters, I beheld the wretch—the miserable monster whom I had created. He held up the curtain, and his eyes—if eyes they may be called—were fixed on me. His jaws opened, and he muttered some *inarticulate sounds* while a grin wrinkled his cheeks. He might have spoken, but I did not hear—one hand was stretched out to detain me, but I escaped and rushed down stairs. I took refuge in a court-yard belonging to the house which I inhabited, where I remained *during* the rest of the night, walking up and down in the greatest agitation, listening attentively, catching and fearing each sound as if it were to announce the arrival of the dæmoniacal corpse to which I had so miserabl*y* given life.

Oh! no mortal could support the horror of that countenance. A mummy again endued with *animation* could not be so hideous as He.[28] I had gazed on him while unfinished; he was ugly then. But when those muscles and joints were endued with motion, it became a thing such as even Dante could never have conceived.

I passed the night wretchedly—sometimes my pulses beat so quickly and hardly that I felt the palpitation of every artery; at others, I nearly sunk to the ground *through* languor and extreme weakness; and mingled with this horror, I felt the bitterness of disappointment. Dreams that had been my food and rest for so long a space were now become a hell to me. And the change was so rapid, the overthrow so complete.

Morning—dismal and wet—at length dawned, and discovered to my sleepless and aching eyes the church of Ingolstadt, its white steeple and *its* clock which pointed to the sixth hour. The porter opened the gates of the court which had that night been my asylum, and I issued into the streets, pacing *them* with quick steps as if I sought to *avoid* the wretch whom I feared every turning in the street would present to my view. I did not dare return to the apartment which I inhabited but felt impelled to hurry on, although wetted by the rain which poured from a black and comfortless sky.

I continued walking in this manner for some time, endeavouring by bodily exercise to ease the load that weighed upon my mind. I traversed the streets without any clear conception of where I was or what I was doing: my heart palpitated *in the sickness of* fear; and I hurried on with irregular steps, not daring to look about me,

> "Like one who on a lonesome road
> Doth walk in fear and dread,
> And having once turned round walks on
> And turns no more his head,
> Because he knows a frightful fiend
> Doth close behind him tread."[29]

Continuing thus, I came at length opposite *to* the inn at which the diligences and carriages usually stopped. Here I paused, I knew not why, but remained some minutes with my eyes fixed on a coach that was coming towards me from the other end of the street. As it drew nearer, I observed that it was the Swiss diligence; it stopped just where I was standing; and, on the doors being opened, I perceived Henry Clerval, who on seeing me instantly sprung out.

"My dear Frankenstein!" exclaimed he. "How glad I am to see you; how fortunate *that* you should be here at the *very* moment of my alighting."

Nothing could equal my delight on seeing Clerval: his presence brought back to my thoughts my father, Elizabeth, and all those scenes of home so dear to my recollection. I grasped his hand and, in a moment, forgot my horror and misfortune. I felt *suddenly, and* for the first time *during* many months, calm and serene joy. I welcomed my friend, therefore, in the most cordial manner, and we walked towards my college. Clerval continued talking for some time about *our mutual* friends and his *own* good fortune in being allowed to come to Ingolstadt.

"You may believe," said he, "it was not without considerable trouble that I persuaded my father that it is not absolutely necessary for a merchant to know nothing except book-keeping; and, indeed, I believe I left him incredulous to the last, for his constant answer to my applications was the same as *that of* the Dutch schoolmaster in 'The Vicar of Wakefield': 'I have ten thousand florins a year without Greek, I eat heartily without Greek.'[30] But his affection for me at length overcame his dislike for learning, and he permitted me to *under*take a voyage *of discovery* to the land of knowledge."

"And my father, brothers, and Elizabeth?" said I.

"Very well and very happy," replied he, "only a little uneasy that they hear from you so seldom, and, by the bye, I mean to lecture you a little upon their account myself. But my dear Frankenstein," continued he, stopping short and gazing full in my face, "I did not before remark how very ill you are. So thin and pale, you appear as if you had been watching for several nights."

"You have guessed right," I replied; "I have lately been so engaged in *one* occupation that I *have* not allow*ed* myself sufficient rest, as you see; but I hope, I sincerely hope, all those occupations are at an end—I am free now, I hope."

I trembled excessively: I could not bear to think of, and far less to allude to, the occurrences of the preceding night. I walked therefore with a quick pace, and we soon arrived at my college. I then reflected—and the thought made me shiver—that the creature whom I had left in my apartment might be still there, alive and walking about. I dreaded to see him, but I dreaded still more that Henry should behold the monster. Entreat*ing* him *therefore* to remain a few minute*s* at the bottom of the stairs, I darted up towards my own room. My hand was already on the lock before I recovered myself, when I paused, and a cold shivering came over me. I threw the door open as children are accustomed to do when they expect a spectre to stand in waiting for them on the other side. But nothing appeared. I stepped fearfully in—the apartment was empty, and my bedroom was also freed from its hideous guest. I could hardly believe that so great a good fortune could have befallen me; but when I *became* assured that my enemy had indeed fled, I clapped my hands for joy and ran down to Henry.

We ascended into my room, and presently the servant brought breakfast: but I was unable to contain myself. It was not joy only that possessed me; I felt my flesh tingle with the excess of sensitiveness, and my pulse beat rapidly. I was unable to remain for a single instant in the same place; I jumped over the chairs, clapped my hands, and laughed aloud. Clerval at first attributed my unusual spirits to joy on his arrival; but, when he observed me *more attentively*, he saw a wildness in my eyes for which he could not account; and my loud, unrestrained, heartless laughter frightened and astonished him.

"My dear Frankenstein," cried he, "what for God's sake is the matter? Do not laugh so. How ill you are! What is the cause of all this?"

"Do not ask me," cried I, putting my hands before my eyes, for I thought I saw the spectre glide into the room. "He can tell! Oh, save me! save me!" I imagined that the monster seized me; I struggled furiously and fell down in a fit.

Poor Clerval! What must have been his feelings? A meeting which he had anticipated with such joy so strangely turned to bitterness. But I did not witness his grief, for I was lifeless and did not recover my senses for a long, long time.

Chapter 8

This was the commencement of a nervous fever which confined me for several months. During all this time Henry was my only nurse. I afterwards learned that, knowing my father's advanced age and unfitness for so long a journey and how wretched Elizabeth would be, he had spared them this grief by concealing the extent of my disorder. He knew that I could not have a more kind and attentive nurse than himself; and, firm in the hope he had of my recovery, he did not doubt that, instead of doing harm, he performed the kindest action that he could towards them.

But I was in reality very ill, and surely nothing but the unbounded and unremitting attentions of my friend could have restored me to life. The form of the monster on whom I had bestowed life was for ever before *my* eyes, and I raved incessantly concerning him. Doubtless my words surprised Henry: he at first believed them the wanderings of my disordered imagination; but the pertinacity with which I continually recurred to the same subject *persuaded him that my disorder owed its origin to some uncommon and terrible event.*

By very slow degrees and with frequent relapses that alarmed and grieved my friend, I recovered. I remember that the first time I was capable of observing outward objects with any kind of pleasure, I perceived that the fallen leaves had disappeared and that young buds were shooting forth from the trees. It was a divine spring, and the season no doubt contributed greatly to my convalescence. I felt also sentiments of joy and affection revive in *my* bosom, my gloom disappeared, and in a short time I became as cheerful as before I was attacked by the fatal passion.

"Dearest Clerval," said I, "how kind, how very good you are to me. This whole winter, instead of spending it in study as you promised yourself, has been consumed in my sick room: how shall I ever repay you? I feel the greatest remorse for the disappointment I have been the occasion of. But you will forgive me."

"You will repay me," replied Henry, "if you do not discompose yourself; but get well as fast as you can. And since you appear in such good spirits, I may speak to you on one subject, may I not?"

I trembled. One subject! What could it be? Could he allude to an object on whom I dared not even think? "Do not frighten yourself," said Clerval, who observed my change of colour, "I will not mention it if it agitates you. But your father and cousin would be so happy if they received a letter from you in your own hand. They hardly know how ill you have been and are uneasy at your long silence."

"Is that all?" I said smiling. "My dear Henry, how could you suppose that my first thoughts would not fly towards those dear, dear friends whom I love and who are so deserving of my love."

"If this is your present temper," said Henry, "you will be glad perhaps to see a letter that has been lying here some day*s*: it is from your cousin, I believe."

He then put the[31] following letter into my hands.

"To V. Frankenstein.

"Geneva, March 18th, 17—.

"My dear Cousin,

"I cannot describe to you the uneasiness we have all felt concerning your health. We cannot help imagining that your friend Clerval conceals the extent of your disorder, for it is now several months since we have seen your handwriting; and all this time you have been obliged to dictate to Henry. Surely, Victor, you must have been very ill; and this makes us very wretched, as much so nearly as after the death of your dear mother. My father was almost persuaded *that you were indeed dangerously ill* and could hardly *be* res*t*rain*ed* from *undertaking* a journey to Ingolstadt. Clerval always writes that you were getting better; I eagerly hope you will confirm this *intelligence* soon in your own handwriting, for indeed, indeed Victor, we are all very miserable on this account. Relieve us from this fear, and we shall be the happiest creatures in the world. My uncle's health is now so vigorous that he appears ten years younger since last winter. Ernest also is so much improved that you would hardly know him; he is now nearly sixteen, you know, and has lost that sickly appearance that he had some years ago; he is quite well and hearty, if I may use that term, for it is very expressive.

"My uncle and I conversed last night a long time about what profession Ernest should follow. His constant ill health when young has deprived him of the habit of application; and now that he enjoys good health, he is continually in the open air, climbing the hills or rowing on the lake. I therefore proposed that he should *be* a farmer, which you know, cousin, is a favourite scheme of mine. A farmer's is a very healthy, happy life—and the least hurtful, or rather the most beneficial, profession *of any*. My uncle had an idea of his being *educated as* an advocate, *that* through his interest *he might become* a judge. But, besides that he is not at all fit for such an occupation, it is certainly *more creditable* to cultivate the earth for the sustenance of man than to be the confidant and sometimes *the accomplice* of *his* vices, which is the employment of a lawyer. I said that *the occupation of a prosperous* farmer, if it were not a more honourable, it was at least a happier employment than that of a judge, whose misfortune it was always to meddle with the dark side of human nature. My uncle smiled and said that I ought to be an advocate myself, which put an end to the conversation on that subject.

"And now I must tell you a little story that will please you. Do you not remember Justine Moritz?[32] Perhaps you do not; I will therefore tell you her story in few words. Madame Moritz, her mother, was a widow with four children of whom Justine was the third. This girl had always been the favourite of her father; but, *through* an odd perversity, her mother could not endure her and, after the death of M. Moritz, treated her very ill. My aunt observed this and, when Justine was twelve years old, prevailed on her mother to allow her to live at our house. *The republican institutions of our country have produced simpler and happier manners than those which prevail in the great monarchies that surround it. Hence there is less distinction between the classes into which human beings have been divided: and the lower orders, being neither so poor nor so despised, are more refined and moral. A servant at Geneva does not mean the same thing as a servant in France or England—Justine was thus received into our family to learn the duties of a servant, which in our fortunate country does not include a sacrifice of the dignity of a human being.* I dare say that you now remember all about it, for Justine was a great favourite of yours; and I *recollect* you once said that if you were in an ill humour one glance from Justine could dissipate it *for* the same reason that Ariosto gave concerning the beauty of Angelica[33]—she looked so frank-hearted and happy. My aunt *conceived an attachment for her, by which she was* induced to give her an education superior to that which she *had* at first intended. *This benefit* was fully repaid; Justine was the most grateful little creature in the world. I do not mean that she made any professions—I never heard one pass her lips—but you could see by her eye that she almost adored her protectress. Although very gay, and in many respects inconsiderate, yet she paid the greatest attention to every gesture of my aunt—she thought her the *model* of *all excellence* and endeavoured to imitate her words and even her manners, so that *even* now she often reminds me of her.

"When my dearest aunt died, every one was too much occupied in their own grief to notice poor Justine, who had attended her during her illness with the greatest affection.

Poor Justine was very ill, but other trials were reserved for her.

"One by one her brothers and sister had died; and her mother was now, with the exception of her neglected daughter, left childless. The conscience of the woman was troubled, and she began to think that the deaths of her favourites was a judgement *sent* from heaven to *chastise* her partiality. She was a Roman Catholic, and I believe her confessor encouraged the idea *which she had conceived*. Accordingly, a few months after your departure for Ingolstadt, Justine was called home by her repentant mother. Poor girl! she wept when she quitted our house; she was much altered since the death of my aunt; grief had given softness and a winning mildness to her manners, which had before been remarkable for vivacity. Nor was her residence at her mother's house of a nature to restore her gaiety. The poor woman was very vacillating in her repentance. She sometimes begged Justine to forgive her unkindness, but much oftener accused her as having caused the deaths of her brothers and sister. Perpetual fretting at last threw Madame Moritz into a decline, which at first encreased her irritability, but she is now at rest for ever: she died on the first approach of cold at the beginning of this last winter. Justine has returned to us, and I assure you I love her tenderly. She is very clever and extremely mild and pretty; and, as I mentioned before, her *mien* and *her* expressions continually remind me of my dear aunt.

"I must say a few words to you also, my dear Victor, of little darling William. I wish you could see him. He is very tall of his age with sweet, laughing blue eyes, dark eye-lashes, and curling hair. When he smiles, two little dimples appear on his cheeks, which are rosy with health—his chin comes down in a beautiful oval. After this description I can only say what our visitors say a thousand times a day: 'He is too pretty for a boy.' He has already had one or two little wives, but Louisa Biron is his favourite—a pretty little girl of five years old.

"Now, dear Victor, I dare say you wish to be indulged in a little gossip about your acquaintance. The pretty Miss Mansfeld has already received the congratulatory visits on her approaching marriage with a young Englishman, John Melbourne, Esq. Her ugly sister Manon married M. Hofland, the rich banker, last autumn. Your favourite schoolfellow, Louis Manoir, has suffered several misfortunes since the departure of Clerval from Geneva. But he has already recovered his spirits, and he is reported to be on the point of marrying a very lively, pretty Frenchwoman, Madame Tavernier. She is a widow and much older than Manoir, but she is much admired and a favourite with every body.

"I have written myself into good spirits, dear cousin, yet I cannot conclude without again anxiously enquiring concerning your health. Dear Victor, if you are not very ill, write yourself and make your father and all of us happy or——I cannot bear to think on the other side of the question; my tears already flow; write, dearest Victor.

"Your very affectionate cousin,
"Elizabeth Lavenza."

"Dear, dear Elizabeth!" I exclaimed when I had read her letter, "I will write instantly and relieve them from the great pain they must feel."

I wrote, and this exertion greatly fatigued me; but my convalescence had commenced and *proceeded* regularly—in another fortnight I was able to leave my chamber.

Chapter 9

One of my first duties on my recovery was to introduce Clerval to the several professors of the university. And in doing this, I underwent a kind of rough usage ill befitti*ng* the wounds that my mind had sustained. Ever since the fatal night—the end of my labours and the beginning of my misfortunes—I had conceived a violent antipathy even to the name of natural philosophy. When I was otherwise quite restored to health, the sight of *a* chemical instrument *renewed* all *the agony of* my nervous symptoms. Henry saw this and had removed all my apparatus from my view; he had also changed my apartment, for he perceived that I had *acquired* a dislike to the room which had previously been my workshop. But these cares of Clerval were *made of no avail* when I visited the professors. Even my excellent M. Waldman inflicted torture when he praised, with kindness and warmth, the astonishing progress that I had made in the sciences. He soon perceived *that I* dislike*d* the subject; but, not guessing the real cause, he attributed *my feelings* to modesty and changed the subject from my improvement to the science itself, with a desire as I evidently saw of drawing me out. What could I do? He meant to please, and he tormented me. I felt as if he placed carefully, one by one, in my view those instruments which were to be afterwards used in putting me to a slow and cruel death. I writhed under his words, yet dared not shew the pain I felt. Clerval, whose eyes and feelings were always quick in discerning the sensations of others, declined the subject, alleging his ignorance; and the conversation took a more general turn. I thanked him from my heart, but I did not speak. I plainly saw that he was surprised, but he never attempted to draw my secret from me; and, although I loved him with a mixture of affection and reverence that knew no bounds, yet I could never persuade myself to confide to him that event which was so often present to my thoughts, but which I feared the detail to another would only impress more deeply.

M. Krempe was not equally docile; and *in my then condition of almost insupportable sensitiveness*, his harsh blunt encomiums gave me even more pain than the benevolent approbation of M. Waldman. "Damn the fellow," cried he. "Why, M. Clerval, I tell you he has outstript us all—aye, stare if you please, but it is nevertheless true. A youngster who but three years ago believed Cornelius Agrippa as firmly as the gospel has now set himself at the head of the university; and if he is not soon pulled down, we shall all be out of countenance.—Aye, aye," continued he, observing my face expressive of suffering, "M. Frankenstein is modest, an excellent quality in a young man. Young men should be diffident of themselves, you know, M. Clerval; I was myself when young, but one soon grows out of that."

M. Krempe had now commenced an eulogy on himself, and that happily turned the conversation from the subject that was so *agonizing* to me.

Clerval was no natural philosopher. His imagination was too vivid for the minutiæ of science. Languages were his principal study, for he wished to open a field for self-instruction on his return. Persian, Arabic, and Hebrew gained his attention *so soon as* he had become perfectly master of the Greek and Latin languages. For my own part, idleness had ever been irksome to me; and now that I wished to fly from reflection and hated my former studies, I found great relief in being the fellow-pupil with my friend and found not only instruction but consolation in the works of the orientalists. Their melancholy is soothing, and their joy elevating to a degree I never before experienced in studying *the authors of* any other country. When you read their writings, life appears to consist in a warm sun and gardens of roses—in the smiles and frowns of a fair enemy, and the fire that consumes your own heart. How different from the manly and *heroical* poetry of Greece and Rome.

Summer passed away in these occupations, and my return to Geneva was fixed for the latter end of autumn; but being delayed by several accidents, winter and snow arrived, the roads were deemed impassable, and my journey *was* retarded until the *ensuing* spring. I felt this delay very bitterly, for I longed to see my native town and my beloved friends. My return had only been delayed so long from an unwillingness to leave Clerval in a strange town before he had become acquainted with its inhabitants. The winter, however, was spent cheerfully; and although the spring was uncommonly late when it came, its beauty compensated for its dilatoriness. The month of May was already completed, and I expected daily the letter that was to fix the date of my departure, when Henry proposed a pedestrian tour in the environs of Ingolstadt that I might bid farewell to the country I had so long inhabited. I acceded with pleasure to this proposition: I was fond of exercise, and Clerval had always been my favourite companion in the rambles of this nature that I had taken among the scenes of my native country. We passed a fortnight in these perambulations. My health and spirits had long been restored, and they gained additional vigour from the salubrious air I breathed, *the natural incidents of our progress*, and the conversation of my friend. Study had before rendered me unsocia*l*—I *had* shunned the company of my fellow-beings. But Clerval called forth the better feelings of my heart; he again taught me to love the aspect of nature and the cheerful faces of children. Excellent friend! How sincerely did you love me and endeavour to elevate my mind until it was on a level with your own. A selfish pursuit had cramped and narrowed me until your gentleness and affection warmed and opened my senses. I became the same happy creature who a few years ago, loving and beloved by all, had no sorrow or care—when happy, inanimate nature had the power of bestowing on me the most delightful sensations. A serene sky and verdant fields filled me with ecstacy. The present season was indeed divine—the flowers of spring bloomed in the hedges while those of summer were already in bud. I was not disturbed by thoughts that during the preceding year pressed upon me, notwithstanding my endeavours to throw them off *with an invincible burthen*. Henry rejoiced in my gaiety and sincerely sympathized in my feelings: he exerted himself to amuse me, while he expressed the feelings that filled his soul. The resources of his mind on this occasion were truly astonishing. His conversation was full of imagination; and very often, in imitation of the Persian and Arabic writers, he invented tales of wonderful fancy and interest. At other times, he repeated my favourite poems or drew me out into arguments which he supported with great ingenuity.

We returned to our college on a Sunday: the peasants were dancing, and every one we met appeared joyful and happy. My own spirits were high, and I bounded along with feelings of unbridled joy and hilarity.

Chapter 10

On my return I found the following letter from my father.

"To V. Frankenstein.

"Geneva, June 2nd, 17—.

"My dear Victor,

"You have probably waited impatiently for a letter to fix the date of your return, and I was at first tempted to write a few lines, merely mentioning the day on which I should expect you—but that would be a cruel kindness, and I dare not do it. What would be your surprise, my son, when you expected a happy and gay welcome, to behold, on the contrary, tears and wretchedness. And how, Victor, can I relate our misfortune? Absence cannot have rendered you callous to our joys and griefs. And how can I inflict pain on an absent child? I wish to prepare you for the woeful news, but I know it is impossible; even now your eye skims over the page to seek the words which are to convey to you the horrible tidings.

"William is dead! That sweet child whose smiles delighted and warmed me, who was so gentle yet so gay, Victor, he is murdered!

"I will not attempt to console you but will simply relate the circumstances of the transaction.

"Last Thursday (May 28th)[34] I, my niece, and your two brothers went to walk in Plainpalais. The evening was warm and serene, and we prolonged our walk farther than usual. It was already dusk before we thought of returning; and then we discovered that Ernest and William, who had gone on before, were not to be found. We accordingly rested on a seat until they should return. Presently Ernest came and enquired for his brother: he said that he had been playing with him, and that William had run away to hide himself, and that he had vainly sought for him and afterwards waited a long time, but that he did not return.

"This rather alarmed us, and we continued to search for him until night fell, when Elizabeth conjectured that he might have returned to the house; he was not there. We returned again with torches, for I could not rest when I thought my sweet child had lost himself and was exposed to all the damps and dews of night; Elizabeth also suffered extreme anguish. About seven[35] in the morning I discovered my lovely boy, whom the night before I had seen blooming and active in health, stretched on the grass, livid and motionless —the print of the murderer's finger was on his neck.

"He was conveyed home, and the anguish that was visible in my countenance revealed the secret to Elizabeth. She was very earnest to see the corpse. *At first I attempted to prevent her*; but she persisted and, entering the room where it lay, hastily examined the neck of the victim and, clasping her hands, exclaimed, 'Oh God! I have murdered my darling infant.'

"She fainted and was restored with extreme difficulty; when she again lived, it was only to weep and sigh. She told me that that same evening William had teazed her to let him wear a very valuable miniature she possessed of your mother. This picture is gone and was doubtless the temptation which urged the murderer to the deed. We have no trace at present of him, *although* our exertions *to discover him* are unremitted; but they will not restore my beloved William.

"Come, dearest Victor, you alone can console Elizabeth. *She* weeps *continually* and accuses herself unjustly *as the cause of his death*—yet her words pierce my heart. We are all unhappy; but will not that be an additional motive for you, my son, to *return* and be our comforter? Your dear Mother! Alas, Victor! I now say, Thank God she did not live to witness the cruel, miserable death of her youngest darling.

"Come, Victor, not brooding thoughts of vengeance against the assassin, but with feelings of peace and gentleness that will heal instead of festering the wound of our minds. Enter the house of mourning, my son and friend, but with kindness and affection for those who love you, and not with hatred for your enemies.

"Your affectionate and afflicted father,
"Alphonse Frankenstein."

Clerval, who had watched my countenance as I read this letter, was surprised in observing the despair that succeeded to the joy I expressed on receiving new*s* from my friends. I threw the letter on the table and covered my face with my hands.

"My dear Frankenstein," exclaimed Henry when he saw me weep with bitterness, "are you always to be unhappy? My dear friend, what has happened?"

I motioned to him to take up the letter, while I walked up and down the room in the most extreme agitation. Tears also gushed from the eyes of Clerval as he read the account of my misfortune. "I can offer you no consolation, my friend," said he; "your disaster is irreparable. What do you intend to do?"

"To go instantly to Geneva; come with me, Clerval, to order the horses."

During our walk Henry endeavoured to raise my spirits. He did not do this by the common topics of consolation but by shewing the truest sympathy. "Poor William," said he, "that dear child; he now sleeps with his angel mother. His friends mourn and weep, but he is at rest: he does not now feel the murderer's grasp; a sod covers his gentle form, and he knows no pain. He can no longer be a subject for pity; his survivors are the greatest sufferers, and for them time is the only consolation. Those maxims of the Stoics, that death was no evil and that the mind of man ought to be superior to despair on the eternal absence of a beloved object, ought not to be urged—even Cato wept over the dead body of his brother."[36]

Clerval spoke thus as we hurried through the streets, the words impressed themselves on my mind, and I remembered them afterwards in solitude. But now, as soon as the horses arrived, I hurried into a cabriolet[37] and bade farewell to my friend.

My journey was very melancholy. At first I wished to hurry on, for I longed to console and sympathize with my loved and sorrowing friends; but when I drew near my native town, I slackened my *progress*. I could hardly sustain the multitude of feelings that crowded into my mind. I passed through scenes familiar to my youth, but which I had not seen for nearly five years.[38] How altered every thing might be *since* that time? One great, sudden, and desolating change had taken place; but a thousand little circumstances might have by degrees worked other alterations which, although it might be done more tranquilly, would not be less decisive. Fear overcame me; I dared not advance, dreading a thousand nameless evils that made me tremble, although I was unable to define them.

I remained at Lausanne for two days, not daring to proceed. I contemplated the lake: the waters were placid; all around was calm; and the snowy mountains, the "Palaces of Nature,"[39] were not changed. By degrees this calm and heavenly scene restored me, and I *continued my journey* towards Geneva. The road ran by the side of the lake, which became narrower as I approached my native town. I discovered more distinctly the black sides of Jura and the *bright* summit of Mont Blanc. I wept like a child. "Dear mountains! my own beautiful lake! how do you welcome your wanderer? Your summits are clear; the sky and lake are blue. Is this to prognosticate peace or to mock *at* my unhappiness?"

I fear, my friend, that I shall render myself tedious by dwelling on these preliminary circumstances; but they were days of comparative happiness, and I think of them with pleasure. My country, my beloved country! who but a native can tell the delight I took in again beholding thy streams, thy mountains, and, more than all, thy lovely lake.

Yet as I drew nearer home, grief and fear overcame me. Night also closed round; and when I could hardly see the dark mountains, I felt still more gloomily. I pictured every evil and persuaded myself that I was destined to become the most wretched of human beings. Alas! I prophesied truly and failed only *in one single circumstance*: that, in all the misery I imagined and dreaded, I did not conceive the hundredth part of the anguish I was destined to endure.

Chapter II

Night had closed in when I arrived; the gates of Geneva were already shut; and I determined to remain that night at Secheron, *a village half a league to the eastward of the city.* The *sky* was *serene*;

and, as I was unable to rest, I resolved to *visit* the spot where my poor William had been murdered; as I walked, I perceived a storm collecting on the other side of the lake. I saw the lightnings play in the most beautiful figures and gained a summit that I might observe its progress. It advanced, and I soon felt the rain coming slowly in large drops, but its violence quickly encreased.

I quitted my seat and walked on, although the darkness and storm augmented every minute, and the thunder burst with a terrific crash over my head. It was echoed from Salêve, *the Jura*, and the Alps of Savoy; vivid flashes of lightning dazzled my eyes, illumin*ating* the lake; then, for an instant, every thing seemed of a pitchy darkness until the eye recovered itself from the preceding flash. The storm, as is often the case in Switzerland, appeared at once in various parts of the heavens. The most violent storm *hung* exactly north of the town *over* that part *of the* lake *which lies between* the promontory of Belrive and *the village of Copêt*. Another storm enlightened Jura with faint flashes; and another darkened and sometimes disclosed the Môle, a peaked mountain to the east of the lake.

While I watched the storm—so beautiful, yet terrific—I wandered on with a hasty step. This noble war in the sky elevated my spirits; I clasped my hands and exclaimed aloud, "William, dear angel, this is thy funeral, this thy dirge!" As I said these words, I perceived in the gloom a figure which stole from behind a clump of trees near me. I stood fixed, gazing intently; I could not be mistaken; a flash of lightning illumined the object and discovered to me its gigantic stature; *and the* deformity *of its aspect*, more hideous than belongs to humanity, instantly informed me who it was. It was the wretch, the filthy dæmon to whom I had given life. What did he there? Could he be (I shuddered at the conception) the murderer of my brother? No sooner did that idea cross my imagination than I became convinced of its truth—my teeth chattered, and I was forced to lean against a tree for support. The figure quickly passed me, and

I lost it in the gloom. He therefore was the murderer! *Nothing in human shape could have destroyed that fair child. He was the murderer! I could not doubt it. The mere presence of the idea was an irresistible proof of the fact.* I thought of pursuing the devil, but it would have been in vain, for another flash discovered him to me *hanging among the rocks of the* nearly perpendicular ascent of Mont Salêve; he soon reached the summit and disappeared.

I remained motionless; the thunder ceased, but the rain still continued, and the scene was enveloped in an impenetrable darkness. I revolved in my mind the events which I had, until now, sought to forget: *the whole train of my progress towards my creation*; the appearance of the *work of my own hands, alive* at my bed side; *and* its departure. Two years had now nearly elapsed since the night on which he first received life, and was this his first crime? Alas! I had turned loose in the world a depraved wretch whose delight was in murder and wretchedness: *f*or had he not murdered my brother?

No one can conceive of the anguish I suffered during the remainder of the night, which I spent cold and wet in the open air. But I did not feel the inconvenience of the weather; my imagination was busy in scenes of evil and despair. I considered the *being* whom I had cast in among mankind *and endowed with the will and the power to effect* purposes of *horror, such as the deed which he had now done*, nearly in the light of my vampire, my own spirit let loose from the grave and forced to destroy all who were dear to me.

Day dawned, and I directed my steps towards the town; the gates were open, and I hastened to my father's house. My first thought was to discover what I knew of the murderer and cause instant pursuit to be made. But I paused when I reflected what the story was that I had to tell. A *being*, whom I myself had created and endued with life, *had met me at midnight among the precipices of an inaccessible mountain*. The tale was utterly improbable, and I knew well that if any other had communicated such a relation to me, I should have looked upon it as the ravings of delirium. Besides, the strange nature of the animal would elude pursuit, even if I were *so far* credited *as to persuade my relatives to commence it. Besides, of what use would be pursuit? Who could arrest* a creature *capable of* scal*ing* the *overhanging* sides of Mont Salêve? These reflections determined me, and I resolved to remain silent.

It was about five in the morning when I entered my father's house. I told the servants not to disturb the family and went into the library to attend their usual time of rising. Five years[40] had elapsed—passed as a dream but for one indelible trace—and I stood in the same place where I had last embraced my father before my departure for Ingolstadt. Beloved and respectable parent! He still remained to me. I gazed on a picture of my mother, which stood over the mantelpiece. It was an historical piece, painted to please my father, and represented Caroline Beaufort[41] in an agony of despair kneeling by the coffin of her dead father. Her garb was rustic, and her cheek pale; but there was an air of dignity and beauty that hardly permitted the *sentiment* of pity. Below this picture was a miniature of William, and my tears flowed when I looked upon it. While I was thus engaged, Ernest entered—he had heard me arrive and hastened to welcome me. He expressed the greatest delight on seeing me. "Welcome, my dearest Victor," said he, "ah, I wish you had come three months ago, and then you would have found us all joyous and delighted. But we are now so unhappy that I am afraid tears instead of smiles will be your welcome. Our father looks so sorrowful, and it seems to have revived in his mind his sorrow for the death of Mamma, and poor Elizabeth is quite inconsolable." Ernest began to weep as he said these words.

"Do not you," said I, "welcome me thus; try to be more calm *that I may not be* absolutely miserable the moment I enter my father's house after so long an absence. But tell me, how *does* my father support his misfortunes? and how is my poor Elizabeth?"

"She indeed requires consolation," replied Ernest. "She accused herself of having caused the death of my brother, and that made her very, very wretched; but since the murderer has been discovered———"

"The murderer discovered!" exclaimed I: "Good God! how can that be? Who could attempt to pursue him? It is impossible; one might as well try to overtake the winds or confine a mountain stream with a straw!"

"I do not know what you mean," replied Ernest. "But we were all very unhappy when she was discovered. No one would believe it at first; and even now *Elizabeth*[42] will not be convinced, notwithstanding all the evidence. Indeed, who could have believed that Justine Moritz, who was so amiable and fond of all the family, could all at once become so extremely wicked?"

"Justine Moritz!" cried I, "poor, poor girl, is she then accused? But it is wrongfully; every one knows that. No one believes it, surely, Ernest?"

"No one did at first," said my brother, "but several circumstances came out that *forced conviction upon us*; and her own behaviour *has been* so confused *as to add to the evidence of facts a weight that*, *I fear*, *leaves no hope for doubt*; but she will be tried today, and you will then hear all."

He related that, the morning on which the murder of poor William had been discovered, Justine had been taken ill and confined to her bed; and, after several days, one of the servants, happen*ing* to examine the apparel she had worn on the night of the murder, had discovered in her pocket the picture of my mother which had been judged to be the temptation of the murderer. The servant instantly shewed it to one of the others, *who*, without saying a word to any of the family, went to a magistrate who sent to apprehend Justine. On being charged with the fact, she confirmed the suspicion in a great measure by her extreme confusion.

This was a strange tale, but it did not shake my faith; and I replied earnestly: "You are all mistaken. I know the murderer. Justine, poor, good Justine, is innocent."

At that instant my father entered. I saw unhappiness deeply impressed on his countenance, but he endeavoured to welcome me cheerfully and, *after we had exchanged our mournful greetings, he* would have spoken on some other topic than that of our disaster, had not Ernest exclaimed, "Good God, Papa! Victor says that he knows the murderer of poor William."

"We do also, unfortunately," replied my father; "for indeed I had rather have been for ever ignorant than have discovered so much depravity and ingratitude in one whom I valued so highly."

"My dear father," exclaimed I, "you are mistaken. Justine is innocent!"

"If she is," replied my father, "God forbid that she should suffer as guilty. She is to be tried today, and I hope, I sincerely hope, that she will be acquitted."

This speech calmed me. I was firmly convinced in my own mind that Justine and indeed every human being was guiltless of this murder. I had no fear, therefore, that any circumstantial evidence could be brought forward strong enough to convict her; and in this assurance I calmed myself, expecting the trial with eagerness but without prognosticating an evil result.

Chapter 12

We were soon joined by Elizabeth. Time had made great alterations in her form since I had last beheld her. Five years[43] before she was a pretty, good-humoured girl, whom every one loved and caressed. She was now a woman in stature and expression of countenance which was uncommonly lovely. An open and capacious forehead gave indications of a good understanding joined to great frankness. Her eyes were hazel and expressive of uncommon mildness, now through recent affliction allied to sadness. Her hair was of a rich dark auburn, her complexion fair, and her figure sli*ght* and graceful. She welcomed me with the greatest affection. "Your arrival, my dearest cousin," said she, "fills me with hope. You perhaps will find out some means to justify my poor guiltless Justine. Alas! Who is safe if she were convicted *of crime*? I rely on her innocence as certainly as I do *upon* my own. Our misfortune is doubly hard to us. We have not only lost that lovely darling boy, but this poor girl, whom I sincerely love, is to be torn away by even a worse fate. Alas, if she is condemned, I shall never know joy more! But she will not, I am sure she will not; and then I shall be happy again, even after the sad death of my little William."

"She is innocent, my Elizabeth," said I, "and that shall be proved; fear nothing, but let your spirits be cheered by the assurance of her acquittal."

"How kind you are," replied Elizabeth, "every one else believes in her guilt, and that made me wretched; for I knew *that it was* impossible, and to see every one else prejudiced in so deadly a manner rendered me hopeless and despairing." She wept. "Sweet niece," said my father, "dry your tears; if she is, as you believe, innocent, rely on the justice of our judges and the activity with which I shall prevent the slightest shadow of partiality."

We passed a few sad hours until eleven o'clock when the trial was to commence. The rest of the family being obliged to attend as witnesses, I accompanied them to the court. During the whole of this wretched mockery of justice, I suffered living torture. It was to be decided whether the result of my curiosity and lawless *devices* would cause the death of two of my fellow-beings: one a smiling babe full of innocence and joy; the other far more dreadfully murdered with every aggravation of infamy that could make that murder *memorable in horror*. Justine also was a girl of merit and possessed qualities which promised to render her life happy; now all was to be obliterated in an ignominious grave—and I the cause! A thousand times rather would I have confessed myself guilty of the crime ascribed to Justine; but I was absent when it was committed, and such a declaration would have been considered as the ravings of a madman and could not have exculpated her who suffered through me.

The appearance of Justine was calm. She was dressed in mourning; and her countenance, always engaging, was rendered by the solemnity of her feelings exquisitely beautiful. Yet she appeared confident in innocence and did not tremble, although gazed at and execrated by thousands. For all the kindness which her beauty might have gained from others was obliterated by the remembrance of the enormity she was supposed to have committed. She was tranquil, yet her tranquillity was evidently constrained; and as her confusion had before been adduced as a proof of her guilt, she worked up her mind to an appearance of courage. When she entered the court, she threw her eyes round it and quickly discovered where we were seated. A tear seemed to dim her eye when she saw us; but she recovered herself, and a look of sorrowful affection seemed to attest her utter guiltlessness.

The trial began; and after the advocate against her had stated the charge, several witnesses were called. Several strange facts combined against her, which would have staggered any one who had not such proof of her innocence as I had. She had been out the whole of the night on which the murder had been committed, and towards morning had been perceived by a market-woman not far from the spot where the body of the murdered child had been afterwards found. *The woman* asked her what she did there—*but* she looked very strangely and only returned a confused *and unintelligible* answer. She returned to the house about eight o'clock; and when some one enquired where she had passed the night, she replied that she had been looking *for* the child and demanded earnestly if any thing had been heard concerning him. When the body was brought into the house, she fell into violent hysterics and kept her bed for several days. The picture was then produced which the servant had found in her pocket; and when Elizabeth, in a faltering voice, proved that it was the same *which*, an hour before the child had been missed, *she had* placed round his neck, a murmur of indignation and horror filled the court.

Justine was then called on for her defence. As the trial had proceeded, her countenance had altered. Surprise, horror, and misery were strongly expressed. Sometimes she struggled with her tears; but when she was desired to speak, she collected her powers and spoke in an audible although variable voice.

"God knows," she said, "how entirely I am innocent. But I do not pretend to be acquitted on account of my protestations: I rest my innocence on a simple explanation of the facts which have been adduced against me; and I hope the character I have always borne will incline my judges to a favourable interpretation where any circumstance appears doubtful or suspicious."

She then related that, by the permission of Elizabeth, she had passed the evening of the night on which the murder was perpetrated at the house of an aunt who resided in Chêne, a village about a league from Geneva. On her return at about nine o'clock, she met a man who asked her if she had seen any thing of the child who was lost. She was frightened at this account and passed several hours in looking for him, when the gates of Geneva were shut, and she *was forced to* remain several hours of the night in a cottage; but, unable to rest or sleep, she rose early that she might again endeavour to find my brother. If she had gone near the spot where his body lay, it was without her knowledge. *That if she had been bewildered* when questioned by the market-woman was *not* surprising, when she was so wretched *for* the loss of poor William. Concerning the picture she could give no account. "I know," continued the unhappy victim, "how heavily and fatally this one circumstance weighs against me, but I have no power of explaining it; and when I have expressed my utter ignorance, I am only left to conjecture concerning the probabilities by which it might have been placed in my pocket. But here also I am checked. I believe that I have no enemy on earth—and none surely who could have been so wicked as to destroy me wantonly. Did the murderer place it there? I know of no opportunity afforded him for so doing; or if I had, why should he have stolen the jewel to part with it again so soon?

"I commit my cause to the justice of my judges, yet I see no room for hope. I beg permission to have a few witnesses examined concerning my character; and if the*ir testimony shall not overweigh* my supposed guilt, I *must* be condemned, although I would pledge my salvation on my innocence."

Several witnesses were called who had known her for many years, and they spoke well of her; but fear and hatred of the crime of which they supposed her guilty rendered them timorous and unwilling. Elizabeth saw even this last resource, her excellent and irreproachable dispositions and conduct, about to fail the accused, when, although violently agitated, she desired permission to speak. "I am," said she, "the cousin of the unhappy child who was murdered—or rather his sister, for I was educated by and lived with his parents ever since and long before his birth; it may therefore be judged indecent in me to come forward on this occasion; but when I see a fellow-creature about to perish through the cowardice of her pretended friends, I wish to be allowed to speak that I may say what I know of her character. I am well acquainted with it. I have lived in the same house with her—at one time for five, and afterwards for nearly two years. During all that period she appeared to me a most amiable and benevolent creature. She nursed my aunt in her last illness with the greatest affection and care, and afterwards attended her own mother during a long and tedious illness in a manner that excited the admiration of all who knew her. After which she again lived in my uncle's house, where she was beloved by all the family.

She was warmly attached to the child who has been murdered and acted towards him like a most affectionate mother. For my own part, I do not hesitate to say that, notwithstanding all the evidence produced against her, I believe and rely on her perfect innocence. She had no temptation for such an action; as to the bauble on which the chief proof rests, if she had earnestly wished for it, I should have willingly given it her, so much do I esteem and value her."

Excellent Elizabeth! A murmur of approbation was heard; but it was *excited by her generous interference* and not in favour of poor Justine, on whom the public indignation *was* turned with renewed violence, charging her with the blackest ingratitude. She herself wept as Elizabeth spoke, but she did not answer. My own agitation and anguish was extreme during the whole of the trial. I believed in her innocence; I knew it. Could the monster who had (I did not for a minute doubt) murdered my brother also in his hellish sport have betrayed the innocent to death and ignominy? I could not sustain the horror of my situation; and when I saw that the popular voice and the countenance of the judges had already condemned my unhappy victim, I rushed out of the court in agony. The tortures of the accused did not equal mine; she was sustained by innocence, but the fangs of remorse tore my bosom. I passed a night of unmingled wretchedness. In the morning I went to the court; my lips and throat were parched. I dared not ask the fatal question; but I was known, and the officer guessed the cause of my visit—the ballots had been thrown, they were all black, and Justine was condemned.

Chapter 13

I cannot attempt to describe what I then felt. I had *experienced* sensations of horror before; and I have endeavoured to bestow on them adequate expressions, but now words cannot convey any idea of the heart-sickening despair that I endured. The person to whom I had addressed myself also added that Justine had already confessed her guilt. "That evidence," he observed, "was hardly required in so glaring a case, but I am glad of it; and, indeed, none of our judges like to condemn a criminal upon circumstantial evidence, be *it* ever so decisive."

When I returned home, Elizabeth eagerly demanded the result. "My cousin," replied I, "it is decided as you may have suspected: all judges had rather that ten innocent should suffer than that one guilty should escape; but she has confessed."

This was a dire blow to poor Elizabeth, who had relied with firmness on her innocence. "Alas!" said she, "how shall I ever again believe in human benevolence? Justine, whom I loved and esteemed as my sister, how could she put on those smiles of innocence only to betray? Her mild eyes seemed incapable of any severity or ill humour, and yet she has committed a murder."

Soon after, we heard that the poor victim had expressed a wish to see my cousin. My father wished her not to go but said that he left it to her own judgement and feelings to decide. "Yes," said Elizabeth, "I will go, although she is guilty; and you, Victor, shall accompany me—I cannot go alone." The idea of this visit was torture to me, yet I could not refuse.

We entered the gloomy prison chamber and beheld Justine sitting on some straw at the further end; her hands were manacled, and her head rested on her knees; she rose on seeing us; and, when we were left alone with her, she threw herself at the feet of Elizabeth, weeping bitterly.

My cousin wept also. "Oh, Justine!" said she, "why did you rob me of my last consolation? I relied on your innocence; and although I was very wretched, I was not so miserable as I am now."

"And do you also believe that I am so very, very wicked?" cried Justine. "Do you also join with my enemies to crush me?" Her voice was suffocated with sobs.

"Rise my poor girl," said Elizabeth, "why do you kneel if you are innocent? I am not one of your enemies; I believed in your innocence, notwithstanding every evidence, until I heard that you had yourself declared your guilt. That report, you say, is false; and be assured, my dear Justine, nothing can for a minute shake my confidence in you but your own confession."

"I did confess," said Justine, "but I confessed a lie. I confessed that I might obtain absolution, but now that falsehood lies heavier at my heart than all my other sins. The God of heaven forgive me! Ever since I was condemned, my confessor has besieged me; he threatened and menaced until I almost began to think that I was the wicked wretch he said I was. He threatened excommunication and hell fire in my last moments, if I continued obdurate. Dear lady, I had none to support me—all looked on me as a wretch doomed to ignominy and perdition. What could I do? In an evil hour I subscribed to a lie, and now only I am truly miserable." She paused, weeping, and then continued: "I thought with horror, my sweet lady, that you should believe that your Justine, whom your blessed aunt had so highly honoured and whom you loved, was a wretch capable of a crime which none but the devil himself could have perpetrated. Dear William, dearest blessed child, I soon shall see you again in heaven and glory; and that consoles me, going as I am to suffer ignominy and death."

"Oh, Justine!" cried the weeping Elizabeth, "forgive me for having for one moment distrusted you. Why did you confess? But do not mourn, my dear girl, I will every where proclaim your innocence and will force belief. Yet you must die—you, my companion, my playfellow, my more than sister—die—I never, never can survive so horrible a misfortune."

"Dear sweet lady, do not weep," replied Justine. "You ought to raise me with thoughts of a better life, and elevate me from the petty cares of this world of injustice and strife. Do not you, excellent Elizabeth, drive me to despair."

Elizabeth embraced the sufferer. "I will try to comfort you," said she, "but this I fear is an evil too deep and poignant to admit of consolation, for there is no hope. Yet heaven bless thee, my dearest Justine, with resignation and a confidence elevated beyond this world. Oh, how I hate all its shews and mockeries! When one creature is murdered, another is immediately deprived of life in a slow torturing manner, and then the executioners, their hands yet reeking with the blood of innocence, believe that they have done a great deed. They call this retribution—hateful name! When that word is pronounced, I know that greater and more horrid punishments are going to be inflicted than the gloomiest tyrant has ever invented to satiate his utmost revenge. Yet this is not consolation for you, my Justine, unless indeed that you may glory in escaping so miserable a den. Alas! I would I were in peace with my aunt and my sweet William—escaped from light which is hateful to me and the visages of men which I abhor."

Justine smiled languidly. "This, dear lady," said she, "is despair and not resignation. I must not learn the lesson that you would teach me—talk of something else, of something that will bring joy and not encrease of misery."

During this conversation I had retired to a corner of the prison-room where I could conceal the horrid anguish that possessed me. Despair! Who dared talk of that? The poor victim, who on the morrow was to pass the dreary boundary of life and death, felt not as I did—such deep and bitter agony! I gnashed my teeth and ground them together, uttering a groan that came from my inmost soul. Justine started. When she saw who it was, she approached me. "Dear Sir," said she, "you are very kind to visit me; you, I hope, do not believe that I am guilty."

I could not answer. "No, Justine," said Elizabeth, "he is more convinced of your innocence than I was; for even when he heard that you had confessed, he did not credit it."

"I truly thank him," said Justine. "In these last minutes I feel the sincerest gratitude for those who still think of me with kindness. How sweet is the affection of others to such a wretch as I am. It removes more than half my misfortune; and I feel as if I could die in peace, now that my innocence is acknowledged by you, sweet lady, and your cousin."

Thus the poor sufferer tried to comfort others and herself. She indeed gained the resignation she wished for; but I, the true murderer, felt the never-dying worm alive, *which* allowed no hope or consolation. Elizabeth also wept and was unhappy; but hers also was the misery of innocence, which, like a cloud that passes over the fair moon, for a while hides but cannot *destroy* its brightness. Anguish and despair had penetrated into the core of my heart—I bore a hell within me that nothing could *extinguish*.[44]

We stayed several hours with Justine, and it was with great difficulty that Elizabeth tore herself away. "I wish," cried she, "that I were to die with you—I cannot live in this world of misery." Justine assumed an air of cheerfulness while she with difficulty repressed the bitter tears. "Farewell, sweet lady, dearest Elizabeth; may heaven in its bounty bless and preserve you. May this be the last misfortune that you will ever suffer; live and be happy to make others so."

As we returned, Elizabeth said, "You do not know, my dear Victor, how much I am relieved now that I trust in the innocence of this unfortunate girl. I never could again have known peace if I had been deceived in my reliance on her. For the moment that I did believe it, I felt anguish that I could not have long sustained. Now my heart is lightened. The innocent suffers; but she whom I thought amiable and good is not wicked, and I am consoled."

Amiable cousin! Such were your thoughts, mild and gentle as your dear eyes and voice. But I——I was a wretch, and none ever conceived the misery that I then suffered.[45]

Chapter 14

Nothing is more painful *than the dead calmness of inaction and certainty which,* when the mind has been worked up by a quick succession of events, follow*s and* deprives the soul both of hope or fear. Justine died. She rested. And I was alive. The blood flowed freely in my veins, but a weight of despair and remorse pressed on my heart which nothing could remove. Sleep fled from my eyes. I wandered like an evil spirit, for I had committed deeds of mischief beyond description horrible, and more, much more (I persuaded myself) was yet in store. Yet my heart overflowed with kindness and goodness. I had begun life with benevolent intentions and thirsted for the moment when I could put them in practise and make myself useful to my fellow-beings. Now all was blasted. Instead of serenity of conscience, which allowed me to look back on my actions with self-satisfaction and from thence *to gather promise of* new hopes, I was seized by remorse and guilt and hurried away to a hell *of intense tortures such as* no language can describe.

This state of mind *preyed upon* my health, which had entirely recovered from the first shock it had sustained. I shunned the face of man; all sound of joy or complacency was torture to me; solitude was my only consolation—deep, dark, death-like solitude. My father observed with pain *the alteration perceptible in* my dispositions and habits, and endeavoured to reason with me on the folly of giving way to immoderate grief. "Do you think, Victor," said he, "that I do not suffer also? No one could love a child more than I *loved* your brother"—tears came into his eyes as he said this—"but is *it* not *a* duty to the survivors *that we should refrain from augmenting* their unhappiness by an appearance of immoderate grief? It is also a duty owed to yourself; for excessive sorrow prevents improvement or enjoyment, or even the discharge of dai*ly* usefulness without which no man is fit for society."

This advice, although good, was utterly inapplicable to my case; I should have been the first to hide my grief and console my friends if remorse had not mingled its bitterness with my other sensations. Now I could only answer my father with a look of despair and endeavour to hide myself from his view. About this time we retired to our house at Belrive. This change was very agreeable to me in particular. The shutting of the gates of the town regularly at ten o'clock and the impossibility of *remaining* on the lake after that hour rendered our residence within the walls of Geneva very irksome to me. I was now free. Often, after the rest of the family had retired for the night, I took the boat and passed the night upon the water: sometimes, with my sails set, I was carried by the wind; and sometimes, after rowing into the middle of the lake, I left the boat to pursue its own course and gave way to my own miserable reflections. I was often tempted—when all was at peace around me and I the only unquiet thing that wandered restless in a scene so beautiful and heavenly, if I except alone some bat or the *frogs*, *whose* harsh and interrupted croaking *was* heard only when I approached the shore—often, I say, I was tempted to plunge into the silent lake *that* the water*s might* close over me and my calamities for ever. But I was restrained when I thought of the heroic and suffering Elizabeth whom I tenderly loved, and whose existence was bound up in mine. And then I thought also of my father and surviving brother; should I not by my base desertion leave them exposed and unprotected to the malice of the fiend whom I had let loose among them? At these moments I wept bitterly, and wished that peace would revisit my mind *only* that I might afford them consolation and happiness—but that could not be: remorse *extinguished* every hope. I had been the *author* of unalterable evil, and I lived in daily fear *lest* the monster whom I had created might perpetrate *some new wickedness*. I had a*n obscure* feeling that all was not over and that he would still commit some signal crime which by its enormity would almost efface the recollection of the past. *There was always scope for fear so long as* *any thing that I loved remained alive*. My abhorrence of this fiend cannot be conceived. When I thought of him, I gnashed my teeth, my eyes became inflamed, and I ardently wished to extinguish that life which I had so thoughtlessly bestowed. When I reflected on his crimes and malice, my hatred and revenge burst all bounds of moderation. I would have made a pilgrimage to the highest *peak of the* Andes, could I when there have precipitated him to their *base*; I wished but to see him again that I might wreak the utmost extent of anger on his head and avenge the deaths of William and Justine.

Our house was the house of mourning. My father's health was deeply shaken by the horror of the recent events. Elizabeth was sad and desponding; she no longer took delight in her ordinary occupations; all pleasure seemed to her sacrilege towards the dead; eternal woe and tears she then thought was the just tribute she should pay to innocence so blasted and destroyed. She was no longer that happy creature *who in earlier youth had* wandered with me on the banks of the lake and talked with ecstacy of our future prospects. She *had become* grave and often conversed of the inconstancy of fortune and the instability of human life. "When I reflect, my dear cousin," she said, "on the miserable death of Justine Moritz, I no longer see the world and its works in the same light as they before appeared to me. Before, I looked upon the accounts of vice and injustice that I read in books or heard from others as tales of ancient days or imaginary evils; *at least they were remote and more familiar to reason than to imagination*; but now misery has come home, and men appear to me as monsters thirsting for each other's blood. Yet I am certainly unjust. Every one believed that poor girl to be guilty; and if she *could have committed the crime for which she suffered, assuredly she* would have been the most depraved of *human* creatures. For the sake of a few jewels, to have murdered the son of her benefactor and friend, a child whom she had nursed from its birth and appeared to love as if it had been her own. I could not consent to the death of any human being, but certainly I should have thought such a *being unfit to remain in the society of men*. Yet she was innocent. I know, I feel she was innocent. You are of the same opinion, and that confirms me. Alas, Victor! when falsehood can look so like the truth, who can assure themselves of certain happiness? I feel as if I were walking on the edge of a precipice towards which thousands are crowding and endeavouring to plunge me into the abyss. William and Justine were assassinated, and the murderer escapes, wearing human lineaments; he walks about the world free and perhaps respected. But even if I were condemned to suffer on the scaffold for the same crimes, I would not change places with such a wretch."

I listened to this discourse with the extremest agony. I, not in deed but in effect, was the true murderer. Elizabeth read my anguish in my countenance and, kindly taking my hand, said, "My dearest cousin, you must calm yourself; these events have affected me, God knows how deeply! but I am not so wretched as you are. There is an expression of misery and sometimes of revenge in your countenance that makes me tremble; be calm, my beloved Victor; I would sacrifice my life to your peace. We surely shall be happy: quiet in our native country and not mingling in the world, what can disturb our tranquillity?"

She shed tears as she said this, *distrusting the very solace which she gave*, but at the same time smiled that she might chase away the fiend that lurked in my heart. My father, who saw in the unhappiness that was painted in my face only an exaggeration of that sorrow which I might naturally feel, thought that an amusement suited to my taste would be the best means of restoring to me my wonted serenity. It was from this cause that he had removed to the country; and, induced by the same reasons, he now proposed that we should all take a journey to the valley of C*h*amounix. I had been there before, but Elizabeth and Ernest never had; and both had often expressed a wish to see this place, which had been described to them as so wonderful and sublime. Accordingly, we departed from Geneva on this tour about the middle of the month of August, nearly two months after the death of Justine.[46]

The weather was beautiful; and if mine had been a sorrow to be chased away by any fleeting circumstance, this voyage would certainly have had the effect *intended by* my father. As it was, I was *somewhat* interested *in the scene*: *it sometimes lulled*, *it could not extinguish my grief. During* the first day we travelled in a carriage. In the morning we had seen the mountains at a distance to which we gradually advanced. We perceived that the valley through which we wound, and which was formed by the Arve whose course we followed, closed upon us by degrees; and when the sun had set, we saw immense mountains and precipices overhanging *us* on *every* side and heard the sound of *the river raging among rocks* and the dashing of *the* waterfalls *around*.

The next day we pursued our journey on mules; and as we ascended still higher, the valley assumed a more beautiful and verdant appearance. Ruined castles *hanging on the precipices of* piny mountains, the impetuous Arve, and cottages every here and there peeping from among the trees formed a scene of singular beauty. But it was augmented and rendered sublime by the mighty Alps whose white and shining pyramids and domes towered above all like another earth—the habitations of another race of beings. We passed the bridge of Pelissier, where the ravine which the river forms opened before us, and we began to ascend the mountain which overhung it. Soon after, we entered the valley of Chamounix. This valley is more wonderful and sublime, but not so beautiful and picturesque as that of Servox, through which we had just passed. The high and snowy mountains were its boundaries, but we saw no more ruined castles or fertile fields. Immense glaciers approached the road; we heard the rumbling thunder of the falling avalanche and marked the smoke of its passage. Mont Blanc, the *supreme and magnificent* Mont Blanc, raised itself from the surrounding aiguilles,[47] and its tremendous dome overlooked the valley.

During this journey I sometimes joined Elizabeth and exerted myself to point out to her the various beauties of the scene. And often I suffered my mule to lag behind and indulged in the misery of reflection. At other times I spurred on the animal before my companions that I might forget them, the world, and, more than all, myself. When at a distance, I alighted and threw myself on the grass, weighed down by horror and despair. At eight in the evening we arrived at Chamounix. My father and Elizabeth[48] were very much fatigued. Ernest, who accompanied us, was delighted and in high spirits. The only circumstance that detracted from his pleasure was the south wind and the rain that that wind seemed to promise for the next day.

We retired early to our apartments, but not to sleep: at least I did not. I remained many hours at the window watching the *pallid* lightning that played above Mont Blanc—and listening to the rushing of the Arve, which ran before my window.

Chapter 15

The next day, contrary to the prognostics of our guides, was fine, although clouded. We visited the source of the Arveiron and rode about the valley *until evening*. These sublime and magnificent scenes afforded me the greatest consolation that I was capable of receiving. They elevated me from all littleness of feeling; and although they did not remove my grief, they subdued and tranquillized it. In some degree, also, they diverted my mind from the thoughts *over which* it had brooded for the last month. I returned in the evening, fatigued but less unhappy, and conversed with the family with more cheerfulness than had been *my custom* for some time. My father was pleased, and Elizabeth overjoyed. "My dear cousin," said she, "you see what happiness you diffuse when you are *happy*; do not relapse again!"

The following morning the rain poured down in torrents, and thick mists hid the summits of the mountains. I rose early but felt unusually melancholy. The rain depressed me, my old feelings recurred, and I was miserable. I knew how my father would be disappointed at this sudden change, and I wished to avoid him until I had recovered myself so far as to conceal the feelings that overpowered me. I knew that they would remain that day at the inn; and, as I had ever inured myself to rain and cold, I resolved to go to the summit of Montanvert alone. I remembered the effect the view of the tremendous and ever moving glacier had *produced* upon my mind when I first saw it. *I*t had then filled me with a sublime ecstacy that gave wings to the soul and allowed it to soar from the *obscure* world to light and joy. The sight of the awful and majestic in nature had indeed always the effect of solemnizing my mind and causing me to forget the passing cares of life. I determined to go alone, for I was well acquainted with the path, and the presence of another would destroy the solitary grandeur of the scene.

The ascent is precipitous, but the path is cut into continual and short windings which enable you to surmount the perpendicularity of the mountains. It is a scene terrifically desolate. In a thousand places the traces of the winter avalanche may be perceived, where trees lie broken and strewed on the ground: some, entirely destroyed; others, bent leaning upon the jutting *rocks* of the mountain or *transversely* upon other trees. The path as you ascend higher is inters*ected by* ravines *of* snow, down which stones continually roll from above; one of the them is particularly dangerous, as the slightest sound, such as *even* speaking in a loud voice, *produces* a concussion of air sufficient to draw destruction upon the head of the speaker. The pine*s* here are not tall or luxuriant, but they are sombre and add an air of *severity* to the scene. I looked on the valley beneath; vast mists were rising from the river, which ran through *it*, and curling in thick wreaths around the opposite mountains whose summits were hid in the *uniform* clouds, while rain poured from the dark sky and added to the melancholy impression I received from the objects around me. Alas! why does man boast of sensibilities above those apparent in the brute; it only renders them more necessary[49] beings. If our impulses were confined to hunger, thirst, and desire, we might be nearly free; but now we are moved by every wind that blows and by every chance word or scene that that wind[50] may convey to us.

> We rest, a dream has power to poison sleep.
>   We rise, one wand'ring thought pollutes the day.
> We feel, conceive, or reason; laugh, or weep,
>   Embrace fond woe, or cast our cares away;
> It is the same: for, be it joy or sorrow,
>   The path of its departure still is free.
> Man's yesterday may ne'er be like *h*is morrow;
>   Nought may endure but mutability![51]

It was noon when I arrived at the top of the ascent. For some time I sat upon the rock that overlooks the sea of ice.[52] A mist covered both that and the surrounding mountains. Presently a breeze dissipated the mist, and I descended on the glacier. The surface is very uneven, rising like the waves of a troubled sea, descending low, and interspersed by rifts that sink deep. The *field of* ice is a league *in width*, but I was nearly two hours *in* crossing it. The opposite mountain is a bare perpendicular rock. From that side where I now stood, Montanvert was exactly opposite at the distance of a league, and above it rose Mont Blanc in awful majesty. I remained in a recess of the rock, gazing on this wonderful and stupendous scene. *The sea, or rather the vast river of ice, wound among its dependant mountains whose aerial summits hung over its recesses. Their icy and glittering peaks shone in sunlight over the clouds.* My heart, *which* before *was sorrowful*, *now* swelled with something like joy. I exclaimed—"Wandering spirits, if indeed ye wander and do not rest in your narrow beds, allow me this faint happiness or take me as your companion away from the joys of life." As I said this, I suddenly beheld the figure of a man at some distance advancing towards me with superhuman speed. He bounded over the crevices in the ice, *among* which I had walked with caution; his stature also, as he approached, seemed to exceed that of man. I was troubled—a mist covered my eyes, and I felt *faintness seize me.* The cold breeze of the mountains quickly restored me. I perceived as *the shape* came nearer (sight tremendous and abhorred) that it was the wretch whom I had created. I trembled with rage and horror. *I* resolv*ed* to wait his approach and then close with him in mortal combat. He approached; his countenance bespoke bitter anguish combined with disdain and malignancy. But I scarcely observed this; anger and hatred had at first deprived me of utterance, and I recovered only to overwhelm him with words expressive of utter detestation and contempt. "Devil!" I exclaimed, "do you dare approach me? and do not you dread the fierce vengeance of my arm wreaked on your miserable head? Begone, vile insect! or rather stay that I may trample you to dust! and oh, that I could, with the *extinction of* your miserable existence, restore those creatures whom you have diabolically murdered!"

"I expect*ed* this reception," said the dæmon. "All men hate the wretched—how then must I be hated who am miserable beyond *all living things.* Yet you, my creator, hate me and spurn me, thy creature, to whom thou art bound with ties only dissoluble by the death of one of us. *You purpose* to kill me. How dare you sport thus with life? Do your duty towards me, and I will do mine towards you and the rest of mankind. If you comply with my conditions, I will leave them and you at peace; but if you refuse, I will glut the maw of death until *it* be satiated even with your dearest friends."

"Abhorred monster!" cried I furiously, "fiend that thou art, the tortures of hell are too *mild a vengeance for thy crimes.* Wretched devil! you reproach me with your creation; come, that I may extinguish the spark that I so negligently bestowed." My rage was without bounds. I sprung on him, *impelled by all the feelings which can arm one being against the existence of another.* He eluded *me easily* and said, "Be calm! I entreat you to hear me, before you give vent to your hatred *up*on my devoted head. Have I not suffered enough that you wish to encrease my misery? Life, although it be only an accumulation of anguish, is dear to me, and I will defend it. Remember thou hast made me more powerful than thyself: my height is superior to yours; my joints more supple. But I *will not be tempted to set myself in opposition to thee.* I am thy creature and will *even* be mild and docile to *thee*, my *natural* master *and king*, if *thou* will perform *thy part also*, *the* duti*es which thou owest* me. Oh, Frankenstein! do not *be* equitable to every other and trample upon me *alone*, to whom thy justice and even *thy clemency*, *thy affection*, is most due. Remember that I am thy creature—*I ought to be* thy Adam—*but I am* rather the fallen angel, *whom thou drivest from joy for no misdeed*; every where I see bliss *from* whic*h* I alone am irrecoverably *excluded*. I was benevolent and good: misery made me a fiend. *M*ake me happy, and I shall again be virtuous."

"Begone!" replied I—"I will not hear you. There can be no community between you and me. We are enemies. Begone! or let us try our strength in a fight in which one must fall."

"How can I move you?" said the fiend. "Will no entreaties cause you to turn a favourable eye upon thy creature who implores thy goodness and compassion? Believe me, Frankenstein: I was benevolent—my soul glowed with love and humanity; but am I not alone, miserably alone? You, my creator, abhor me. What hope *can* I *gather* from your fellow-creatures *who owe me nothing*? They spurn and *hate* me. The desert mountains and mournful glaciers are my refuge. I have wandered here many days. The caves of ice, which I only do not fear, are a dwelling to me and the only one which man does not grudge. These bleak skies I hail, for they are kinder to me than your fellow-beings. *If the multitude of mankind* knew of my existence, *they* would as you do arm themselves for my destruction. Shall I not then hate them who abhor me? I will keep no terms with my enemies. I am miserable, and they shall share my wretchedness. Yet it is in your power to recompense me and deliver them from an evil which it *only remains for you to make so great, that not only you and your family but thousands of others shall be swallowed up in the whirlwinds of its rage*. Let your compassion and justice be moved, and do not disdain me. Listen to my tale! when you have heard that, deny or commiserate me as you shall judge *that* I deserve. But hear me. The guilty are allowed by human laws, bloody as they *may be*, to speak in their *own* defence *before they are condemned*. Listen to me, Frankenstein. You accuse me of murder, and yet you would with a satisfied conscience destroy *thine own* creature. Oh, praise the eternal justice of man! Yet I ask you not to spare me; listen and then, if you *can and if you* will, destroy the work of your hands."

"Why," cried I—"do you call to my remembrance circumstances *of* which I shudder to reflect *that I have been the miserable origin and author*. Cursed be the day in which you first saw light, cursed (although I curse myself) be the hands that formed you! You have made me wretched beyond expression. *You have left me no power to consider whether I am just to you or no*. Begone, relieve me from *your* sight."

"Thus I relieve you, Creator," he replied and placed his abhorred hands before my eyes which I flung from me with violence, "from the sight of one whom you abhor. Still you can listen to me and grant me your compassion. By the virtues I once possessed, I demand this of you. Hear my tale. It is long and strange, and the temperature of this place is not fitting to your fine sensations; come to the hut on the mountain. The sun is yet high in the heavens; before it descends to hide itself behind *yon* mountains and illumin*at*es another world, you will have heard my story and can decide. On you it rests whether I quit for ever the habitations of man and lead a harmless life, or become the scourge of your fellow-creatures *and the author of your own speedy ruin.*"

As he said this, he led the way across the ice. I followed. My heart was full, and *I* did not answer him; but *as I proceeded*, I weighed the various arguments which he had used, *and* I *determined at least* to listen to his tale. I was partly urged by curiosity, and compassion confirmed me. I had hitherto supposed him to be the murder*er* of my brother, and I *eagerly sought a confirmation or denial of this opinion*. For the first time, also, I felt what the duties of a creator towards his creature were, and that I ought to render him happy before I complained of his wickedness. These motives urged me to comply with his demand. We crossed the ice, therefore, and ascended the opposite rock. The air was cold, and the rain began again to descend. We entered the hut—the fiend with an air of exultation, I with a heavy heart and depressed spirits. But I consented to listen; and, *seating myself* by the fire which he lighted, he thus began his tale.

Frankenstein

or

The Modern Prometheus

VOLUME II

Chapter 1

"It is with difficulty that I remember the æra of my being. All the events of that period appear confused and indistinct. A strange sensation seized me. I saw, felt, heard, and smelt at the same time; and it was indeed a long time before I learned to distinguish between the operations of my various senses. By degrees I remember a stronger light pressed upon my nerves so that I was obliged to close my eyes. Darkness then came over me and troubled me. But hardly had I felt this, when (by opening my eyes, as I now suppose) the light poured in upon me again. I walked and, I believe, descended; but presently I found a great alteration in my sensations. Before, dark opaque bodies had surrounded me, impervious to my touch or sight; and I now found that I could wander on at liberty with no obstacles which I could not either surmount or avoid. The light became more and more oppressive to me, and, the heat wearying me as I walked, I sought a place where I could *receive* shade. This was the forest near Ingolstadt; and here by the side of a brook I lay for some hours resting from my fatigue, until I felt tormented by hunger and thirst. This roused me from my nearly dormant state, and I ate some berries which I found *hanging* on the trees or lying on the ground. I slaked my thirst by the brook; and then, again lying down, I was overcome by sleep. It was dark when I awoke; I felt cold also, and half-frightened *as it were instinctively*, on finding myself so desolate. Before I had quitted your apartment, on a sensation of cold I had covered myself with some clothes; but these were *in*sufficient to secure me from the dews of night. I was a poor, helpless, miserable wretch. I knew and could distinguish nothing; but feeling pain invade me on all sides, I sat down and wept.

"Soon a gentle light stole over the heavens and gave me a sensation of pleasure. I started up and beheld a radiant form rise from among the trees. I gazed with a kind of wonder. It moved slowly; but it enlightened my path, and I again went out in search of berries. I was still cold when, under one of the trees, I found a huge cloak with which I covered myself, and sat down on the ground. No distinct ideas occupied my mind; all was confused. I felt the light, and hunger, and thirst, and darkness; innumerable sounds rung in my ears, and on all sides various scents saluted me; the only object that I could distinguish was the bright moon, and I fixed my eyes on that with pleasure. Several changes of day and night passed, and the orb of night had greatly lessened when I began to distinguish my sensations *from each other.* I *gradually* saw *plainly* the clear stream that supplied me with drink and the trees that shaded me with their foliage. I was delighted when I first discovered that a pleasant sound, *which* often saluted my ears, proceeded from the throats of the little *winged* animals who often intercepted the light from my eyes. I began also to see with greater accuracy the forms that surrounded me and to perceive the boundaries of the radiant light which canopied me. Sometimes I tried to imitate the pleasant songs of the birds, but was unable. Sometimes I wished to express my sensations in my own mode, but *the* uncou*th* and inarticulate sound *which* broke from me frightened me into silence again.

"The moon had disappeared from the night, and again with a lessened form it shewed itself while I still remained in the forest. My sensations were by this time become distinct, and my mind received every day additional ideas. My eyes became accustomed to the light, and to perceive objects in their right forms: I distinguished the insect from the herb and, by degrees, one herb from another. I found that the sparrow uttered none but harsh notes, *whilst* those of the blackbird were sweet and enticing. One day, when I was oppressed by cold, I found a fire that had been left by some wandering beggars and was overcome with delight *at the warmth which I experienced from it.* In my joy I thrust my hand into the live embers but quickly drew it away with a cry of pain. How strange, I thought, that the same cause should at once produce such opposite effects. I examined the materials of the fire and, to my joy, found it to be wood. I quickly collected some branches, but they were wet and would not burn. I was pained at this and sat still watching the operation of the fire. The wet wood I had placed near the heat dried and itself became *inflamed.* I reflected on this; and by touching the various branches, I discovered the cause and busied myself in collecting a great *quantity* of wood that I might dry it and have a plentiful supply *of fire.* When night came on and *brought with it* sleep, I was in the greatest fear lest my fire should be extinguished. I covered it carefully with dry wood and leaves and then placed upon that wet branches; and then, spreading my cloak, I lay on the ground and sunk into sleep. It was morning when I awoke, and my first care was to visit the fire. I uncovered it, and a gentle breeze quickly fanned it into a flame. I observed this also and contrived a fan of branches, which roused the embers when they were nearly extinguished. When night again came, I found with pleasure that the fire gave light as well as heat; and the discovery of this element was useful to me also in my food, for I found some of the offals that the travellers had left had been roasted and tasted much more savoury than the berries I gathered. I tried therefore to dress my food in the same manner, placing them on the live embers. I found that the berries were spoiled by this operation, and the nuts much improved. Food, however, became very scarce, and I often spent a day searching in vain for a few acorns to assuage the pangs of hunger. When I found this, I resolved to quit the place which I had hitherto inhabited and to seek for *one* where the few wants I experienced would be more easily satisfied. In this emigration, I exceedingly lamented the loss of my fire. I had obtained it by strange means and knew not how to *re*produce it. This *deficiency* obtained my serious consideration for several hours, but I was obliged to *relinquish all attempts to supply* it; and, wrapping myself up in my cloak, I struck across the wood towards the setting sun. I passed three days in these rambles and at length discovered the open country. A great fall of snow had taken place the night before, and the fields were of one uniform white; the appearance was disconsolate, and I found my feet chilled by the cold damp substance that covered the ground. It was about seven in the morning, and I longed to obtain food and shelter. At length I perceived a small hut which had doubtless been built for the convenience of some shepherd. This was a new sight to me, and I examined the structure of it with great curiosity. Finding the door open, I entered. An old man sat in it, near a fire *over* which he was preparing his breakfast. He turned on hearing a noise and, perceiving me, shrieked loudly and, quitting the hut, ran across the fields with a speed of which his debilitated form hardly appeared capable. His flight somewhat surprised me, but I was enchanted with the appearance of the hut. Here the snow and rain could not penetrate; the ground was dry; and it presented to me then as exquisite and divine a retreat as Pandemonium appeared to the dominions of hell *after their suffocation in the lake of fire*. I greedily devoured the remnants of the shepherd's breakfast, which consisted of bread, cheese, milk, and Rhenish wine—the latter of which, however, I did not like. Then overcome by fatigue, I lay down among some straw and fell asleep.

"It was noon when I awoke; and, allured by the warmth of the sun, I determined to recommence my travels; and, depositing the remains of the peasant's breakfast in a wallet I found, I proceeded across the fields for several hours, until at sunset I *arrived at* a village. How miraculous did this appear. The huts, the neater cottages, and statelier houses engaged my admiration by turns. The vegetables in the gardens and the milk and cheese that I saw placed at the windows of some of the cottages *allured me*.

One of the best of these I entered, but I had hardly placed my foot *within* the door before the children shrieked and one of the women fainted. The village was roused: some fled; some attacked me until, grievously bruised by stones and many other kinds of missile weapons, I escaped to the open country and fearfully took refuge in a low *hovel*, quite bare and making a wretched appearance after the palaces I had beheld in the village. This *hovel*, however, adjoined a cottage of a neat and pleasant appearance; but after my late *dearly* bought experience, I dared not enter it. My place of refuge was constructed of wood, but so low that I could with difficulty sit upright in it. No wood, however, was placed on the earth which formed the floor of the cottage, but it was dry; and although the wind entered by innumerable chinks, I found it an agreeable asylum from the snow and rain. Here then I retreated and lay down, happy to have found a shelter from the inclemency of the season and still more from the barbarity of man."

Chapter 2

"As soon as morning dawned, I crept from my asylum that I might view the adjacent cottage and discover if I could remain in the kennel that I had found. It was situated against the back of the cottage and surrounded on the sides which were exposed by a pigstye and clear pool of water. One part was open, and by that I had crept in; but now I covered every crevice by which I might be discovered with stones and wood, yet in such a manner that I could move them on an occasion to pass out; all the light I enjoyed came through the stye, and that was sufficient for me.

"Having thus arranged my dwelling and carpeted it with clean straw, I retired, for I saw the figure of a man at a distance; and I remembered too well my treatment the night before to trust myself in his power. I had first, however, provided for my sustenance for that day by a loaf of coarse bread which I purloined and a cup with which I could drink, more conveniently than from my hand, of *the* pure water which flowed by my *retreat*. The floor was a little raised so that it was kept perfectly dry; and by its vicinity to the chimney of the kitchen fire of the cottage, it was tolerably warm. Being thus provided, I determined to reside in this hovel until something should occur which might alter my determination. It was indeed a paradise compared to the bleak forest (my former residence), the rain-dropping branches, and the dank earth. I ate my breakfast with pleasure and was about to remove a plank to procure myself a little water when I heard a step, and, looking through a small chink, I beheld a young creature with a pail on her head passing before my hovel. The girl was young and of gentle demeanour, unlike what I have since found cottagers and farm-house servants to be. Yet she was meanly dressed, a coarse blue petticoat and a linen jacket being her only garb; her fair hair was plaited but not adorned; she looked patient yet sad. She passed away but in a quarter of an hour returned, bearing the pail which was now partly filled with milk. As she walked along seemingly incommoded by the burthen, a young man met her, whose countenance expressed a deeper despondency; uttering a few sounds with an air of melancholy, he took the pail from her head and bore it into the cottage himself. She followed, and they disappeared. Presently I saw the young man again with some tools in his hand cross the field opposite the cottage, and the girl was also busied—sometimes in the cottage, and sometimes in the yard, where she fed some chickens. While I examined my dwelling, I discovered that part of the cottage window had formerly occupied a corner of it, but the panes had been filled up with wood. In one of these was a small and almost imperceptible chink, through which the eye could just penetrate; *through this chink* a small room *was visible*, whitewashed and clean but very bare of furniture. In one corner near a small fire *sat* an old man leaning his head on his hand in a disconsolate attitude. The young girl was occupied in arranging the cottage; but presently she took something out of a drawer, which employed her hands, and sat down beside the old man, who, taking up an instrument, began to play and to produce sounds sweeter than the voice of the thrush or nightingale. It was a lovely sight even to me, poor wretch, who had never beheld aught beautiful before. The silver hairs and benevolent countenance of the aged cottager won my reverence, while the gentle manners of the girl enticed my love. He played a sweet mournful air, which I perceived drew tears from the eyes of his amiable companion, of which the old man took *no*[53] notice until she sobbed audibly. He then pronounced a few sounds, and the poor creature, leaving her work, knelt at his feet. He raised her and smiled with such kindness and love that I felt *sensations of a peculiar and overpowering nature*: they were a mixture *of pain and pleasure*, *such as I had* never *experienced* either *from hunger or cold*, *or warmth or food*; *and I withdrew* from my station *unable to bear these emotions*.[54]

"Soon after this, the young man returned, bearing on his shoulders a load of wood. The girl met him at the door, helped to relieve him of his burthen, and, taking some of it into the cottage, placed it on the fire; then she and the youth went apart into a nook of the cottage, and he shewed her a large loaf and a piece of cheese. She seemed pleased and went into the garden for some roots and plants, which she placed in water and then upon the fire. She afterwards continued her work, *whilst* the young man went into the garden and appeared busily employed in digging and pulling up roots. After he had been employed thus about an hour, the young woman joined him, and they returned to the cottage together. The old man in the mean time had been pe*n*sive; but, on the approach of his companions, he assumed a *more* cheerful air, and they sat down to eat. The meal was quickly dispatched; the young woman was again occupied in arranging the cottage;

the old man walked before the door in the sun for a few minutes, leaning on the arm of the youth. Nothing could exceed in beauty the contrast between these two excellent creatures. One was old, with silver hairs and a countenance beaming with benevolence and love; the younger was slight and graceful in his figure, and his features were moulded with the finest s*ym*metry—yet his eyes and attitude expressed the utmost sadness and despondency. The old man returned to the cottage; and the youth, with tools different from those *which* he had used in the morning, directed his steps across the fields. Night quickly shut in, but to my extreme wonder I found that the cottagers had a means of prolonging light by the use of tapers and was pleased to find that setting of the sun did not put an end to the pleasure I experienced in watching my human neighbours. In the evening, the young girl and her companion were employed in various occupations *which* I did not then understand, and the old man again took that instrument which produced the divine sound*s* that had enchanted me in the morning. *So soon as* he had finished, the youth began, not to play, but to utter sounds which were monotonous and neither resembling the harmony of the old man's instrument or the songs of the birds; I since found that he read *aloud*, but at that time I knew nothing of the science of words or letters. The family soon extinguished their lights and retired, as I conjectured, to rest.

"I lay on my straw, but I could not sleep. I thought of the occurrences of the day. What chiefly struck me was the gentle manners of these people, and I longed to join them but dared not. I remembered too well the treatment I had suffered the night before from the barbarous villagers and resolved, whatever course of conduct I might hereafter consider it proper to pursue, that for the present I would remain quietly in my hovel, watching and endeavouring to discover the motive of their actions.

"The cottagers arose the next morning before the sun. The young woman arranged the cottage and prepared the food; and the youth, mounted on a large strange animal, rode away. This day was passed in the same routine *as* the preceding one. The young man was constantly employed out of doors, and the girl in various laborious occupations *within*. The old man, whom I soon perceived to be blind, employed his leisure hours in playing on his instrument or in contemplation. Nothing could exceed the love and respect that the younger cottagers *shewed* towards this venerable old man. They performed towards him every little office of *affection* and duty with gentleness; and he rewarded them by his benevolent smiles.

"They were not, however, entirely happy. The young man and his companion often retired into a corner of their common room and wept. I saw no cause for this unhappiness, but I was deeply affected by it. If such lovely creatures were miserable, it was less strange that I, an imperfect and solitary being, should be wretched. Yet why were these gentle beings unhappy? They possessed a delightful house (for such it was in my eyes) and every luxury; they had a fire to warm them when chill and delicious viands when hungry; they were dressed in excellent clothes; and, still more, they enjoyed one another's company and speech—and interchanged each day looks of affection and kindness. What did their tears mean? Did they really express pain? I was at first unable to solve these questions, but perpetual attention and time explained to me many of the appearances which at first seemed *enig*matic."[55]

Chapter 3

"A considerable period elapsed before I discovered one *of the* causes of the uneasiness of this amiable family. It was poverty—and they suffered that evil in a very distressing degree. Their nourishment consisted entirely of bread, the vegetables of their garden, and the milk of one cow, which gave very little during the winter, when its masters could scarcely procure any food for it. They often, I believe, suffered the pangs of hunger very poignantly, especially the *two* younger cottagers,[56] for several times they placed food before the old man when they had none for themselves. This trait of kindness moved me sensibly. I had been accustomed during the night to steal a part of their store for my own consumption; but when I found that in doing this I inflicted pain on the cottagers, I abstained and satisfied myself with berries, nuts, and roots which I *gathered from* a neighbouring wood. I discovered also another means by which I was able to assist their labours. I found that the youth spent a great part of each day in collecting wood for the family fire; and during the night, I often took his tools, the use of which I quickly discovered, and brought home firing sufficient for the consumption of several days.

"I remember the first time *that* I did this, the young woman who opened the door in the morning *appeared* greatly *astonished* to see a great pile of wood on the outside. She said some words in a loud voice, and presently the youth joined her, who also appeared astonished. I observed with pleasure that he did not go to the forest that day but spent it in repairing the cottage and in cultivating the garden.

"By degrees also I made another discovery of still greater moment *to me*. I found that these people *possessed* a *method* of communicating their *experience and feelings* to one another by articulate sounds which they uttered. I perceived that the words they spoke sometimes produced pleasure or pain, smiles or sadness, in the minds and countenances of the hearers. This was indeed a godlike science, and I ardently desired to become acquainted with it. But I was baffled in every attempt I made for this purpose. Their pronunciation was quick; and, the words they uttered not having any apparent connection with visible objects, I was unable to discover any clue by which I could unrable[57] the mystery of their *reference*. By great application, however, and after having remained *during the space of* several revolutions of the moon in my hovel, I discovered the names that were given to some of the most familiar objects *of discourse*: I learned and applied the words fire, milk, bread, and wood. I learned also the names of the cottagers themselves. The youth and his companion had each of them several, but the old man had only one, which was Father. The girl was called sister or Agatha, and the youth Felix, brother, or son. I cannot describe the delight I felt when I learned the ideas appropriated to each of these sounds and was able to pronounce them. I distinguished several other words without being able *as yet* to understand or apply them—such as good, dearest, unhappy.

"I spent the winter in this manner. The gentle manners and beauty of the cottagers greatly endeared them to me. When they were unhappy, I felt depressed; and I sympathized in their joys. I saw few human beings besides them; and if any other happened to enter the cottage, their harsh manners and rude gait only enhanced to me the superior advantages of my friends. The old man, I could perceive, often endeavoured to encourage his children, as I sometimes found that he called them, *to cast off their melancholy*. He would talk in a cheerful accent with an expression of goodness that bestowed pleasure even on me. Agatha listened with respect; her eyes sometimes filled with tears, which she endeavoured to wipe away unperceived; but I generally found that her manners and tone were more cheerful after having listened to the exhortations of her father. It was not thus with Felix. He was always the saddest of the group; and, even to my unpractised senses, he appeared to have suffered more deeply than his friends. But if his countenance was more sorrowful, his voice was more cheerful than that of his sister, especially when he addressed the old man.

"I could mention innumerable instances which, although slight, marked the dispositions of these amiable cottagers. In the midst of poverty and want, Felix carried with pleasure to his sister the first little white flower that peeped out from beneath the *snowy* ground. Early in the morning before she had risen, he cleared away the snow that obstructed her path to the milk-house, drew water from the well, and brought the wood from the outhouse, *where, to his perpetual astonishment, he found his store always replenished by an invisible hand.* In the day, I believe he worked sometimes for a neighbouring farmer, *because* he often went *forth* and did not return until dinner, yet brought no wood with him. At other times he worked in the garden; but, as there was little to do in the frosty season, he often read to the old man and Agatha. This reading had puzzled me extremely at first; but, by degrees, I discovered that he uttered many of the same sounds when he read as when he talked; I conjectured therefore that he found on the paper signs for speech which he understood, and I ardently longed to comprehend these also. But how was that[†] possible, when I did not even understand the sounds for which they stood as signs? I improved, however, sensibly in this science, but not sufficiently to follow up any kind of conversation, although I applied my whole mind to the endeavour: for I easily perceived that, although I eagerly longed to discover myself to the cottagers, I ought not to make the attempt until I had first become master of their language; which knowledge might enable me to make them overlook the deformity of my figure; for with this also the contrast perpetually presented to my eyes had made me acquainted.

"I had admired the perfect forms of my cottagers—their grace, beauty, and delicate complexions: but how was I terrified, when I viewed myself in a transparent pool! At first I started back, unable to believe that it was indeed I who was reflected in the mirror; and when I became fully convinced that I was in reality the monster that I am, I was filled with the bitterest sensations of despondence and mortification. Alas! I did not yet entirely know the fatal effects of this miserable deformity.

---

† Manuscript missing from this point to end of Ch. 4 on p. 147: text supplied from *1818*.[58]

"As the sun became warmer, and the light of day longer, the snow vanished, and I beheld the bare trees and the black earth. From this time Felix was more employed; and the heart-moving indications of impending famine disappeared. Their food, as I afterwards found, was coarse, but it was wholesome; and they procured a sufficiency of it. Several new kinds of plants sprung up in the garden, which they dressed; and these signs of comfort increased daily as the season advanced.

"The old man, leaning on his son, walked each day at noon, when it did not rain, as I found it was called when the heavens poured forth its waters. This frequently took place; but a high wind quickly dried the earth, and the season became far more pleasant than it had been.

"My mode of life in my hovel was uniform. During the morning I attended the motions of the cottagers; and when they were dispersed in various occupations, I slept: the remainder of the day was spent in observing my friends. When they had retired to rest, if there was any moon, or the night was star-light, I went into the woods, and collected my own food and fuel for the cottage. When I returned, as often as it was necessary, I cleared their path from the snow, and performed those offices that I had seen done by Felix. I afterwards found that these labours, performed by an invisible hand, greatly astonished them; and once or twice I heard them, on these occasions, utter the words good spirit, wonderful;[59] but I did not then understand the signification of these terms.

"My thoughts now became more active, and I longed to discover the motives and feelings of these lovely creatures; I was inquisitive to know why Felix appeared so miserable, and Agatha so sad. I thought (foolish wretch!) that it might be in my power to restore happiness to these deserving people. When I slept, or was absent, the forms of the venerable blind father, the gentle Agatha, and the excellent Felix, flitted before me. I looked upon them as superior beings, who would be the arbiters of my future destiny. I formed in my imagination a thousand pictures of presenting myself to them, and their reception of me. I imagined that they would be disgusted, until, by my gentle demeanour and conciliating words, I should first win their favour, and afterwards their love.

"These thoughts exhilarated me, and led me to apply with fresh ardour to the acquiring the art of language. My organs were indeed harsh, but supple; and although my voice was very unlike the soft music of their tones, yet I pronounced such words as I understood with tolerable ease. It was as the ass and the lap-dog; yet surely the gentle ass, whose intentions were affectionate, although his manners were rude, deserved better treatment than blows and execration.

"The pleasant showers and genial warmth of spring greatly altered the aspect of the earth. Men, who before this change seemed to have been hid in caves, dispersed themselves, and were employed in various arts of cultivation. The birds sang in more cheerful notes, and the leaves began to bud forth on the trees. Happy, happy earth! fit habitation for gods, which, so short a time before, was bleak, damp, and unwholesome. My spirits were elevated by the enchanting appearance of nature; the past was blotted from my memory, the present was tranquil, and the future gilded by bright rays of hope, and anticipations of joy."

Chapter 4

"I now hasten to the more moving part of my story.[60] I shall relate events that impressed me with feelings which, from what I was, have made me what I am.

"Spring advanced rapidly; the weather became fine, and the skies cloudless. It surprised me, that what before was desert and gloomy should now bloom with the most beautiful flowers and verdure. My senses were gratified and refreshed by a thousand scents of delight, and a thousand sights of beauty.

"It was on one of these days, when my cottagers periodically rested from labour—the old man played on his guitar, and the children listened to him—I observed that the countenance of Felix was melancholy beyond expression: he sighed frequently; and once his father paused in his music, and I conjectured by his manner that he inquired the cause of his son's sorrow. Felix replied in a cheerful accent, and the old man was recommencing his music, when some one tapped at the door.

"It was a lady on horseback, accompanied by a countryman as a guide. The lady was dressed in a dark suit, and covered with a thick black veil. Agatha asked a question; to which the stranger only replied by pronouncing, in a sweet accent, the name of Felix. Her voice was musical, but unlike that of either of my friends. On hearing this word, Felix came up hastily to the lady; who, when she saw him, threw up her veil, and I beheld a countenance of angelic beauty and expression. Her hair of a shining raven black, and curiously braided; her eyes were dark, but gentle, although animated; her features of a regular proportion, and her complexion wondrously fair, each cheek tinged with a lovely pink.

"Felix seemed ravished with delight when he saw her, every trait of sorrow vanished from his face, and it instantly expressed a degree of ecstatic joy, of which I could hardly have believed it capable; his eyes sparkled, as his cheek flushed with pleasure; and at that moment I thought him as beautiful as the stranger. She appeared affected by different feelings; wiping a few tears from her lovely eyes, she held out her hand to Felix, who kissed it rapturously, and called her, as well as I could distinguish, his sweet Arabian. She did not appear to understand him, but smiled. He assisted her to dismount, and, dismissing her guide, conducted her into the cottage. Some conversation took place between him and his father; and the young stranger knelt at the old man's feet, and would have kissed his hand, but he raised her, and embraced her affectionately.

"I soon perceived, that although the stranger uttered articulate sounds, and appeared to have a language of her own, she was neither understood by, or herself understood, the cottagers. They made many signs which I did not comprehend; but I saw that her presence diffused gladness through the cottage, dispelling their sorrow as the sun dissipates the morning mists. Felix seemed peculiarly happy, and with smiles of delight welcomed his Arabian. Agatha, the ever-gentle Agatha, kissed the hands of the lovely stranger; and, pointing to her brother, made signs which appeared to me to mean that he had been sorrowful until she came. Some hours passed thus, while they, by their countenances, expressed joy, the cause of which I did not comprehend. Presently I found, by the frequent recurrence of one sound which the stranger repeated after them, that she was endeavouring to learn their language; and the idea instantly occurred to me, that I should make use of the same instructions to the same end. The stranger learned about twenty words at the first lesson, most of them indeed were those which I had before understood, but I profited by the others.

"As night came on, Agatha and the Arabian retired early. When they separated, Felix kissed the hand of the stranger, and said, 'Good night, sweet Safie.' He sat up much longer, conversing with his father; and, by the frequent repetition of her name, I conjectured that their lovely guest was the subject of their conversation. I ardently desired to understand them, and bent every faculty towards that purpose, but found it utterly impossible.

"The next morning Felix went out to his work; and, after the usual occupations of Agatha were finished, the Arabian sat at the feet of the old man, and, taking his guitar, played some airs so entrancingly beautiful, that they at once drew tears of sorrow and delight from my eyes. She sang, and her voice flowed in a rich cadence, swelling or dying away, like a nightingale of the woods.

"[61]When she had finished, she gave the guitar to Agatha, who at first declined it. She played a simple air, and her voice accompanied it in sweet accents, but unlike the wondrous strain of the stranger. The old man appeared enraptured, and said some words, which Agatha endeavoured to explain to Safie, and by which he appeared to wish to express that she bestowed on him the greatest delight by her music.

"The days now passed as peaceably as before, with the sole alteration, that joy had taken place of sadness in the countenances of my friends. Safie was always gay and happy; she and I improved rapidly in the knowledge of language, so that in two months I began to comprehend most of the words uttered by my protectors.

"In the meanwhile also the black ground was covered with herbage, and the green banks interspersed with innumerable flowers, sweet to the scent and the eyes, stars of pale radiance among the moonlight woods; the sun became warmer, the nights clear and balmy; and my nocturnal rambles were an extreme pleasure to me, although they were considerably shortened by the late setting and early rising of the sun; for I never ventured abroad during daylight, fearful of meeting with the same treatment as I had formerly endured in the first village which I entered.

"My days were spent in close attention, that I might more speedily master the language; and I may boast that I improved more rapidly than the Arabian, who understood very little, and conversed in broken accents, whilst I comprehended and could imitate almost every word that was spoken.

"While I improved in speech, I also learned the science of letters, as it was taught to the stranger; and this opened before me a wide field for wonder and delight.

"The book from which Felix instructed Safie was Volney's Ruins of Empires.[62] I should not have understood the purport of this book, had not Felix, in reading it, given very minute explanations. He had chosen this work, he said, because the declamatory style was framed in imitation of the eastern authors. Through this work I obtained a cursory knowledge of history, and a view of the several empires at present existing in the world; it gave me an insight into the manners, governments, and religions of the different nations of the earth. I heard of the slothful Asiatics; of the stupendous genius and mental activity of the Grecians; of the wars and wonderful virtue of the early Romans—of their subsequent degeneration—of the decline of that mighty empire; of chivalry, Christianity,[63] and kings. I heard of the discovery of the American hemisphere, and wept with Safie over the hapless fate of its original inhabitants.

"These wonderful narrations inspired me with strange feelings. Was man, indeed, at once so powerful, so virtuous, and magnificent, yet so vicious and base? He appeared at one time a mere scion of the evil principle, and at another as all that can be conceived of noble and godlike. To be a great and virtuous man appeared the highest honour that can befall a sensitive being; to be base and vicious, as many on record have been, appeared the lowest degradation, a condition more abject than that of the blind mole or harmless worm. For a long time I could not conceive how one man could go forth to murder his fellow, or even why there were laws and governments; but when I heard details of vice and bloodshed, my wonder ceased, and I turned away with disgust and loathing.

"Every conversation of the cottagers now opened new wonders to me. While I listened to the instructions which Felix bestowed upon the Arabian, the strange system of human society was explained to me. I heard of the division of property, of immense wealth and squalid poverty; of rank, descent, and noble blood.

"The words induced me to turn towards myself. I learned that the possessions most esteemed by your fellow-creatures were, high and unsullied descent united with riches. A man might be respected with only one of these acquisitions; but without either he was considered, except in very rare instances, as a vagabond and a slave, doomed to waste his powers for the profit of the chosen few. And what was I? Of my creation and creator I was absolutely ignorant; but I knew that I possessed no money, no friends, no kind of property. I was, besides, endowed with a figure hideously deformed and loathsome; I was not even of the same nature as man. I was more agile than they, and could subsist upon coarser diet; I bore the extremes of heat and cold with less injury to my frame; my stature far exceeded their's. When I looked around, I saw and heard of none like me. Was I then a monster, a blot upon the earth, from which all men fled, and whom all men disowned?

"I cannot describe to you the agony that these reflections inflicted upon me; I tried to dispel them, but sorrow only increased with knowledge. Oh, that I had for ever remained in my native wood, nor known or felt beyond the sensations of hunger, thirst, and heat!

"Of what a strange nature is knowledge! It clings to the mind, when it has once seized on it, like a lichen on the rock. I wished sometimes to shake off all thought and feeling; but I learned that there was but one means to overcome the sensation of pain, and that was death—a state which I feared yet did not understand. I admired virtue and good feelings, and loved the gentle manners and amiable qualities of my cottagers; but I was shut out from intercourse with them, except through means which I obtained by stealth, when I was unseen and unknown, and which rather increased than satisfied the desire I had of becoming one among my fellows. The gentle words of Agatha, and the animated smiles of the charming Arabian, were not for me. The mild exhortations of the old man, and the lively conversation of the loved Felix, were not for me. Miserable, unhappy wretch!

"Other lessons were impressed upon me even more deeply. I heard of the difference of sexes; of the birth and growth of children; how the father doated on the smiles of the infant, and the lively sallies of the older child; how all the life and cares of the mother were wrapt up in the precious charge; how the mind of youth expanded and gained knowledge; of brother, sister, and all the various relationships which bind one human being to another in mutual bonds.

"But where were my friends and relations? No father had watched my infant days, no mother had blessed me with smiles and caresses; or if they had, all my past life was now a blot, a blind vacancy in which I distinguished nothing. From my earliest remembrance I had been as I then was in height and proportion. I had never yet seen a being resembling me, or who claimed any intercourse with me. What was I? The question again recurred, to be answered only with groans.

"I will soon explain to what these feelings tended; but allow me now to return to the cottagers, whose story excited in me such various feelings of indignation, delight, and wonder, but which all terminated in additional love and reverence for my protectors (for so I loved, in an innocent, half painful self-deceit, to call them)."

Chapter 5

"Some time elapsed before I learned the history of my friends.[64] It was one *which* could not fail to impress itself deeply *on* my mind, unfolding as it did a number of circumstances, each interesting and wonderful to one so utterly inexperienced as I was.

"The name of the old man was De Lacey. He was descended from a good family in France, where for many years he had lived in affluence, respected by his superiors and beloved by his equals. His son was bred in the service of his country, and Agatha had ranked with ladies of the highest distinction. A few months *before* my arrival, they had lived in a large and luxurious city called Paris, surrounded by friends and possessed of every enjoyment *which* virtue *and refinement of intellect and taste*, accompanied with a competent fortune, could afford.

"The father of Safie had been the cause of their *ruin*. He was a Turkish merchant and had inhabited Paris for many years, when his person became *for some reason which I could not learn* obnoxious to the government. He was seized and cast into prison the very day that Safie arrived from Constantinople to join him. He was tried and condemned to death. The injustice of his sentence was very flagrant. All Paris were indignant, and it was judged that his religion and wealth, rather than the crime alleged against him, *had been the cause of his condemnation*. Felix was present at his trial; his horror and indignation *were* uncontrollable when he heard the *decision of the court*. He made at that moment a solemn vow to deliver him and then looked around for the means. After many fruitless attempts to gain admittance to the *prison*, he found a strongly grated window in an unguarded part of the *building*, which lighted the dungeon of the unfortunate Mahometan, who, loaded with chains, waited in despair the execution of the barbarous sentence. Felix visited the grate at night and made known to the prisoner his intentions in his favour. The Turk, amazed and delighted, endeavoured to *kindle* the zeal of his deliverer by promises of reward and wealth. Felix rejected his offers with contempt. Yet when he saw the lovely Safie, who was allowed to visit her father and who by her gestures expressed her lively gratitude, the youth could not help owning to his own mind that the captive possessed a treasure which would fully reward his toil and hazard.

"The Turk quickly perceived the impression that his daughter had made on the heart of Felix and endeavoured to secure him more entirely by the promise of her hand in marriage. Felix was too delicate to accept this *offer*, yet he looked forward to the probability of that event as the consummation of his happiness.

"During the ensuing days, while the preparations were going forward for the escape of the merchant, the zeal of Felix was warmed by several letters that he received from this lovely girl, who found means to express her thoughts in the language of her lover by the aid of an old man, a servant of her father who understood French. She thanked him in the most ardent terms for his intended kindness, and at the same time she gently deplored her own fate. I have copies of these letters, for I found means during my residence in the hovel to procure the implements of writing, and they were often in the hands of Felix or Agatha. Before I depart, I will give them to you; they will prove to you the truth of my tale; but at present, as the sun already begins to decline, I shall only have time to repeat the substance to you. Safie related that her mother was a Christian Arab seized and made a slave by the Turks. Recommended by her beauty, she had won the heart of the father of Safie, who married her. The young girl spoke in high and enthusiastic terms of her mother, who, born in freedom, spurned the bondage to which she was now *reduced*. She instructed her daughter in the tenets of her religion and taught her to aspire to higher powers of intellect and an independence of spirit forbidden to the female followers of Mahomet. This lady died, but her lessons were indelibly impressed in the mind of Safie, who sickened at the prospect of again returning to *Asia* and the being immured in walls of a haram, allowed only to occupy herself with puerile amusements ill-suited to the temper of her soul now accustomed to grand ideas and a noble emulation for virtue. The prospect of marrying a Christian and remaining in a country where women were allowed to take a rank in society was enchanting to her.

"The day for the execution of the Turk was fixed; but on the night previous to it, he had quitted prison and, before morning, was distant many leagues from Paris. Felix had procured passports in the name of his father, sister, and himself. He communicated his plan to the former, who aided the deceit by quitting his house under the pretence of a journey and concealed himself with his daughter in an obscure part of Paris. Felix conducted the fugitives through France to Lyons and across Mont Cenis when he arrived at Leghorn, where the merchant *had decided* to wait a favourable opportunity of passing over to Africa. He could not deny himself the pleasure of remaining a few days in the society of the Arabian, who exhibited towards him the simplest and tenderest affection. They conversed with one another by the aid of an interpreter, and Safie sang to him the divine airs of her native country. The Turk allowed this intimacy to take place and encouraged the hopes of the youthful lovers, while in his heart he had formed far other plans. He loathed the idea that his daughter should be united to a Christian, but he feared the resentment of Felix if he should appear lukewarm, for he knew that he was still in the power of his deliver*er* if he should choose to betray him to the Italian state which they at that time inhabited. He revolved a thousand plans by which he should be enabled to prolong the deceit until it was no longer necessary—and then *to* carry his daughter to Africa with him. His plans were greatly facilitated by the news *which* arrived from Paris.

"The government of France were greatly enraged at the escape of their victim and spared no pains to discover and punish his deliverer. The plot of Felix was quickly discovered, and De Lacey and Agatha were thrown into prison. The news reached Felix and roused him from his dream of pleasure. His blind and aged father and his gentle sister lay in a noisome dungeon, while he enjoyed the free air and the society of her he loved. This idea was torture to him. He arranged with the Turk that, if the latter should find a favourable opportunity for escape before Felix could return to Italy, Safie should remain as a boarder in a convent at Leghorn; and then, quitting the lovely Arabian, he hastened to Paris and delivered himself up to the vengeance of the law, hoping to free De Lacey and Agatha by this proceeding.

"He did not succeed. They remained confined for five months before the trial took place, the result of which deprived them of their fortune and *condemned them to a perpetual exile* from their native country.

"They found a miserable asylum in the cottage in Germany where I found them. Felix learned that the treacherous Turk, for whom he and his family endured such unheard of oppression, on *discovering* that his deliverer was *thus reduced to poverty and impotence*, became a traitor to good feeling and honour and had quitted Italy with his daughter, insultingly sending Felix a pittance of money to aid him, as he said, in some plan of future maintenance.

"Such were the events that preyed on the heart of Felix and rendered him, when I first saw him, the most miserable of his family. He could have endured poverty; and when this distress had been the meed of his virtue, he would have gloried in it. But the ingratitude of the Turk and the loss of his beloved Safie were misfortunes more bitter and irreparable. The arrival of the Arabian now infused new life into his soul.

"When the news *reached her* that Felix was deprived of his wealth and rank, the merchant commanded his daughter to think no more of her lover but to prepare to return to her native country with him. The generous nature of Safie was outraged by this command. She attempted to expostulate with her father, but he left her angrily, reiterating his tyrannical command.

"A few days after, the Turk entered his daughter's apartment and told her hastily that he had reason to believe that his residence in Leghorn had been divulged and that he *sh*ould speedily be delivered up to the French government. He had consequently hired a vessel to convey him to Constantinople, *for* which *city* he should sail in a few hours. He intended to leave his daughter under the care of a servant to follow at her leisure with the greater part of his property, which had not yet arrived at Leghorn.

"Safie revolved in her own mind the plan of conduct that it would become her to pursue *in this emergency*. A residence in Turkey was abhorrent to her; her religion and feelings were alike adverse to it. By some papers of her father that fell into her hands, she heard of the exile of her lover and learned the name of the spot where he resided. She hesitated some time, but at length she formed her resolution. Taking with her some jewels that belonged to her and a small sum of money, she quitted Italy with an attendant, a native of Leghorn but who understood *Arabic*, and departed for Germany. She arrived in safety at a town about twenty leagues from the cottage of De Lacey; her attendant then fell dangerously ill. Safie nursed her with the most devoted affection; but the poor girl died, and the Arabian was left alone, unacquainted with the language of the country and utterly ignorant of the customs of the world. She fell, however, into good hands. The Italian had mentioned the name of the spot for which they were bound; and, after her death, the woman of the house in which they had lived took care that Safie should arrive safely at the cottage of her lover."

Chapter 6

"Such was the history of my beloved cottagers.[65] It impressed me deeply. I learned from *the views of social life which it developed* to admire their virtues and to deprecate the vices of mankind. As yet I looked upon crime as a distant evil; benevolence and generosity were ever present before me, *inciting me to desire to become an actor* in the busy scene where so many admirable qualities were called forth and displayed. But in giving an account of the progress of my intellect, I must not omit a circumstance *which occurred* in the beginning of the month of August of *the same* year.

"One night, during my accustomed visit to the neighbouring wood where I collected my own food and brought home firing for my protectors, I found on the ground a leathern portmanteau containing several articles of dress and some books. I eagerly seized the prize and returned with it to my hovel. The books were fortunately written in the language *the elements of which* I had learned at the cottage; they consisted of 'Paradise Lost,' a volume of 'Plutarch's Lives,' and the 'Sorrows of Werter.'[66] The possession of these treasures gave me extreme delight; I could continually study and *exercise* my mind upon the*se histories* when my friends were employed in their ordinary occupations. I can hardly describe to you the effect *of* these books. They produced in me an infinity of new images and ideas that sometimes raised me to ecstacy but more frequently sunk me to the lowest dejection. In the 'Sorrows of Werter,' besides the interest of its simple and affecting story, so many opinions are canvassed and so many lights thrown upon what had hitherto been to me *obscure* subjects, that I found in it a never-ending source of speculation *and astonishment.* The gentle and domestic manners it described, combined with lofty sentiments and feelings *which had for their object something out of self,* accorded well with my experience among my protectors *and with the wants which were for ever alive within my own bosom.* But I thought Werter himself a more divine being than I had ever beheld *or imagined.* His character contained no pretension, but it sunk deep. The disquisitions upon death and suicide were calculated to fill me with *wonder.* I did not pretend to enter into the merits of the case; yet I inclined towards the opinion of the hero, whose extinction I wept *without precisely* understand*ing* it. As I read, however, I applied much personally to my own feelings and condition. I found myself similar yet at the same time strangely unlike the beings concerning whom I read and to whose conversation I was a listener. I sympathized with and partly understood them, but I was unformed in mind; I was dependant on none, and related to none. 'The path of my departure was free,'[67] and there was none to lament my annihilation. My person was hideous, and my stature gigantic. What did this mean? Who was I? What was I? *Whence did I come? What was my destination?* These questions continually recurred, but I was unable to solve them.

"The volume of 'Plutarch's Lives' which I possessed contained the histories of the first founders of the ancient republics. This book had a far different effect upon me from the letters of Werter. I learned from *Werter's imaginations* despondency and gloom; but Plutarch taught me high thoughts: he elevated me above the wretched sphere of my own reflections to admire and love the heroes of past ages. Many things I read surpassed my understanding and experience. I had a very confused knowledge of kingdoms and wide extents of country, mighty rivers, and boundless seas. But I was perfectly unacquainted with towns and large assembl*ag*es of men. The cottage of my protectors had been the only school *in which* I *had* studied human nature. But this book developed new and mightier scenes of action. I read of men concerned in public affairs governing or massacring their species. I felt the greatest ardour for virtue rise within me and abhorrence for vice, as far as I understood the signification of those terms, relative as they were, as I applied them, to pleasure and pain alone. Induced by these feelings, I was of course led to admire peaceable lawgivers, Numa, Solon, and Lycurgus, more than Romulus and Theseus.[68] The patriarchal lives of my protectors caused these impressions to take a firm hold on my mind; perhaps, if my first *introduction to humanity* had been *made by* a young soldier burning for glory and slaughter, I should have been imbued with different sensations.

"But 'Paradise Lost' excited different and far deeper emotions. I read it, as I had *read* the other volumes which had fallen into my hands, as a true history. It moved every feeling of wonder and awe that the picture of an omnipotent God warring with his creatures was capable of exciting. I often referred the several situations, as their similarity struck me, to my own. Like Adam, I was created apparently as I had been, but united by no link to any other being *in existence*; but his state was different from mine in every other respect. He had come forth from the hands of God a perfect creature, happy, prosperous, and guarded by the especial care of his creator. He was allowed to converse and acquire knowledge from beings of a superior nature; but I was wretched, helpless, and alone. Many times I considered Satan as my fitter mate; for often, like him, when I viewed the bliss of my protectors, the bitter gall of envy rose within me.

"Another circumstance strengthened and confirmed these feelings. Soon after my arrival in the hovel, I discovered some papers in the pocket of the dress *which* I had taken from your study. At first I *had* neglected them; but now that I was able to decypher the characters in which they were written, I began to study them with diligence. It was your journal of the four months that preceded my creation. You minutely described in *these papers* every step you took in the progress of your work; this *history* was mingled with accounts of domestic occurrences. You doubtless recollect these papers. Here they are. Every thing is related in them *which bears reference to my accursed origin*; *the whole detail of that series of* disgusting circumstance*s which produced it* is set in view; the minutest description of my odious and loathsome person *is given in language which painted your own horrors and has rendered mine ineffaceable*. I sickened as I read. 'Hateful day when I received life!' I exclaimed in agony. 'Cursed Creator! Why did you form a monster so hideous that even you turned from me in disgust? God in pity made man beautiful and alluring. I am more hateful to the sight than the bitter apples of hell to the taste. Satan has his companions, fellow-devils, to admire and encourage him; but I am solitary and detested.'

"These were my reflections in my hours of despondency and solitude; but when I contemplated the virtues of the cottagers, their amiable and benevolent dispositions, I persuaded myself that when they *should* become acquainted with my admiration of their virtues, they would pity me and overlook my personal deformity. Could they turn from their door one, however monstrous, who solicited their compassion and friendship? I resolved at least not to despair but in every way to fit myself for an interview which would decide my fate. I postponed this attempt for some months longer, for the importance attached to its *success* inspired me with a dread *lest it should not succeed.* Besides, I found that my understanding improved so much with every day's experience that I was unwilling to commence this undertaking until a few more months should have added to my wisdom.

"Several changes in the mean time took place in the cottage. The presence of Safie diffused happiness among its inhabitants, and I also found that a greater degree of plenty reigned there. Felix and Agatha spent more time in amusement and conversation and were assisted in their labours by servants. They did not appear rich, but they were contented and happy. Their feelings *were serene and peaceful*, while *mine* became every day more miserable. Encrease of knowledge only discovered to me more clearly what a wretched outcast I was. I cherished hope, it is true, but it vanished when I beheld my person reflected in water or even my shadow in the moonshine. I endeavoured to crush these fears and to fortify myself for the trial which in a few months I resolved to undergo; and sometimes I allowed my thoughts, unchecked by reason, to ramble in the fields of Paradise and dared to fancy amiable and lovely beings sympathizing with my feelings and cheering my gloom. Their angelic countenances breathed smiles of consolation. But it was all a dream. No Eve soothed my sorrows or shared my thoughts. I was alone. I remembered Adam's supplication to his creator,[69] but where was mine? He had abandoned me, and in the bitterness of my heart I cursed him.

"Autumn passed thus. I saw, with surprise and grief, the leaves decay and fall, and nature again assume the barren and bleak appearance it had when I first beheld the woods and the lovely moon. I did not heed the bleakness of the weather. I was more fitted by my constitution for the sufferance of cold than heat. But my only joys were the sight of flowers and birds, and all the gay apparel of summer; when those deserted me, I turned with more attention towards the cottagers. Their happiness was not decreased by the absence of summer. They loved and sympathized with one another, and their joys, depending on each other, were not *interrupted* by the casualties that took place around them. The more I saw of them, the greater became my desire to claim their protection and kindness. My heart yearned to be known and loved by these amiable creatures, to see their sweet looks directed towards me in kindness. I dared not think that they would turn *them* from me with disdain or horror. The poor that stopped at their door were never driven away. I asked, it is true, for greater treasures than a little food or rest. I required kindness and sympathy, but I did not believe myself utterly unworthy of it."

Chapter 7

"The winter advanced,[70] and an entire revolution of the seasons had taken place since I awoke into life. My attention at this time was solely directed towards my plan of introducing myself into the cottage of my protectors. I revolved many projects, but that on which I finally fixed was to enter their dwelling when the blind old man *should be* alone. I had sagacity enough to discover that the unnatural hideousness of my person was the chief object of horror with those who had formerly beheld me. My voice, although harsh, had nothing terrible in it. I thought, therefore, that if, in the absence of his children, I could gain the goodwill of the old De Lacey, I might by his means be tolerated by my younger protectors.

"One day, when the sun shone on the red leaves that strewed the ground and diffused cheerfulness although it denied warmth, Safie, Agatha, and Felix set out on a long country walk, and the old man at his own desire was left alone in the cottage. When his children had departed, he took up his guitar and played several mournful but sweet airs, *more sweet and mournful than I had ever* heard him play before. At first his countenance was illuminated with pleasure, but, as he continued, thoughtfulness and sadness succeeded; and laying down the instrument, he sat absorbed in reflection.

"My heart beat quick. This was the hour and moment of trial which would decide my hopes. The servants were gone to a neighbouring fair. All was silent in and around the cottage. It was an excellent opportunity; yet when I *proceeded* to execute my plan, my limbs failed me, and I sunk to the ground. Again I rose and, exerting all the firmness of which I was master, removed the planks which I had placed before my hovel to conceal my retreat. The fresh air revived me, and with renewed determination I approached the door of the cottage. I knocked. 'Who is there?' said the old man—'come in.' I entered. 'Pardon this intrusion,' said I, 'I am a traveller, in want of a little rest. You would greatly oblige me if you would allow me to remain a few minutes before your fire.' 'Enter,' said De Lacey, 'and I will try in what manner I can relieve your wants; but, unfortunately, my children are *from home*, and, as I am blind, I am afraid I shall find it difficult to procure food for you.' 'Do not trouble yourself, my kind host,' I replied, 'I have food; it is warmth and rest only that I need.' I sat down and a silence ensued. I knew very well that every minute was precious to me, yet I remained irresolute in what manner to commence the interview, when the old man addressed me. 'By your language, stranger, I suppose you are my countryman—are you French?' 'No,' replied I, 'but I was educated by a French family and understand that language only. I am now going to claim the protection of some friends, whom I sincerely love and of whose favour I have some hopes.' 'Are these Germans?' asked De Lacey. 'No—they are French. But let us change the subject. I am an unfortunate and deserted creature. I look around, and I have no relation or friend on earth. These amiable people to whom I go have never seen me and know little of me. I am full of fears; for if I fail there, I am an outcast in the world for ever.'

"'Do not despair,' said the old man. 'To be friendless is indeed to be unfortunate: but the hearts of men, when unprejudiced by obvious self-interest, are full of brotherly love and charity. Rely therefore on your hopes; and if these friends are good and amiable, do not despair.' 'They are kind,' I answered. 'They are the most excellent creatures in the world, but, unfortunately, they are prejudiced against me. I have good dispositions; I love virtue and knowledge; my life has been hitherto harmless and in some degree beneficial; but a fatal prejudice clouds their eyes; and, where they ought to see a feeling and kind friend, they behold only a detestable monster.'

"'That is indeed unfortunate,' replied De Lacey, 'but if you are really blameless, cannot you undeceive them?'

"'I am about to undertake that task. And it is on that account that I feel so many overwhelming terrors. I love these friends tenderly; I have, unknown to them, been for many months in the habits of daily kindness towards them; but they believe that I wish to injure them, and it is that prejudice which I wish to overcome.'

"'Where do these friends reside?' said De Lacey.

"'Near here—*on* this spot.'

"The old man paused a moment and then continued. 'If you will unreservedly confide to me the particulars, I perhaps may be of use in undeceiving them. I am blind and cannot judge of your countenance, but there is something in your words *which* persuades me that you are sincere. I am poor and an exile, but it will afford me true pleasure to be in any way serviceable to a *human* creature.'

"'Excellent man!' exclaimed I, 'I thank you and accept your generous offer. You raise me from the dust by this kindness, and I trust that I shall not be driven from the society and sympathy of my fellow-creatures.'

"'Heaven forbid! even if you were really criminal—for that can only drive you to desperation and not instigate you to virtue. I also am unfortunate. I and my family have been condemned, although innocent: judge, therefore, if I do not feel for your misfortunes.'

"'How can I thank you, my best and only benefactor—from your lips first have I heard the voice of kindness directed towards me. I shall be for ever grateful, and your present humanity assures me of success with the friends whom I am on the point of meeting.'

"'May I know the names and residence of those friends?' asked De Lacey.

"I paused. This was the moment of decision which was to rob me of or bestow happiness on me for ever. I struggled vainly for firmness sufficient to answer him; the effort destroyed all my remaining strength; I sank on a chair and sobbed aloud. At that moment I heard the steps of my younger protectors. I had not a moment to lose; but, seizing the hand of the old man, I cried—'Now is the time!—save and protect me! You and your family are the friends whom I seek. Do not you desert me in the hour of trial!'

"'Great God!' exclaimed the old man. 'Who are you?'

"At that instant the cottage door opened, and Felix, Safie, and Agatha entered. Who can describe their horror and astonishment on beholding me? Agatha fainted; and Safie, unable to attend to her friend, rushed out of the cottage. Felix darted forward and with supernatural strength tore me from his father, to whose knees I clung. In a transport of fury, he dashed me to the ground and struck me violently with a stick. I saw him on the point of repeating the blow when, overcome by pain and anguish, I quitted the cottage and, in the general tumult, escaped unperceived to my hovel.

"Cursed, Cursed Creator! Why did I live? Why in that instant did I not extinguish the spark of existence which you had so wantonly bestowed? I know not. Despair had not yet taken possession of me;

my feelings were those of rage and revenge. I could with pleasure have destroyed the cottage and its inhabitants—and glutted myself with their shrieks and misery. When night came on, I quitted my retreat and wandered to the wood. No longer restrained by the fear of discovery, I gave vent to my anguish in fearful howlings. I was like a wild beast in the toils,[71] destroying the objects that obstructed me and ranging through the wood with stag-like swiftness. Oh! what a miserable night I passed! The cold stars shone in mockery, the bare trees waved their branches above me, and now and then the sweet voice of a bird burst forth amidst the universal stillness. All, save I, were at rest or in enjoyment. I, like the arch-fiend, bore a hell within me;[72] and, finding myself unsympathized with, I wished to tear up the trees, spread havoc and destruction, and then have sat down and enjoyed the ruin.

"But this was a luxury of sensation that could not endure. I became fatigued with excess of bodily exertion and sank on the damp grass in the despondency of despair. There was no one among the myriads of men that existed that would pity or assist me—and should I feel kindness towards my enemies? No! from that moment I declared everlasting war against the species and, more than all, against h*im* who had formed me and sent me forth to *this insupportable* misery.

"The sun rose. I heard the voices of men and knew that it was impossible to return to my retreat *during* that day; accordingly, I hid myself in some thick underwood, determin*ing* to devote the ensuing hours to reflection on my situation. The pleasant sunshine and pure air of day restored me to some degree of tranquillity; and when I considered what had passed at the cottage, I could not help believing that I was too hasty in my conclusions. I had certainly acted imprudently. It was apparent that my conversation *h*ad softened the father, and I was a fool for having exposed my person to the horror of his children. I ought to have familiarized the old De Lacey to me and, by degrees, have discovered myself to the rest of the family when they should have been prepared for my approach. But I did not believe my errors irretrievable; and, after much consideration, I resolved to return to the cottage, seek the old man, and, by my representations, win him to my party.

"These thoughts calmed me, and in the afternoon I sunk into a profound sleep; but the fever of my blood did not allow of peaceful dreams. The horri*ble* scene of the preceding day was for ever acting before my eyes: the females were flying, and the enraged Felix tearing me from his father's feet. I awoke exhausted; and, finding that it was already night, I crept from my hiding-place and went in search of food."

Chapter 8

"When my hunger was appeased, I directed my steps towards the well-known path that conducted to the cottage. All there was at peace. I crept into my hovel and remained in silent expectation of the accustomed hour when the family arose. That *hour* passed, and the sun mounted high in the heavens, but the cottagers did not appear. I trembled violently, apprehending some dreadful misfortune. The inside of the cottage was dark, and I heard no motion. I cannot describe the agony I felt during this suspense.

"Presently two countrymen passed by; but, pausing near the cottage, they entered into conversation, using violent gestures. I did not understand what they said, for their language differed from that of my protectors. Soon after, however, Felix approached with another man. I was surprised, as I knew that he had not quitted the cottage that morning, and waited anxiously to discover by his discourse the meaning of these unusual appearances. 'Do you consider,' said his companion to him, 'that you will be obliged to pay three months' rent and to lose the produce of your garden? I do not wish to take any unfair advantage, and I beg therefore that you will take some days to consider of your determination.'

"'It is utterly useless,' replied Felix, 'we can never again inhabit that cottage. The life of my father is in the greatest danger owing to the dreadful circumstance that I have related. My wife and sister will never recover their horror. I entreat you not to reason with me any more. Take possession of your tenement, and let me fly from this place.'

"Felix trembled violently as he said this. He and his companion entered the cottage, in which they remained for a few minutes, and then departed. I never again saw any *more* of the family of De Lacey.

"I continued in my hovel for the remainder of the day in a state of utter and stupid despair. My protectors had departed and had broken the only link that held me to the world. For the first time the feelings of revenge and hatred filled my bosom, and I did not strive to control them; but, allowing myself to be borne away by the stream, I bent my mind towards injury and death. When I thought of my friends—of the mild voice of De Lacey, the gentle eyes of Agatha, and the exquisite beauty of the Arabian—these thoughts vanish*ed*, and a gush of tears somewhat soothed me. But, again, when I reflected that they had spurned and deserted me, anger returned; and unable to injure any thing human, I turned my fury towards inanimate objects. As night advanced, I placed a variety of combustibles around the cottage; and, after having destroyed every vestige of cultivation in the garden, I waited with forced patience[73] until the moon had sunk to commence my operations. As the night advanced, a fierce wind arose from the woods and quickly dispersed the clouds that had loitered in the heavens—the blast tore along like a mighty avalanche and produced a kind of insanity in my spirits that burst all bounds of reason or reflection. I lighted a dry branch of tree and danced with fury around the devoted cottage, my eyes still fixed on the western horizon, the edge of which the moon nearly touched. Part of its orb was at length hid, and I waved my brand; it sunk, and, with a loud scream, I fired the straw and hay that I had collected. The wind fanned the fire, and the cottage was quickly enveloped by the flames which clung to it and licked it with their forked *and destroying* tongues. As soon as I was convinced that no assistance could save any part of the habitation, I quitted the scene and sought for refuge in the wood.

"And now with the world before me, whither should I bend my steps?[74] I resolved to fly far from the scene of my misfortunes. But to me, hated and despised, every country must be equally horrible. At length the thought of you crossed my mind. I learned from your papers that you were my creator; and to whom could I apply with more fitness than to h*im* who had given me life? Among the lessons that Felix had bestowed on Safie, geography had not been omitted. From these I had learned the relative situations of the different countries of the earth. You had mentioned Geneva as the name of your native town, and towards this place I resolved to proceed.

"But how was I to direct myself? I knew that I must travel *in a* south-west*erly direction* to reach my destination, but the sun was my only guide. I did not know the names of the towns I was to pass through, nor could I ask information from a single human being. But I did not despair. From you only could I hope for succour, although towards you I felt *no* sentiment *than that* of *hate*. Unfeeling, heartless creator! You had endowed me with perceptions and passions and then cast me abroad for the scorn and horror of mankind. But on you only had I any claim, and from you I determined to seek that justice which I vainly attempted to gain from *any other being that wore the human form*.

"My travels were long, and the suffering*s* I endured intense. It was late in autumn when I quitted the district where I had so long resided. I travelled only at night, fearful of meeting the visage of a human being. Nature decayed around me, and the sun became heatless; rain and snow poured around me, and I found no shelter—Oh, Earth! how often did I imprecate curses on the cause of my being. The mildness of my nature had fled, and all within me was turned to gall and bitterness. The nearer I approached to your habitation, the more deeply did I feel the spirit of revenge *become kindled in* my heart. Snow fell around me, and the waters were hardened, but I rested not. A few incidents now and then directed me right, but I often wandered wide from my path. *The agony of my grief allowed me no respite. No incident occurred from which my rage and misery could not extract its food. But a circumstance* that happened when I arrived on the confines of Switzerland, when the sun had recovered a part of its heat and the earth again began to look green, confirmed in a*n especial* manner the bitterness and horror of my feelings.

"I generally rested *during* the day and travelled only when I was secured by night from the view of man. One morning, however, finding that my path lay through a deep wood, I ventured to continue my journey after the sun had risen. The day, which was one of the first of spring, cheered even me by the loveliness of its sun*shine* and the gentleness of the breeze. I felt emotions of softness and pleasure that had long appeared dead revive within me; half-surprised with these new sensations, I allowed myself to be borne away by them and, forgetting my solitude and deformity, dared to be happy. Tears of gentleness again bedewed my cheeks, and I even raised my humid eyes with thankfulness towards the blessed sun which bestowed such joy upon me.

"I continued to wind among the paths of the wood until I came to its boundary, which was skirted by a deep and rapid river, into which many of the trees bent their branches now budding with the fresh spring. Here I paused, not exactly knowing what course to pursue, when I heard voices that induced me to conceal myself under the shade of cypress. I was scarcely hid when a young girl came running towards the spot where I was concealed, laughing as if she ran from some one in sport. She continued her course along the precipitate sides of the river, when suddenly her foot slipt, and she fell into the rapid stream. I rushed from my hiding-place and, with extreme labour from the force of the current, saved her and dragged her to shore. She was senseless; and I endeavoured by every means in my power to restore *animation*, when I was suddenly interrupted by the approach of a rustic, who was probably the person from whom she had playfully fled. On seeing me, he darted towards me and, tearing the girl from my arms, hastened towards the deeper parts of the forest. I followed speedily, I hardly knew why; but when the man saw me draw near, he aimed a gun, which he carried, at my body and fired. I sunk to the ground, and with encreased swiftness he escaped into the wood.

"This then was the reward of my benevolence. I had saved a human being from destruction, and, as a recompense, I now writhed under the miserable pain of *a* wound *which shattered the flesh and bone*. The feelings of kindness and gentleness, which I had entertained but a few moments before, gave place to hellish rage and gnashing of teeth—inflamed by pain, I vowed eternal hatred and vengeance to all mankind. But the agony of my wound overcame me, my pulses paused, and I fainted.

"For some weeks I led a miserable life in these woods, endeavouring to cure the wound *which* I had received. The ball had entered my shoulder, and I knew not whether it had remained there or passed through; at any rate, I had no means of extracting it. My sufferings were augmented also by the oppressive sense of *the* injustice and ingratitude *of their infliction*. My daily *vows* rose for revenge—a deep and deadly revenge, such as would alone compensate for the *outrages and the anguish I had endured*.

"After some weeks my wound healed, and I continued my journey. The labours I endured were no longer to be alleviated by the bright sun or gentle breezes of spring; all joy was but *a* mockery to me, *which insulted my desolate state*, and made me feel more painfully that I was not made for enjoyment. But my toils now drew near a close, and two months from this time I reached the environs of Geneva.[75]

"It was evening when I arrived in the outskirts of that town, and I retired to a hiding-place among the fields that surround it, to consider in what manner I should apply to you. I was oppressed by fatigue and hunger, and far too unhappy to enjoy the gentle breezes of evening or the prospect of the sun setting behind the stupendous mountains of the Jura. At this time a slight sleep relieved me, which was disturbed by the approach of a beautiful child, who came running into the recess I had chosen with all the sportiveness of infancy. Suddenly, as I gazed on him, an idea seized me—that this little creature was unprejudiced and had lived too short a time to have imbibed a horror of deformity. If therefore I could seize him and educate him as my companion and friend, I should not be so desolate in this peopled earth. Urged by this impulse, I seized on the boy as he passed and drew him towards me. As soon as he beheld my form, he placed his hand before his eyes and uttered a shrill scream. I drew his hand forcibly from his face and said, 'Child, what is the meaning of this? I do not intend to hurt you; listen to me.' He struggled violently. 'Let me go,' he cried. 'Monster! ugly wretch! You wish to eat me and tear me to pieces—you are an ogre—let me go, or I will tell my papa.' 'Boy,' said I, 'you will never see your father again—you must come with me.' He burst into loud cries: 'hideous monster! let me go. My papa is a syndic—he is M. Frankenstein—let me go—you dare not keep me.' 'Frankenstein!' cried I, 'you belong then to my enemy, to him towards whom I have sworn eternal revenge, and you shall be my first victim.' The child still struggled and loaded me with epithets which carried despair to my heart. I grasped his throat to silence him, and in a moment he lay dead at my feet.

"I gazed on my victim, and my heart swelled with exultation and hellish triumph—clapping my hands, I exclaimed, 'I too can *make desolate.* My enemy is not impregnable; this death will carry despair to him, and a thousand thousand[76] other miseries shall torment and destroy him. As I fixed my eyes on the child, I saw something glittering on his breast. I took it. It was the portrait of a most lovely woman. In spite of my malignity, it softened and attracted me. For a few moments I gazed with delight on her dark, *deep* eyes and lovely lips, but presently my rage returned: I remembered that I was for ever deprived of the delights such beautiful creatures could bestow; and that she whose resemblance I contemplated would, in regarding me, have changed that air of divine benignity to one of horror and detestation.

"Can you wonder that such thoughts transported me with rage? I only wonder that at that moment, instead of venting my sensations in useless exclamations and agony, I did not rush among mankind and perish in the attempt to destroy them. While I was overcome by these feelings, I left the spot where I had committed the murder and sought a more secluded hiding-place. At that moment I perceived a woman passing near me—she was young, not indeed so beautiful as her whose portrait I held, but of an agreeable aspect and blooming in the loveliness of health and youth. And here, I thought, is one of those whose smiles are bestowed on all but me. She shall not escape my vengeance; thanks to the lessons of Felix and the sanguinary laws of man, I *have learned* how to work mischief. I approached her unperceived and placed the portrait securely in one of the folds of her dress.

"For some days I haunted the spot where these scenes had taken place, sometimes wishing to see you, sometimes resolved to quit the world and its miseries for ever. At length I wandered towards these mountains and have ranged *through* their immense recesses, consumed by a burning passion which you alone can gratify. And we may not part until you have promised to comply with my requisitions. I am alone and miserable. Man will not associate with me, but one as deformed and horrible as myself would not deny herself to me. This being you must create."

Chapter 9

The creature finished speaking and fixed his *looks* on me in expectation of a reply. But I was bewildered and perplexed and unable to arrange my ideas sufficiently to understand the meaning of his proposition. He continued—

"You must create a female for me with whom I can live in the interchange of those sympathies necessary for my being. This you alone can do, and I demand of you as a right which you must not refuse."

As he said this, I could no longer suppress the anger that burned within me. "I do refuse it," I replied, "and no torture shall ever extort a consent from me. You may render me the most miserable of men, but you shall never make me base in my own eyes. Shall I create another like yourself whose joint wickedness would desolate the world? Begone! I have answered you. You may kill me, but I will never consent."

"You are in the wrong," replied he; "and, instead of threatening, I am content to reason with you. I am malicious because I am miserable. Am I not shunned and hated by all mankind? You, my creator, would tear me to pieces and triumph. Remember that—and tell me why I should pity man more than he pities me. You would not call it murder if you precipitated me into one of those ice rifts and destroyed my frame, the work of your own hand. Shall I respect man when he contemns me? Let him live with me in the interchange of kindness, and, instead of injury, I would bestow every benefit *upon him* with tears of gratitude at his acceptance. But that cannot be; the human senses are insurmountable barriers to our union. But mine shall not be the submission of abject slavery. I will revenge my injuries; if I cannot inspire love, I will cause fear; and chiefly towards you my arch-enemy, because my creator, do I swear *inextinguishable* hatred. I will work and destroy, nor finish until I desolate your heart so that you curse the hour of your birth." A fiendish rage animated him as he said this; his face was wrinkled into contortions too horrible for human eyes to behold; but presently he calmed himself and proceeded.

"I intended to reason. This passion is detrimental to me, for you do not reflect that you are the *sole* cause *of its excesses*. If any being felt emotions of benevolence towards me, I should return then[77] an hundred and an hundred fold; for that one creature's sake, I would make peace with the whole kind. But I now indulge in dreams of bliss that cannot be realized. What I ask of you is reasonable and moderate. I demand a creature of another sex, but as hideous as myself. The gratification is small, but it is all that I can receive, and it shall content me. It is true we shall be monsters cut off from all the world, but on that account we shall be more attached to one another. Our lives will not be happy, but they will be harmless and free from *the* misery *which* I now feel. Oh! my creator, make me happy; let me feel gratitude towards you for one benefit. Let me see that I excite the sympathy of one creature. Do not deny me my request."

I was moved. I shuddered when I thought of the possible consequences of my consent, but I felt that there was some justice in his argument. His tale and the feelings he now expressed proved him to be a creature of fine sensations; and did not I, as his maker, owe him all the portion of happiness that it was in my power to bestow? He saw my change of feeling and continued.

"If you consent, neither you nor any human creature shall ever see us again. I will go to the vast wilds of America.[78] My food is not that of man; I do not destroy the lamb or the kid to glut my appetite. Acorns and berries afford me sufficient nourishment. My companion will be of the same nature as myself and will be content with the same fare. We shall make our bed of dried leaves; the sun will shine on us as on man and will ripen our food. You are moved. The picture I present to you is peaceful and human, and you must feel that you could deny it only in the wantonness of power and cruelty. Pitiless as you are towards me, I see compassion in your eyes. Let me seize the favourable moment and persuade you to promise what I so ardently desire."

"You promise," replied I, "to quit the habitations of man and to inhabit those wilds where the beasts of the field will be your only companions. How can you, who long for the love and sympathy of man, persevere in this exile? You will return and seek their kindness, and you will meet their detestation; your evil passions will be renewed, and you will then have a companion to aid you in your task of destruction. Begone; I cannot consent."

The monster replied with fervour: "How inconstant are your feelings; but a moment ago you were moved by my representations, and why do you again harden yourself to my complaints? I swear by the earth which I inhabit, and by you that made me, that with the companion you bestow I will quit the neighbourhood of man and dwell, as it may chance, in the most savage places. My evil passions will have fled, for I shall meet with sympathy. My life will flow quietly away, and in my dying moments I shall not curse my maker."

His words had a strange effect upon me. I compassionated him and sometimes felt a wish to console him; but when I looked on him, when I saw the filthy mass that moved and talked, my heart sickened, and my feelings were altered to those of horror and hatred. I tried to stifle them. I thought that, as I could not sympathize with him, I had no right to refuse him the small portion of happiness that I had it in my power to bestow. "You swear," I said, "to be harmless, but have you not already shewn a degree of malice that would reasonably make me distrust you? May not even this be a feint that will encrease your triumph *by affording a wider scope to your* revenge?"

"How is this," cried he; "I thought I had moved your compassion, and yet you still refuse to bestow on me the only benefit that *can* soften my heart and render me harmless. If I have no ties and no affections, hatred and vice must be my portion. The love of another will destroy the cause of my crimes, and I shall become a thing of whose existence every one will be ignorant. My vices are the children of a forced solitude that I abhor, and my virtues will necessarily arise when I *shall* receive the sympathy of an equal. I shall feel *the* affections *of a living being* and become linked to the chain of existence and events from which I am now excluded."

I paused some time to reflect on all he had related and the various arguments *which* he had *employed*. I thought of the *promise of* virtues *which* he had displayed on the opening of his existence; and *the* subsequent blight *of all kindly feelings inspired* by the detestation and horror that his protectors had manifested towards him. His power and threats were not omitted in my calculations: a creature who could exist among the ice caves of the glaciers and hide himself from pursuit in the ridges of inaccessible precipices was a being possessing faculties it would be vain to cope with. After a long pause of reflection, I concluded that the justice due both to him and my fellow-creatures demanded of me that I should comply with his request. Turning to him, therefore, I said—

"I consent to your demand on your solemn oath to quit Europe, and every other place in the neighbourhood of man, as soon as I shall deliver into your hands a female who is to accompany you in your exile."

"I swear," he cried, "by the sun and by the blue sky of heaven, that while they exist you shall never behold me. Depart then to your home and commence your labours. I shall watch their progress with unutterable anxiety; and fear not but that when you are ready for me I shall appear."

Saying this, he suddenly quitted me, fearful perhaps of any change in my sentiments. I saw him descend the mountain with greater speed than the flight of the eagle and quickly lost him among the undulations of the sea of ice.

His tale had occupied the whole day, and the sun was upon the verge of the horizon when he departed. I knew that I ought to hasten to descend to the valley, as I should soon be encompassed in darkness. But my heart was heavy, and my steps slow. The labour of winding among the little paths and fixing my feet firmly as I advanced teazed me, occupied as I was by the feelings *which* the occurrences of the day had produced. It had long been night when I came to the half-way resting place and seated myself beside the fountain. The stars shone at intervals as the clouds passed from over them. The dark pines rose before me, and every here and there a broken tree lay on the ground; it was a scene of wonderful solemnity and stirred strange thoughts within me. I wept bitterly, and, clasping my hands in agony, I exclaimed, "Oh! stars, and clouds, and wind, ye are all about to mock me. If ye really pity, crush me; but if not, depart; depart and leave me to darkness." These were wild and miserable thoughts, but I cannot describe to you how the eternal twinkling of stars weighed upon me, and I listened to every blast of wind as if it were a dull ugly siroc[79] on its way to consume me.

It was morning before I arrived at the village of Chamounix; but my presence, so haggard and strange, hardly calmed the fears of my family who had waited the whole night in anxious expectation of my return.

The following day we returned to Geneva. The intention of my father in coming had been to divert my mind and to restore to me my lost tranquillity. But the medicine had been fatal; and, unable to account for the excess of misery I appeared to suffer, he hastened to return home, hoping that the quiet and calm of a domestic life would by degrees alleviate my sufferings from whatsoever cause they might spring.

For myself, I was passive in all their arrangements, and the gentle affection of my beloved Elizabeth was inadequate to draw me from the depth of my despair. The promise I had made to the dæmon weighed upon my mind like Dante's iron cowl on the head of the hellish hypocrites.[80] All pleasures of earth or sky passed before me as a dream, and that one thought only had to me the reality of life. Can you wonder that sometimes a kind of insanity possessed me, or that I saw about me a multitude of filthy animals inflicting on me incessant torture that often extorted screams and bitter groans?

By degrees, however, these feelings became calmed. I entered again into the every day of life, if not with interest, at least with some degree of tranquillity.[81]

Chapter 10

Day after day, week after week, passed away on my return to Geneva, and I had not the courage to commence my work. I feared the vengeance of the disappointed fiend, yet I *was unable to* overcome my repugnance *to the task*. I found also that I was unable to compose a female without again devoting several months to study and laborious disquisition. I had heard of some discoveries having been made by an English philosopher, the knowledge of which was material to my success, and I sometimes thought of obtaining my father's consent to visit England for this purpose; but I clung to *every* pretence of delay and could not resolve to interrupt my returning tranquillity.[82] My health, which had hitherto declined, was now much restored; and my spirits, when unchecked by the memory of my unhappy promise, rose proportionably. My father saw this with pleasure, and he turned his thoughts towards the best method of eradicating the remains of my melancholy, which every now and then would return by fits and, with a devouring blackness, overcast the approaching sunshine. At these moments I took refuge in the most perfect solitude: I passed whole days on the lake, alone in a little boat, watching the clouds and *listening to* the ripp*ling* of the waves, silent and listless. But the fresh air and bright sun seldom failed *to* restore me to some degree of composure, and on my return I met the salutations of my friends with a readier smile and *a* more cheerful heart.

It was after my return from one of the*se* rambles that my father, calling me aside, thus addressed me—

"I am happy to remark, my dear son, that you have resumed your former pleasures and seem to be returning to yourself. And yet you are still unhappy and still avoid our society. For some time I was lost in conjecture as to the cause of this; but yesterday an idea struck me, and if it is well-founded, I conjure you to avow it. Secrecy on such a point would *not only* be useless *but draw* down treble misery on us all."

I trembled violently at this exordium, and my father continued. "I confess, my son, that I have always looked forward to your marriage with your cousin as the tie of our domestic comfort and the stay of my declining years. You were attached to each other from your earliest infancy; you studied together and appeared in dispositions and tastes entirely suited for one another. But so blind is the experience of man, that what I conceived to be the best assistants to my plan may have entirely destroyed it; you perhaps regard her as your sister, without any wish that she might become your wife. Nay, you may have met with another whom you may love; *and*, considering yourself as bound in honour to your cousin, this feeling may occasion the poignant misery *which* you appear to feel."

"My dear Father, reassure yourself. I love my cousin tenderly and sincerely. I never saw any woman who excited, as Elizabeth does, my warmest admiration and affection. My future hopes and prospects are entirely bound up in the expectation of our union."

"The expression of your sentiments on this subject, my dear Victor, gives me more pleasure than I have for some time experienced. If you feel thus, we shall assuredly be happy, however present events may cast a gloom over us. But[83] it is this gloom, which appears to have taken too strong a hold of your mind, that I wish to dissipate. Tell me, therefore, whether you object to an immediate solemnization of the marriage. We have been unfortunate, and recent events have drawn us from that every-day tranquillity befitting my years and infirmities. You are younger; yet I do not suppose, possessed as you are of a competent fortune, that an early marriage would at all interfere with any future plans of honour and utility that you may have formed. Do not suppose, however, that I wish to dictate happiness to you, or that a delay on your part would cause me any *serious* uneasiness. Interpret my words with candour and answer me, I conjure you, with confidence and sincerity."

I listened to my father in silence and remained for some time without offering any reply. I revolved rapidly in my mind a multitude of thoughts and endeavoured to come to some conclusion. Alas! to me the idea of an immediate union with my cousin was one of horror and dismay. I was bound by a solemn promise which I had not yet fulfilled and dared not break; or, if I did, what manifold miseries might not impend over me and my devoted family! Could I enter into a festival with this deadly weight yet hanging round my neck and bowing me to the ground? *I must* perform my engagement and let the monster depart with his mate before I allowed myself to enjoy the delight of a union *from which I expected* peace. I remembered also the necessity I was under of either *journeying* to England or entering into a long correspondence with the *philosophers* of that country, whose knowledge and discoveries *were* of *indispensable* use to me in my present undertaking. The latter method of obtaining the desired intelligence was dilatory and unsatisfactory; besides, any change of scene was agreeable to me, and I was delighted with the idea of spending a year or two *in change of scene and variety of occupation in absence* from my family, during which time some event might happen which would restore me to them in peace and happiness. My promise might be fulfilled, and the monster have departed; or some accident might occur to destroy him and put an end to my slavery for ever. These feelings dictated my answer to my father. I expressed a wish to visit England; but, concealing *the* true reasons *of this* request, I clothed my desires under the guise of wishing to travel and see the world before I sat down for life within the walls of my native town.

I urged my *entreaty* with earnestness, and my father was easily induced to comply—for a more indulgent *or a* less dictatorial parent did not exist upon earth. Our plan was soon arranged. I should travel to Strasbourg where Clerval would join me, and we should proceed down the Rhine together. Some short time would be spent in the towns of Holland, but our principal stay would be in England. We should return by France. It was agreed that this tour should occupy the space of two years.

My father pleased himself with the reflection that I should be united to Elizabeth immediately on my return to Geneva. "These two years," said he, "will pass swiftly, and it will be the last delay that will oppose itself to your happiness. And, indeed, I earnestly desire that period to arrive when we shall all be united, and neither hopes nor fears arise to disturb our domestic calm."

"I am content," I replied, "with your arrangement. By that time we shall both have become wiser, and I hope happier, than we at present are." I sighed, but my father kindly forbore to question me *further* concerning the cause of my dejection. He hoped that new scenes and the amusement of travelling would restore my tranquillity.

I now *made arrangements* for my journey, but one feeling haunted me which filled me with fear and agitation. During my absence I should leave my friends unconscious of the existence of their enemy and unprotected from his attacks, exasperated as he might be by my departure. But he had promised to follow me wherever I might go, and would he not accompany me to England? This *imagination* was dreadful in itself, but soothing in as much as it *supposed the safety of* my friends. I was agonized with the *idea of a* possibility that the reverse of this might happen. But through the whole period during which I was the slave of my creature, I allowed myself to be governed by the impulses of the moment; and my present sensations strongly intimated that the fiend would follow me and *exempt* my *family* from the danger *of his machinations.*

It was in the latter end of August that I departed to pass two years of exile. Elizabeth approved of the reasons of my departure and only regretted that she had not the same opportunities of enlarging her experience and cultivating her understanding. She wept, however, as she bade me farewell and entreated me to return happy and tranquil. "We all," said she, "depend upon you; and if you are miserable, what must be our feelings?"

I threw myself into the carriage that was to convey me away, hardly knowing whither I was going and careless of what was passing around. I remembered only, and it was with a bitter anguish that I reflected on it, to order that my chemical instruments should be packed to go with me. For I resolved to fulfil my promise while abroad and return, if possible, a free man. Filled with dreary imaginations, I passed through many beautiful and majestic scenes, but my eyes were fixed and unobserving; I could only think of the bourne of my travels and the work which was to occupy me whilst they endured. After some days spent in listless indolence, during which I traversed many leagues, I arrived at Strasbourg, where I waited two days for Clerval. He came; alas, how great was the contrast between us! He was alive to every new scene: joyful when he saw the beauties of the setting sun, and more happy when he saw it rise and recommence a new day. He pointed out to me the shifting colours of the landscape and the appearances of the sky. "This is what it is to live," he cried; "now I enjoy existence. But you, my dear Frankenstein, *wherefore* are *you* desponding and sorrowful?" Indeed, I was occupied by gloomy thoughts, and neither saw the descent of the evening star nor the golden sunrise reflected in the Rhine; and you, my friend, would be far more amused with the journal of Clerval, who observed the scenery with an eye of feeling and delight, than to listen to my reflections—I, a miserable wretch haunted by a curse that shut up every avenue to enjoyment.

We had agreed to go down the Rhine in a boat from Strasbourg to Rotterdam, whence we might take shipping for London. During this voyage, we passed by many willowy islands and saw several beautiful towns. We stayed a day at Manheim *and*, on the fifth from our departure from Strasbourg, arrived at Mayence. The course of the Rhine below Mayence becomes much more picturesque. The river descends rapidly and winds between hills, not high, but steep, and of beautiful forms. We saw many ruined castles standing on the edges of precipices, surrounded by black woods, high and inaccessible. This part of the Rhine, indeed, presents a singularly variegated landscape. In one spot you view rugged hills, ruined castles overlooking tremendous precipices, with the dark Rhine rushing beneath. And on the sudden turn of a promontory, flourishing vineyards and populous towns, and a meandering river with green sloping banks, occupy the scene. We travelled at the time of the vintage and heard the song of the labourers as we glided down the stream. Even I, depressed in mind, and my spirits continually agitated by gloomy feelings, even I was pleased. I lay at the bottom of the boat; and, as I gazed on the cloudless blue sky, I seemed to drink in a tranquillity to which I had long been a stranger. And if these were my sensations, who can describe those of Henry? He felt as if he had been transported to fairy land and enjoyed a happiness seldom tasted by man. "I have seen," he said, "the most beautiful scenes of my own country. I have been on the lakes of Lucerne and Uri, where the snowy mountains descend almost perpendicularly to the water, casting black and impenetrable shades which would cause a gloomy and mournful appearance, were it not for the most verdant islands that relieve the eye by their gay appearance. I have seen this lake agitated by a tempest, when the wind tore up whirlwinds of water and gave you an idea of what the water-spout must be on the great ocean—and the waves dash with fury *on* the *base* of the mountain, where the priest and his mistress were overwhelmed by an avalanche and where their dying voices are still said to be heard amid the pauses of the night wind.[84] I have seen the mountains of La Valais and the Pays de Vaud, but this country, Victor, pleases me more than all those wonders. The mountains of Switzerland are more majestic and strange, but there is a charm in the banks of this divine river that I never before saw equalled. Look at that castle which overhangs *yon* precipice; and that also, on the island, almost concealed among the foliage of those lovely trees; and now that group of labourers coming from among their vines; and that village half-hid in the recess of the mountain. Oh! surely the spirit that inhabits and guards this place has a soul more in harmony with man than those who pile the glacier or retire to the inaccessible peaks of the mountains of our own country."

I[85] smiled at the enthusiasm of my friend and remembered with a sigh the period when my eyes would have glistened with joy to behold the scenes *which* I now viewed. But the recollection of those days was too painful; I must shut out all thought to enjoy tranquillity, and that reflection alone is sufficient to poison every pleasure.

At Cologne we descended to the plains of Holland, and we resolved to post the remainder of our way, for the wind was contrary, and the stream of the river was too gentle to aid us. We now arrived at very different country. The soil was sandy, and the wheels sunk deep in it. The towns of this country are the most pleasing part of the scene. The Dutch are extremely neat, but there is an awkwardness in their contrivances that often surprised us. In one place, I remember, a windmill was situated in such a manner that the postillion[86] was obliged to guide the carriage close to the opposite side of the road to escape from the sweep of its sails. The way often led between two canals, where the road was only broad enough to allow one carriage to pass; and when we met another vehicle, which was frequently the case, we were rolled back sometimes for nearly a mile until we found one of the drawbridges which led to the fields, down on which one carriage remained while the other passed on. They soak their flax also in the mud of their canals and place it against the trees along the road-side to dry. When the sun is hot, the scent *which* this exhales is not very easily endured. Yet the roads are excellent and the verdure beautiful.

From Rotterdam we went by sea to England. It was on a clear morning in the latter *days* of September[87] that I first saw the white cliffs of Britain. The banks of the Thames presented a new scene; they were flat but fertile, and almost every town was marked by some story. We saw Tilbury Fort and remembered the Spanish Armada; Gravesend, Woolwich, Greenwich—places which I had heard of even in my country. At length we saw the numerous steeples of London, St. Paul's towering above all, and the Tower famed in English history.

Chapter II

London was our present point of rest; we determined to remain several months in this wonderful and celebrated city.[88] Clerval desired the intercourse of the men of genius and talent who flourished at that time; but this was, with me, a secondary *object*; I was principally occupied with the means of obtaining the information necessary for the completion of my promise, and quickly availed myself of the letters of introduction that I had brought with me, addressed to the most distinguished natural philosophers. If this journey had taken place during my days of study and happiness, it would have afforded me inexpressible pleasure. But a blight had come over my existence, and I only visited these people for the sake of the information they might give me on the subject in which I was so deeply interested. Company was irksome to me;

when alone, I could fill my mind with the sights of heaven and earth; the voice of Henry soothed me; and I could cheat myself into a transitory peace. But busy, uninteresting, joyous faces brought back despair to my heart. I saw an insurmountable barrier placed between me and my fellow-men; this barrier was sealed with the blood of William and Justine, and to reflect on those events filled my soul with anguish. But in Clerval I saw the image of my former self; he was inquisitive and anxious to gain experience and instruction. The difference of manners *which* he observed was to him an inexhaustible source of *observation and* amusement. He was for ever busy, and the only check to his enjoyments was my sorrowful and dejected mien. I tried to conceal this as much as possible, that I might not debar him from the pleasures natural to one who was entering on a new scene of life, undisturbed by any care or bitter recollection. I often refused to accompany him, alleging another engagement, that I might remain alone. I now also began to collect the materials necessary for my new creation, and this was to me like the torture of single drops of water continually falling on the head. Every thought that was devoted to it was an extreme anguish, and every word that I spoke in allusion to it caused my lips to quiver and my heart to palpitate.

After passing some months in London, we received a letter from a person in Scotland who had formerly been our visitor at Geneva. He mentioned the beauties of his native country and asked us if those were not sufficient allurements to induce us to prolong our journey as far north as Perth, where he resided. Clerval eagerly desired to accept this invitation; and I, although I abhorred society, wished to view again mountains and streams and all the wondrous works of nature in her chosen dwelling places. We had arrived in England at the beginning of October, and it was now February; we accordingly determined to commence our journey towards the north at the expiration of another month. In this expedition we did not intend to follow the great road to Edinburgh, but to visit

Windsor, Oxford, Matlock, and the Cumberland lakes, resolving to arrive at the completion of this tour about the end of July. I packed my chemical instruments and the materials which I had collected, resolving to finish my labours in some obscure nook in the country.

We quitted London on the 27th of March and remained a few days at Windsor, rambling in its beautiful forest. This was a new scene to us mountaineers; the majestic oaks, the quantity of game, and the flocks of lovely deer were all novelties to us. From thence we proceeded to Oxford. We[89] were charmed with the appearance of the town. The colleges are ancient and picturesque, the streets broad, and the landscape rendered perfect by the lovely Isis, which spreads into broad and placid expanse of water and runs south of the town. We had letters to several of the professors, *who* received *us* with great politeness and cordiality. We found that the regulations of this university were much improved since the days of Gibbon,[90] but there is still in fashion a great deal of bigotry and devotion to established rules that constrains the mind of the students and leads to slavish and narrow principles of action. Many enormities are also practised which, although they might excite the laughter of a stranger, were looked upon in the world of the university as matters of the utmost consequence. Some of the gentlemen obstinately wore light-coloured pantaloons when it was the rule of the college to wear dark: the masters were angry and their scholars resolute, so that *during our stay* two of the students were on the point of being expelled on this very question.[91] The threatened severity caused a considerable change in the costume of the gentlemen for several days.

Such, to our infinite astonishment, we found to be the principal topic of conversation when we arrived in the town. Our minds had been filled with the remembrance of the events that had been transacted here above a century *and a half* before.[92] It was here that Charles I had collected his forces; this town had been faithful to him when the whole nation had forsaken him to join the standard of parliament and liberty. It was strange to us, *as we* enter*ed* the town, our thoughts *were* occupied by the memory of the unfortunate king, the amiable Falkland, and the insolent Goring,[93] *but we found* it filled with gownsmen and students who think of nothing less than these events. Yet there are some relics to remind you of ancient times; among others, we regarded with curiosity the press instituted by the author of the history of the troubles.[94] We were also shewn a room which Friar Bacon,[95] the discoverer of gunpowder, had inhabited and which, as it was predicted, would fall in when a man wiser than that philosopher should enter it. A short, round-faced, prating professor who accompanied us refused to pass the threshold, although we ventured inside in perfect security, *and probably he might have done the same.*

Matlock, which was our next place of rest, resembled to a great degree the scenery of Switzerland; but every thing is on a lower scale, and the green *hills* want the crown of distant white Alps, which always attend on the piny mountains of our country. We visited the wondrous cave and the little cabinets of natural history, where the curiosities are disposed in the same manner as in the collections at Servox and Chamounix. The latter name made me tremble when pronounced by Henry, and I hastened to quit Matlock where the scenes were thus associated.

From Derby, still journeying northward, we passed two months *in* Cumberland and Westmoreland. I could now almost fancy myself among the Swiss mountains. The little patches of snow which yet lingered on the north*ern* sides of the mountains, the lakes, and the dashing of the rocky streams were all familiar and dear sights to me. Here also we made some acquaintances who almost contrived to cheat me into happiness. The delight of Clerval was proportionably greater than mine; his mind expanded in the company of men of talent, and he found in himself greater capacity and feeling than he could have imagined himself to have possessed while he associated with his inferiors. "I could pass my life here," said he to me, "and among these mountains I should hardly regret Switzerland and the Rhine."

But he found that a traveller's life is one that includes much pain amidst its enjoyments. His feelings are for ever on the stretch; and when he begins to sink into repose, he finds himself obliged to quit it for something new, which again engages his attention and which also *he* forsakes for *other* novelt*ies.* We had scarcely visited the various lakes of Cumberland and Westmoreland and conceived an affection for some of the inhabitants, when the period of our appointment with our Scotch friend approached, and we left them to travel on. For my own part I was not sorry. I had now neglected my promise for some time, and I feared the effects of the dæmon's disappointment. He might remain in Switzerland and wreak his vengeance on my relatives; this idea pursued me and tormented me at every moment when I might otherwise have snatched repose and peace. I waited for my letters with feverish impatience: if they were delayed, I was miserable and overcome by a thousand fears; and when they arrived, and I saw the superscription of Elizabeth or my father, I hardly dared to read and ascertain my fate. Sometimes I thought that the fiend followed me and might remind me *by* murdering my companion. *When* these thought*s* *possessed me*, I would not quit Henry for a moment but followed him as his shadow to protect him from the fancied rage of his destroyer. I felt as if I had committed some great crime, the consciousness of which haunted me. I was guiltless, but I had *indeed* drawn down a horrible curse *upon* my head, *as mortal as that of crime.*

I visited Edinburgh with languid eyes and mind, and yet that city might have interested the most unfortunate being. Clerval did not like it so well as Oxford, for the antiquity of th*e latter* city was pleasing to him. But the beauty and regularity of the new town *of Edinburgh* delighted him; its environs are also the most beautiful in the world—Arthur's Seat, St. Bernard's Well, and the Pentland Hills. But I was impatient to arrive at the termination of my journey. We left Edinburgh in a week, passing through Cupar, St. Andrews, and along the banks of the Tay to Perth, where our friend expected us. But I was not in the mood to laugh and talk with strangers, or enter into their feelings or plans with the good humour expected from a guest; and accordingly I told Clerval that I wished to make the tour of Scotland *alone*. "Do you," said I, "enjoy yourself, and let this be our rendezvous. I may be absent a month or two, but do not interfere with my motions, I entreat you; leave me to peace and solitude for a short time; and when I return, I hope it will be with a lighter heart, more congenial to your own temper." Henry wished to dissuade me but, seeing me bent on this plan, *ceased to remonstrate. He* entreated me to write often. "I had rather be with you," he said, "in your solitary rambles than with these Scotch people, whom I do not know; hasten then, my dear friend, to return that I may again feel myself somewhat at home, which I cannot do in your absence."

Chapter 12

Having parted from my friend, I determined to visit some remote spot of Scotland and finish my work in solitude. I did not doubt but that the monster followed me and would discover himself *to me* when I should have finished, *that he might* receive his companion. With this resolution I traversed the northern highlands and fixed on one of the Orkney Islands for the scene of my labours. It was a place fitted for such a work, being hardly more than a rock whose high sides were continually beaten upon by the waves. The soil was barren, hardly affording pasture for a few miserable cows and oatmeal for its inhabitants, which consisted of five person*s*, whose gaunt and scraggy limbs gave tokens of their sorry fare. Vegetables and bread, when they indulged in such luxuries, and even fresh water was to be procured from the main land, which was about five miles distant. On the whole island there were but three miserable huts, and one of these was vacant when I arrived. This I hired. It contained but two rooms, and these exhibited all the squalidness of the most miserable p*enury*. The thatch had fallen in, the walls *were* unplastered, and the door was off its hinges. I ordered it to be repaired, bought some furniture, and took possession—an incident which would have doubtless occasioned some surprise, had not all the senses of the cottagers been benumbed by want and squalid poverty. As it was, I lived ungazed at and unmolested, hardly thanked for the pittance of food and clothes which I gave, so much does suffering blunt even the coarsest sensations of men.

In this retreat I devoted the morning to labour, but in the evening, when the weather permitted, I walked on the stony beach of the sea to listen to the waves as they roared and dashed at my feet. It was a monotonous yet ever-changing scene. I thought of Switzerland; it was far different from this desolate and appalling landscape. Its hills are covered with vines, and its cottages are scattered thick*ly* in the plains. Its fair lakes reflect a blue and gentle sky; and, when troubled by the winds, it is but the play of a lively infant when compared to the roarings of the giant ocean.

In this manner I distributed my occupations when I first arrived; but as I proceeded in my work, it became every day more horrible and irksome to me. Sometimes I could not prevail on myself to enter my laboratory for several days, and at other times I *toiled* day and night in order to *complete* it. It was indeed a filthy work in which I was engaged. During my first experiment, a kind of enthusiastic frenzy *had* blinded me to the horror of my employment; my mind was intently fixed on the sequel of my labour, and my eyes were shut to the horror of my proceedings. But now I went to it in cold blood, and my heart often sickened at the work of my hands.

Thus situated, employed in the most detestable occupation, in a solitude where nothing could for an instant call my attention from the actual scene in which I was engaged, my spirits were unequal. I became restless and nervous. Every moment I feared to meet my persecutor. Sometimes I sat with my eyes fixed on the ground, fearing to raise them lest they should meet *the object which* I so much dreaded to *behold*. I feared to wander from the sight of my fellow-creatures, lest when alone he should come to claim his companion. In the mean time I worked on, and my labour was already considerably advanced. I looked with pleasure towards *its* completion, yet freedom from the curse I endured was a joy I never dared promise myself.[96]

One evening I sat in my workshop; the sun had set, and the moon was just rising from the sea. I had not light sufficient for my employment, and I sat idle in a pause of consideration of whether I should leave my labour for the night or hasten its conclusion by an unremitting attention to it. As I sat, a train of reflection occurred to me which led me to consider the effects of what I was now doing. Three years before, I had been engaged in the same manner and had created a fiend whose unparalleled barbarity had desolated my heart and filled it for ever with the bitterest remorse. I was now about to form another being of whose dispositions I was alike ignorant. She might be ten thousand times more malignant than her mate and delight in murder and wretchedness. He had sworn to quit the neighbourhood of man and hide himself in deserts, but she had not; and she who was in all probability to become a thinking and reasoning animal might refuse to comply with a compact made before her creation. They might even hate one another. The creature who already lived loathed his own deformity, and might he not conceive a greater abhorrence for it when it came before his eyes in the female form? She also might turn with disgust from him to the superior beauty of man. She might quit him, and he be again alone, *exasperated by* the fresh provocation of being deserted by one of his own species.

Even if they were to leave Europe and inhabit the deserts of the new world, it was their intention to have children, and a race of devils would be propagated *up*on the earth from whose form and mind man shrunk with horror. Had I *any* right for my own benefit to inflict this curse to everlasting generations? I had before been moved by the sophisms of the being whom I had created; I had been moved by his fiendish threats; and now, for the first time, the wickedness of my promise burst upon me. I shuddered to think that future ages might curse me as their pest, whose selfishness had not hesitated to buy its own peace at the price perhaps of the *existence of* the whole human race. I trembled, and my heart failed within me, when on looking up I saw by the light of the moon the dæmon *at the casement*. A ghastly grin wrinkled his lips, *as he* gazed on me *where* I sat. Yes, he had followed me in my travels; he had loitered in forests, hid himself in caves, or taken refuge in wide and desert heaths; and he now came to view my progress and claim the fulfilment of my promise. As I looked on him, his countenance appeared to express the utmost extent of malice and *treachery*. I thought with a sensation of madness *on* my promise of creating another like to him and, trembling with passion, tore to pieces the thing on which I was engaged. The wretch saw me destroy the creature on whose future existence he depended for happiness and, with a howl of devilish despair *and revenge*, withdrew.

I left the room and, locking the door, made a vow in my own heart never to resume my labours; and then, with trembling steps, I sought my own apartment. I was alone. None were near me to dissipate the gloom and relieve me from the most terrible reveries. Several hours passed, and I remained near my window gazing on the sea. It was almost motionless, for the winds were hushed, and all nature reposed under the eye of the quiet moon. A few fishing vessels alone specked the water, and now and then the gentle breeze wafted the sound of the voices as the *fisher*men called to one another. I felt the silence, although I was hardly conscious of its extreme profundity, until my ear was suddenly arrested by the paddling of oars near the shore, and a person landed close to my house. In a few minutes after, I heard the creaking of my door as if some one endeavoured to open it softly. I trembled from head to foot; I felt a presentiment of who it was and wished to rouse one of the peasants who dwelt in a cottage not far from mine. But I was overcome by the sensation *of* helplessness, so often felt in a frightful dream when you in vain endeavour to fly the impending danger, and was rooted to the spot. Presently I heard the sound of footsteps along the passage, *the* door opened, and the wretch whom I dreaded appeared. Shutting the door, he approached me and said in a smothered voice: "You have destroyed the work that you began; what is it that you intend? Do you dare break your promise? I have endured toil and misery. I left Switzerland with you; I crept along the shores of the Rhine, among its willow islands and *over* the summits of its hills. I have dwelt many months in the heaths of England and among the deserts of Scotland. I have endured incalculable fatigue and cold and hunger. Do you dare destroy my hopes?"

"Begone," I replied; "I do break my promise; never will I create another like yourself, equal in deformity and wickedness."

"Slave," said the wretch, "I before reasoned with you, but you have proved yourself unworthy of my condescension. Remember that I have power; you believe yourself miserable, but I can make you so wretched that the light of day will be hateful to you. You are my creator, but I am your master—Obey!"

"Wretch," said I, "the hour of my weakness is past, and the period of your power is arrived. Your threats cannot move me to do an act of wickedness, but they confirm me in a resolution of not creating you a companion in vice. Shall I in cold blood set loose upon the earth a dæmon whose delight is in death and wretchedness? Begone! I am firm, and your words will only exasperate my rage."

The monster saw my determination in my face and gnashed his teeth in the impotence of anger. "Shall each man," cried he, "find his equal, and each beast have his mate, and I be alone? I had feelings of affection, and they were returned by detestation. Man, you may hate, but beware! Your hours will pass in dread and misery, and soon the bolt will fall which will ravish from you your happiness for ever. Are you to be happy while I grovel in the intensity of my wretchedness? You *can blast* my other passions; but revenge remains—revenge dearer than light or food. I may die, but first you, my tyrant and tormentor, shall curse the sun that gazes on your misery. Beware, for I am fearless and therefore powerful. I will watch with the wiliness of a snake that I may sting with its venom. Man, you shall repent of the injuries you inflict."

"Devil," I cried. "Cease, and do not poison the air with those sounds of malice. I have declared my resolution to you, and I am no coward to bend beneath words. Leave me; I am inexorable."

"It is well," said he. "I go; but remember! I shall be with you on your marriage night."

Chapter 13

I started forward and exclaimed—"Villain, before you sign my death-warrant, be sure that you are yourself safe." I would have seized him; but he eluded me, quitting the house with precipitation—in a few moments I saw him in his boat, which shot across the waters with an arrowy swiftness and was soon lost amidst the waves.

All was again silent; but his words rung in my ears. I burnt with rage to pursue the murderer of my peace and precipitate him into the ocean. I walked up and down my room hastily and perturbed; my imagination conjured before me a thousand images to torment and sting me. Why had I not followed him and closed with him in mortal strife? But I had suffered him to depart, and he had directed his course towards the main land. I shuddered to suppose who might be the next victim sacrificed to his insatiate revenge. And then again I thought of his words—"I will be with you on your marriage night." That then was the period fixed for the fulfilment of my destiny. In that hour I should die and at once satisfy and extinguish his malice. The prospect did not move me to fear; yet when I thought of my beloved Elizabeth—of her tears and endless sorrow when she should find her lover so barbarously snatched from her—tears, the first I had shed for many months, streamed from my eyes, and I resolved not to fall before my enemy without a bitter struggle.

The night passed away, and the sun rose from the ocean. My feelings became calmer, if it may be called calmness when the violence of rage sinks into the depths of despair. I left the house, the horrid scene of the last night's contention, and walked on the beach of the sea, which I almost regarded as an insuperable barrier between me and my fellow-creatures. Nay, a wish that *such* was the fact stole across me; I *wished that I* might pass my life on this barren rock, wearily, it is true, but uninterrupted by any sudden shock of misery. If I returned, it was to be sacrificed—or to see those I most loved die under the grasp of a dæmon whom I had myself created. I walked about the isle like a restless spectre separated from all it loved and miserable in the separation. When it became noon and the sun rose higher, I lay down on the grass and was overpowered by a deep sleep. I had been awake the whole of the preceding night: my nerves were agitated, and my eyes inflamed with watching and misery. The sleep into which I now sunk refreshed me; and when I awoke, I again felt as if I belonged to a race of human beings like myself, and I began to reflect upon what had passed with greater composure. Yet still the words of the fiend rung in my ears like a death knell; they appeared like a dream, yet distinct and oppressive as a reality.

The sun was far descended, and I still sat on the shore, satisfying my *ap*petite, which was become ravenous, with an oaten cake, when I saw a fishing boat land close to me, and one of the men brought me a packet; it contained letters from Geneva, and one from Clerval entreating me to join him. He said that nearly a year had elapsed since we had quitted Switzerland, and France was yet unvisited. He entreated me, therefore, to leave my solitary isle and meet him at Perth in a week from that time, when we might arrange the plan of our future proceedings. This letter completely recalled me to life, and I determined to quit my island at the expiration of two days.

Yet before I departed there was a task to perform on which I shuddered to reflect: I must pack my chemical instruments; and for that purpose I must enter the room which had been the scene of my odious work; and I must handle the utensils, the sight of which were sickening to me. The next morning at daybreak I summoned sufficient courage and unlocked the door of my work room. The remains of the half-finished creature whom I had destroyed lay scattered on the floor, and I almost felt as if I *had* mangled the living flesh of a human being. I paused to collect myself and then entered the chamber. With trembling hands, I conveyed the instruments out of the room; but I reflected that I ought not to leave the relics of my work to excite the horror *and suspicion* of the peasants, and I accordingly put them into a basket with a great quantity of stones and, tying it up, determined to throw them into the sea that very night; and in the mean time I sat on the beach, employed in cleaning and arranging my chemical apparatus.

Nothing could be more complete than the alteration that had taken place in my feelings since the night of the appearance of the dæmon. I had before regarded my promise with gloomy despair as a thing that must, with whatever consequences, be fulfilled; but I now felt as if a film had been taken from before my eyes and that I now, for the first time, saw clearly. The idea of renewing my labours did not for an instant occur to me. The threat I had heard weighed on my thoughts, but I did not reflect that a voluntary act of mine might avert it. I had resolved in my own mind that to create another like the fiend I had first made would be an act of the basest and most atrocious selfishness, and I banished from my mind every thought that could lead to a different conclusion.

Between two and three in the morning the moon rose, and I then, putting my basket into a little skiff, sailed out about four miles from the shore. The scene was perfectly solitary; a few boats were returning towards land, but I sailed away from them. I felt as if I was about the commission of a dreadful crime and avoided with shuddering anxiety any encounter with my fellow-creatures. At one time the moon, which had before been clear, was suddenly overspread by a thick cloud, and I took advantage of the moment of darkness and cast the basket into the sea. I listened to the gurgling sound as it sunk and then sailed away from the spot. The sky had become clouded; but the air was pure, although chilled by the north-east breeze that was rising. But it refreshed and filled me with such agreeable sensations that I resolved to prolong my stay on the water and, fixing the rudder in a direct position, stretched myself at the bottom of the boat. Clouds hid the moon, every thing was obscure, and I heard only the sound of the boat as its keel cut through the waves. The sound lulled me, and in a short time I slept soundly.

I do not know how long I remained in this situation, but when I awoke I found that the sun had already mounted considerably. The wind was high, and the waves continually threatened the safety of my little skiff. I found that the wind was north-east and must have driven me far from the coast from which I had embarked. I endeavoured to change my course but quickly found that if I again made the attempt, the boat would be instantly filled with water. Thus situated, my only resource was to drive before the wind. I confess that I felt a few sensations of terror. I had no compass with me and was so little acquainted with the geography of this part of the world that the sun was of little benefit to me. I might be driven into the wide Atlantic and feel all the tortures of starvation—or be swallowed up in immeasurable waters that roared and buffeted around me. I had already been out many hours and felt the tortures of a burning thirst, a prelude to my other sufferings. I looked on the heavens, which were covered by clouds that flew with the wind only to be replaced by others. I looked on the sea. It was to be my grave. "Fiend," I exclaimed, "your task is already fulfilled!" I thought of Elizabeth, of my father, and of Clerval—and sunk into a reverie so despairing and frightful that even now, when the scene is on the point of closing before me for ever, I shudder to reflect on it.

Some hours passed thus. But by degrees, as the sun declined towards the horizon, the wind died away into a gentle breeze, and the sea became free from breakers. But these gave place to a heavy swell; I felt sick and hardly able to hold the rudder, when suddenly I saw a line of high land towards the south. Almost spent as I was by fatigue and misery, this sudden certainty of life rushed like a warm joy to my heart, and tears gushed from my eyes. How mutable are our feelings, and how strange is that clinging love we have of life even in the excess of misery. I constructed another sail with a part of my dress and eagerly steered my course towards the land. It had a wild rocky appearance; but as I approached nearer, I easily perceived the traces of cultivation. I saw vessels near the shore and found myself suddenly transported back to the neighborhood of civilized man. I eagerly *traced* the windings of the *land* and hailed a steeple which I at length saw issuing from behind a small promontory. As I was in a state of extreme debility from fasting, I resolved to go directly towards the town as a place where I could most easily procure nourishment. Fortunately I had money with me.

As I turned the promontory, I discovered a small neat town—and a good harbour which I entered, my heart bounding with joy at my unexpected escape.

As I was occupied in fixing the boat and arranging the sails, several people crowded towards the spot. They appeared very much surprised at my appearance but, instead of offering me any assistance, whispered together with gestures that at any other time might have produced in me a slight sensation of alarm. As it was, I merely remarked that it was English that they spoke, and therefore addressed them: "My good friends," said I, "will you be so kind as to tell me what the name of this town is—and where I am."

"You will know that soon enough," replied a man with a gruff voice. "May be you are come to a place that will not prove much to your taste. But you will not be consulted as to your quarters, I promise you."

I was exceedingly surprised at receiving so rude an answer from a stranger, and I was also disconcerted on perceiving the frowning and angry countenances of his companions. "Why do you answer me so roughly," I replied. "Surely it is not the custom of Englishmen to receive strangers so inhospitably."

"I do not know," said the man, "what the custom of the English may be, but it is the custom of the Irish to hate villains."

While this strange dialogue continued, I perceived the crowd rapidly encrease. Their faces expressed a mixture of curiosity and anger which annoyed and in some degree alarmed me. I enquired the way to the inn, but no one replied. I then moved forward, and a murmuring noise rose from the crowd as they followed and surrounded me—when an ill-looking man, coming forward, tapped me on the shoulder and said: "Come, Sir, you must follow me to Mr. Kirwin's to give an account of yourself."

"Who is Mr. Kirwin," said I, "and why am I to give an account of myself? Is not this a free country?"

"Aye, Sir," replied the man, "free enough for honest folks. Mr. Kirwin is a magistrate, and you are to give an account of the death of a gentleman who was found murdered here last night."

This answer startled me, but I presently recovered myself. I was innocent, and that could easily be proved. Accordingly, I followed my conductor in silence and was led to one of the best houses in *the* town. I was ready to sink from fatigue and hunger; but, being surrounded by a crowd, I thought it politic to rouse all my strength that no physical debility might be construed into apprehension or conscious guilt. Little did I then expect the calamity that would in a few moments overwhelm me and *extinguish* in horror and despair all fear of ignominy or death. I must pause, for *it* requires all my fortitude to recall *the* frightful images *of the events which I am about to relate*, in proper detail, to my recollection.

Chapter 14

I was soon introduced into the presence of the magistrate, an old benevolent man with calm and mild manners. He looked *upon* me, however, with some degree of severity; and then, turning towards my conductors, he asked who appeared as witnesses on this occasion. About half a dozen men came forward; and one being selected by the magistrate, he deposed that he had been out fishing the night before with his son and his brother-in-law, Daniel Nugent, when, about nine o'clock, they observed a strong northerly blast rising, and they accordingly put in for port. It was a very dark night as the moon had not yet risen; they did not land at the harbour but, as they had been accustomed, at a creek about two miles below. He went first carrying a part of the fishing tackle, and his companions followed him at some distance. As he was walking along the sands, he *struck* his foot against something and fell all his length on the ground; his comrades came up to assist him, and by the light of their lantern they discovered that he had fallen on the body of a man who was to all appearance dead.

Their first supposition was that it was the corpse of *some person* who had been drowned and thrown on shore by the waves. But, upon examination, they found that the clothes were not wet and even that the body was not yet cold. They instantly carried it to the cottage of an old woman near *the spot* and endeavoured, *but in vain*, to restore it to life. He appeared to have been a handsome young man about twenty years of age. He had apparently been strangled, for there *was* no sign of any violence except the black mark of fingers on his neck.

The first *part* of this deposition did not in the least interest me; but when the mark of the fingers was mentioned, I remembered the murder of my brother and felt myself extremely agitated; my limbs trembled, and a mist came over my eyes, which obliged me to lean on a chair for support; the magistrate observed me with a keen eye and of course drew an unfavourable augury from my manner.

The son confirmed his father's account. But when Daniel Nugent was questioned, he swore positively that, just before the fall of his companion, he saw a boat with a single man in it at a short distance from the shore; and, as far as he could judge by the light of a few stars, it was the same boat in which I had just landed.

A woman deposed that she lived near the beach and was standing at the door of her cottage waiting for the return *of the fishermen*; about an hour before she heard of the discovery of the body, she saw a boat with only one man in it push off from that part of the shore where the corpse was afterwards found.

Another woman confirmed the account of the fishermen having brought the body into her house. It was not cold, and they put it into a bed and rubbed it; and Daniel went to the town for an apothecary, but life was quite gone.

Several other men were examined concerning my landing, and they agreed that, with the strong north wind that had arisen during the night, it was very probable that I had beaten about for many hours and had been obliged to return nearly to the same spot from which I had departed. Besides, they observed that it appeared I had brought the body from another place; and it was likely that, as I did not appear to know the shore, I might have put into the harbour ignorant of the distance of the town of ——— from the place where I had deposited the corpse.

Mr. Kirwin, on hearing this evidence, desired that I should be taken into the room where the body lay for interment that it might be observed what effect the sight of it *would* produce upon me. This idea was probably suggested by the extreme agitation I had exhibited when the mode of the murder had been described. I was accordingly conducted by the magistrate and several other persons to the inn. I could not help being struck by the strange coincidences that had taken place during this eventful night; but knowing that I had been conversing with several persons in the island I had inhabited about the time that the body had been found, I was perfectly tranquil as to the consequences of the affair.

I entered the room where the corpse lay and was led up to the coffin. How can I describe my sensation? I feel yet parched with horror, nor can I ever reflect on that terrible moment without shuddering and agony that faintly reminds me of the anguish of *the* recognition. The trial, the presence of the magistrate and witnesses, passed like a dream from my memory when I saw the lifeless form of Henry Clerval stretched before me. I gasped for breath; and, throwing myself on the body, I exclaimed, "And have my murderous machinations deprived you also, my dearest Henry, of life? Two I have already destroyed; other victims await their destiny. But you, Clerval, my friend, my benefactor!"——

The human frame could no longer support the agonizing suffering that I endured, and I was carried out of the room in strong convulsions.

A fever succeeded to this. I lay for two months on the point of death. My ravings, as I afterwards heard, were frightful. I called myself the murderer of William, of Justine, and of Clerval.

Sometimes I entreated my attendants to assist me in the destruction of the fiend by whom I was tormented; and, at others, I felt the *fingers* of the monster already grasping my neck, and screamed aloud with agony and terror. Fortunately, as I spoke my native tongue, Mr. Kirwin alone understood me. But my gestures and bitter cries were sufficient to affright the other witnesses.

Why did I not die? More miserable than man ever was before, why did I not sink into rest and forgetfulness? Death snatches away many blooming children, the only hopes of their doating parents. How many brides and youthful lovers have been one day in the bloom of health and hope, and the next a prey for worms and the decay of the tomb! Of what materials was I made that I could thus resist so many shocks which, like the turning of the wheel, continually renewed the torture?

But I was doomed to live and in two months found myself as awaking from a dream, in a prison, stretched on a wretched bed surrounded by gaolers, turnkeys, bolts, and all the miserable apparatus of a dungeon. It was morning, I remember, when I thus awoke. I had forgotten the particulars of what had happened and only felt as if some great misery had overcome me. But when I looked around and saw the barred windows and the squalidness of the room in which I was, all flashed across my memory, and I groaned bitterly. This sound disturbed an old woman who was sleeping in a chair beside me. She was a hired nurse, the wife of one of the turnkeys, and her countenance expressed all those bad qualities which often characterize that class. Her face was hard and rude, like that of persons accustomed to see, without sympathizing in, sights of misery. Her voice expressed her entire indifference. She addressed me in English, and the words struck me as ones that I had heard during *my* suffering*s*. "Are you better now, Sir?" said she.

I replied in the same language, with a feeble voice, "I believe I am; but if it all be true, if indeed I did not dream, I am sorry that I am still alive to feel misery and horror."

"For that matter," replied the old woman, "if you mean about the gentleman that you murdered, I believe that it were better for you if you were dead, for I fancy it will go hard with you. You will be hanged when the next session comes on; however, that is none of my business. I am sent to nurse you and get you well. I do my duty with a safe conscience; it were well if every body did the same."

I turned with loathing from the woman who could utter so unfeeling a speech to a *person* just saved, on the very edge of death; but I felt languid and unable to reflect on all that had passed. *The whole series of my life* appeared as a dream. I sometimes doubted if indeed it was not all true, but it never presented itself to my mind with the force of reality.

As the images that floated before me became more distinct, I grew feverish; a darkness pressed around me; no person was near me who soothed me with the gentle voice of love; no dear hand supported me. The physician came and prescribed medicines, and the old woman prepared them for me; but utter carelessness was visible in the first, and the expression of brutality was strongly impressed on the visage of the second. Who could be interested in the fate of a murderer but the hangman who would gain his fee?

These were my first reflections, but I soon learned that Mr. Kirwin had shewn me extreme kindness. He had caused the best room in the prison to be prepared for me (wretched indeed was the best), and it was he who had provided a physician and attendants for me. It is true he seldom came to see me, for, although he ardently desired to relieve the sufferings of every human creature, he did not wish to be present at the agonies and miserable ravings of a murderer. He came, therefore, sometimes to see that I was not neglected, but his visits were short and at long intervals.

One day when I was gradually recovering, *I was* seated in a chair, my eyes half *open* and my cheeks livid like those of death.

I was overcome by gloom and misery, and often reflected whether I had better not seek death than wait miserably pent up, only to be let loose in a world replete with wretchedness. At one time I considered whether I should not declare myself guilty and suffer the penalty of the law, which in depriving me of life would afford the only consolation that I was capable of receiving. Such were my thoughts, when the door of my prison opened, and Mr. Kirwin entered. His countenance expressed sympathy and kindness: he drew a chair close to mine and addressed me in French.

"I fear that this place is very shocking to you. Can I do any thing to make you more comfortable?"

"I thank you," replied I, "but all that you mention is nothing to me; on the whole earth there is no comfort which I am capable of receiving."

"I know that the sympathy of a stranger can be but little relief to one borne down as you are by so strange a misfortune. But you will, I hope, soon quit this unhappy abode—for, doubtless, evidence can be easily brought to free you from the criminal charge."

"That is my least concern—I am, by a course of strange events, become the most miserable of mortals. Persecuted and tortured as I am and have been, can death be any evil to me?"

"Nothing indeed could be more unfortunate and agonizing than the strange chances that have lately occurred. You were thrown, by some surprising accident, on this shore, renowned for its hospitality. Seized immediately and charged with murder, the first sight that was presented to your eyes was the body of your friend murdered in so unaccountable a manner and placed by some fiend, as it were, across your path."

As Mr. Kirwin said this, notwithstanding the agitation that I endured on this retrospect of my sufferings, I also felt considerable surprise at the knowledge he seemed to possess concerning me. I suppose some astonishment was expressed in my countenance, for Mr. Kirwin hastened to say: "It was not until a day or two after your illness that I thought of examining your dress, that I might discover some trace by which I could send to your relations an account of your misfortune and illness. I found several letters, among others one which I discovered by its commencement to be from your father. I instantly wrote to Geneva. Nearly two months has passed since the departure of my letter. But you are ill—even now you tremble. *You* appear unfit for agitation of any kind."

"This suspense is a thousand times worse than the most horrible event. Tell me what new scene of death has been acted and whose murder I am now to lament."

"Your family are all perfectly well," said Mr. Kirwin with gentleness; "and some one, a friend, is come to visit you."

I do not know by what chain of thought the idea presented itself, but it instantly darted into my mind that the monster had come to mock at my misery and taunt me with the death of Clerval as a new incitement to comply with his hellish desires. I put my hand before my eyes and cried out in agony—"Oh, take him away! I cannot see him; for God's sake, do not let him enter!"

Mr. Kirwin regarded me with a troubled countenance. He could not help regarding my exclamation as a presumption of my guilt and said, in rather severe tone—"I should have thought, young man, that the presence of your father would have been welcome, instead of inspiring such violent repugnance."

"My father," said I, while every feature and every muscle was relaxed from anguish to pleasure. "Is my father indeed come? How kind, how very kind! But where is he, why does he not hasten to me?"

My change of manner surprised and pleased the magistrate; perhaps he thought that my former exclamation was a momentary return of delirium. And now he instantly resumed his former benevolence. He rose and quitted the room with my nurse, and in a minute my father entered it.

Nothing at this moment could have given me greater pleasure than the arrival of my father. I stretched out my hand to him and cried—"Are you then safe—and Elizabeth—and Ernest?"

My father calmed me by his assurances of their welfare and told me that he had not communicated my imprisonment to my cousin but merely mentioned my illness. "And what a place this is that you inhabit, my son," continued he, looking mournfully at the barred windows and the wretched appearance of the room. "You travelled to seek happiness, but a fatality seems to pursue you—and poor Clerval."

The name of my unfortunate and murdered friend was too great an agitation to be endured in my weak state. I shed tears. "Alas, yes, my father," said I, "*some* destiny of the most horrible kind hangs over *me*, and I must live to fulfil it, or surely I should have died on the coffin of Henry."

Chapter 15

We were not allowed to converse for any length of time, for the precarious state of my health rendered every precaution necessary *that could ensure tranquillity*. Mr. Kirwin came in and insisted that my strength should not be exhausted by too much exertion. But the appearance of my father was to me like that of my good angel, and I gradually recovered my health. As my sickness quitted me, I was absorbed by a gloomy and black melancholy that nothing could dissipate. The image of Clerval was for ever before me, ghastly and murdered. More than once the agitation *into which* these reflections threw me made my friends dread a dangerous relapse.

Alas! Why did they preserve so miserable and detested a life? It was surely that I might fulfil my destiny, which is drawing to a close. Soon, oh, very soon, will death extinguish these thro*b*bings and *relieve me from* this mighty weight of anguish that bears me to the dust; and, in executing the award of justice, I shall also sink to rest. Then the appearance of death was distant, although the wish was ever present to my thoughts; and I often sat for hours motionless and speechless, wishing for some mighty revolution that might bury me and my destroyer in its ruins.

The season of the assizes[97] approached. I had already been three months in prison; and, although I was still weak and in continual danger of a relapse, I was obliged to travel nearly a hundred miles to the county town where the court was held. Mr. Kirwin charged himself with every care of collecting witnesses and arranging my defence. I was spared the disgrace of appearing publicly as a criminal, as the case was not brought before the court that decides on life and death. The grand jury rejected the bill on its being proved that I was in the Orkney Island at the hour the body of my friend was found. And a fortnight after my removal, I was liberated from prison. My father was enraptured on finding me freed from the vexations of a criminal charge, and that I was again permitted to breathe the fresh atmosphere and allowed to return to my native country. I did not participate in these feelings, for to me the walls of a dungeon or a palace were alike hateful. The cup of life was poisoned for ever; and, although the sun shone upon me as upon the happy and gay of heart, I saw around me nothing but a dense and frightful darkness, penetrated by no glimmer but the light of two eyes that glared upon me. Sometimes they were the expressive eyes of Henry languishing in death, the dark orbs nearly covered by the lid and the long lashes that fringed it. Sometimes it was the watery clouded eyes of the monster as I first saw them in my chamber at Ingolstadt.

My father tried to awake in me the feelings of affection. He talked of Geneva, which I should soon visit—of Elizabeth and Ernest. But these words only drew from me deep groans. Sometimes, indeed, I felt a wish for happiness, for my beloved cousin and the blue lake which had been so dear to me in early childhood; but my general state of feeling was a torpor, in which a prison was as welcome a residence as the divinest scene in nature; and these fits were seldom interrupted but by paroxysms of anguish and despair. At these moments I often endeavoured to put an end to the existence I loathed, and it required unceasing attendance and vigilance to *restrain me from* committing some dreadful act of violence. I remember, as I quitted the prison, I heard one of the men say—"He may be innocent of the murder, but he has certainly a bad conscience."

These words struck me. A bad conscience! Yes, surely I had one. William, Justine, and Clerval had died through my infernal machinations. "And whose death," cried I, "is to finish the tragedy? Ah! my father, do not let us remain in this wretched country. Take me where I can forget myself, my existence, and all the world." My father easily acceded to my desire; and, after having taken leave of Mr. Kirwin, we hastened to Dublin. I felt as if I was relieved from a heavy weight when the packet set sail with a fair wind from Ireland and I had quitted for ever the country which had been to me the scene of so much misery. It was midnight, my father slept below in the cabin, and I lay on the deck looking at the stars and listening to the dashing of the waves. I hailed the darkness that shut Ireland from my sight, and my pulse beat with a feverish joy when I reflected that I should soon see Geneva. The past appeared to me in the light of a frightful dream; yet the vessel in which I was, the wind that blew me from the detested shore of Ireland, and the sea which surrounded me told me too forcibly that I was deceived by no vision and that Clerval, my friend and dearest companion, had fallen a victim to me and the monster of my creation.

I repassed in my memory my whole life: my quiet happiness when residing with my family in Geneva, the death of my mother, and my departure for Ingolstadt. I remembered with shuddering the mad enthusiasm that hurried me on to the creation of my hideous enemy, and I called to my mind the night on which he first lived. I was unable to *pursue* the train of thought. A thousand feelings pressed upon me, and I wept bitterly.

Ever since my recovery from the fever, I had been in the custom of taking every night a small quantity of laudanum, for it was by means of this drug only that I was enabled to gain the rest necessary for the preservation of life. Oppressed by the recollection of my various misfortunes, I now took a double dose and soon slept profoundly. But, alas, sleep did not afford me respite from thought and misery; my dreams presented a thousand objects that scared me. Towards morning I was possessed by a kind of night-mare. I felt the fiend's grasp on my neck and could not free myself from it. Groans and cries rung in my ears. My father, who was watching over me, perceiving my restlessness, awoke me and pointed to the port of Holyhead, which we were now entering.

We had resolved not to go to London but to cross the country to Portsmouth—and thence to embark to Havre. I preferred this plan principally because I dreaded to see again those places in which I had enjoyed a few moments of tranquillity with my beloved Clerval. And I thought with horror of seeing those men whom we had been accustomed to visit together and who, doubtless, would make enquiries concerning an event, the very remembrance of which made me again feel what I endured when I gazed on his lifeless form.

As for my father, his desires and exertions were bounded to the again seeing me restored to health and peace of mind. His tenderness and attentions were unremitt*ing*, my grief and gloom was obstinate, but he would not despair. Sometimes he thought that I felt deeply the degradation of being obliged to answer a charge of murder, and he endeavoured to prove to me the futility of pride. "Alas! my father," said I, "how little do you know me: human beings, their feelings and passions, would indeed be degraded if such a wretch as I felt pride. Justine, poor unhappy Justine, was as innocent as I, and she suffered the same charge—she died for it. And I am the cause of this—I murdered her. William, Justine, and Henry—they all died by my hand."

My father had often during my late confinement heard me make the same assertion. When *I* thus accuse*d* myself, he sometimes seemed to desire an explanation; and at others he appeared to consider it as caused by delirium, and that during my illness some idea of this kind had presented itself to my imagination, the remembrance of which I preserved in my convalescence. I avoided explanation; I maintained a continual silence concerning the wretch I had created. I had a feeling that I should be supposed mad, and this for ever chained my tongue, when I would have given the whole world to have confided the fatal secret. Upon these occasions, my father said with an expression of unbounded wonder, "What do you mean, Victor, are you mad? My dear son, I entreat you not to make so strange an assertion again."

"I am not mad," I cried energetically, "the sun and the heavens who have viewed my operations can bear witness of my truth. I was the assassin of those most innocent victims—they died by my machinations. A thousand times would I have shed my own blood, drop by drop, to have saved their lives. But I could not, my father, indeed I could not sacrifice the whole human race."

The conclusion of this speech persuaded my father that my ideas were deranged; and *by* instantly chang*ing* the subject of our conversation, *he* endeavoured to alter the course of my thoughts. He wished as much as possible to obliterate the memory of the scenes in Ireland and never again alluded to them or suffered me to speak of my misfortunes. As time passed away, I became more calm; misery had her dwelling in my heart, but I no longer talked in the *same* incoherent manner of my own crimes; sufficient for me was the consciousness of them. By the utmost self-violence, I curbed the imperious voice of wretchedness which desired sometimes to declare itself to the whole world, and my manners were calmer and more composed than they had ever been since my journey to the sea of ice. Even my father, who watched me as the bird does its nestling, was deceived and thought that the black melancholy which had oppressed me was quitting me for ever, and that my native country and the society of my friends would entirely restore me to my former health and vivacity.

We arrived at Havre on the 8th of May[98] and instantly proceeded to Paris, where my father had some business which detained *us* a few weeks. In this city I received the following letter from Elizabeth.

"To Victor Frankenstein.

"Geneva, May 18, 17—."[99]

"My dearest Friend,

"It gave me the greatest pleasure to receive a letter from my uncle dated at Paris. You are no longer at a formidable distance, and I may hope to see you in less than a fortnight. My poor cousin! How much must you have suffered! I expect to see you looking even more ill than when you quitted Geneva. This winter has been passed most miserably; but, although happiness will not shine in our eyes for many months, yet I hope to see peace in your countenance and to find that your heart is not totally devoid of comfort and tranquillity.

"Yet I fear that the same feelings now exist that made you so miserable a year ago, even perhaps augmented by time. I would not at this period disturb you, when so many misfortunes weigh upon you, but a conversation that I had with my uncle previous to his departure renders some explanation necessary before we meet.

"Explanation, you may possibly say, what can Elizabeth have to explain? If you really say this, my questions are answered, and I have no more to do than to sign myself your affectionate cousin. But you are distant from me, and it is possible that you may dread and yet be pleased with this explanation; and, in the probability of this being the case, I dare not postpone any longer to write what, during your absence, I have often wished to express to you but have never had courage to begin.

"You well know, Victor, that our union had been the favourite plan of my aunt and uncle ever since our infancy. We were told this when young and taught to look forward to it as an event that would certainly take place. We were affectionate playfellows during childhood and, I believe, dear and valued friends to one another when we grew older. But as a brother and sister often entertain a lively affection towards one another *without desiring a more intimate union*, may not *such* also be our case? Tell me, dearest Victor. Answer me, I conjure you by our mutual happiness, with simple truth—Do you not love another?

"You have travelled; you have spent several years of your life at Ingolstadt; and I confess to you, my friend, that when I saw you last autumn so unhappy, flying from the society of every creature to solitude and despondency, I could not help supposing that you might regret our connection and believe yourself bound in honour to fulfil the wishes of your parents, although they opposed themselves to your inclinations. But this is false reasoning. I confess to you, my cousin, that I love you and that in my airy castles of futurity you have been my constant friend and companion. But it is your happiness I desire, as well as my own, when I declare to you that our marriage would render me eternally miserable unless it were the dictate of your own free choice. Even now I weep when I think that, borne down as you are by the cruelest misfortunes, you may stifle by the word honour all hope of that love and happiness which would alone *restore you to yourself.* I, who have so disinterested an affection for you, may encrease your miseries tenfold by being an obstacle to your wishes. Ah, Victor, be assured that your cousin and playmate has too sincere a love for you not to be made wretched by this supposition. Be happy, my friend; and if you obey me in this one request, be assured that nothing on earth will have the power to interrupt my tranquillity.

"Do not let this letter disturb you. Do not answer it tomorrow, or the next day, or not even until you come, if it will give you pain. My uncle will send me news of your health; and if I see but one smile on your lips when we meet, occasioned by this letter or any other exertion of mine, I shall need no other happiness. Your affectionate friend,

"Elizabeth Lavenza."

Chapter 16

This letter revived in my memory what I had before forgotten, the threat of the fiend when he visited me at the Orkney Island—"I will be with you on your marriage night." Such was my sentence, and on that night would the dæmon employ every art to destroy me and tear me from the glimpse of happiness *which promised* partly to console my sufferings. On that night he had determined to consummate his crimes by my death. Well, be it so. A deadly struggle would then assuredly take place where, if he was victorious, I should be at peace, and his power over me *be* at an end. If he were vanquished, I should be a free man. Alas! what a freedom—such as the peasant endures when his family have been massacred before his eyes, his cottage burnt, his lands laid waste, and he is turned adrift, homeless, pennyless, and alone—but free. Such would be my liberty, except that in my Elizabeth I possessed a treasure, alas, balanced by the horrors of remorse and guilt which would pursue me until death!

Sweet and beloved Elizabeth! I read and re-read her letter, and some softened feelings stole into my heart and dared whisper paradisaical dreams of love and joy. But the apple was already eaten, and the angel's arm bared ready to chase me from all hope. Yet I would die to make her happy; if the monster executed his threat, *death was inevitable*. Yet again I considered *whether* my marriage would hasten my fate if once the fiend had determined on my death. *My destruction might indeed arrive a few months sooner*; *but*, *if my torturer should suspect that I postponed my marriage on account of his menaces*, *he would surely find other and, perhaps, more dreadful means of revenge*. He had vowed to be with me on my marriage night. Yet he did not consider that threat as binding him to peace in the mean time—for, as if to shew me that he was not yet satiated with blood, he had murdered Clerval *immediately after the enunciation of his threats*. I resolved, *therefore*, that if my immediate union with my cousin would conduce either to hers or my father's happiness, my adversary's threats against my life should not retard it a single hour.

In this state of mind I wrote to Elizabeth. My letter was calm and affectionate. "I fear, my beloved girl," I said, "little happiness remains on earth for us, yet *all that* I may one day enjoy is concentered *in* you. Chase away your idle fears. To you alone do I consecrate my life and my endeavours for content. I have one secret, Elizabeth, a dreadful one. It will chill your frame with horror; and then, far from being surprised at my misery, you will only wonder that I live. I will reveal this tale of misery and terror to you the day after our marriage—for, my sweet cousin, we must have perfect confidence between us. But until then, I conjure you, do not mention or allude to it. This I most earnestly entreat of you, and I know *that* you will comply."

In about a week after *the arrival of Elizabeth's letter*, we returned to Geneva. Elizabeth welcomed me with warm affection; yet tears were in her eyes as she beheld my emaciated frame and feverish *cheeks*. I also saw a change in her. She was thinner and had lost much of that heavenly vivacity that had before charmed me. But her softness and gentle looks of compassion made her more fit for one blasted and miserable as I was.

The calm, however, which I now enjoyed did not last. Recollection brought madness with it. And when I thought of what *had* passed, a real insanity possessed me. Sometimes I was furious and burnt with rage, sometimes low and despondent. I neither spoke nor looked, but sat motionless, bewildered by the multitude of miseries that overcame me. Elizabeth alone had the power to draw me from these fits. Her gentle voice would soothe me when passionate, and inspire me with human feelings when sunk in torpor. She wept with me and for me. When reason returned, she would remonstrate with me and endeavour to inspire me with resignation. Ah, it is well for the unfortunate to be resigned. But for the guilty, there is no peace: the agonies of remorse poison the luxury there otherwise is *sometimes found* in indulging the excess of grief.

Soon after my arrival, my father spoke of my immediate marriage with my cousin. I remained silent.

"Have you then," said my father, "some other attachment?"

"None on earth. I love Elizabeth and look forward to our union with delight. Let the day therefore be named, and on it I will consecrate my life or death to the happiness of my cousin."

"My dear Victor, do not speak thus. Heavy misfortunes have befallen us, but let us only cling closer to what remains and transfer our love for those whom we ha*ve* lost to those who *yet* live. Our circle will be small, but bound close by the ties of affection and mutual misfortune. And when time will have *softened* your despair, new and dear cares will be born to replace those *of* whom *we have been so cruelly* deprived."

Such were the lessons of my father, but to me the remembrance of the threat returned. Nor can you wonder that, omnipotent as the fiend had yet been in his deeds of blood, I should almost regard him as invincible; and that when he had pronounced the words, "I shall be with you on your marriage night," I should regard the threatened fate as unavoidable. But death was no evil to me if the loss of Elizabeth were balanced with it; and I therefore, with contented and even cheerful countenance, agreed with my father that the ceremony should take place, if my cousin would consent, in ten days—and thus put, as I imagined, the seal to my fate.

Great God! If for one instant I had thought what might be the hellish intention of my fiendish adversary, I would rather have banished myself for ever from my country, and *wandered a friendless outcast over the earth*, than have consented to this miserable marriage. But, as if possessed of magic powers, the monster had blinded me to his real resolutions; and, when I thought I prepared only my own death, I hastened that of *a far dearer* victim.

As the time drew nearer for our marriage, whether from cowardice or a prophetic feeling, I felt my heart sink within me. But I concealed *my feelings under* an appearance of hilarity that brought smiles of joy to the countenance of my father but hardly deceived the ever-watchful and nicer eye of Elizabeth. She looked forward to our union with placid content, not unmingled with a little fear, which past misfortunes had impressed, that what now appeared certain and tangible happiness might soon dissipate into an airy dream and leave no trace but deep and everlasting regret.

Preparations were made for the event. Congratulatory visits *were* received, and all wore a smiling appearance. I shut up, as well as I could, in my own heart the anxiety that preyed there and entered with seeming earnestness into the plans of my father, although they might only serve as the decorations of my tragedy. A house was purchased for us near Cologny, by which we should enjoy the pleasures of the country and yet be so near Geneva as to see my father every day, who would still reside within the walls for the benefit of Ernest that he might follow his studies at the university.

In the mean time I took every precaution to defend my person in case the fiend should attack me. I carried pistols and a dagger constantly about me and was ever on the watch to prevent artifice, and by these means gained a great degree of tranquillity. And indeed, as the period approached, the threat appeared more as a delusion, not to be regarded as worthy to disturb my peace, while the happiness I hoped for in my marriage wore an appearance of greater certainty as the period of its solemnization drew near, and I heard it spoken of every day as an occurrence which no accident could possibly prevent.

Elizabeth seemed happy at the change from mirth to content which she saw come over me. But on the day that was to fulfil my wishes and my destiny, she was melancholy; a presentiment of evil pervaded her, and perhaps also she thought of the dreadful secret which I had promised to reveal to her the following day. My father was in the mean time overjoyed and, in the bustle of preparation, only observed in the melancholy of his niece the diffidence of a bride.

After the ceremony was performed, a large party assembled at my father's; but it was agreed that Elizabeth and I should pass the afternoon and night at Evian and set out on our return the next morning. The day was fine; and, as the wind was favourable, we resolved to go by water.

Those were the last moments of my life during which I enjoyed the feeling of happiness. We passed rapidly along; the sun was hot, but we were sheltered by a kind of canopy from its rays while we enjoyed the beauty of scene—sometimes on one side of the lake, where we saw Mont Salêve, the pleasant banks of Montalegre, and, at a distance, surmounting all, the beautiful Mont Blanc and the assemblage of snowy mountains that endeavoured to emulate her. Sometimes coasting the opposite banks, we saw the mighty Jura opposing its dark side to the ambition that would wish to quit its native country, and an almost insurmountable barrier to the conqueror that should dare invade it.

I took the hand of Elizabeth. "You are sorrowful," said I. "Ah! my love, if you knew what I have suffered and what I may still endure, you would endeavour to let me taste the quiet and freedom from despair that this one day at least permits me to enjoy."

"Be happy, my dear Victor," replied Elizabeth; "there is, I hope, nothing to distress you; and be assured that if a lively joy is not painted in my face, my heart is content. Something whispers to me not to depend too much on the prospect which is opened before us, but I will not listen to such a sinister voice. Observe how fast we move along and how the clouds, which sometimes obscure and sometimes rise above the dome of Mont Blanc, render this scene of beauty still more interesting. Look also at the innumerable fish that are swimming in these clear waters, where we can distinguish every pebble that lies at the bottom. What a divine day; how happy and serene all nature appears!"

Thus Elizabeth endeavoured to divert her thoughts and mine from all reflection on melancholy subjects, but her temper was fluctuating. Joy for a few instants shone in her eyes, but it continually gave place to distraction and reverie.

The sun sunk lower in the heavens; we passed by the river Drance and observed[100] its path through the chasm of the mountains and the glens of the lower hills. The Alps here come closer to the lake, and we approached the amphitheatre of mountains that forms its eastern boundary. The spire of Evian shone under the woods that surrounded it, and the range of mountain above mountain *by* which *it was* overhung.

The wind which had hitherto carried us along with amazing rapidity sunk at sunset to a gentle breeze; the light air just ruffled the water and caused a pleasant motion among the trees. As we approached the shore, it wafted the most delightful scent of flowers and hay. The sun sunk beneath the horizon as we landed; and, as I touched the shore, I felt those cares and fears revive which *soon were to clasp me and cling to me for ever.*

Chapter 17

It was eight o'clock when we landed; we walked for a short time on the shore, enjoying the transitory twilight, and then retired to the inn and contemplated the lovely scene of waters, mountains, and woods obscured in darkness, yet still displaying their black outlines. The wind which had fallen in the south now rose with great violence in the west; the moon had reached her summit in the heavens and was beginning to descend; the clouds swept across it swifter than the flight of the vulture and dimmed her rays, while the lake reflected the *scene of the* busy heavens *made* still busier by the *restless* waves that were beginning to rise. Suddenly a heavy storm of rain descended.

I had been calm during the day; but *so soon* as night obscured the shapes of objects, a thousand fears arose in my mind. I was anxious and watchful, while my right hand grasped a pistol which was hidden in my bosom. Every sound terrified *me*, but I resolved that I would sell my life dearly and not *relax the conflict that impended* until *my own life, or that of my adversary, were extinguished.*

Elizabeth observed my agitation for some time in timid and fearful silence. At length she said, "What is it, my dear Victor, that agitates you? What is it you fear?"

"Oh peace, peace, my love!" I replied, "this night and all will be safe—but this night is dreadful, very dreadful."

I passed an hour in this state of mind, when suddenly I reflected how dreadful the combat which I *momently* expected *to* take place would be to my wife; and I earnestly entreated her to retire, resolving not to join her until I had obtained some knowledge as to the situation of my enemy.

She left me, and I continued some time walking up and down the passages of the house and inspecting every corner that might afford a retreat to my adversary. But I saw no trace *of him* and *was* beg*inning* to consider *that some fortunate chance had intervened to prevent the execution of his menace*, when suddenly I heard a shrill and dreadful scream. It came from the room into which Elizabeth had retired. As I heard it, the whole truth rushed to my mind, my arms dropped, the motion of every muscle and fibre was suspended; I could feel the blood trickling in my veins *and tingling in my feet*. This state lasted but an instant, the scream was repeated, and I rushed into the room. Great God! Why did I not then expire? Why am I here to relate the destruction of the best hope and *the* purest creature of earth? She was there, lifeless and inanimate, thrown across the bed, her head hanging down, her pale and distorted features half covered by her hair. Every where I turn, I see the same figure—her bloodless arms and relaxed figure flung by the murderer on its *bridal* bier. Could I behold this and live? Alas! life is obstinate—*it clings closest* where it is most hated. For a moment only did I lose recollection—I fainted.

When I recovered, I found myself in the midst of the people of the inn. Their countenances expressed a breathless terror, but the horror of others appeared *only as* a mockery, *a shadow* of the feelings that oppressed *me*. I escaped from them to the room where lay the body of Elizabeth—my love—my wife—so lately living—so dear—so worthy. She had been moved from the posture in which I had first beheld her; and now as she lay, her head upon her arm and a handkerchief thrown across her face and neck, I might have supposed her asleep. I rushed towards her and embraced her with ardour, but the deathly coldness of the body told me that what I now held in my arms had ceased to be the Elizabeth whom I had loved and cherished; the murderous grasp of the fiend was on her neck, and the breath had ceased to issue from her lips.

While I still held her in my arms in the agony of despair, I happened to look up. The room had before been quite dark, and I felt a kind of panic on seeing the pale yellow light of the moon illuminate the chamber. The shutters had been thrown back; and, with a sensation of horror not to be described, I saw at the open window a figure the most hideous and abhorred. A grin was on the face of the monster; he seemed to jeer as, with his fiendish finger, he pointed towards the corpse of my wife. I rushed towards the window and, drawing a pistol from my bosom, shot—but he eluded me, leapt from his station, and, running with the swiftness of lightning, plunged into the lake. The report of my pistol brought a crowd into the room. I pointed to where he had disappeared, and we followed him with boats and cast nets, but in vain; and, passing several hours in the search, returned hopeless, most of my companions believing it to have been a form conjured by my fancy. However, after having landed, they proceeded to search the country, parties going in different directions among the woods and vines. I did not accompany them.

I was exhausted; a film covered my eyes; and my skin was parched with the heat of fever. In this state I lay on a bed, hardly conscious of what had happened, and my eyes wandered round the room as if to seek something that I had lost. At length I remembered that my father would anxiously expect the return of Elizabeth and myself and that I must return alone. This reflection brought tears into my eyes, and I wept for a long time. I reflected on my misfortunes and their cause, and was bewildered in a cloud of wonder and horror. The death of William, the execution of Justine, the murder of Clerval and now of my wife—even at that moment I knew not that my only remaining friends were safe from the malignity of the fiend: my father even now might be writhing under his grasp, and Ernest might be dead at his feet. This reflection made me shudder and recalled me to action. I started up and resolved to return to Geneva with *all* possible speed. There were no horses to be procured, and I must return by the lake; but the wind was *unfavourable*, and the rain fell in torrents. It was, however, hardly yet morning, and I might reasonably hope to arrive by night. I hired a number of men to row and took an oar myself, for I had always experienced relief from mental *torment* in bodily exercise. But the overflowing misery I now felt, and the excess of agitation that I endured, rendered me incapable of any exertion. I threw down the oar and, leaning my head upon my hands, gave way to every gloomy idea that arose. If I looked up, I saw the scenes which were familiar to me in my happier *time* and which I had contemplated but the day before in the company of her who was now but a shadow and a recollection. Tears streamed from my eyes. I looked on the lake, the rain had ceased for a moment, and I saw the fish play in the waters as I had done but a few hours before—they had then been observed by Elizabeth. Nothing is so painful to the human mind as great and sudden change. The sun might shine, or the clouds might lower—but nothing could appear to me as it had done the day before. A fiend had snatched from me every hope of future happiness. No creature had ever been so miserable as I was; so frightful an event was single upon earth.

But why should I dwell upon the incidents that followed this last overwhelming event? Mine has been a tale of horrors. I have reached their acme; and what I must now relate can but be tedious to you, now[101] that one by one my friends were snatched away, and I was left desolate. My own strength is exhausted, and I must tell in few words what remains of my hideous narration.

I arrived at Geneva. My father and Ernest yet lived, but the former was unable to bear the miserable tidings that I bore. I see him now, excellent and venerable old man. His eyes wandered in vacancy, for they had lost their charm and delight—his niece, his more than daughter, whom he doated on with all the affection of a man who, in the decline of life, having few affections, clings *more earnestly* to those that remain. Cursed, cursed be the fiend that brought misery on his grey hairs and doomed him to *waste* in wretchedness. He could not live under the horrors that were accumulated round him. An apoplectic fit was brought on, and in a few days he died in my arms.

What then became of me? I know not. I lost sensation, and chains and darkness were the only objects that pressed upon me. Sometimes, indeed, I dreamed that I wandered in flowery meadows and pleasant vales with the friends of my youth; but I awoke and found myself in a dungeon. Melancholy followed, but by degrees I regained a clear conception of my miseries and situation, and was then released from my prison. For they had called me mad; and *during* many months, as I understood, a solitary cell had been my habitation. But liberty had been a useless gift to me had I not, as I awakened to reason, at the same time awakened to vengeance. As the memory of past misfortunes pressed upon me, I began to reflect on their cause—the monster whom I had created, the miserable dæmon whom I had sent abroad in the world for my destruction. I was possessed by a maddening rage when I thought of him—and desired and ardently prayed that I might have him within my grasp to wreak *a* great and signal *revenge* on his cursed head.

Nor did my hate long confine itself to useless wishes; I began to reflect on the best means of securing him; and for this purpose, about a month after my release, I repaired to a criminal judge in the town and told him that I had an accusation to make, that I knew the destroyer of my family, and that I required him to exert his whole authority for the apprehension of the murderer.

The magistrate listened to me with attention and kindness. "Be assured, Sir," said he, "no pains or exertions on my part have been or shall be spared to discover the *villain*."

"I thank you," I replied, "listen therefore to the deposition I have to make. It is indeed a tale so strange that I fear you would not credit it, were there not something in truth which, however wonderful, forces conviction. The story is too connected to be mistaken for a dream, and I have no motive for falsehood." My manner as I said this was impressive but calm; I had formed in my own heart the resolution to pursue my destroyer to death; and this purpose quieted my agony and *provisionally* reconciled me to life.

I now related my history briefly, but with firmness and precision, marking dates with accuracy and never deviating into invective or exclamation. The magistrate appeared at first perfectly incredulous, but as I continued he became more attentive and interested. I saw him sometimes shudder with horror; at others, a lively surprise unmi*ngled* with disbelief was painted on his countenance. When I had concluded my narration, I said—

"This is the being whom I accuse and for whose detection and punishment I call upon you *to* exert your whole power. It is your duty as a magistrate, and I believe and hope your feelings as a man do not revolt from the execution of *those* functions on this occasion."

This address caused a considerable change in the physiognomy of my auditor. He had heard my story with that half kind of belief that is given to a tale of spirits and ghosts; but when he was called upon to act officially in consequence of it, the whole tide of his incredulity returned. He, however, answered mildly.

"I would willingly afford you every aid in your pursuit; but the creature of whom you speak appears to have powers which would put all my exertions to defiance. Who can follow an animal *which* can traverse the sea of ice and inhabit caves and dens where no man would venture to intrude? Besides, some months have elapsed since the commission of his crimes, and no one may conjecture to what place he has wandered *or* what *region* he may now inhabit."

"I do not doubt," I replied, "that he hovers near the spot which I inhabit. And if he has indeed taken refuge in the Alps, he may be hunted like the chamois and destroyed as a beast of prey. But I perceive your thoughts: you do not credit my narrative, and do not intend to pursue my enemy with the punishment that is his desert."

As I spoke, rage sparkled in my eyes. The magistrate was intimidated: "You are mistaken," said he, "I will exert myself; and if it is in my power to seize the monster, be assured that he shall suffer punishment proportionate to his crimes. But I fear from what you have yourself described to be his properties that this will prove impracticable and that, while every proper measure is pursued, you should endeavour to make up your mind to a disappointment."

"That cannot be," said I wildly. "But all that I can say will be of little avail. My revenge is of no moment to you; yet, while I allow it to be a vice, I confess that it is the devouring and only passion of my soul; my rage is unspeakable when I reflect that the murderer whom I have turned loose upon society still exists. You refuse my just demand. I have but one resource, and I devote myself either in my life or death to his destruction." I trembled with excess of agitation as I said this; there was frenzy in my manner and something, I doubt not, of that haughty fierceness *which* the martyrs of old were said to have possessed. But to a Genev*ese* magistrate, whose mind was occupied by far other ideas than those of devotion and heroism, this elevation of mind had much the appearance of madness. He endeavoured to soothe me as a nurse does a child, and reverted to my tale as the effects of delirium. "Man," I cried, "how ignorant art thou in thy pride of wisdom! Cease; you know not what it is you say."

I broke from the house and, angry and disturbed, retired to meditate some other mode of action.

Chapter 18

My present situation was *one in which all voluntary thought was swallowed up and lost.* I was hurried away by fury. Revenge alone *endowed* me with strength and *composure.* It modelled my feelings *and* allowed me to be calculating and calm *at periods* when otherwise delirium or death would have been my portion. My first resolution was to quit Geneva for ever. My country which, when I was happy and beloved, was dear to me—now, in my adversity, became hateful. I provided myself with a small sum of money, *together with* a few jewels *which* had belonged to my mother, and departed.

And now my wanderings began, which are to cease but with life. I have traversed a vast *portion* of *the earth* and *have* endured all the hardships *which* travellers in deserts and barbarous countries are wont to meet. How I have lived I hardly know; many times *have* I *stretched my failing limbs* on the sandy plain, exhausted and far from succour, and prayed for death. But revenge kept me alive. I dared not die and leave my adversary in being.

When I quitted Geneva, my first labour was to gain some clue by which I might trace the steps of my fiendish enemy. But my plan was unsettled; and I wandered many hours around the confines of the town, uncertain what path *I should* pursue. As night approached, I found myself at the entrance of the cemetery where William, Elizabeth, and my father reposed. I entered it and approached the tomb which marked their graves. Every thing was silent except the leaves of the trees, which were gently *agitated* by the breeze. The night was nearly dark, and the scene would have been affecting and solemn even to an uninterested observer. The spirits of the departed seemed to flit around and to cast a *shadow, which was felt but seen not*, around the head of the mourner. The deep grief *which this scene had at first excited* quickly gave way to rage and despair. They were dead, and I lived. Their murderer also lived, and to destroy him I must drag out my weary existence. I knelt on the earth and with quivering lips exclaimed, "By the sacred earth *on which* I kneel, by the shades that wander near me, by the deep and eternal grief that I feel, I swear! And by thee, Oh Night, and by the spirits that preside over thee, I swear to pursue the dæmon who caused this misery until he or I shall *perish* in mortal conflict! For this purpose I will preserve my life. To execute this dear revenge, will I again behold the sun and *tread the* green herbage of earth, which otherwise should vanish from my eyes for ever. And I call on you, spirits of the dead, and you, wandering ministers of vengeance, to aid me and conduct me in my work. Let the cursed and hellish monster drink deep of agony. Let him feel the despair that now torments me."

I had begun my adjuration with solemnity and an awe that almost assured me that the shades of my murdered friends heard and approved my devotion. But the furies possessed me as I concluded it, and rage choaked my utterance. I was answered through the stillness of night by a loud and fiendish laugh. It rung in my ears long and heavily; the mountains re-echoed it, and I felt as if all hell surrounded me with mockery and laughing. Surely in that moment I should have been possessed by frenzy and have destroyed my miserable existence, but that my vow was heard, and I was reserved for vengeance. The laughter died away when a well-known and abhorred voice, apparently close to my ear, addressed me in an audible whisper: "I am satisfied—miserable wretch, you have determined to live, and I am satisfied." I darted towards the place from which the sound proceeded, but the *devil* eluded my grasp. Suddenly the broad disk of the moon arose and shone fully upon *his ghastly and distorted shape, as he fled with more than mortal speed.*

I pursued him; and for many months this *pursuit* has been my task. Guided by a slight clue, I followed the windings of the Rhone, but vainly. The Mediterranean appeared, and by a strange chance I saw the fiend enter by night and hide himself in a vessel bound for the Black Sea. I followed him—*I knew the vessel in which he was concealed—and he escaped me I know not how.* Amidst the wilds of Tartary and Russia, although he still *evaded* me, I have ever followed in his track. Sometimes the peasants, scared by his horrid apparition, informed me of his path; sometimes he himself, who feared that if I lost all trace I should despair and die, often left some mark to guide me. The snows descended on my head, and I saw the *print* of his huge step on the white plain. To you who *are fast*[102] entering on life, and care *is new to you and agony unknown,* how can *you understand* what I have felt and still feel? Cold, want, and fatigue were *the* least pains *which I was destined to endure*; I was cursed by some devil and bore about with me my eternal hell. Yet still a spirit of good followed and directed my steps and, when I most murmured, would suddenly extricate me from my seemingly insurmountable difficulties. Sometimes, when nature overcome by hunger sunk under the exhaustion, a repast was prepared for me in the desert that restored and inspirited me. The fare indeed was coarse, such as the peasants of the country *ate*; but I may not doubt that it was set there by the spirits I had invoked to aid me. Often, when all was dry, the heavens cloudless, and I was parched with thirst, a slight cloud would bedim the sky, shed the few drops that revived me, and vanish.

I followed, when I could, the courses of rivers; but the dæmon generally avoided these, as it was here that the population of the country chiefly collected. In other places human beings were seldom seen, and I generally subsisted on the wild animals that crossed my path. I had money with me and gained the friendship of the villagers by distributing it or bringing with me some food that I had killed, which, after taking a small part, I always presented to those who had provided me with fire and utensils for cooking. My life as it passed thus was indeed hateful to me, and it was during sleep alone that I could taste joy. Oh blessed sleep! often, when most miserable, I sunk to repose, and my dreams lulled me even to rapture. The spirit that guarded me had surely provided these moments, or rather hours, of happiness that I might retain strength to fulfil my pilgrimage. *Deprived of this respite*, I should have sunk under my hardships. During the day I was *thus* sustained and inspirited by the hope of night: *for in* sleep I saw my friends, my wife, and my beloved country; again I saw the benevolent countenance of my father, heard the silver tones of my Elizabeth's voice, and beheld Clerval enjoying health and youth. Often when wearied by a toilsome march, I persuaded myself that I was dreaming *until night should come* and that I *should then* enjoy reality in the arms of my dearest friends. What agonizing fondness did I feel for them! how did I cling to their dear forms, as *sometimes* they haunted *even the visions of my waking hours*, and persuade myself that they still lived. At such moments the vengeance that burned within me died in my heart, and I pursued my path towards the destruction of the dæmon more as a task enjoined by heaven, *as the mechanical impulse of some power of which I was unconscious*, than the ardent desire of my soul.

What his feelings were whom I pursued, I *cannot* know. Sometimes, indeed, he left marks in writing on the barks of trees or cut on stone that guided me and instigated my fury. "My reign is not yet over" *was legible in* one of these *inscriptions*: "You live and my power is complete. Follow me—I seek the everlasting ices of the north where you will feel the misery of cold and frost *to which I am impassive*. You will find near this place, if you follow not too tardily, a dead hare; eat and be revived. Come on, my enemy; we have yet to wrestle for our lives, but many hard and miserable hours will you spend until that period arrives."

Scoffing devil! Again do I vow vengeance; again do I devote thee, miserable fiend, to torture and death; never will I *omit* my search until he *or I perish*. And then with what ecstacy shall I join my Elizabeth and those who even now prepare for me *the* reward *of* my tedious and horrible pilgrimage.

As I pursued still my journey to the northward, the snows *thickened*, and cold encreased *in* a degree almost too severe to support. The peasantry were shut up in their hovels, and only a few of the most hardy ventured forth to seize the animals whom starvation had forced forth to seek for prey. The rivers were covered with ice, and no fish could be procured. The triumph of my enemy encreased with the difficulty of my labours. One inscription that he left was in these words: "Prepare! your toils only begin; wrap yourself in furs and provide food, for we shall soon enter on a journey where your sufferings will satisfy my everlasting hatred."

My courage and perseverance were inspired with new strength by these difficulties; I resolved not to fail in my purpose; and, calling heaven to support me, I continued with unabated fervour to traverse immense deserts until the ocean appeared at a distance and formed the utmost boundary of the horizon. Oh! how unlike it was to the blue seas of the south. Covered with ice, it was only to be distinguished from land by its superior wildness and ruggedness. The Greeks wept when they saw the Mediterranean from the hills of Asia, and hailed with rapture the boundary of their toils. I did not weep; but I knelt down and thanked my guiding spirit with a full heart for conducting me safely towards the place where I hoped, notwithstanding my adversary's threat, to meet and grapple with him. Some weeks before *this period* I had procured a sledge and dogs, and thus traversed the snows with inconceivable speed. I know not whether the fiend possessed the same advantages; but I found that, as before I had daily lost the advantage in my pursuit, I now gained on him so much that, when I for the first time saw the ocean, he was but one day's journey in advance, and I hoped soon to intercept him. With new courage, therefore, I pressed on and in two days arrived at a wretched hamlet on the sea-shore. I enquired concerning the fiend and gained every information. A gigantic *monster*, they said, had arrived the night before. Armed with a gun and many pistols and putting to flight the inhabitants of a solitary cottage through fear of his terrific appearance, *he* had *carried off* their store of winter food; and placing it in a sledge, to draw which he had seized on a numerous drove of trained dogs, he had harnessed them—and the same night, to the joy of the horror-struck villagers, *had* pursued his journey across the sea in a direction that led to no land; and they conjectured that he must be speedily destroyed in the breaking of the ice or frozen by the eternal frost.

On hearing this information, I suffered a temporary fit of despair. He had escaped me; and I must now commence a destructive and almost endless journey across the mountainous ices of the ocean—amidst cold that few of the inhabitants could long endure and *which* I, *the* native of a genial and sunny climate, *could not* hope to survive. Yet at the idea that the fiend should live and be triumphant, my rage and vengeance returned and, like a mighty tide, overwhelmed every other feeling. After a slight repose, during which the spirits of the dead hovered round me and instigated me to toil and revenge, I prepared for my journey.

I exchanged my land sledge for one fashioned for the ruggedness of the *frozen* ocean; and, purchasing a plentiful stock of provisions, I departed from land. How many days have passed since then I know not, but I have endured misery *which* nothing but the eternal sentiment *of a just revenge* burn*ing* within my heart could have enabled me to support. Immense and rugged mountains of ice often barred up my passage, and I often heard the *earthquake and the thunder of the* ground-sea which threatened my destruction, but again a frost came *and made the paths of the sea secure*. By the *quantity* of provision *which I have consumed*, I should guess that I had passed *three weeks* in this journey. And despondency and grief often wrung bitter drops from my eyes. Despair indeed had almost secured her prey, and I should soon have sunk under this misery. When once, after the poor animals that carried me had with incredible toil gained the summit of an ice mountain, they paused to rest—and one, unable to move, sinking under the toil, died—I viewed the expanse before, with anguish; when suddenly my eye was arrested by a dark speck on the dusky plain, I strained my sight to *discover* what it could be and uttered *a* wild cry of ecstacy when I distinguished a sledge, dogs, and *the distorted proportions of a well-known* form within. Oh, with what a burning gush did hope revisit my heart! Warm tears filled my eyes, which I hastily wiped away that they might not intercept the view I had of the fiend. I followed—but still the dew dimmed my sight until, giving way to the emotions that oppressed me, I wept aloud.

But this was not the time for delay. I disincumbered the dogs of their dead companion, gave them a plentiful portion of food, and, after an hour's repose which was absolutely necessary and yet which was bitterly irksome to me, I continued my path. The sledge was still visible; nor did I again lose sight of it, except at the moments when for a short time some ice rock *concealed* it *with its intervening crags*. I indeed perceptibly gained on *the object of my pursuit*. And after about another *day's* journey, I beheld myself at no more than *half a mile* distant. My heart bounded within me. But now, when I appeared almost within grasp of my enemy, my hopes were suddenly extinguished, and I lost all trace of him more utterly than I had ever done before. A ground-sea was heard—the thunder of it*s progress*, as the waters rolled and swelled beneath me, became every moment more ominous and terrific. I pressed on, but in vain. The wind arose; the sea roared; and, with the mighty shock of an earthquake, it split and cracked with a tremendous and overwhelming sound. The work was soon finished: in a few minutes a mighty ocean rolled between me and my enemy. And I was left drifting on a scattered piece that was every moment lessening and thus preparing for me a hideous death. In this manner many hours passed; several of my dogs died; and I myself *was about to* sink under the accumulation of hardships, when I saw your vessel riding at anchor and holding forth to me hopes of succour and life. I had no conception that vessels ever came so far north and was astounded at the sight. I quickly destroyed *part of* my sledge *to* construct oars and by these means was able, with infinite fatigue, to move my ice-raft in the direction of your *vessel*. I had resolved that, if you were going southward, still to trust myself to the mercy of the seas rather than abandon my purpose. I hoped to be able to move you to grant me a boat and some provision with which I could still seek my enemy. But your direction was northward. You took me on board when my vigour was exhausted, and I should soon have sunk under my multiplied hardships to a death *which* I *still* dread, for my task is unfulfilled. Oh! when will my guiding spirit, in conducting me to him, allow me the rest I so much desire? or must I die, and he yet live? If I do, swear to me, Walton, that he shall not escape, that you will seek him and satisfy my vengeance in his death. Yet, do I dare ask you to undertake my pilgrimage, to endure the hardships that I have undergone? No, I am not so selfish; yet, when I am dead, if he should appear, if the ministers of vengeance should conduct him to you, swear that he shall not live—swear that he shall not triumph over my accumulated miseries and live to make another such a wretch as I am. Oh! he is eloquent and persuasive, and once his words had even power over my heart—but trust him not. His soul is as hellish *as his form*, full of *treachery* and fiend-like malice—hear him not. Call on the manes[103] of William, Justine, Clerval, Elizabeth, my father, and of the wretched Victor; and thrust your *sword into* his heart. I will hover near you and direct the steel aright.

Walton—in continuation.

August 26th.[104]

You have read this strange and terrific story, Margaret, and do not you feel your blood congealed with horror *like that which even now curdles mine*? *Sometimes*, seized with *sudden* agony, he could not continue *his tale*; *at others*, his voice, broken yet piercing, *uttered the words of which it is composed*. His fine and lovely eyes *were now* lighted up with indignation, *now* subdued *to downcast* sorrow and infinite wretchedness. Sometimes he commanded his countenance and tones and related the most horrible incidents with a *tranquil* voice, suppressing every mark of agitation—*then*, like a volcano bursting forth, his face would suddenly change to an expression of the wildest rage as he shrieked *out* his imprecations on his persecutor.

His tale is connected and told with an appearance of the simplest truth; yet I own to you, my sister, that the letters of Felix and Safie which he shewed me, and the apparition of the monster seen from our ship, brought to me a greater conviction of the truth of his narrative than his asseverations, *however earnest and connected.* Such a monster *has* then real exist*ence*; I *cannot* doubt it; yet I *am* lost in surprise and admiration. Sometimes I endeavoured to gain from Frankenstein the particulars of his formation, but on this point he was impenetrable. "Are you mad, my friend?" said he, "or whither does your senseless curiosity lead you? Would you also create for yourself and *for* the world a dæmoniacal enemy, or to what do your questions tend? Peace, peace! learn my miseries, and do not seek to encrease your own."

Frankenstein discovered that I detailed or made notes concerning his history; he asked to see them, and himself corrected and augmented them in many places, but principally in giving the life and spirit of the conversations he held with his enemy. "Since you have made an account," said he, "I would not that a mutilated one should go down to posterity."

Thus has a week[105] passed away while I have listened to the strangest tale that ever imagination formed. My thoughts and every feeling of my soul *have* been drunk up by the interest *for* my guest *which this tale and his own elevated and gentle manners have created.* I wish to soothe him, yet *can* I *counsel* one so infinitely miserable, so destitute of every hope of consolation, to live? Oh, no! the only joy he *can now know will be when he* compose*s* his shattered feelings to peace and death. Yet he enjoys one comfort, the *offspring* of solitude and delirium: he believe*s* that when in dreams he *holds converse with* his friends, *and derives from that communion consolation for* his miseries or *excitement* to *his* vengeance, that they *are* not the creations of his fancy but the real beings *who visit him from the regions of a remoter world.* This *faith* give*s* a solemnity to his reveries that renders them *to me almost as imposing and interesting as truth.*

Our conversations *are* not always confined to his own history and misfortunes. On every point of general literature he displays unbounded knowledge and a quick and piercing apprehension. His eloquence is forcible and touching; nor can I hear him when he narrates a pathetic incident, or endeavours to move the passions *of* pity and love, without tears. What a glorious creature must he have been in his days of prosperity when he is thus noble and godlike in ruin. He seems to feel his own worth and the greatness of his fall. "When younger," said he, "I felt as if I was destined for some great enterprise. My feelings are profound, but I possessed a coolness of judgement that fitted me for *illustrious achievements*. This sentiment of the worth of my nature supported me when others would have sunk, for I deemed it criminal to throw away in useless grief those talents that might be useful to my fellow-creatures. When I reflected on the work that I had completed, no less a one than the creation of a sensitive and rational animal, I could not rank myself with the herd of common projectors. But this feeling which supported me now serves only to *plunge* me lower in the dust. All my speculations and hopes are as nothing; and, like the Archangel who aspired to omnipotence, I am chained in an eternal hell. My imagination was vivid, yet my powers of application were intense—by the union of these qualities I conceived the idea and executed the creation of a man. Even now I cannot recollect without passion my reveries while the work was incomplete—I trod heaven in my thoughts—now exulting in my powers—now burning with the idea of their consequences. From my infancy I was imbued with high hopes and a lofty ambition, but how am I sunk! Oh my friend! if you had known me as I once was, you would not recognize me in this state of degradation. Despondency rarely visited my heart; a high destiny seemed to bear me on—until I fell, oh! never, never *again* to rise."

Must I lose this admirable being? I have longed for a friend; *I have sought* one who would sympathize with and love me. Behold, on these desert seas I have found *such a* one; but I fear I *have* gained him but to know his value and lose him. I would reconcile him with life, but he repulses the thought. "I thank you, Walton," he said, "for your kind intentions towards so miserable a wretch; but when you speak of new ties and *fresh* affections, think *you that* any can replace those *which are gone*? Can any man be to me as Clerval was; or any woman, another Elizabeth? Even where the affections are not strongly moved by any superior excellence, the companions of our childhood always possess a certain power over our mind that hardly any other later friend can obtain. They know our infantine feelings, which, however they may be afterwards modified, are never eradicated; and they can judge of our actions with greater certainty. A sister or brother can never, unless indeed such symptoms have been shewn early, suspect the other *of* fraud or false dealing, when another friend, however strongly he may be attached, may be, in spite of himself, invaded by suspicion. But I enjoyed friends, dear not only by association but for their own sake—and, wherever I am, the soothing voice of my Elizabeth or the conversation of Clerval will be ever whispered in my ear. They are dead, and but one feeling *can* in such a *solitude persuade me to preserve my life*. If I were engaged in any high undertaking or design fraught with extensive utility to my fellow-creatures, then could I live to fulfil it. But such is not my destiny. I must pursue and destroy the being to whom I gave existence; then my task will be fulfilled, and I may die."

September 2d.[106]

My beloved Sister,

I write to you encompassed by peril and ignorant if I am ever doomed to see again dear England and the dearer friends that inhabit it. I am surrounded by mountains of ice which admit of no escape and threaten every moment to crush my vessel. The brave fellows whom I persuaded to be my companions look at me for aid, but I have none to bestow. There is something terribly appalling in our situation. Yet my courage and hopes do not desert me. We may survive; and if we do not, I will repeat the lessons of my Seneca[107] and die with a good heart.

Yet what, Margaret, will be your state? You will not hear of my destruction, and you will anxiously await my return. Years will pass, and you will have visitings of despair and yet be cheered by hope. Oh! my beloved sister, the sickening failings of your heart-felt expectations are, in prospect, more terrible to me than my own death. But you have a husband and lovely children; you may be happy. Heaven bless you, and make you so!

My unfortunate guest regards me with the tenderest compassion. He endeavours to fill me with hope and talks as if life were a thing which he loved. He reminds me how often the same accidents have happened to other navigators who have attempted the same sea. In spite of myself, he fills me with cheerful auguries. Even the sailors feel the benefit of his eloquence—when he speaks, they no longer despair—he rouses their energies, and they believe these vast mountains of ice *are* mole hills which will vanish before the resolutions of man. This is but transitory, and each day's expectation delayed fills them with fear; and I almost dread *the* mutiny *of despair*.

September 5th.[108]

A scene has just passed of such *uncommon* interest that, although it is highly probable that the papers may never reach you, my dear Margaret, yet I cannot forbear recording it. We are still surrounded by *mountains of* ice, still in imminent danger *of being crushed in their conflict*. The cold is excessive, and many of my unfortunate comrades have already found a grave amidst this scene of desolation. Frankenstein has declined daily in health; a feverish fire still glimmers in his eyes; but he is ex*h*austed, and, when suddenly roused to any exertion, he speedily sinks again *into* apparent lifelessness.

I mentioned in my last letter the fears I had of mutiny. This morning, as I sat watching the wan countenance of my friend, his eyes half closed and his limbs hanging listlessly, I was roused by half a dozen of the sailors who desired admission into the cabin. They entered, and their leader addressed me. He told me that he and his companions had been chosen by the other sailors to come in deputation to me to make a demand which in justice I could not refuse. We were immured by ice and would probably never escape; but they feared that if, as was possible, the ice should be dissipated and a free passage opened, I should be rash enough to continue my voyage and lead them to fresh dangers after they *might* happily *have* surmounted this. They desired, therefore, that I should make a solemn promise, if the vessel should be freed, *that* I would instantly direct my course to *Archangel*.[109]

This speech troubled me. I had not despaired; nor had I yet conceived the idea of returning, if set free. Yet could I in justice, or even in possibility, refuse th*is demand*? I hesitated before I answered, when Frankenstein, who had at first been silent and indeed appeared hardly to have force enough to attend, now roused himself. His eyes sparkled, and his cheek *was* flushed with momentary vigour. Turning to the men, he said: "What do you mean? What do you demand of your captain? Are you then so easily turned from your design? Did you not call this a glorious expedition, and *wherefore* was it *glorious*? Not because the way was smooth and placid as a *southern sea*, but because it was full of dangers and terror—because at every new incident your fortitude was to be called forth, and your courage exhibited—because death and danger surrounded you, and these you were to brave and overcome. For this, was it a glorious—for this, was it an honourable undertaking. You were to be hereafter hailed as the benefactors of your species—your names adored as the brave men who encountered death for honour and *the benefit of mankind*. And now behold, with the first *imagination of danger*—or, if you will, the first mighty and terrific trial of your courage—you shrink away and are content to be handed down as men who had not strength to endure cold and peril. And so, poor souls, they were chilly and returned to their warm firesides. Why, that requires not this preparation. Ye need not have come thus far and dragged your captain to the shame of a defeat to prove yourselves cowards. Oh! be men, or be more than men; be steady to your purposes and firm as rock. This ice is not made of such stuff *as your hearts might be*; it is mutable and cannot withstand you, if you say that it shall not. Do not return to your families with the stigma of disgrace marked on your brows; return as heroes who have fought and conquered and who know not what it is to turn their backs on the foe."

He spoke thus with a voice so modulated to the different feelings expressed in his speech, with an eye so full of high design and heroism, that can you wonder that the men were moved. They looked at one another and were unable to reply. I spoke. I told them to retire and consider of what had been said: that I would not lead them further north if they strenuously desired the contrary; but that I hoped that with reflection their courage would return. They retired; and I turned to my friend, but he was sunk in languor and almost deprived of life.

How all this will terminate I know not. But I had rather die than return shamefully, my purpose unfulfilled. Yet I fear *such* will be my fate. The men unsupported by the ideas of glory and honour can never willingly continue to endure their present hardships.

September 7th.

The die is cast. I have consented to return if we are not destroyed. Thus are my hopes blasted by cowardice and indecision. I come back ignorant and disappointed. It requires more philosophy than I possess to bear this injustice with patience.

September 12th.[110]

It is past. I am returning to *Archangel*.[111] I have lost my hopes of utility and glory—I have lost my friend. But I will endeavour to detail the bitter circumstances to you, my dear sister. And, while I am wafted towards England and towards you, I will not despair.

September 9th:[112] The ice began to move, and roarings like thunder were heard at a distance as the *islands* split and cracked in every direction. We were in the most imminent peril. But as we could only remain passive, my chief attention was occupied by my unfortunate guest, whose illness encreased to such a degree that he was entirely confined to his bed. The ice cracked behind us and was driven with force towards the north—a breeze sprung from that quarter—*and* on the 11th the passage towards the south *became* free. When the sailors saw this, and that their return towards their native country was apparently assured, a shout of tumultuous joy broke from them loud—and long continued. Frankenstein, who was dozing, awoke and asked the reason *of the tumult*. I was unable to reply. He asked again. "They shout," I said, "because they will soon return to England."

"Do you then really return?"

"Alas, yes! I cannot withstand their demands. I cannot lead them unwillingly to danger, and I must return."

"Do so if you will, but I will not. You may give up your purpose, but mine is assigned to me by heaven, and I dare not. I am weak, but surely the spirits who assist my vengeance will endow me with sufficient strength." Saying this, he endeavoured to spring from the bed, but the exertion was too great for him; he fell back and fainted. It was long before he was restored; I often thought that life was entirely extinct. At length he opened his eyes, but he breathed with difficulty and was unable to speak. The *surgeon* gave him a composing draught and ordered us to leave him undisturbed. In the mean time he told me that my friend had certainly not many hours to live.

His sentence was pronounced, and I could only grieve and be patient. I sat by his bed watching him—his eyes were closed, and I thought he slept. But presently he called to me in a feeble voice and, bidding me come near, said—"Alas! the strength I relied on is gone; I feel that I shall soon die, and he, my enemy and persecutor, may still be in being. Think not, Walton, that in the last moments of my existence I feel that burning hatred and ardent desire of revenge that I once expressed; but I feel myself justified in desiring the monster's death. During these last days I have been occupied in examining my past conduct; nor do I find it blameable. In a fit of enthusiastic madness, I created a rational creature and was bound towards him to assure, as far as in me lay, his happiness and well-being. This was my duty, but there was one still paramount to this. My duties towards my fellow-creatures had greater claims because they included a greater portion of happiness or misery. Urged by this view, I refused, and I did right in refusing to create a companion for the first creature. He shewed unparalleled malignity. He destroyed my friends—he devoted to destruction beings who *possessed exquisite* sensations, happiness, and wisdom. Nor do I know where this thirst for vengeance may end. Miserable himself, that he may render no other wretched, he ought to die. The task of his destruction was mine, but I have failed. Once when actuated by selfish and vicious motives, I asked you to undertake my unfinished work; and I renew this request now, when I am only induced to make it by reason and virtue.

"Yet I cannot ask you to renounce your country and friends to fulfil this *task*. And now that you are returning to England, you have little chance of meeting *with* him. But the consideration of these points, and the well-balancing of what you may esteem your duties, I leave to you. My judgement and ideas are already disturbed by *the near approach of* death. I dare not ask you to do what I think right, for I may still be misled by passion.

"That[113] he should live to be the means of misery disturbs me, else this hour when I momentarily expect *my release* is the only happy one I have enjoyed for several years. The forms of the beloved dead flit before me, and I hasten to their arms. Farewell, Walton. Seek happiness in tranquillity and avoid ambition, even if it be only the apparently innocent one of shining in science and discoveries. Yet why do I say this? I have myself been blasted in these hopes, but another may succeed."

His voice became fainter; and, exhausted with *his* effort, he sunk into silence. About half an hour afterwards he endeavoured to speak, but was unable; he pressed my hand feebly, and his eyes closed while a gentle smile played on his lips.

Margaret—What can I say? Can I make any comment on the death of this glorious creature? Alas! all that I can express must be inadequate and feeble. My tears flow. But I journey towards England, and I may there find consolation.

I am interrupted. What do these sounds portend? It is midnight, the breeze blows fairly, and the watch on deck scarcely stir. Again there is a sound, and it comes from the cabin where the remains of Frankenstein still lie. I must *arise* and examine. Good night, my sister.

Great God! What a scene has just taken place. I am yet dizzy with the remembrance of it. I hardly know whether I shall have the power to detail it; yet I will try, for the tale I have recorded is incomplete without this final and wonderful catastrophe.

I entered the cabin where lay the remains of my miserable guest. Over him hung a form which I cannot find words to describe, gigantic in stature, yet uncouth and distorted. His face was hid, as he hung over the coffin, by long locks of ragged hair; but his extended hand appeared like those of the mummies, for to nothing else can I compare its colour and apparent texture. When he heard a noise and saw me enter, he ceased his exclamations of grief and sprung towards the window. Never was any thing so hideous as his face, so disgusting yet appalling. I shut my eyes involuntarily while I called on him to stay. He paused. Looking at me with wonder and then again turning towards the lifeless form of his creator, he seemed to forget my presence, while every feature and gesture seemed instigated by the wildest rage. "That is also my victim," he exclaimed. "In his murder my crimes are consummate. Oh, Frankenstein! Generous and self-devoted creature, dare I ask *thee* to pardon me? I who destroyed thee by destroying those *thou* loved*st*. Alas! he is dead and may not answer me."

His voice seemed suffocated; and my first impulse, which had been to obey the dying request of my friend in destroying his enemy, now *was overwhelmed* in a mixture of curiosity and pity. I approached him, yet I dared not look on him: there was something so scaring and unearthly in his ugliness. I attempted to speak, but the words died away on my lips. The monster continued to utter wild and incoherent self-reproaches. At length I said, "Your repentance is now useless. If you had felt the stings of remorse before you urged your diabolical vengeance to *this* extremity, Frankenstein would yet have lived."

"And do you think," said the dæmon, "that I was then dead to anguish and remorse? He," he continued, pointing to the corpse, "he suffered not more in the completion of the deed than I did in its execution. A frightful selfishness hurried me on while my heart was torn with agony. Think ye that the groans of Clerval were music to my ear? My heart was made for love and sympathy; and, when wrenched by misery to vice and hatred, it did not endure the violence of the change without torture *such as you cannot even imagine*. When Clerval died, I returned to Switzerland heart-broken and overcome. I pitied Frankenstein and his bitter sufferings; my pity amounted to horror; I abhorred myself. But when I saw that he again dared to hope for happiness—that, while he heaped wretchedness and despair on me, he sought his own enjoyment in feelings and passions from the indulgence of which I was for ever barred—I was again roused to indignation and revenge. I remembered my threat and resolved to execute it. Yet when she died—nay, then I was not miserable—I cast off all feeling and all anguish. I rioted in the extent of my despair; and, being urged thus far, I resolved to finish my dæmoniacal design. And it is now ended. There is my last victim."

I was touched by the expressions of his misery, yet I remembered what Frankenstein had said of his eloquence and persuasion; and, when I again cast my eyes on the form of my friend, my indignation was kindled. "Wretch," I said, "it is well that you come here to whine over the misery you have created. You throw a torch among a pile of buildings; and, when they are consumed, you sit amid the ruins and lament their fall. Hypocritical fiend! If he whom you lament still lived, still would you pursue him with your accursed vengeance. It is not pity that you feel—it is sorrow that your power of mischief is annihilated."

"It is not thus," said the dæmon, "and yet such must be your impression, since such appears to have been the purport of my actions. But I do not seek for a fellow-feeling in my misery—I feel it deeply and truly—and for sympathy that I may never find. When I first sought it, it was the love of virtue, it was feelings of happiness and content, that I wished to be participated. But now that virtue is to me merely a shadow, and happiness and content are turned into despair, shall I seek for sympathy in that? No—I am content to suffer alone while I do suffer. And when I die, I am satisfied that hatred and opprobrium should load my memory. Once my fancy was soothed by dreams of virtue, of fame, and of enjoyment. Once I hoped to meet with one who, pardoning my outward form, would love me for the excellent qualities *which* I *was so eminently capable of bringing forth.* I was then filled with high thoughts of honour and self-devotion. But now vice has sunk me below the meanest animal—no crimes can equal mine; and, when I call over the frightful catalogue, I cannot believe that I am he whose thoughts were once filled with sublime and transcendant visions of loveliness. But it is even so. The fallen angel becomes a malignant devil. Yet he, even he, man's enemy, had friends and associates; I am quite alone.

"You who call Frankenstein your friend seem to have a knowledge of my crimes and his misfortunes. But, in the detail that he gave of them, he could not sum up the hours and months of misery that I endured burning with impotent rage. For when I destroyed his hopes, I did not satisfy my own desires. They were as craving and ardent as before. Still I desired love and fellowship, and I was still spurned. Was there no injustice in this? And am I the only criminal, while all mankind sinned against me? Why do you not hate Felix who drove his friend from his door? or the man who would have destroyed the saviour of his child? Nay, they are virtuous and immaculate beings—while I, the miserable and trampled on, am *an abortion* to be spurned and kicked and hated! Even now my blood boils at the memory of this injustice.

"But it is true that I am a wretch. I have murdered the lovely and the helpless. I have seized the innocent as they slept and grasped his throat to death who never injured me. I devoted my creator to misery and have followed him even to his destruction. You hate me, but your abhorrence cannot equal mine for myself. I look on my hands that executed the deed, I think of the heart that formed the plans, and I loathe myself. Fear not that I shall do more mischief; my work is nearly complete. It needs not yours or any man's death to consummate it, but it requires my own. And do not think that I shall be slow to perform that sacrifice. I shall quit your vessel; and, on the ice-raft that brought me, I shall seek the most northern extremity of land that the globe affords. I shall collect my funeral pile and consume myself to ashes, that my remains may afford no light to any curious and unhallowed wretch who would create such another. I shall die. I shall no longer feel the anguish that now consumes me, or be the prey of feelings unsatisfied yet unquenched. He is dead who created me; and when I die, the remembrance of me will be lost for ever. I shall no longer see the sun or stars *or* feel the winds play on my cheeks. Light, feeling, and sense will die. And in this must I find my happiness. Some years ago, when the images this world affords first opened on me, when I felt the cheering warmth of summer and heard the rustling of leaves and the chirping of birds—and these were all to me—I should have wept to die; and now it is my only consolation. Stained by crimes and torn by the bitterest remorse, where can I find rest but in death?

"Farewell; I leave you and, with you, the last of men that these eyes will ever behold. Farewell, Frankenstein! If a desire for revenge remains to you in death, it would be better satisfied in my life than in my destruction. But it was not so. You wished for my extinction that I might not cause greater wretchedness to others, and now you will not desire my life for my own misery. *Blasted* as you were, my agony is superior to yours, for remorse is the bitter sting that rankles in my wounds and tortures me to madness.

"But soon," he cried, clasping his hands, "I shall die, and what I now feel will no longer be felt; soon these thoughts—these burning miseries—will be extinct. I shall ascend my pile triumphantly, and the flame that consumes my body will give *enjoyment or tranquillity* to my mind."

He sprung from the cabin window, as he said this, *upon* an ice-raft that lay close to the vessel; and pushing himself off, he was carried away by the waves, and I soon lost sight of him in the darkness and distance.

NOTES

1 The four initial Walton letters and the first section of Ch. 1 are not in the Draft manuscript, hence the text, punctuation and paragraphing on pp. 44–62 are reproduced from the *1818* first edition—except for the ragged-right margins here introduced for the four letters.

2 The inside address for this and the next three introductory letters is represented without the italics used in *1818*, in which readers would encounter the formatting of '*To Mrs.* SAVILLE, *England*.'

3 This word, italicized in *1818*, is represented here with an underline; italics in this edition of *1816–1817 MWS/PBS* are reserved for PBS words in the text. The word 'keeping' refers to the harmony of elements within the composition of a painting.

4 MWS quotes from and alludes to 'The Rime of the Ancient Mariner' (1798; 1800) by Samuel Taylor Coleridge (1772–1834).

5 Lacking in *1818*, concluding quotation marks are here supplied.

6 The chapter number, Roman numeral 'I.' in *1818*, is here represented as Arabic number '1' in accord with the sequencing and formatting used in this edition based on the *1816–1817 Draft*.

7 The reading in *1818* is 'her', an error that MWS corrected in *1818 Thomas* and subsequent editions.

8 The first word of the extant *1816–1817 Draft*. All text prior to this point (pp. 44–62) is printed from *1818*; hereafter, with one exception (pp. 139–47), this new edition is based on the Draft manuscript, and it represents PBS's contributions in italics.

9 The first of the two places in this paragraph of the Draft where MWS cancelled 'Carignan' (the apparent surname for Henry in the ur-text of the novel) and substituted 'Clerval'. See 'Naming in The *Frankenstein* Notebooks', in *1816–1817 Facsimile*, pp. lvii–lx.

10 MWS frequently altered dates and years in the Draft—and also between the Draft and *1818*—suggesting that she kept and refined a chronology of the action in the novel. In this case, 'eleven years old' in the Draft became 'thirteen years of age' in *1818*, thus making Victor's birth date two years earlier or making him two years older when he first read Agrippa. The latter is more likely; see note 15 below to compare this change in age with the change in age when he experienced the thunderstorm that caused him to devote his life to a study of natural philosophy.

11 Cornelius Agrippa (1486–1535), German writer on the occult and on alchemy.

12 The Swiss Paracelsus (1493–1541) and the German Albertus Magnus (*c.*1193–1280) were philosophers also associated with the occult and alchemy.

13 Alphonse's censure of Agrippa was 'definite' (the reading in the Draft) rather than 'indefinite' (the reading in *1818*).

14 Although MWS's 'distillation' in the Draft is printed as 'Distillation' in *1818*, PBS cancelled the 'di', underlined 'stillation', and wrote two letters or symbols beneath the underline. If the two letters form 'no', PBS may have rejected his alternate word 'stillation' and reverted to the original 'distillation'. But see *1816–1817 Facsimile*, p. 23n, where I once

suggested instead that 'no' might comment on the word 'utterly' immediately below; see also David Ketterer, '"The Wonderful Effects of Steam": More Percy Shelley Words in *Frankenstein*?', *Science-Fiction Studies*, 25 (1998): 566–8, for interpreting the apparent and misformed word 'no' as containing an alchemical symbol for gold that somehow might comment on distillation and the effects of steam. As a final possibility, the two apparent letters of 'n' and 'o' may have been an amateurish attempt to represent either the alchemical symbol for distillation or the separate alchemical symbols for lead and gold.

15 MWS first wrote 'twelve years old' in the Draft, then corrected it to 'fourteen', and eventually printed in *1818* that Victor was 'fifteen' years old during this thunderstorm, thereby changing the year of Victor's birth or making him older when he became interested in natural philosophy. The change from 'fourteen' in Draft to 'fifteen' in *1818* is related to other changes in the chronology of the action—see notes 10, 17, and 18.

16 Both Pliny the Elder (AD 23–79) and George-Louis Leclerc, Comte de Buffon (1707–1788), were famous scientists who wrote extensively about natural history.

17 PBS did not finish his inserted phrase 'the age of', but 'seventeen' is given as Victor's age at this point in *1818*, and MWS specified that Victor was 'seventeen' in the first sentence of Chapter 3 in the Draft.

18 Changed to 'six' years younger in *1818*.

19 The University of Ingolstadt (1472–1800), located on the Danube in Upper Bavaria, had a medical school to which Victor Frankenstein would have been attracted. Moreover, Ingolstadt also suggested progressive or revolutionary thought because the society of the Illuminati had been founded there in 1776.

20 One of the places in the Draft where PBS restored what MWS had cancelled: she had written and then cancelled 'renew the spirit', replacing it with 'cast a gleam', which PBS then cancelled and replaced with 'renew the spirit'.

21 'The Old Familiar Faces' (1798), a poem by Charles Lamb (1775–1834).

22 MWS in the Draft initially wrote 'W.–' and then wrote 'aldham' above the dash; she then wrote the name as 'Waldham' three more times in Chapter 4. In Chapter 5 and throughout *1818*, she spelled the name 'Waldman', the spelling used throughout this edition.

23 PBS wrote this extended passage in pencil, which MWS then inked over; however, MWS chose not to ink over 'natural' in PBS's pencilled phrase of 'modern natural philosophers'. She similarly did not accept PBS's pencilled change of '*expressed to them*' for MWS's 'exhibited' that introduced this extended passage.

24 MWS added these fourteen words from 'I listened' to 'then added' after PBS inserted his remarks on modern philosophers—by adding these transitional remarks, MWS attempted to make PBS's editorial additions seem seamless in her narrative.

25 Although printed as 'petty' in *1818* (also the reading in *1823* and *1831*), 'pretty' (the reading in Draft) is appropriate in an ironic context and is retained here.

26 See Sinbad's fourth voyage in the *Arabian Nights Entertainments*.

27 In the Draft, PBS changed the order of MWS's original phrase 'labour and difficulty'.

28 The double underline emphasizes 'He' and may have instructed the compositor to print the word in small caps.

29 Coleridge's "Ancient Mariner" [*MWS's note*].

30 From Chapter 20 of *The Vicar of Wakefield* (1766) by Oliver Goldsmith (1730–1774).

31 Just above 'the' in the Draft, MWS wrote 'Ch V—113' to indicate the new chapter division in the three-volume Fair Copy (and in *1818*): '113' would have referred to p. 113 in the missing Volume I of the Fair Copy that MWS wrote out in April 1817. Because the

pagination in the Fair Copy was nearly identical to the pagination in *1818*, this sentence begins on p. 114 of Volume I of *1818*.

32 MWS in this chapter of the Draft initially wrote 'Justine Martin' (and 'Mad. Martin' for her mother and 'M. Martin' for her father); of the four references to 'Martin' here, two were cancelled and 'Moritz' substituted. In Chapters 11 and 14 of Volume I, MWS wrote the name as 'Moritz', the name used throughout this edition and in *1818*.

33 The heroine of *Orlando Furioso* (1532) by Ludovico Ariosto (1474–1533).

34 The Draft once again proves that MWS was very mindful of her chronology—she initially wrote May '26' but then immediately cancelled it for '28th', suggesting that she was using a perpetual calendar in order to fix the date of William's death in the year 17[95], when the 28th would have fallen on a Thursday. Although she changed the date in *1818* to May '7th', the date still allows for the year 17[95].

35 MWS in the Draft initially wrote 'four' in the morning, which she then cancelled for 'seven'. *1818* prints the time as 'five in the morning'.

36 Despite embracing a Stoicism that preached emotional control, Marcus Porcius Cato (95–46 BC), denominated Cato the Younger, was devastated by the death of his half-brother Caepio. MWS would have read about Cato in Plutarch's *Lives*, one of the books the monster read.

37 A two-wheeled carriage drawn by one horse.

38 The first of three places in the Draft where Victor specifies that a five-year period had elapsed since his departure from Geneva (see pp. 102 and 104 for the other instances), a period that is changed to six years in *1818*. Again, MWS was clearly concerned about the chronology in her narrative.

39 In the margin to her Draft, MWS wrote but then cancelled 'Lord Byron', thereby not publicly identifying this phrase from *Childe Harold's Pilgrimage*, Canto III (1816), stanza 62.

40 The second of three places in the Draft where Victor specifies that a five-year period had elapsed since his departure from Geneva (see pp. 98 and 104 for the other instances), a period that is changed to six years in *1818*.

41 The reading in the Draft is 'Caroline Beaumont' rather than 'Caroline Beaufort', the name printed here and throughout Volume I, Chapter 1, in *1818*. MWS could have miswritten 'Beaumont' here, or later changed the name in the Fair Copy or proofs for *1818*.

42 MWS in the Draft mistakenly wrote 'Myrtella', which PBS later cancelled for 'Elizabeth'. This is the first of the two places where MWS wrote 'Myrtella' (which may have been the name for Elizabeth in the ur-text of the novel)—see 'Naming in The *Frankenstein* Notebooks', in *1816–1817 Facsimile*, pp. lvii–lx.

43 The third of three places in the Draft where Victor specifies that a five-year period had elapsed since his departure from Geneva (see pp. 98 and 102 for the other instances), a period that is changed to six years in *1818*.

44 Compare Satan and 'the hot hell that always in him burns' in Milton's *Paradise Lost*, IX.467.

45 The end of Volume I in *1818*.

46 MWS and PBS left records of a similar journey they took to the valley of Chamonix in late July 1816—see Michael Erkelenz (ed.), *The Geneva Notebook of Percy Bysshe Shelley: Bodleian MS. Shelley adds. e. 16 and MS. Shelley adds. c. 4, Folios 63, 65, 71, and 72*, The Bodleian Shelley Manuscripts, Volume XI (New York: Garland, 1992), pp. 98–101; *The Letters of Percy Bysshe Shelley*, ed. Frederick L. Jones (Oxford: Clarendon Press, 1964),

I.495–502; MWS *Journal*, pp. 112–21; and MWS, *History of a Six Weeks' Tour through a Part of France, Switzerland, Germany, and Holland: with Letters Descriptive of a Sail round the Lake of Geneva, and of the Glaciers of Chamouni* (London: T. Hookham, Jun., and C. and J. Ollier, 1817), pp. 141–72. See also notes 52 and 100 below.

47 Mountain peaks.

48 MWS in the Draft mistakenly wrote 'Myrtella', which she then cancelled for 'My father & Elizabeth'—see note 42 above.

49 According to the *OED*, 'necessary' in opposition to 'free': 'Impelled by the natural force of circumstances upon the will; having no independent volition', an obsolete definition of 'necessary' (*OED* III.8.a&b).

50 Although printed as 'word' in *1818* (also the reading in *1823* and *1831*), 'wind' (the reading in Draft) is more appropriate in this context and is retained here.

51 The third and fourth stanzas of PBS's 'Mutability', published in *Alastor; or, The Spirit of Solitude: and Other Poems* (London: Baldwin, Cradock, and Joy, 1816), pp. 59–60. Because the punctuation and formatting of these lines are different in the Draft and in *Alastor*, I here print the lines as they appear in *1818*, for which the Shelleys read and corrected proofs.

52 MWS called the 'Mer de Glace', the glacier that the Shelleys visited during their excursion to Chamonix and the Alps in July 1816, 'the most desolate place in the world' (MWS *Journal*, p. 119)—very fitting for the meeting between Victor and his monster.

53 PBS's pencilled 'no' inked over by MWS.

54 PBS cancelled MWS's phrasing, pencilled in his suggested revisions, some but not all of which MWS inked over to accept. In effect, MWS edited PBS's prose after he edited her prose.

55 PBS in pencil cancelled MWS's misspelled 'igmmatic', replaced it with 'enigmatic' (later inked over by MWS), and addressed MWS with her pet name, 'o you pretty Pecksie!'

56 The word 'cottagers', the reading in *1818*, is conjectural and barely perceptible in the Draft.

57 MWS's word 'unrable', unnecessarily changed to 'unravel' in *1818*, is a perfectly good word: it is based on 'rable', meaning to speak in a rapid and confusing manner (*OED*). MWS had initially written 'unrable the mystery of their sounds'.

58 There is a noticeable 'trauma' to the text at this point: the rest of Chapter 3 (from the word 'that') and all of Chapter 4 are not in the Draft manuscript—hence the text on these pages (139-47) is printed from *1818* (with any variation noted). This missing section in the Draft that deals with the monster learning to speak and read (possibly resulting from PBS's direct advice on linguistic matters) is followed in the Draft by two sets of Inserts ('X' and 'Y', a total of eleven rewritten pages) denominated 'another Chapter [Chapter 5]' by PBS and recasting the narrative about the involvement of the De Lacey family with Safie and her father in Paris. 'Safie', whose name first appears in Chapter 4 (for which there is no Draft) and then reappears in Insert 'Y' of Chapter 5, initially appears in Insert 'X' as 'Maimouna', then 'Amina', and finally 'Safie'. MWS's cancellations of the other two names give evidence for dating these Inserts (see *1816–1817 Facsimile*, pp. 317–19). These two Inserts (on pages not sequentially linked to the rest of the narrative in Notebook A) also serve as the bridge between Notebook A and the beginning of Chapter 6 that starts Notebook B in the Draft.

59 These words, italicized in *1818*, are represented here with an underline; italics in this edition of *1816-1817 MWS/PBS* are reserved for PBS words in the text.

60 The chapter number 'V' that precedes this sentence in *1818* is here represented as Arabic

number '4' in accord with the sequencing and formatting used in this edition based on the *1816–1817 Draft.*

61 The compositor in *1818* mistakenly omitted the double quotation marks at the beginning of this and three other paragraphs in this chapter (the next two paragraphs and the paragraph beginning 'While I ...').

62 This title, italicized in *1818*, is represented here with an underline; italics in this edition of *1816–1817 MWS/PBS* are reserved for PBS words in the text.

63 Spelled with lower case in *1818*—changed here to 'Christianity' in accord with the spelling used elsewhere in this edition of *1816–1817 MWS/PBS.*

64 The extant *1816–1817 Draft* resumes with this sentence, following the missing section that deals with the monster learning to speak and read (see note 58). This new 'Chapter 5' is unnumbered in the Draft, it begins on the first page of Insert 'Y' to Notebook A, and it is designated 'another Chapter' by PBS, a heading he supplied as he was reading MWS's Insert 'Y' (which revised and replaced portions of her Insert 'X')—see the textual commentary in *1816–1817 Facsimile*, pp. 317, 319.

65 The first sentence of an unnumbered chapter (here designated Chapter 6) that begins Notebook B of the Draft.

66 Milton, *Paradise Lost* (1667; 1674); Plutarch (46–?120), *Parallel Lives*; J. W. von Goethe (1749–1832), *The Sorrows of Young Werter* (1774; first translated into English in 1779).

67 Adaptation of line 14 of PBS's 'Mutability', published in *Alastor; or, The Spirit of Solitude*, p. 60—see also note 51. The quotation is followed by a *signe de renvoi* in the Draft, but there is no explicit identification of the quotation or its author in the margin or on the page.

68 The monster read biographies of each in Plutarch's *Parallel Lives.*

69 See the epigraph from *Paradise Lost* on the title page of the novel in Appendix A below.

70 This phrase means that it was still autumn, which 'advanced towards winter'. MWS had originally written the 'season advanced'; the 'entire revolution of the seasons' since his creation would make it November; and in the next chapter the monster recalled that he left the cottage 'late in autumn' (see p. 164), that is, late November or early December, a year after his creation.

71 Nets or a snare that entraps wild beasts.

72 Recalling Milton's *Paradise Lost*, IV.20.

73 Although printed as 'forced impatience' in *1818* (also the reading in *1823* and *1831*), 'forced patience' (the reading in Draft) is appropriate in this context and is retained here.

74 Echoing 'The World was all before them' and 'with wand'ring steps and slow/ Through Eden took their solitary way' from the conclusion of Milton's *Paradise Lost*, XII.646, 648–69.

75 At this point in the Draft, MWS revealed her concern for chapter divisions as she brought the monster's actions to a climax: she finished Chapter 8 in the middle of p. 87 of Notebook B (the chapter already nine manuscript pages long) and headed p. 88 with 'Chap. 9th', but she soon thereafter wrote at the bottom of the text on p. 87 'The same chapter continued'; she then cancelled the chapter heading on p. 88, and continued Chapter 8 for three more pages through to p. 90. She then on p. 91 wrote 'Chap. 9th' and began with the words, 'The creature finished speaking ...' (see *1816–1817 Facsimile*, pp. 392–401).

76 The Draft reading of 'thousand thousand' that acts as an intensifier was ultimately printed as 'thousand' in *1818.*

77 Although printed as 'them' in *1818* (also the reading in *1823* and *1831*), 'then' (the reading in Draft) is appropriate in this context and is retained here.

78 Changed to 'South America' in *1818*.

79 Variant spelling of sirocco, an oppressively hot wind that blows from North Africa over the Mediterranean and Southern Europe.

80 See *The Divine Comedy* by Dante Alighieri (1265–1321), specifically the *Inferno*, Canto 23: the hypocrites in hell actually wear 'leaden' caps and hoods.

81 The end of Volume II in *1818*.

82 MWS wrote this and the preceding sentence sometime between 9 and 17 April 1817 (when she was making her final corrections to the Draft), as evidenced by the sentences being drafted on the verso of the address leaf of a letter from William Godwin to MWS that was postmarked 9 April 1817. This important passage, which emphasizes Victor's own initiative in travelling to England, results from PBS's advice to MWS on p. 100 of Volume II of the Draft: 'I think the journey to England ought to be Victor's proposal.—that he ought to go for the purpose of collecting knowledge, for the formation of a female. He ought to lead his father to this in the conversations—the conversation commences right enough.' MWS followed PBS's advice, inserted this important passage about 'obtaining my father's consent', cancelled two-and-a-half pages of the original Draft in which Alphonse had been the one to suggest that Victor accompany Clerval to England, and then drafted four-and-a-quarter substitute pages (some of which directly rework phrasing from the cancelled pages). For further information on this substitute text, see the following note; see also *1816–1817 Facsimile*, pp. xlii, 416–41.

83 The substitute pages, occasioned by MWS accepting PBS's suggestion that Victor propose the trip to England, begin with 'But it is this gloom' in this paragraph and extend for five additional paragraphs, at which point the original Draft resumes with the paragraph beginning 'It was in the latter end of August ...'.

84 The Shelleys alluded to this same legend in *History of a Six Weeks' Tour*, pp. 48–9, which was published eight weeks before *Frankenstein*.

85 This and most of the next paragraph (both of which repeat the substance of a description of Holland in *History of a Six Weeks' Tour*, pp. 74–7) survived in the text of the novel until the proof stage in late October 1817, at which point paragraphs lamenting Clerval's death were substituted. For information on this substitution, see *1816–1817 Facsimile*, pp. xc–xci (the entry for 24 October 1817).

86 Variant spelling of 'postilion', the person riding the horse drawing the carriage.

87 The 'latter *days* of September' is consistent with Victor's remark in the next chapter that he 'arrived in England [meaning London] at the beginning of October' (see p. 182)—but note the error and inconsistency in *1818* that specifies seeing the 'white cliffs' in the 'latter days of December' (Volume III, Chapter 1, page 20).

88 The chapter number '11' that precedes this sentence in *1816–1817 Draft* is renumbered by MWS as chapter '2' to indicate its position in Volume III of the reconfigured three-volume novel in Fair Copy and in *1818*.

89 Most of the remaining part of this paragraph and most of the following paragraph survived in the text of the novel until the proof stage in late October 1817, at which point paragraphs defining Victor's fall from his youthful idealism were substituted. That text contained a description of John Hampden's monument that was based on MWS's visit there on 20 October 1817. For information on this substitution, see *1816–1817 Facsimile*, pp. xc–xci (the entries for 20 and 24 October 1817).

90 Edward Gibbon (1737–1794), best known for his *History of the Decline and Fall of the Roman*

Empire (1776–88), had complained in his memoirs about the bigotry, idleness and lack of discipline at Oxford University during his fourteen months at Magdalen College in 1752–53. The Shelleys had read *Miscellaneous Works of Edward Gibbon, Esq., with Memoirs of his Life and Writings Composed by Himself* (1796)—see entries on and around 2 February 1815, MWS *Journal*, p. 62.

91 PBS had been expelled from Oxford in March 1811 after publishing *The Necessity of Atheism*. MWS may have been recalling what she learned about Oxford when she visited there with PBS, her stepbrother Charles Clairmont, and Thomas Love Peacock at the end of summer in 1815, when they 'saw the Bodleian Library, the Clarendon Press, & walked through Quadrangles of the different Colleges'—see *Clairmont Correspondence*, vol. I, p. 14. This letter from Charles Clairmont to his sister Claire Clairmont, dated 13–20 September 1815, also anticipates elements of *Frankenstein*: 'We visited the very rooms where the two noted Infidels [Percy] Shelley and [Thomas Jefferson] Hogg ... poured with the incessant & unwearied application of an Alchemyst over the artificial & natural boundaries of human knowledge; brooded over the perceptions which were the offspring of their villainous & impudent penetration & even dared to threaten the World with the horrid & diabolical project of telling mankind to open its eye. I am sure you will duely apreciate the sagacity & rigid justice of the directors, whose anxiety for the commonweal led them to excommunicate such impious monsters.'

92 This important reference dates the action of the novel in the early or mid-1790s—that is, a century and a half earlier in 1642, Charles I (1600–1649) had withdrawn his forces to Oxford during the English Civil War. (MWS initially wrote 'above a century before'; she then altered it to 'above two centuries before'; then PBS corrected the phrase to 'above a century *and a half* before'.)

93 'Gower' in the Draft and *1818*. In *1823* and *1831*, the name was corrected to 'Goring', namely George, Baron Goring (1608–1657), a general who supported Charles I, whose 'amiable' secretary of state was Lucius Carey, second Viscount Falkland (1610–1643).

94 The Clarendon Press or Clarendon Building, home at the time of Oxford University Press and named after Edward Hyde, first Earl of Clarendon, whose *History of the Rebellion and Civil Wars in England* (1702–04) MWS had read in September–October 1816—see MWS *Journal*, pp. 137–42.

95 MWS had initially written in the Draft 'Lord Chancellor Bacon', but corrected the name after PBS addressed her in the margin: 'no sweet Pecksie—'twas friar Bacon the discoverer of gunpowder'—namely Roger Bacon (1214–?1292).

96 When MWS decided to transform the two-volume novel into a three-volume novel, she wrote 'Finish Chap. 2 here' at the end of this paragraph (where, in fact, Chapter 2 of Volume III ends in *1818*). See also note 88 above.

97 More likely the winter assizes in that Victor's release a fortnight after the trial allowed him to reach Havre by 8 February, well before the spring assizes. But because MWS changed the arrival date in Havre from '8 February' to '8 May', her redoing of the chronology allows for the trial at the spring assizes.

98 The Draft again demonstrates MWS's concern for chronology: she initially wrote '8th of February' but then changed 'February' to 'May'—see previous note.

99 MWS initially wrote 'Feb. 18' but changed the date of Elizabeth's letter to 'May 18'.

100 Although the words from 'observed' to the end of the paragraph are in MWS's hand, they are nearly a verbatim transcription of PBS's description of the same scene in the Geneva Notebook from his June 1816 tour with Lord Byron—see Erkelenz, *The Geneva Notebook*, pp. 126–7; and *1816–1817 Facsimile*, p. lxxix, and p. 561 and n.

101 MWS in the Draft correctly wrote 'now' but in the Fair Copy incorrectly wrote 'no', which was corrected in the Fair Copy by an unidentified hand to 'Know', the reading in *1818*—see *1816–1817 Facsimile*, pp. 572–3, 690–91.

102 MWS's apparent misreading of PBS's syntactically incomplete rephrasing ('To you *are fast* entering on life, & care *is new to you*') as 'To you *first* entering on life, & care *is new to you*' caused MWS to rewrite the phrase in the Fair Copy: 'To you first entering on life to whom care is new', the reading in *1818*—see *1816–1817 Facsimile*, pp. 716–17.

103 Spirits of the dead.

104 The reading of 'August 13th' in the Draft is here altered to 'August 26th' in keeping with readings in the Fair Copy and in *1818*. This emendation to the Draft is necessary because Walton wrote to his sister on 19 August (see the introductory Letter IV) that Victor would 'commence his narrative the next day', thus indicating that a week elapsed during the narrative and its transcription between 20 and 26 August—see note 105 below.

105 The reading of 'have ten days' in the Draft is here altered to 'has a week' (the reading in the Fair Copy and in *1818*) in keeping with Victor beginning his narrative on 20 August and concluding it on 26 August—see note 104 above.

106 The reading of 'August 27th' corrected to 'August 31th' in the Draft is here altered to 'September 2d.' (the reading in *1818*) in keeping with the other date changes in this final chapter.

107 Lucius Annaeus Seneca (*c.*4 BC–AD 65), Roman Stoic and natural philosopher.

108 The reading of 'September 6th' in the Draft is here altered to 'September 5th' (the reading in *1818*) in keeping with the other date changes in this final chapter.

109 Although MWS initially wrote 'England', PBS changed the destination to '*Archangel*', whence the ship originated. The Fair Copy is not extant for this page, but *1818* begs the question by the phrase 'direct my course southward'.

110 MWS in the Draft first wrote '17th' but changed the date to '12th' by superimposing a '2' over the previously written '7'.

111 Again, MWS wrote 'England', and PBS corrected it to '*Archangel*'. Although the Fair Copy is not extant, 'England' is the restored reading in *1818*. Walton could have taken a route back to England, but it would have been more in keeping for him to return to Archangel, where he had hired the ship and engaged the crew. However, PBS seems to concede the plot direction (or to give up making the changes), for he does not challenge or change any of the four remaining references to returning to England—moreover, when he fair-copied the last pages of the Draft, he wrote 'England' as the point of destination.

112 This date of 'September 9th' within the 'September 12th' entry (for which there is no Fair Copy evidence) was apparently read by a compositor as a date 'of' an entry and incorrectly changed to 'September 19th' in *1818* so that it would postdate the entry of 'September 12th'.

113 From this point until the end of the novel, this edition of the Draft retains MWS's (or Walton's and the monster's) original voice; this same concluding text in *1818* is dominated more by PBS's voice, for he fair-copied and embellished the last twelve-and-three-quarter pages of the Draft. For an explanation of this collaboration and a comparison of these Draft and Fair Copy texts, see *1816–1817 Facsimile*, pp. lxxxv, 810–17.

occupation. The leaves of that year
were withered before my work drew
near a close, and now every day shewed
me more plainly how well I had succeeded. But my enthusiasm was
checked by my ~~ann~~ anxiety and I appeared
rather like one doomed by slavery
to toil in the mines or any other
unwholsome trade than an artist
occupied in his favourite employment.
Every ~~day~~ night a slow fever oppressed
me and I became ~~nervous~~ nervous to a ~~degree~~
most painful degree; a ~~fever~~ a disease I regretted the more because I had
hitherto enjoyed excellent health &
~~my nerves were fi~~ had always
boasted of ~~my~~ the firmness of my nerves. But I
believed that exercise and amusement
would soon ~~dri~~ drive away ~~these~~ such symptoms and I promised myself both
of these when my creation should be
compleated. ~~I had then determined to~~
~~go to Geneva as soon as this should be~~
~~done and a in the midst of my~~
~~family find ease~~

Mary Shelley

NOTE ON THE TEXT

The following version of *Frankenstein*, which is based on the *1816–1817 Draft*, presents a text that removes PBS's interventions from the novel. To that end, all words, phrases and sentences that PBS added to the Draft notebooks are eliminated, and all MWS words, phrases and sentences that PBS cancelled are restored. Nearly all of the punctuation in the Draft is represented here, even if redundant or misplaced, and whether supplied by MWS or PBS.

In order to suggest what MWS brought to the writer's table, as it were, this new text of *Frankenstein* reproduces MWS's text as faithfully as possible: MWS's word order and paragraphing are followed; misspellings are retained if the intended word is recognizable; the minimal punctuation and sometimes inconsistent capitalization are reproduced, although I eliminate the running quotation marks in the left margin that MWS occasionally used for an extended quotation. Whenever the reader might be confused by the text, an editorial apparatus supplies missing letters, words and punctuation in angle brackets; identifies redundant or misplaced words and punctuation in curly brackets; and provides commentary on the manuscript Draft in square brackets. All of these editorial interventions are kept at a minimum so that the reader can more directly experience MWS's narrative voice in *1816–1817 MWS* and have a base text by which to evaluate the reading text of *1816–1817 MWS*/PBS in this volume.

The running foots in this *1816–1817 MWS* text are keyed to the reading text of *1816–1817 MWS*/PBS so that the reader can compare the two texts and thereby better understand the Shelleys' collaboration and the editorial processes that ultimately led to the 'finished' Draft of *Frankenstein*. Notes supplied for the reading text of *1816–1817 MWS/PBS* are not repeated below, but a few daggered footnotes explain irregularities in the Draft.

<word>—missing word supplied to complete sense (supplied words come from PBS emendations, from MWS words mistakenly cancelled, or from text of *1818*, *1823* or *1831*)

<part of word>—letters supplied to prevent confusion resulting from an incorrectly spelled word or from a word with letters torn from the manuscript

<punctuation>—punctuation supplied to prevent syntactical or grammatical confusion in MWS text

{word}—redundant or misplaced word that needs to be cancelled to prevent confusion

{part of word}—incorrectly added letters that need to be cancelled to prevent a word from being misunderstood

{punctuation}—incorrectly added or placed punctuation that needs to be cancelled to prevent syntactical or grammatical confusion

[*for* word]—word supplied that otherwise might not be understood by MWS's spelling

[?word]—conjectural word

[*editorial comment*]—comment on the Draft manuscript

Frankenstein

or

The Modern Prometheus

VOLUME I

Chapter 1

servants had any request to make it <was> always through her intercession[†] We agreed perfectly although there was a great dissimilitude in our characters. I was more calm and philosphical than my companion Yet I was not so mild or yielding. My application was of longer endurance but it was not so severe as hers while it lasted<:> my amusements were studying old books of chemistry and natural magic<;> those of Elizabeth were drawing & music.

My brothers were considerably younger than myself but I had a friend in one of my schoolfellows who compensated for this. Henry Clerval was the son of a merchant of Geneva and an intimate friend of my father's—he was a boy of singular talent & fancy<.> I remember when he was only nine years old he wrote a fairy tale which was the delight and amazement of all his companions. Like Don Quixote his favourite study was books of chivalry & romance and we used to act plays composed by him out of his favourite books, the principal characters of which were Orlando<,> Robin Hood, Amadis and St. George—No youth could {could} be more happy than mine.—My parents were indulgent, and my companions amiable. Our studies were never forced, and by some means we always had an end placed in view which excited us to ardour. It was by this & not by emulation that we were urged. Elizabeth was not told to apply herself to drawing or her companions would outstrip her, but she knew how pleased her Aunt would be by a painting

† For the four introductory Walton letters in the frame tale and for the beginning of Chapter 1, all of which are missing from the Draft manuscript (which begins with this unpunctuated sentence), see pp. 44–62 in this edition.

Compare p. 62

of some of her favourite scenes done by her own hand. We learned Latin & English to read the writers of those languages and so far from study being rendered odious to us through punishment, we loved application and our amusements were the labours of other children. perhaps we did not read so many books or learn languages so quickly as another child but what we learned was impressed on our memory. In this description of our domestic circle I include Henry Clerval, for he was constantly with us. he went to school with me and generally passed the afternoon at our house for being an only child, and destitute of companions at home, his father was pleased that he should find associates at our house and we were never completely happy when Clerval was absent.

Chapt. 2

Those events which materially influence our future destinies are often caused by slight or trivial occurences. Natural philosophy is the genius that has regulated my fate<.> I wish therefore in this account of my early years to state those facts which led to my predeliction for that science. When I was eleven years old we all went on a party of pleasure to the baths near Thonon and the inclemency of the weather obliged us to remain a day confined to the inn. In this house I chanced to find a volume of the works of Cornelius Agrippa. I opened it with apathy<;> the theory that he attempted to demonstrate and the wonderful facts that he relates soon changed this feeling into enthusiasm. A new light dawned upon my mind and bounding with joy I communicated my discovery to my father. I cannot help here remarking the many opportunities instructors have of directing the attention of their pupils to useful knowledge, which they utterly neglect. My father looked carelessly at the title page of my book—and said Ah! Cornelius Agrippa!—My dear Victor do not waste your

 Compare pp. 62–4

time upon this—it is sad trash. If instead of this remark or rather exclamation my father had taken the pains to explain to me that the principles of Agrippa had been entirely exploded{.} and that a modern system of science had been introduced which possessed much greater power than the ancient because the powers of the ancient were pretended and chimerical, while those of the moderns are real and practical; Under such circumstances I should certainly have thrown Agrippa aside, and with my imagination warmed as it was should probably have aplied myself to the more rational theory of chemistry which has at present the approbation of the learned. But the cursory glance my father had taken of my volume by no means assured me that he was acquainted with its contents; and I continued to read with the greatest avidity.

When I returned home, my first care was to procure the works of this author and afterwards those of Paracelsus and Albertus Magnus. I read and studi<ed> the wild fancies of the authors with delight, they appeared to me treasures known to few besides myself; and, althoug<h> I often wished to discover these secret stores of knowledge to my father yet his definite censure of my favorite Agrippa, always withheld me. I disclosed my secret to Elizabeth therefore, under a strict promise of secrecy; but she did not interest herself in them and I was left by her to pursue my studies alone.—

It may appear very strange that a desciple of Albertus Magnus should arise in the eighteenth century, but our family was not scientifical, and I did not attend any of the lectures given at Geneva. My dreams were therefore undisturbed by reality, and I entered with the greates<t> diligence into the search of the philosophers stone and the elizer vitæ. But the latter obtained my most undived [*for* undivided] attention; wealth was an inferior object but what would be the glory of the discovery if I could banish disease from the human frame and render man invunerable to any but violent death.

Compare pp. 64–5

Nor were these my only visions; the raising of ghosts or devils was also a favourite pursuit and If I never saw any I attributed it rather to my own inexperience and mistake, than want of skill in my instructor.

The natural phænonema that takes place every day before our eyes did not escape my exanimations. distillation of which my favorite authors were utterly ignorant excited my astonishment, but my utmost wonder was caused by an air pump which I saw used by a gentleman whom we were in the habit of visiting.

The ignorance of my philosopheres on these and several other points, served to decrease credit with me—but I could not entirely throw them aside before any other system occupied their place.

When I was about fourteen years old we were at our house near Belrive when we witnessed {the} a violent at [*for* and] terrible thunder storm<.> it advanced from behind Jura and the thunder burst at once with frightful loudness from various quarters of the heavens. I {and} remained while it lasted at the door watching its {its} progress with curiosity & delight. When it was most violent, I beheld the fire issue from an old and beautiful oak about twenty yards from our house and when the dazzling light vanished, the oak had dissapeared an [*for* and] nothing remained but a blasted stump. When we visited it the next morning we found the tree shattered in a singular manner. It was not splintered by the shock, but entirely reduced to thin ribands of wood. I never saw any thing so utterly destroyed. The catastrophe of the tree excited my extreme astonishment.

And I eagerly enquired of my father what thunder and lightning was. He replied, electricity; describing at the same time the effect of that power. He made a small electrical machine and exhibited a few experiments and made a kite with a wire string and drew down that fluid from the clouds.

This last stroke compleated the overthrow of Cornelius Agrippa, Albertus Magnus and Paracelsus, who had so long reigned the lords

Compare pp. 65–6

of my imagination. But by some fatality I did not feel enclined to commence any modern system and this inclination was influenced by the following circumstance.

My father expressed a wish that I should attend a course of lectures upon natural philosophy, to which I consented and one evening that I spent in town at the house of Clerval's father I met M. P<,> a proficient in Chemistry who left the company at an early hour to give his lecture upon that science enquiring as he went out if any one would go with him—I went but this lecture was unfortunately nearly the last in his course—the professor talked with the greatest fluency of potassium & Boron—of sulphats and oxids and displayed so many words to which I could not affix any idea: that I was disgusted with a science that appeared to me to contain only words.

From this time untill I went to Colledge I entirely neglected my formerly adored study of the science of chemistry although I still read with delight Pliny and Buffon{s} authors that stood about on a par in my estimation

My occupations at this age were principally the mathematics, and most of the branches of study appertaining to that science. I was also busily employed in learning languages Latin was familiar to me and I began to read without the help of the dictionary some of the easiest greek authors.—I also understood English & german perfectly: this is <a> list of my accomplishments at that time and you may conceive that my hours were fully employed in acquiring and maintaining a knowledge of this various literature.

Another task also devolved upon me when I became the instructor of my brothers. Ernest was five years younger than myself, and was my principal pupil. He had been aflicted with ill health from his infancy & Elizabeth and I had been his constant nurses<;> his disposition was gentle but he was incapable <of> any severe application. William the younger of our family was quite a child and the most beautiful little fellow in the world, his lively

Compare pp. 66–7

blue eyes dimpled cheeks and endearing manners inspired the tenderest affection. Such was our domestic circle from which care and pain seemed for ever banished. My father directed our studies and my mother partook of our enjoyments. neither of us possessed an envied preheminence over the other<,> the voice of command was never heard among us<,> but mutual affection engaged us all to comply with & obey the slightest desire of each other.

Chapter 3

When I had attained the age of seventeen my parents resolved that I should go to the university of Ingolstadt. I had hitherto attended the schools of Geneva, but my father thought it necessary for the completion of my education that I should be acquainted with other customs besides those of my native country. My departure was therefore fixed at an early date. But before the day resolved upon could arrive the first misfortune of my life occurred: as if an omen of my future misery if I should prosecute my journey.

Elizabeth had caught the scarlet fever but her illness was not severe and she quickly recovered. During her confinement many arguments had been urged to persuade my mother not to attend upon her. She had yielded to these but when she heard that her favourite was recovering, she would no longer debar herself from her society, and entered her sick chamber long before it was safe. The consequences of this imprudence were fatal: on the third day my mother sickened. Her fever was very malignant, and the looks of her attendants prognosticated the worst evil. On her death bed the fortitude and benignity of my mother did not desert her. She joined the hands of Elizabeth and myself. "My children said she it was on your union that my firmest hopes of future happiness were placed. It will now be the consolation of your father. Elizabeth,

 Compare pp. 67–8

my love, supply my place to your young cousins. Alas! I almost regret being taken from you, and happy and beloved, as I am is it not hard to quit you all? But these are not thoughts befitting me I will endeavour to resign myself cheerfully to death and will indulge a hope my beloved creatures of meeting you in another world."

She died calmly and her features expressed affection even in death. I need not describe the feelings of those whose dearest ties are rent by that most irreperable evil; the void that every where presents itself to the soul—and the despair that is exhibited on the countenance. It is so long before the mind can persuade itself that she, whom they saw every day, and whose very existence appeared a part of theirs, can have departed for ever: That the brightness of a loved eye can have faded and the sound of a voice so familiar and dear to the ear can be hushed, never more to be heard. These are the reflections of the first days. But when the lapse of time proves the reality of the evil then the bitterness of grief commences. But who has not had some dear connection rent away by that rude hand and why need I describe a sorrow which all have felt, and must feel? But the time at length arrives when grief is rather an indulgence than a necessity and the smile that plays on the lips, although it is deemed sacriledge, is not Banished.—My mother was dead but we had still duties which we ought to perform we must continue our course with the rest & bless God if nothing worse happens. And the idleness generated by grief would become a bad habit if further indulged

My journey to Ingolstadt which had been deferred by these events was now again determined upon, and all that I could obtain from my father was respite of some weeks. This time was spent sadly. My mothers death and my speedy departure depressed our spirits but Elizabeth endeavoured to cast a gleam of cheerfullness in our little society. Since the death of her aunt her mind had acquired new firmness and vigour. She determined to fulfil her duties with

Compare pp. 68–9

the greatest exactitude and her most imperious duty was to render her uncle and cousins happy. She consoled me, amused her uncle, instructed my brothers and I never beheld her so enchanting as at this time when she was continually endeavouring to contribute to the happiness of others entirely forgetful of herself.

The day of my departure at lenghth arrived—I had taken leave of all my friends excepting Clerval, who spent the last evening with us. He bitterly lamented that he was not able to accompany me But his father could not bear to part with him<;> besides he intended him to become a partner with him in his business, and he said he did not see of what use learning could be to a merchant. Henry had a refined mind he did not wish to be idle and was well pleased to become his father's partner but he believed that a man might be a very good trader and yet have a cultivated understanding.

We sate late listening to his complaints, and making many little arrangements for the future. The next morning early I departed. Tears gushed from the eyes of Elizabeth they proceeded partly from sorrow at my departure, and partly because she reflected that the same journey was to have taken place three months before when a mothers blessing would have accompanied me

I threw myself into the chaise that was to convey me away and indulged in the most melancholy reflections. I who had ever been surrounded by amiable companions, continually engaged in endeavouring to give mutual pleasure; I was now alone. In the university whither I was going I must form my own friends and be my own introduction. My life had hitherto been remarkably retired and domestic and this had given me an invincible repugnance to new countenances. I loved my brothers Elizabeth and Clerval these were "old familiar faces" but I believed myself totally unfitted for the company of strangers. Such were my reflections as I commenced my journey But as I proceeded my spirits and hopes rose. I ardently desired knowledge and I often when at home thought how hard it was to remain during my youth cooped up in one place and longed

 Compare pp. 69–70

to enter into the world and take my station among other human beings. And now my desires were complyd with & it would indeed be folly to repent.

I had plenty of leisure for these and many other reflections during my journey to Ingolstadt which was long and fatiguing—at length the steeples of the town met my eyes. I alighted and was conducted to my solitary apartment to spend the evening as I pleased.

Chap. 4

The next morning I delivered my letters of introduction and paid a visit to some of the principal professors. and among others to M. Krempe Professor of natural philosophy. He received me with politeness, and asked me several questions concerning my progress in the different branches of science appertaining to natural philosophy. I mentioned, it is true with fear and trembling, the only authors I had ever read upon those subjects. The professor stared. "Have you really" said he "spent your time in studying such nonsence?" I replied in the affirmative.

"Every minute"—continued M. Krempe with warmth, "every instant that you have wasted upon those books is utterly and entirely lost. You have burdened your memory with exploded systems and useless names. Good God in what desart land have you lived where no one was kind enough to inform you that these fancies which you have so greedily imbibed are a thousand years old and as musty as they are ancient. I little expected in this enlightened and scientific age to find a disciple of Albertus Magnus and Paracelsus. My dear sir you must begin your studies entirely anew." So saying he stessed [*for* stepped] aside, and wrote down a list of several books upon natural philosophy which he desired me to procure and

Compare pp. 70–71

dismissed me after mentioning that in the beginning of the next week he intended to commence a course of lectures upon natural philosophy and that M. Waldham a fellow professor would lecture upon chemistry the alternate days which he missed.

I returned home not dissapointed for I had long considered the authors useless which the professor had so strongly reprobated—but I did not feel very much enclined to study those books which at his recommondation I had procured. M. Krempe was a little squat man with a gruff voice and repulsive countenance and the teacher did not prepossess me in favour of his science. Besides I had a contempt for the uses of modern natural philosophy. It was very different when the masters of the science sought immortality and wealth;—such views although futile were grand; but now it was all changed. and the expulsion of chimera overthrew at the same time all greatness in the science

Such were my reflections during two or three days spent almost in solitude: but as the ensueing week commenced I thought of the information Mr. Krempe had given me concerning the lectures. and although I could not consent to go and hear that little conceited fellow deliver sentences out of a pulpit I recollected what he had said of Mr. Waldham, whom I had never seen as he had been hitherto out of town.

Partly from curiosity and partly from idleness I went into the lecturing room which Mr. Waldham entered shortly after. This Professor was a very different man from his colleague. He was about fifty but with aspect expressive of the greatest benevolence<;> a few grey hairs covered his temples but those at the back of his head were nearly black. He was short in person but remarkably erect and his voice the sweetest I had ever heard. He began his lecture with a kind of history of chemistry and the various improvements made by various men of learning pronoucing with fervour the names of the greatest discoverers. He then took a cursory view of the present state of chemistry and explained many of its terms made a

 Compare pp. 71–2

few preparatory experiments and concluded with a panegyric upon modern chemistry the words of which I shall never forget.

"The ancient teachers of this science" said he, "promised impossibilities and performed nothing. The modern masters promise very little. They know that metals cannot be transmuted and that the elixir of life is a chimæra. But these philosophers whose hands appear only made to dabble in dirt and their eyes to pore over the microscope or cruscible, have indeed performed miracles. They penetrate into the recesses of nature and show how she works in her hiding places. They ascend into the heavens;—they have discoverd how the blood circulates, and the nature of the air we breathe. The [*for* they] have acquired new and almost unlimited powers;—They can command the thunders of heaven, mimick the earthquake, and even mock the invisible world with its own shadows."

I departed highly pleased with the professor and his lecture & paid him a visit the same evening. His manners in private were even more mild & attractive than in public. For there was a certain dignity in his manner during his lectures which was replaced by the greatest affability and kindness in his own house. He heard my little narration concerning my studies with attention <and> smiled at the names of Cornelius Agrippa and Paracelsus but without the contempt that Mr Krempe had exhibited. I ended by saying that his lecture had removed my prejudice against modern chemists and I requested at the same time his advice concerning the books I ought to procure

"I am happy" said Mr. Waldham, "To have gained a desciple and if {if} your application equals your ability I have no doubt of your success. Chemistry is that branch of natural philosophy in which the greatest improvements have & may be made. It is on that account that I chose it for my peculiar study. But at the same time I did not neglect the other sciences. A man would make a very sorry chemist if he atteneded to that department alone. If

Compare pp. 72–3

your wish is really to become a man of science and not merely a pretty experimentalist I should advice you to apply to every branch of natural philosophy and Mathematics."

He then took me into his laboratory and explained to me his various machines telling me what I ought to procure and promising me the use of his when I should have advanced far enough in the study not to derange their mechanism. He also gave me the list of books which I had requested and I took my leave.

Thus ended a day memorable to me for it decided my destiny.

Chap. 5

From this day natural philosophy and particularly chemistry became nearly my sole study. I read with ardour those books so full of genius and discrimination that have been written on these subjects. I attended the lectures, and cultivated the acquaintance of the men of science of the university; and I found even in Mr. Krempe a great deal of sound sense & real information combined it is true with a repulsive phisiognomy & manners, but not on that account the less valuable. In M. Waldman I found a true friend. His gentleness was never tinged by dogmatism and his instructions were given with an air of frankness and good nature that banished ever [*for* every] idea of pedantry. It was perhaps the amiable character of this man that enclined me more to the study of that branch of natural philosophy which he professed than an intrinsic love for the science itself. But this was only in the first steps towards knowledge; as I entered more fully into philosophy the more I studied it for its own sake. That application which at first had been a matter of duty now became so ardent and eager that the stars often dissapeared while I was yet labouring in my labrotary.

 Compare pp. 73–4

As I applied so closely, it may be easily conceived that I improved rapidly. My ardour was indeed the astonishment of the students, and my proficiency that of the master, and Professor Krempe often asked me with a sly smile how Cornelius Agrippa went on. Two years passed in this manner during which I paid no visit to Geneva, but was engaged heart and soul in the pursuit of some discoveries which I hoped to make. None but those who have experienced it can conceive of the enticements of science—In other studies you go as far as others have done before you and there is nothing more to learn, but in a scientific pursuit there is continual food for discovery and wonder. A mind of moderate capacity who closely pursues one study must infallibly arrive at great proficiency in that study—And I who continually applied to one thing and wrapt up as I was in this I improved so rapidly that at the end of the two years I made one or two trifling discoveries in the improvement of some chemical machines which procured me great esteem and admiration at the university. When I arrived at this point, that my residence at Ingolstadt was no longer conducive to my improvement, I thought of returning to my friends and to my native town, when an incident happened that protracted my stay.

One of those phænonoma which had peculiarly attracted my attention was the structure of the human frame; and indeed that of any animal endued with life. Whence I often asked myself did this principle of life proceed. It was a bold question, and one that has ever been considered as a mystery. Yet how many things are we on the brink of becoming acquainted with if cowardice or carelessness did not restrain us. I revolved these circumstances in my mind and determined from thenceforth to apply myself more particularly to that branch of natural philosophy which treats of phisiology. Unless I had been animated by an almost supernatural enthusiasm, my application to this study would have been irksome and almost intolerable. To examine the causes of life we must first have recourse to death. I became acquainted with the science of

Compare pp. 74–5

anatomy but this was not sufficient. I must also observe the natural decay & corruption of the human body. In my education my father had taken the greatest precautions that my mind should not be impressed by supernatural horrors. I do not ever remember having trembled at a ghost story or to have feared the apparition of <a> spirit. Darkness had no effect upon my fancy and a churchyard was to me merely the receptacle of bodies deprived of life and becoming<,> from being the seat of beauty & strength<,> food for the worm. But now I was obliged to examine the cause & progress of this decay and forced to spend days and nights in vaults and Charnel houses. {I} My attention was fixed upon every horror of which the human feelings are susceptable—I saw how the fine form of man was degraded and wasted. I beheld the corruption of death succeed to the blooming cheek of life—how the worm succeeded to the wonders of the eye and brain. I paused, examined and analyzed every minutiæ of causation untill from the midst of this darkness a sudden light broke in upon me. A light so brilliant & wondrous yet so simple that while it intoxicated me I was surprised that I among so many men of genius who had applied to the same science that I alone should discover this astonishing secret.

Remember I am not recording the vision of a madman—the sun does not more certainly shine in the heavens than that what I now record is true. Some miracle might have produced it. But the stages of discovery were distinct and probable. After days and nights of incredible toil and fatigue I succeeded in discovering the cause of generation & life. Nay more, I was myself capable of bestowing animation upon lifeless matter.

The surprise that I at first experienced on this discovery soon gave place to delight and rapture. After so much time spent in painful labour to arrive at onece at the summit of my desires was the most gratifying circumstance that could have occurred. But this discovery was so great and overwhelming that all the steps that progressively led to it were obliterated. and I beheld only the

 Compare pp. 75–6

result. What had been the study and desire of the wisest men since the creation of the world was now in my grasp; Not that, like a magic scene it all opened upon me at once; on the contrary the information I had obtained was rather one that would direct my endeavours than show me the prospect with any precise certainty. I was like the Arabian who had been buried with the dead, and found a passage to life aided only by one glimmering and seemingly ineffectual light.

I see by your eargerness and the wonder and hope which your eyes express, my friend, that you expect to be informed of the secret with which I am acquainted: but you are mistaken. Listen patiently to the end of my story and you will easily perceive why I am reserved upon that subject.—I will not lead you on, unguarded and ardent as I then was, to your destruction & infallible misery. Learn from me, if not by my precepts at least by my example, how dangerous is the acquirement of knowledge and how much happier that man is who believes his native town the world, than he <who> aspires to become greater than his nature will allow.

Chapter 6.

When I found this astonishing power placed in my hands, I hesitated a long time concerning the use I should make of it. Although I possessed the capacity of bestowing animation yet to prepare a creature for the reception of it with all its intricacies of fibres muscles & veins must be a work of inconceivable labour & difficulty. I doubted at first whether I should attempt the creation of a being like myself or one of simpler organization; but my imagination was too much exalted by my first success to permit me to doubt of my ability to create an animal as complex and wonderful as man. Yet when I considered my materials they hardly appeared

Compare pp. 76–7

adequate to so ardous an undertaking; but I did not despair. I allowed that my first attempts might be futile, my operations fail or my work be imperfect, but I looked around on the improvement that every day takes place in science and mechanics although I could not hope that my attempts would be in every way perfect but I did not think that the magnitude and grandeur of my plan was any argument of its impracticability. And it was with these feelings I began the creation of a human being. As the smallness of the parts were a great hindrance to my speed I resolved, contrary to my first intention, to make him of a gigantic stature; that is to say about seven or eight feet in height, and proportionably large. And after having formed this determination and having spent some months in collecting of my materials, I began.

No one can conceive the variety of feelings which pressed upon me during this time. When success raised me to enthusiasm life and death appeared to me ideal bounds, which I should first break and pour a torrent of light into our dark world. A new creation would bless me as its creator and source; many happy and excellent creatures would owe their existence to me in a manner no father could claim the gratitude of his child And pursueing my reflections I thought that if I could bestow animation upon lifeless matter I might in process of time (although I now found it impossible) renew life where death had apparently devoted the body to corruption.

These thoughts supported my spirits while I pursued my undertaking with unremitting ardour. My cheek was pale with study, and my person emaciated by confinement. sometimes on the very brink of certainty I fail<e>d yet I still clung to the hope which the next day or the next hour might realize. One secret which I alone possessed was the hope to which I clung and the moon gazed on my midnight labours while with unrelaxed & breathless eagerness I pursued nature to her most secret hiding places. But who shall know my secret operations as I dabbled among the

 Compare pp. 77–8

unhallowed damps of the grave, or tortured the living animal to animate my lifeless clay? Now my limbs tremble and my eyes swim with the rememberance, but then a resistless and almost frantic <impulse> urged me on; I seemed to have lost all soul or sensation but for one pursuit. It was indeed a passing trance that only made me feel with renewed acuteness when the unnatural stimulus ceased to operate, and I had returned to my old habits. I collected bones from Charnel houses and with profane fingers meddled with the secrets of the human frame. In a solitary chamber—or rather cell at the top of the house and seperated from all other appartments by a gallery and staircase I kept my workshop of filthy creation; my eyeballs were starting from their sockets in attending to the minutiæ of my employment. The dissecting room and the slaughter house furnished many of my materials, and often did my human nature turn from my occupation but I was still urged on by an eagerness which encreased, as my work drew near a conclusion.

The Summer months passed while I was thus employed heart and soul, in one pursuit. It was a most beautiful season: never did the fields bestow a more plentiful harvest, or the vines yeild a more luxuriant vintage. But my eyes were shut to the charms of nature & the same feelings which made me neglect the scenes around me caused me also to forget those friends who were so many miles absent and whom I had not seen for so long a time. I knew that my silence disquieted them and I well remembered the words of my father. "I know that while you are pleased with yourself you will think of us with affection and we shall hear regularly from you. And you must pardon me if I regard any interruption in your corespondence, as a proof that your other studies are equally neglected" I knew well therefore what his opinion would be but I could not tear my thoughts from my occupation loathsome in itself but which had taken a strong hold of my imagination. I wished as it were to procrastinate my feelings of affection, untill the great object of my affection was compleated.

Compare pp. 78–9

I then thought that my father would be unjust if he ascribed my neglect to vice or faultiness on my part; but I am now convinced that he was in the right in conceiving that I should not be altogether free from blame. A human being in perfection ought always to preserve a calm and peaceful mind and never to allow passion or a transitory desire to disturb his tranquillity. I do not think that the pursuit of knowledge is any exception to this rule. If the study to which you apply yourself has a tendency to weaken your affections and to destroy your taste for those simple pleasures in which no alloy can possibly mix then that study is certainly unlawful that is to say not befitting the human mind. If this rule was always observed; if no man allowed any pursuit whatsoever to interfere with his tranquillity and domestic affections Greece had never been enslaved, Cæsar would have spared his country, America would have been discovered more gradually, and the Empires of Mexico & Peru had not been destroyed.

But I forget that I am moralizing in the most interresting part of my tale; and your looks remind me to proceed.

My father made no reproach in his letters, and only took notice of my silence by enquiring more particularly than before what my occupations were. Winter spring and summer passed away during my labours but I did not watch the blossom or the expanding leaves—sights which before had alway<s> yeilded me supreme delight. so much was I taken up with my occupation. The leaves of that year were withered before my work drew near a close. And now every day shewed me more plainly how well I had succeeded. But my enthusiasm was checked by my anxiety and I appeared rather like one doomed by slavery to toil in the mines or any other unwholsome trade than an artist occupied in his favourite employment. Every night a slow fever oppressed me and I became nervous to a most painful degree; a {a} disease I regretted more because I had hitherto enjoyed excellent health & had always boasted of my firm nerves. But I believed that

 Compare pp. 79–80

exercise and amusement would soon drive away these symtoms and I promised myself both of these when my creation should be compleated.

Chapter 7th

It was on a dreary night of November that I beheld my man compleated; And with an anxiety that almost amounted to agony I collected instruments of life around me that I might infuse a spark of being in to the lifeless thing that lay at my feet. It was already one in the morning, the rain pattered dismally against the window panes, & my candle was nearly burnt out, when by the glimmer of the half extinguished light I saw the dull yellow eye of the creature open.—It breathed hard, and a convulsive motion agitated its limbs.

How can I describe my emotion at this catastrophe; or how delineate the wretch whom with such infinite pains and care I had endeavoured to form. His limbs were in proportion and I had selected his features as handsome. Handsome; Great God! His yellow skin scarcely covered the work of muscles and arteries beneath; his hair was flowing and his teeth of a pearly whiteness but these luxuriancies only formed a more horrid contrast with his watry eyes that seemed almost of the same colour as the dun white sockets in which they were set, his shrivelled complexion and strait black lips.

The different accidents of life are not so changeable as the feelings of human nature. I had worked hard for nearly two years for the sole purpose of infusing life into an inanimate body. For this I had deprived myself of rest and health. I had desired it with an ardour that far exceed<ed> moderation; but now that I had succeeded these dreams vanished and breathless horror and disgust filled my heart.

Compare pp. 80–81

Unable to endure the aspect of the creature I had created, I rushed out of the room and remained a long time traversing my bed chamber unable to compose my mind to sleep. At lenght lassitude succeeded to the tumult I had before endured, and I threw myself on my bed in my clothes endeavouring to seek a few moments of forgetfullness. But it was in vain; I slept indeed but I was disturbed by the wildest dreams—I saw Elizabeth in the bloom of health walking in the streets of Ingolstadt; delighted & surprised I embraced her but as I imprinted the first kiss on her lips they became lurid with the hue of death; her features appeared to change and I thought that I held the corpse of my dead mother in my arms: a shroud envolepped her form & I saw the grave worms crawling in the folds of the flannel; I started from my sleep with horror, a cold dew covered my forehead<,> my teeth chattered and every limb was convulsed, when, by the dim and yellow light of the moon as it forced its way through the window shutters, I beheld the wretch—the miserable monster whom I had created; he held up the curtain, and his eyes; if eyes they may be called, were fixed on me—His jaws opened and he muttered some words while a grin wrinkled his cheeks. He might have spoken but I did not hear—one hand was stretched out to detain me but I escaped and rushed down stairs—I took refuge in a court-yard belonging to the house which I inhabited; where I remained the rest of the night walking up and down in the greatest agitation; listening attentively, catching and fearing each sound as if it were to announce the arrival of the demoniacal corpse to which I had so miserable given life.

Oh! no mortal could support the horror of that countenance. A mummy again endued with life could not be so hideous as He. I had gazed on him while unfinished; he was ugly then. But when those muscles and joints were endued with motion it became a thing such as even Dante could never have conceived.

I passed the night wretchedly—sometimes my pulses beat so quickly and hardly that I felt the palpitation of every artery: At

 Compare pp. 81–2

others I nearly sunk to the ground with languor and extreme weakness. And mingled with this horror I felt the bitterness of disappointment: Dreams that had been my food and rest for so long a space were now become a hell to me—And the change was so rapid, the overthrow so complete.

Morning—dismal and wet—at length dawned, and discovered to my sleepless and aching eyes the church of Ingolsstadt its white steeple & clock which pointed to the sixth hour. The porter opened the gates of the court which had that night been my assylum and I issued into the streets, pacing with quick steps as if I sought to <avoid> the wretch whom I feared every turning in the street would present to my view. I did not dare return to the appartment which I inhabited but felt impelled to hurry on although wetted by the rain which poured from a black and comfortless sky.

I continued walking in this manner for some time endeavouring by bodily exercise to ease the load that weighed upon my mind. I traversed the streets without any clear conception of where I was or what I was doing: my heart palpitated with fear and I hurried on with irregular steps: not daring to look about me,

> "Like one who on a lonesome road
> Doth walk in fear and dread
> And having once turned round walks on
> And turns no more his head
> Because he knows a frightful fiend
> Doth close behind him tread".*
>
> *Coleridge's "Ancient Mariner".

Continueing thus, I came at lenght opposite the Inn at which the diligences and carriages usually stopped. Here I paused I knew not why but remained some minutes with my eyes fixed on a coach that was coming towards me from the other end of the street. As it drew nearer I observed that it was the Swiss diligence; it

Compare pp. 82–3

stopped just where I was standing, and on the doors being opened I perceived Henry Clerval, who on seeing me instantly sprung out.

"My dear Frankenstien," exclaimed he "How glad I am to see you; how fortunate you should be here at the moment of my alighting."

Nothing could equal my delight on seing [*for* seeing] Clerval: his presence brought back to my thoughts my father, Elizabeth and all those scenes of home so dear to my recollection. I grasped his hand, and in a moment forgot my horror and misfortune. I felt for the first time for many months, calm and serene joy. I welcomed my friend therefore in the most cordial manner & we walked towards my colledge. Clerval continued talking for some time about my friends and his good fortune in being allowed to come to Ingolstadt.

"You may believe," said he, "it was not without considerable trouble that I persuaded my father that it is not absolutely necessary for a merchant to know nothing except bookeeping and indeed I believe I left him incredulous to the last<,> for his constant answer to my applications was the same as the dutch schoolmaster in the Vicar of Wakefield—"I have ten thousand florins a year without greek—I eat heartily without greek<."> But his affection for me at length overcame his dislike for learning, and he permitted me to take a voyage to the land of knowledge."

"And my father, brothers & Elizabeth" said I

"Very well & very happy" replied he "only a little uneasy that they hear from you so seldom, & by the bye, I mean to lecture you a little upon their account myself—But my dear Frankenstein" continued he stopping short & gazing full in my face "I did not before remark how very ill you are. So thin and pale; you appear as if you had been watching for several nights."

"You have guessed right" I replied "I have lately been so engaged in several occupations that I did not allow myself sufficient rest as

Compare pp. 83–4

you see; but I hope, I sincerely hope all those occupations are at an end—I am free now I hope."

I trembled excessively: I could not bear to think of, & far less to allude to the occurences of the preceeding night. I walked therefore with a quick pace, and we soon arrived at my colledge. I then reflected—and the thought made me shiver that the creature whom I had left in my appartment might be still there—alive and walking about. I dreaded to see him but I dreaded still more that Henry should behold the monsther. I therefore entreated him to remain a few minute<s> at the bottom of the stairs, while I darted up towards my own room. My hand was already on the lock before I recovered myself, when I paused and a cold shivering came over me. I threw the door open as children are accustomed to do when they expect a spectre to stand in waiting for them on the other side. But nothing appeared. I stepped fearfully in—the appartment was empty, and my bedroon [*for* bedroom] was also freed from its hideous guest. I could hardly believe that so great a good fortune could have befallen me; but when I was assured that my enemy had indeed fled, I clapped my hands for joy and ran down to Henry.

We ascended into my room & presently the servant brought breakfast: but I was unable to contain myself. It was not joy only that possessed me; I felt my flesh tingle with the excess of sensitiveness and my pulse beat rapidly. I was unable to remain for a single instant in the same place—I jumped over the chairs, clapped my hands & laughed aloud. Clerval at first attributed my unusual spirits to joy on his arrival—but when he observed me he saw a wildness in my eyes for which he could not account and my loud unrestrained heartless laughter frightened and astonished him.

My dear Frankenstein," cried he "What for God's sake is the matter do not laugh so—How ill you are! What is the cause of all this?

Compare pp. 84–5

Do not ask me cried I, putting my hands before my eyes, for I thought I saw the spectre glide into the room—He can tell! Oh save me save me"—I imagined that the monster seized me I struggled furiously & fell down in a fit.

Poor Clerval! What must have been his feelings. A meeting which he had anticipated with such joy so strangely turned to bitterness. But I did not witness his grief for I was lifeless and did not recover my senses for a long, long time.

Chap. 7 [*for* 8]

This was the commencement of a nervous fever which confined me for several months.[†] And during all this time Henry was my only nurse. I afterwards learned that knowing my fathers advanced age and unfitness for so long a journey & how wretched Elizabeth would be<,> he had spared them this grief by concealing the extent of my disorder. He knew that I could not have a more kind & attentive nurse than himself, and firm in the hope he had of my recovery he did not doubt that instead of doing harm he performed the kindest action that he could towards them.

But I was in reality very ill & surely nothing but the unbounded & unremitting attentions of my friend could have restored me to life. The form of the monster on whom I had bestowed life was for ever before <my> eyes, and I raved incessantly concerning him. Doubtless My words surprised Henry—he at first believed them the wanderings of my disordered imagination but the pertinacity with which I continually recurred to the same subject astonished him.

It was by very slow degrees and with frequent relapses that alarmed & grieved my friend that I recovered. I remember that

† MWS misnumbered this and subsequent chapters in Notebook A.

Compare pp. 85–6

the first time I was capable of observing outward objects with any kind of pleasure, I perceived that the fallen leaves had disappeared and that young buds were shooting forth from the trees. It was a divine spring & the season no doubt contributed greatly to my convalescence. I felt also sentiments of joy and affection revive in <my> bosom, my gloom disappeared and in a short time I became as cheerful as before I was attacked by the fatal passion.

"Dearest Clerval," said I "How kind, how very good you are to me. This whole winter instead of spending it in study as you promised yourself, has been consumed in my sick room: how shall I ever repay you? I feel the greatest remorse for the disappointment I have been the occasion of—But you will forgive me."

"You will repay me," replied Henry, "if you do not discompose yourself; but get well as fast as you can. And since you appear in such good spirits I may speak to you on one subject; may I not?"

I trembled; one subject! What could it be? Could he allude to an object on whom I dared not even think. Do not frighten yourself," said Clerval, who observed my change of colour, "I will not mention it if it agitates you. But your father and cousin would be so happy if they received a letter from you in your own hand—They hardly know how ill you have been, and are uneasy at your long silence."

Is that all?" I said smiling "My dear Henry how could you suppose that my first thoughts would not fly towards those dear, dear friends whom I love and who are so deserving of my love."

"If this is your present temper" said Henry "you will be glad perhaps to see a letter that has been lying here some day it is from your cousin I believe."†

He then put the following letter into my hands.

---

† At this point in the Draft, MWS wrote 'Ch V— 113', referring to the chapter and page number in Volume I of the restructured three-volume Fair Copy that she wrote out in April/May 1817.

Compare pp. 86–7

"To V. Frankenstien

Geneva March 18th 17—

"My dear Cousin

"I cannot describe to you the uneasiness we have all felt concerning your health. We cannot help imagining that your friend Clerval conceals the extent of your disorder, for it is now several months since we have seen your handwriting and all this time you have been obliged to dictate to Henry—Surely Victor you must have been very ill and this makes us very wretched as much so nearly as after the death of your dear mother. My father was almost persuaded of this and could hardly refrain from a journey to Ingolstadt. but I entreated him not<,> for although his health is better now than it has been since the death of My beloved Aunt, yet the fatigue might make him very ill. And Clerval always writes that you were getting better; I eagerly hope you will confirm this soon in your own handwriting for indeed, indeed Victor we are all very miserable on this account. Relieve us from this fear and we shall be the happiest creatures in the world.—My uncles health is now well & <so> vigorous that he appears ten years younger since last winter. Ernest also is so much improved, that you would hardly know him; he is now nearly sixteen you know and has lost that sickly appearance that he had some years ago—he is quite well & hearty if I may use that term for it is very expressive.

"My uncle and I conversed last night a long time about what profession Ernest should follow. His constant ill health when young has deprived him of the habit of application and now that he enjoys good health he is continually in the open air climbing the hills or rowing on the lake. I, therefore, proposed that he should <be> a farmer which you know cousin is a favourite scheme of

 Compare pp. 87–8

mine—A farmer's is a very healthy happy life; and the least hurtful or rather the most benificial of any profession. My uncle had an idea of his being an advocate, & through his interrest a judge. But besides that he is not at all fit for such an occupation, it is certainly better to cultivate the earth for the sustenance of man than to be the confidant & sometimes a helpmate of their vices; which is the employment of a Lawyer. I said that a rich farmer if it were not a more honourable it was at least a happier employment than that of a judge, whose misfortune it was always to meddle with the dark side of human nature My uncle smiled and said that I ought to be an advocate myself; which put an end to the conversation on that subject.

And now I must tell you a little story that will please you. Do you not remember Justine Moritz? Perhaps you do not<;> I will therefore tell you her story in few words. Mad. Martin [*earlier and unchanged surname for* Moritz] her Mother was a widow with four children of whom Justine was the third. This girl had always been the favourite of her father but by an odd perversity her Mother could not endure her and after the death of M. Moritz treated her very ill. My Aunt observed this, and when Justine was twelve years old prevailed on her mother to allow her to live at our house. Where she was taught all the duties of servant & was very kindly treated. I dare say that you now remember all about it, for Justine was a great favourite of yours & I remember you once said, that if you were in an ill humour one glance from Justine could dissipate it from the same reason that Ariosto gave concerning the beauty of Angelica:—she looked so frank hearted and happy. My Aunt was very fond of her which induced her to give her and [*for* an] education superior to that which she at first intended and she was fully repaid; for Justine

Compare pp. 88–9

was the most grateful little creature in the world. I do not mean that she made any professions—I never heard one pass her lips but you could see by her eye that she almost adored her protectress. Although very gay, and in many respects inconsiderate, yet she paid the greatest attention to every gesture of my Aunt—she thought her the miracle of perfection and endeavoured to imitate her words and even her manners, so that now she often reminds me of her. You did not observe all this, nor did I at the time but it struck me afterwards when I reflected on the subject.

When my dearest Aunt died every one was too much occupied in their own grief to notice poor Justine who had attended her during her whole illness with the greatest affection. Poor Justine was very ill but other tryals were reserved for her.

One by one her brothers & sister had died and her mother was now with the exception of her neglected daughter left childless. The conscience of the woman was troubled and she began to think that the deaths of her favourites was a judgement from heaven to punish her partiallity<;> she was a roman Catholic and I believe her confessor encouraged the idea. Accordingly, a few Months after your departure for Ingolstadt, Justine was called home by her repentant Mother. Poor girl she wept when she quitted our house<;> she was much altered since the death of my aunt: grief had given softness and a winning mildness to her manners which had before been remarkable for vivacity. Nor was her residence at her Mothers house of a nature to restore her gaiety. The poor woman was very vacillating in her repentance. She sometimes begged Justine to forgive her unkindness but much oftenor accused her as having caused the deaths of her brothers & sister. Perpetual fretting at last threw Mad. Martin [*earlier and*

 Compare pp. 89–90

unchanged name for Moritz] into a decline, which at first encreased her irritability, but she is now at rest for ever; she died on the first approach of cold at the beginning of this last winter. Justine has returned to us and I assure you I love her tenderly. She is very clever and extremely mild & pretty and as I mentioned before her air and expressions continually remind me of my dear Aunt.

I must say a few words to you also, my dear Victor, of little darling William. I wish you could see him. He is very tall of his age with sweet laughing blue eyes dark eyelashes and curling hair When he smiles two little dimples appear on his cheeks which are rosy with health—his chin comes down in a beautiful oval After this description I can only say what our visitors say a thousand times a day—'He is too pretty for a boy.' He has already had one or two little wives but Louisa Biron <is> his favourite—a pretty little girl of five years old

Now, dear Victor I dare say you wish to be indulged in a little gossip about your acquaintance. The pretty Miss Mansfeld has already received the congratulatory visits on her approaching marriage with a young Englishman, John Melbourne Esq. Her ugly sister Manon married M. Hofland the rich banker last autumn. Your favourite schoolfellow Louis Manoir has suffered several misfortunes since the departure of Clerval from Geneva But he has already recovered his spirits and he <is> reported to be on the point of marrying a very lively pretty frenchwoman—Mad. Tavernier—She is a widow and much older than Manoir but she is much admired and a favourite with every body.

I have written myself into good spirits, dear Cousin yet I can not conclude without again anxiously enquiring concerning your health—Dear Victor, if you are not very ill write yourself and make your father and all of us happy

Compare pp. 90–91

or——I cannot bear to think on the other side of the question<;> my tears already flow<;> write—dearest Victor

Your very affectionate Cousin
Elizabeth Lavenza

"Dear, dear Elizabeth" I exclaimed when I had read her letter— "I will write instantly and relieve them from the great pain they must feel."

I wrote, and this exertion greatly fatigued me; but my convalescence had commenced and went on regularly—in another fortnight I was able to leave my chamber.

Chap. 8th [*for* 9th]

one of my first duties on my recovery was to introduce Clerval to the several professors of the university. And in doing this I underwent a kind of rough usage that ill befitted the wounds that my mind had sustained. Ever since the fatal night—the end of my labours & the beginning of my misfortunes<—>I had conceived a violent antipathy even to the name of Natural Philosophy. When I was otherwise quite restored to health the sight of <a> Chemical instrument brought on again all my nervous symtoms. Henry saw this and had removed all my apparatus from my view<;> he had also changed my appartment, for he perceived that I had a dislike to the room which had previously been my workshop. But these cares of Clerval were thrown away when I visited the professors. even my excellent M. Waldman inflicted torture when he praised with kindness and warmth the astonishing progress that I had made in the sciences. He soon perceived my dislike of the subject, but not guessing the real cause he attributed it to modesty on hearing myself praised and changed the subject from my improvement, to

Compare pp. 91–2

the science itself, with a desire as I evidently saw of drawing me out. What could I do? He meant to please & he tormented me I felt as if he placed carefully one by one in my view those instruments which were to be afterwards used in putting me to a slow and cruel death. I writhed under his words, yet dared not shew the pain I felt. Clerval, whose eyes and feelings were always quick in dicerning the sensations of others declined the subject alledging his ignorance & the conversation took a more general turn. I thanked him from my heart, but I did not speak. I plainly saw that he was surprised, but he never attempted to draw my secret from me, and although I loved him with a mixture of affection and reverence that knew no bounds, yet I could never persuade myself to confide to him that event which was so often present to my thoughts, but which I feared the detail to another would only impress more deeply.

Mr. Krempe was not equally docile<;> & weak as my illness had made me his harsh blunt econiums [*for* encomiums] gave me even more pain than the benevolent approbation of M. Waldman—"Damn the fellow," cried he "Why Mr. Clerval I tell you he has outstript us all—ay stare if you please but it is nevertheless true—A youngster who but three years ago believed Cornelius Agrippa as firmly as the gospel has now set himself at the head of the university & if he is not soon pulled down we shall all be out of countenance.—Aye, Aye, continued he observing my face expressive of suffering "Mr. Frankenstein is modest an excellent quality in a young man; Young men should be diffident of themselves you know<,> Mr. Clerval; I was myself when young but one soon grows out of that."

Mr. Krempe had now commenced an eulogy on himself and that happily turned the conversation from the subject that was so painful to me.

Clerval was no natural philosopher. His imagination was too vivid for the minutiæ of science. Languages were his principal study for he wished to open a field for self-instruction on his

Compare pp. 92–3

return—Persian Arabic & Hebrew gained his attention when he had become perfectly master of the Greek & Latin languages. For my own part idleness had ever been irksome to me and now that I wished to fly from reflection and hated my former studies I found great relief in being the fellow pupil with my friend and found not only instruction but consolation in the works of the orientalists. Their melancholy is soothing and their joy elevating to a degree I never before experienced in studying any other books. When you read their writings life appears to consist in a warm sun and gardens of roses—in the smiles & frowns of a fair enemy and the fire that consumes your own heart How different from the manly & warlike poets of Greece & Rome.

Summer passed away in these occupations & my return to Geneva was fixed for the latter end of Autumn<;> but being delayed by several accidents<,> winter & snow arrived, the roads were deemed impassable and my journey retarted [*for* retarded] untill the spring. I felt this delay very bitterly for I longed to see my native town and my beloved friends<;> my return had only been delayed so long from an unwillingness to leave Clerval in a strange town before he had become acquainted with its inhabitants. The winter however was spent cheerfully and although the spring was uncommonly late when it came<,> its beauty compensated <for> its dilatoriness. The month of May was already compleated, and I expected daily the letter that was to fix the date of my departure, When Henry proposed a pedestrian tour in <the> environs of Ingolstadt that I might bid farewell to the country I had so long inhabited.—I acceeded with pleasure to this proposition—I was fond of Exercise and Clerval had always been my favourite companion in the rambles of this nature that I had taken among the scenes of my native country. We passed a fortnight in these perambulations. My health and spirits had long been restored and they gained additional vigour from the salubrious air I breathed and the conversation of my friend. Study had before rendered

 Compare pp. 93–4

me unsociable,—I shunned the company of my fellow beings But Clerval called forth the better feelings of my heart. he again taught me to love the aspect of nature and the cheerful faces of children. Excellent Friend! How sincerely did you love me and endeavour to elevate my mind untill it was on a level with your own. A selfish persuit had cramped and narrowed me untill your gentleness & affection warmed & opened my senses. I became the same happy creature who a few years ago, loving & beloved by all, had no sorrow or care—when happy<,> inanimate nature had the power of bestowing on me the most delightful sensations—A serene sky and verdant fields filled me with extasy.—The present season was indeed divine—the flowers of spring bloomed in the hedges while those of summer were already in bud—I was not disturbed by thoughts that during the preceeding year pressed upon me not withstanding my endeavours to throw them off<.> Henry rejoiced in my gaiety and sincerely sympathized in my feelings—he exerted himself to amuse me, while he expressed the feelings that filled his soul. The resources of his mind on this occasion were truly astonishing. his conversation was full of imagination and very often, in imitation of the persian & Arabic writers, he invented tales of wonderful fancy and interrest. At other times he repeated my favourite poems or drew me out into arguments which he supported with great ingenuity.

We returned to our colledge on a sunday—the peasants were dancing and every one we met appeared joyful and happy—my own spirits were high and I bounded along with feelings of unbridled joy and hilarity.

Chap. 9th [*for* 10th]

On my return I found the following letter from my father.

Compare pp. 94–5

To V.— Frankenstein

Geneva—June 2nd—17—

My dear Victor

You have probably waited impatiently for a letter to fix the date of your return and I was at first tempted to write a few lines {to} merely mentioning the day on which I should expect you—but that would be a cruel kindness and I dare not do it. What would be your surprise, my son, when your [*for* you] expected a happy and gay welcome to beheld [*for* behold] on the contrary tears and wretchedness. And how, Victor, can I relate our misfortune? absence cannot have rendered you callous to our joys and griefs and how can I inflict pain on an absent child? I wish to prepare you for the woeful news but I know it is impossible; even now your eye skims over the page to seek the words which are to convey to you the horrible tidings.

William is dead! That sweet child whose smiles delighted & warmed me who was so gentle yet so gay, Victor, he is Murdered!

I will not attempt to console you but will simply relate the circumstances of the transaction.

Last thurday (May 28th) I; my niece and your two brothers went to walk in Plainpalais. The evening was warm and serene, and we prolonged our walk farther than usual. It was already dusk before we thought of returning and then we discovered that Ernest and William who had gone on before, were not to be found. We accordingly rested on a seat untill they should return. Presently Ernest came & enquired for his brother he said that he had been playing with him and that William had run away to hide himself and that he had vainly sought for him & afterwards waited a long time but that he did not return.

This rather alarmed us and we continued to search

 Compare pp. 95–6

for him untill night fell; when Elizabeth conjectured that he might have returned to the house: but he was not there—We returned again with torches for I could not rest when I thought my sweet child had lost himself, and was exposed to all the damps & dews of night; Elizabeth also suffered extreme anguish. About seven in the morning I discovered my lovely boy whom the night before I had seen blooming & active in health stretched on the grass livid and motionless—the print of the murderers finger was on his neck.

He was conveyed home and the anguish that was visible in my countenance revealed the secret to Elizabeth. She was very earnest to see the corpse which <I> for a long time refused but she persisted, and entering the room where it lay hastily examined the neck of the victim<,> and clasping her hands exclaimed—Oh God! I have murdered my darling infant.

She fainted and was retored [*for* restored] with extreme difficulty; and when she again lived it was only to weep and sigh—She told me that that same evening William had teazed her to let him wear a very valuable miniature she possessed of your Mother. This picture is gone and was doubtless the temptation which urged the murderer to the deed. We have no trace at present of him, but our exertions are unremitted; but they will not restore my beloved William.

Come, dearest Victor, you alone can console Elizabeth who weeps & accuses herself so unjustly, and yet her words pierce my heart. We are all unhappy but will not that be an additional motive for you, my son, to come and be our comforter. Your dear Mother! Alas, Victor! I now say Thank God she did not live to witness this grief—the cruel miserable death of her youngest darling.

Compare pp. 96–7

Come, Victor; not brooding thoughts of vengeance against the assassin but with feelings of peace and gentleness that will heal instead of festering the wound of our minds. Enter the house of mourning, my son & friend but with kindness and affection for those who love you & not with hatred for your enemies.

Your affectionate & afflicted father

Alphonse Frankenstein

Clerval who had watched my countenance as I read this letter was surprised in observing the despair that succeeded to the joy I expressed on receiving new [*for* news] from my friends. I threw the letter on the table and covered my face with my hands.

"My dear Frankenstien," exclaimed Henry when he saw me weep with bitterness "are you always to be unhappy? my dear friend, what has happened?"

I motioned to him to take up the letter while I walked up & down the room in the most extreme agitation. tears also gushed {also} from the eyes of Clerval as he read the account of my misfortune—"I can offer you no consolation, my friend," said he "your disaster is irreperable. What do you intend to do?"

"To go instantly to Geneva come with me, Clerval, to order the horses"

During our walk Henry endeavoured to raise my spirits—He did not do this by the common topics of consolation but by shewing the truest sympathy. "Poor William" said <he> "that dear child he now sleeps with his angel mother. His friends mourn and weep but he is at rest he does not now feel the murderers grasp—a sod covers his gentle form and he knows no pain—He can no longer be a subject for pity his survivors are the greatest sufferers and for them time is the only consolation. Those maxims of the stoics that death was no evil and that the mind of man ought to be superior to despair on the eternal absence of a beloved object

Compare pp. 97–8

ought not to be urged—even Cato wept over the dead body of his brother."

Clerval spoke thus as we huried through the streets the words impressed themselves on my mind and I remembered them afterwa<r>ds in solitude. But now, as soon as the horses arrived I hurried into a Cabriolet and bad farewell to my friend.

My journey was very melancholy. At first I wished to hurry on for I longed to console & sympathize with my loved and sorrowing friends but when I drew near my native town I slackened my pace. I could hardly sustain the multitude of feelings that crowded into my mind. I passed though [*for* through] scenes familiar to my youth but which I had not seen for nearly five years, how altered every thing might be during that time? one great sudden and desolating change had taken place but a thousand little circumstance might have by degrees worked other alterations which although it might be done more tranquilly would not be less decisive. Fear overcame me<;> I dared not advance dreading a thousand nameless evils that made me tremble although I was unable to define them.

I remained at Lausanne for two days not daring to proceed. I contemplated the lake—the waters were placid—all around was calm and the Snowy mountains the "Palaces of Nature" were not changed. By degrees this calm and heavenly scene restored me, and I proceeded towards Geneva. The road ran by the side of the lake which became narrower as I approached my native town—I discovered more distinctly the black sides of Jura; and the summit of Mont Blanc—I wept like a child—Dear mountains my own beautiful lake how do you welcome your wanderer Your summits are clear the sky and lake are blue is this to prognosticate peace or to mock my unhappiness?

I fear, my friend that I shall render myself tedious by dwelling on these preliminary circumstances but they were days of comparative happiness and I think of them with pleasure—My Country my beloved country who but a native can tell the delight I took in

Compare pp. 98–9

again beholding thy streams thy mountains and more than all thy lovely lake

Yet as I drew nearer home grief and fear overcame me—night also closed round and when I could hardly see the dark mountains I felt still more gloomily I pictured every evil and persuaded myself that I was destined to become the most wretched of human beings—Alas! I prophesied truly and failed only that in all the misery I imagined and dreaded, I did not conceive the hundredth part of the anguish I was destined to endure.

Chapter 10th [*for* 11th]

Night had closed in when I arrived<,> the gates of Geneva were already shut<,> and I determined to remain that night at Secheron. The night was very fine and as I was unable to rest I resolved to walk towards the spot where my poor William had been murdered; as I walked I perceived a storm collecting on the other side of the lake. I saw the lightnings play in the most beautiful figures and gained a summit that I might observe its progress. It advanced and I soon felt the rain coming slowly in large drops but its violence quickly encreased.

I quitted my seat and walk<ed> on, although the darkness and storm augmented every minute and the thunder burst with a terrific crash over my head—It was echoed from Salêve and the Alps of Savoy—vivid flashes of lightning dazzled my eyes, and illumined the lake; and then, for an instant every thing seemed of a pitchy darkness untill the eye recovered itself from the preceeding flash. The storm as is often the case in Switzerland appeared at once in various parts of the heavens. The most violent storm was exactly north of the town and at that part where <the> lake turns the promontory of Belrive and<,> changing its course

 Compare pp. 99–100

from South to north which it before pursues<,> proceeds from west to east—another storm enlightened Jura with faint flashes and another darkened and sometimes disclosed the Mole—a peaked mountain to the east of the lake.

While I watched the storm—so beautiful yet terrific I wandered on with a hasty step—this noble war in the sky elevated my spirits; I clasped my hands & exclaimed aloud "William, dear angel, this is thy funeral, this thy dirge!"—As I said these words I perceived in the gloom a figure which stole from behind a clump of trees near me—I stood fixed gazing intently, I could not be mistaken<;> a flash of lightning illumined the object, and discovered to me its gigantic stature, its deformity more hideous than belongs to humanity instantly informed me who it was. It was the wretch, the filthy dæmon to whom I had given life. What did he there? Could he be (I shuddered at the conception<)> the murderer of my brother. No sooner did that idea cross my imagination than I became convinced of its truth—my teeth chattered and I was forced to lean against a tree for support—The figure quickly passed me and I lost it in the gloom. He therefore was the murderer! I could not doubt it I was agonized by the bare probability—I thought of pursueing the devil, but it would have been in vain for another flash discovered him to me climbing up the steep and nearly perpendicular ascent of Mont-Salêve; he soon reached the summit and dissapeared.

I remained motionless the thunder ceased but the rain still continued & the scene was inveloped in an impenetrable darkness. I revolved in my mind the events which I had, untill now, sought to forget. The appearance of the creature at my bed side—its departure. two years had now nearly elapsed since the night on which he first received life, and was this his first crime—Alas! I had turned loose in the world a depraved wretch whose delight was in murder & wretchedness: For had he not murdered my brother?

No one can conceive of the anguish I sufferred during the

Compare pp. 100–101

remainder of the night which I spent cold & wet in the open air. But I did not feel the incovenience of the weather my imagination was busy in {in} scenes of evil and despair I considered the wretch whom I had cast in among mankind for purposes of mischief nearly in the light of my vampire; my own spirit let loose from the grave and forced to destroy all who were dear to me.

Day dawned and I directed my steps towards the town—the gates were open and I hastened to my father's house.—My first thought was to discover what I knew of the murderer & cause instant pursuit to be made. But I paused when I reflected what the story was that I had to tell. A creature whom I myself had created and endued with life The tale was utterly improbable and I knew well that if any other had communicated such a relation to me I should have looked upon it as the ravings of delirium Besides<,> the strange nature of the animal would elude pursuit, even if I were credited which was utterly impossible—the common people would believe it to be a real devil and who could attempt a creature that could scale the steep sides of Mont-Salêve? These reflections determined me, and I resolved to remain silent.

It was about five in the morning when I entered my fathers house. I told the servants not to disturb the family, and went into the library to attend their usual time of rising. Five years had elapsed—passed as a dream but for one indelible trace, and I stood in the same place where I had last embraced my father before my departure for Ingolstadt. Beloved and respectable parent! He still remained to me. I gazed on a picture of my mother which stood over the mantlepiece. It was an historical piece painted to please my father and represented Caroline Beaumont in an agony of despair kneeling by the coffin of her dead father. Her garb was rustic, & her cheek pale but there was an air of dignity and beauty that hardly permitted the feeling of pity. Below this picture was a miniature of William, and my tears flowed when I looked upon it—While I was thus engaged Ernest entered—he had heard me

 Compare pp. 101–2

arrive and hastened to welcome me. He expressed the greatest delight on seeing me—"Welcome my dearest Victor," said he, ah I wish you had come three months ago and then you would have found us all joyous & delighted—But we are now so unhappy that I am afraid tears instead of smiles will be your welcome<;> our father looks so sorrowful and it seems to have revived in his mind his sorrow for the death of Mamma<,> and poor Elizabeth is quite inconsolable." Ernest began to weep as he said these words.

"Do not you" said I, "welcome me thus; and try to be more calm and preveng [*for* prevent] my being absolutely miserable the moment I enter my fathers house after so long an absence. But tell me, How my father supports his misfortunes; and how is my poor Elizabeth?"

She indeed requires consolation," replied Ernest—"She accused herself of having caused the death of my brother and that made her very, very wretched; but since the murderer has been discovered{"}———"

"The murderer discovered!" Exclaimed I—"Good God how can that be? Who could attempt to pursue him? It is impossible, one might as well try to overtake the winds or confine a mountain stream with a straw!

"I do not know what you mean" replied Ernest, But we were all very unhappy when she was discovered—No one would believe it at first and even now Myrtella [*error for* Elizabeth] will not be convinced notwithstanding all the evidence. Indeed who could have believed that Justine Moritz, who was so amiable and fond of all the family could all at once become so extremely wicked."

"Justine Moritz!" cried I, "poor, poor girl is she then accused—but it is wrongfully every one knows that. No one believes it surely, Ernest?"

"No one did at first," said my brother, "but several circumstances came out, and her own behaviour was so confused but she will <be> tried today and you will then hear all?"

Compare pp. 102–3

He related that the morning on which the murder of poor William had been discovered Justine had been taken ill and confined to her bed, and after several days one of the servants happened to examine the apparel she had worn on the night of the murder & had discovered in her pocket the picture of my mother which had been judged to be the temptation of the murderer. The servant instantly shewed it to one of the others, and without saying a word to any of the family they went to a magistrate who sent to apprehend Justine, on being charged with the fact she confirmed the suspicion in a great measure by her extreme confusion.

This was a strange tale but it did not shake my faith and I replied earnestly. "You are all mistaken. I know the murderer<.> Justine, poor, good Justine is innocent."

At that instant my father entered and I saw unhappiness deeply impressed on his countenance but he endeavoured to welcome me cheerfully and would have spoken on some other topic than that of our disaster had not Ernest exclaimed Good God, Papa! Victor says that he knows the murderer of poor William.

"We do also, unfortunately," replied my father for indeed I had rather have been for ever ignorant than have discovered so much depravity & ingratitude in one whom I valued so highly.

"My dear father" exclaimed I—"You are mistaken. Justine is innocent."

"If she is" replied my father "God forbid that she should suffer as guilty—She is to be tried today and I hope I sincerely hope that she will be acquitted

This speech calmed me. I was firmly convinced in my own mind that Justine and indeed every human being was guiltless of this murder. I had no fear therefore that any circumstantial evidence could be brought forward strong enough to convict her and in this assurance I calmed myself expecting the trial with eagerness but without prognosticating an evil result.

 Compare pp. 103–4

Chap. 11 [*for* 12]

We were soon joined by Elizabeth. Time had made great alterations in her form since I had last beheld her. Five years before she was a pretty, good humoured girl Whom every one loved, and caressed. She was now a woman in stature and expression of countenance which was uncommonly lovely—An open & capacious forehead gave indications of a good understanding joined to great frankness. Her eyes were hazel and expressive of uncommon mildness now through recent affliction allied to sadness—Her hair was of a rich dark auburn her complexion fair and her figure slim and graceful. She welcomed me with the greatest affection "Your arrival, my dearest cousin," said she, "fills me with hope. You perhaps will find out some means to justify my poor guiltless Justine. Alas Who is safe is [*for* if] she were convicted for I rely on her innocence as certainly as I do on my own. Our Misfortune is doubly hard to us. We have not only lost that lovely darling boy but this poor girl whom I sincerely love, is to be torn away by even a worse fate—Alas if she is condemned I shall never know joy more But she will not I am sure she will not and then I shall be happy again even after the sad death of my little William."

"She is innocent, my Elizabeth," said I and that shall be proved—fear nothing but let your spirits be cheered by the assurance of her aquittal.

"How kind you are," replied Elizabeth, "every one else believes in her guilt, and that made me wretched for I knew it to be impossible, and to see every one else prejudiced in so deadly a manner rendered me hopeless and despairing." She wept—"Sweet niece" said my father dry your tears<;> if she is as you believe innocent rely on the justice of our judges & the activity with which I shall prevent the slightest shadow of partiality.

Compare pp. 104–5

We passed a few sad hours untill eleven o'clock when the trial was to commence. {My} the rest of the family being obliged to attend as witnesses I accompanied them to the court. During the whole of this wretched mockery of justice I sufferred living torture. It was to be decided whether the result of my curiosity and lawless desires would cause the death of two of my fellow beings. One a smiling babe full of innocence and joy, the other far more dreadfully murdered with every agravation <of> infamy that could make that murder more terrible. Justine also was a girl of merit and possessed qualities which promised to render her life happy; now all was to be obliterated in an ignominious grave;—And I the cause! A thousand times rather would I have confessed myself guilty of the crime ascribed to Justine, but I was absent when it was committed and such a declaration would have been considered as the ravings of a madman and could not have exculpated her who suffered through me.

The appearance of Justine was calm. She was dressed in mourning and her countenance, always engaging, was rendered by the solemnity of her feelings exquisitely beautiful. Yet she appeared confident in innocence and did not tremble although gazed at and execrated by thousands. For all the kindness which her beauty might have gained from others was obliterated by the rememberance of the enormity she was supposed to have committed. She was tranquil yet her tranquillity was evident<ly> constrained—and as her confusion had before been adduced as a proof of her guilt she worked up her mind to an appearance of courage. When she entered the court she threw her eyes round it and quickly discovered where we were seated—a tear seemed to dim her eye when she saw us but she recovered herself and a look of sorrowful affection seemed to attest her utter guiltlessness.

The trial began and after the advocate against her had stated the charge several witnesses were called. Several strange facts combined against her which would have staggered any one who had not such pro<o>f of her innocence as I had. She had been out

 Compare pp. 105–6

the whole of the night on which the murder had been committed and towards morning had been perceived by a market-woman not far from the spot where the body of the murdered child had been afterwards found. She asked her what she did there?—for she looked very strangely and only returned a confused answer. She returned to the house about eight o'clock and when some one enquired where she had passed the night she replied that she had been looking of the child and demanded earnestly if any thing had been heard concerning him. When the body was brought into the house she fell into violent hysterics and kept her bed for several days. The picture was then produced which the servant had found in her pocket and when Elizabeth in a faltering voice proved that it was the same she had, an hour before the child had been missed, placed round his neck<,> a murmur of indignation and horror filled the court.

Justine was then called on for her defence. As the trial had proceeded her countenance had altered. Surprise horror and misery were strongly expressed. Sometimes she struggled with her tears but when she was desired to speak she collected her powers and spoke in an audible although variable voice.

"God knows," she said, "how entirely I am inocent. but I do not pretend to be acquitted on account of my protestations<.> I rest my innocence on a simple explanation of the facts which have been adduced against me, and I hope the character I have always borne will encline my judges to a favourable interpretation where any circumstance appears doubtful or suspicious.

She then related that by the permission of Elizabeth she had passed the evening of the night on which the murder was perpetrated at the house of an aunt who resided in Chêne a village about a league from Geneva. On her return at about nine o'clock she met a man who asked her if she had seen any thing of the child who was lost. She was frightened at this account, and passed several hours in looking for him when the gates of Geneva were shut and

Compare pp. 106–7

she remained several hours of the night in a cottage, but unable to rest or sleep, she rose early that she might again endeavour to find my brother. If she had gone near the spot where his body lay it was without her knowledge and she had been confused when questioned by the market woman, was that surprising when she was so wretched on the loss of poor William. Concerning the picture she could give no account. "I know," continued the unhappy victim "how heavily and fatally this one circumstance weighs against me but I have no power of explaining it and when I have expressed my utter ignorance I am only left to conjecture concerning the probabilities by which it might have been placed in my pocket. But here also I am checked I believe that I have no enemy on earth and none surely who could have been so wicked as to destroy me wantonly. Did the murderer place it there? I know of no opportunity afforded him for so doing or if I had why should he have stolen the jewel to part with it again so soon?

"I commit my cause to the justice of my judges yet I see no room for hope. I beg permission to have a few witnesses examined concerning my character and if then my supposed guilt is apparent I shall be condemned although I would pledge my salvation on my innocence."

Several witnesses were called who had known her for many years and they spoke well of her but fear and hatred of the crime of which they supposed her guilty rendered them timorous and unwilling to come forward. Elizabeth saw even this last resource, her excellent and irreproachable dispositions & conduct, about to fail the accused, when although violently agitated she desired permission to speak. "I am" said she "the cousin of the unhappy child who was murdered or rather his sister for I was educated by and lived with his parents ever since and long before his birth; it may therefore be judged indecent in me to come forward on this occasion but when I see a fellow creature about to perish through the cowardice of her pretended friends I wish to be allowed to speak that I may say what I know of

 Compare pp. 107–8

her character. I am well acquainted with it. I have lived in the same house with her at one time for five and afterwards for nearly two years. During all that period she appeared to me a most amiable and benevolent creature. She nurst my aunt in her last illness with the greatest affection and care and afterterwards attended her own mother during a long & tedious illness in a manner that excited the admiration of all who knew her. After which she again lived in my uncle's house where she was beloved by all the family. she was warmly attached to the child who has been murdered and acted towards him like a most affectionate Mother. for my own part I do not hesitate to say that not withstanding all the evidence produced against her I believe and rely on her perfect innocence. She had no temptation for such an action<;> as to the bauble on which the chief proof rests if she had earnestly wished for it I should have willingly given it her so much do I esteem and value her."

Excellent Elizabeth! A murmur of approbation was heard, but it was on her account & not in favour of poor Justine on whom the public indignation turned with renewed violence, charging her with the blackest ingratitude. She herself wept as Elizabeth spoke but she did not answer. My own agitation & anguish was extreme during the whole of the trial. I believed in her innocence I knew it. Could the monster who had (I did not for a minute doubt) murdered my brother, al<s>o in his hellish sport have betrayed the innocent to death and ignominy. I could not sustain the horror of my situation and when I saw that the popular voice and the countenance of the Judges had already condemned my unhappy victim I rushed out of the court in agony. The tortures of the accused did not equal mine<;> she was sustained by innocence but the fangs of remorse tore my bosom—I passed a night of unmingled wretchedness. In the morning I went to the court; my lips and throat were parched. I dared not ask the fatal question—but I was known and the officer guessed the cause of my visit—the ballots had been thrown they were all black & Justine was condemned.

Compare pp. 108–9

Chapter 12 [*for* 13]

I cannot attempt to describe what I then felt—I had had sensations of horror before and I have endeavoured to bestow on them adequate expressions but now words cannot convey any idea of the heart sickening despair that I endured. The person to whom I had addressed myself also added that Justine had already confessed her guilt. "That evidence" he observed—"was hardly required in so glaring a case but I am glad of it; and indeed none of our judges like to condemn a criminal upon circumstantial evidence let it be ever so decisive."

When I returned home Elizabeth eagerly demanded the result. "My cousin" replied I, "it is decided as you may have suspected—all Judges had rather that ten innocent should suffer than that one guilty should escape: but she has confessed."

This was a dire blow to poor Elizabeth who had relied with firmness on her innocence. "Alas!" said she "How shall I ever again believe in human benovolence—Justine, whom I loved and esteemed as my sister. How could she put on those smiles of innocence only to betray—her mild eyes seemed incapable of any severity or ill humour and yet she has committed a murder."

Soon after we heard that the poor victim had expressed a wish to see my cousin. My father wished her not to go but said that he left it to her own judgement and feelings to decide. "Yes," said Elizabeth "I will go although she is guilty—and you Victor shall acco<m>pany me—I cannot go alone." The idea of this visit was torture to me yet I could not refuse.

We entered the gloomy prison chamber and beheld Justine sitting on some straw at the further end; her hands were mannacled and her head rested on her knees,—she rose on seeing us and when we were left alone with her she threw herself at the feet of Elizabeth weeping bitterly.

 Compare pp. 109–10

My cousin wept also—Oh Justine said she, why did you rob me of my last consolation—I relied on your innocence and although I was very wretched I was not so miserable as I am now."

"And do you also believe that I am so very very wicked?" Cried Justine Do you also join with my enemies to crush me? Her voice was suffocated with sobs.

"Rise my poor girl," said Elizabeth "why do you kneel if you are innocent I am not one of your enemies, I believed in your innocence notwithstanding every evidence untill I heard that you had yourself declared your guilt. That report you say is false, and be assured my dear Justine nothing can for a minute shake my confidence in you but your own confession—"

"I did confess" said Justine "but I confessed a lie. I confessed that I might obtain absolution but now that falsehood lies heavier at my heart than all my other sins. The God of heaven forgive me! Ever since I was condemned my confessor has besieged me; he threatened and menaced untill I almost began to think that I was the wicked wretch he said I was. He threatened excomunication and Hell fire in my last moments if I continued obdurate. Dear Lady, I had none to support me—all looked on me as a wretch doom<ed> to ignominy and perdition; what could I do? In an evil hour I subscribed to a lie and now only I am truly miserable." She paused, weeping, and then continued. "I thought with horror, my sweet lady, that you should believe that your Justine whom your b<l>essed aunt had so highly honoured and whom you loved, was a wretch capable of a crime which none but the devil himself could have perpetrated. Dear William, dearest blessed child, I soon shall see you again in heaven & glory and that consoles me going as I am to suffer ignominy and death."

"Oh Justine" cried the weeping Elizabeth, "forgive me for having for one moment distrusted you—why did you confess? But do not mourn my dear girl, I will every where proclaim your innocence and will force belief. Yet you must die—you my companion, my

Compare pp. 110–11

playfellow, my more than sister—die—I never never can survive so horrible a misfortune".

"Dear Sweet lady," do not weep"—replied Justine "—you ought to raise me with thoughts of a better life, and elevate me from the petty cares of this world of injustice and strife—Do not you, excellent Elizabeth drive me to despair."

Elizabeth embraced the sufferer "I will try to comfort you," said she, but this I fear is an evil too deep and poignant to admit of consolation for there is no hope Yet heaven bless thee, my dearest Justine, with resignation and a confidence elevated beyond this world. Oh how I hate all its shews and mockeries.—When one creature is murdered another is immediately deprive<d> of life in a slow torturing manner & then the executioners<,> their hands yet reeking with the blood of innocence<,> believe that they have done a great deed. They call this retribution; hateful name! When that word is pronounced I know that greater and more horrid punishments are going to be inflicted than the gloomiest tyrant has ever inventented to satiate his utmost revenge. Yet this is not consolation for you, my Justine, unless indeed that you may glory in escaping so miserable a den. Alas! I would I were in peace with my aunt & my sweet William—escaped from light which is hateful to me and the visages of men which I abhor."

Justine smiled languidly. "This, dear Lady said she is despair and not resignation. I must not learn the lesson that you would teach me—talk of somthing else of somthing that will bring joy and not encrease of misery."

During this conversation I had retired to a corner of the prison-room where I could conceal the horrid anguish that possessed me—Despair! Who dared talk of that? The poor victim who on the morrow was to pass the dreary boundary of life & death felt not as I did—Such deep & bitter agony I gnashed my teeth and ground them together uttering a groan that came from my inmost soul. Justine started<;> when she saw who it was she approached me. "Dear Sir," said she, "you are very kind to visit me; you I hope do not believe that I am guilty."

I could not answer—"No Justine" said Elizabeth; "he is more convinced of your innocence than I was<,> for even when he heard that you had confessed he did not credit it."

"I truly thank him"—said Justine "In these last minutes I feel the sincerest gratitude for those who still think of me with kindness. How sweet is the affection of others to such a wretch as I am—It removes more than half my misfortune and I feel as if I could die in peace now that my innocence is acknowledged by you, sweet lady, and your cousin."

Thus the poor sufferer tried to comfort others and herself. She indeed gained the resignation she wished for but I the true murderer felt the never dying worm alive and I was allowed no hope or consolation. Elizabeth also wept and was unhappy but hers also was the misery of innocence which like a cloud that passes over the fair moon & for a while hides but cannot disturb its brightness<;> anguish and despair had penetrated into the core of my heart—I bore a hell within me that nothing could diminish.

We staid several hours with Justine and it was with great difficulty that Elizabeth tore herself away "I wish" cried she that I were to die with you—I cannot live in this world of misery." Justine assumed an air of Cheerfullness while she with difficulty repressed the bitter tears—"Farewell sweet lady, dearest Elizabeth may heaven in its bounty bless and preserve you May this be the last misfortune that you will ever suffer.—live & be happy to make others so.

As We returned Elizabeth said, You do not know, my dear Victor, how much I am relieved now that I trust in the innocence of this unfortunate girl. I never could again have known peace if I had been deceived in my reliance on her. For the moment that I did believe it I felt anguish that I could not have long sustained. Now my heart is lightened. The innocent suffers—but she whom I thought amiable and good is not wicked and I am consoled."

Compare pp. 112–13

Amiable Cousin! Such were your thoughts mild and gentle as your dear eyes and voice. but I.——I was a wretch & none ever conceived the misery that I then sufferred.

Chap. 13th [*for* 14th]

Nothing is more painful when the mind has been worked up by a quick succession of events, for a dead calm of inaction and certainty to follow which deprives the soul both of hope or fear. Justine died—She rested. & I was alive the blood flowed freely in my veins but a weight of despair & remorse pressed on my heart which nothing could remove—Sleep fled from my eyes. I wandered like an evil spirit for I had committed deeds of mischief beyond description horrible, and more much more (I persuaded my self) was yet in store. Yet my heart overflowed with kindness and goodness—I had begun life with benevolent intentions and thirsted for the moment when I could put them in practise and make myself useful to my fellow beings. Now all was blasted; Instead of serenity of conscience which allowed me to look back on my actions with self satisfaction, and from thence new hopes like gay sweet-smelling flowers to spring up with regard to futurity. I was seized by remorse and guilt, and hurried away to a hell no language can describe.

This state of mind altered my health which had entirely recovered from the first shock it had sustained. I shunned the face of man; all sound of joy or complacency was torture to me; Solitude was my only consolation deep, dark, death-like solitude. My father observed with pain how my dispositions & habits were altered and endeavoured to reason with me on the folly of giving way to immoderate grief. "Do you think, Victor" said he "That I do not suffer also—no one could love a child more than I did

 Compare pp. 113–14

your brother—(tears came into his eyes as he said this) but is not our duty owed to their survivors not to add to their unhappiness by an appearance of immoderate grief. It is also a duty owed to yourself; for excessive sorrow prevents improvement or enjoyment, or even the discharge of day [*for* daily] usefullness without which no man is fit for society."

This advice, although good, was utterly innaplicable to my case; I should have been the first to hide my grief and console my friends if remorse had not mingled its bitterness with my other sensations. Now I could only answer my father with a look of despair and endeavour to hide myself from his view. About this time we retired to our house at Belrive. This change was very agreable to me in particular. The shutting of the gates of the town regularly at ten o'clock and the impossibility of staying on the lake after that hour rendered our residence within the walls of Geneva very irksome to me. I was now free: often, after the rest of the family had retired for the night I took the boat and passed the night upon the water: sometimes with my sails set I was carried by the wind and sometimes after rowing into the middle of the lake I left the boat to pursue its own course and gave way to my own miserable reflections. I was often tempted when all was at peace around me and I the only unquiet thing that wandered restless in a scene so beautiful & heavenly; if I except alone some bat, or the harsh and interrupted croaking of the frogs which I heard only when I approached the shore; often I say, I was tempted to plunge into the still and silent lake and let the water close over me & my calamities for ever. But I was restrained when I thought of the heroic & suffering Elizabeth whom I tenderly loved, and whose existence was bound up in mine. And then I thought also of my father and surviving brother; should I not by my base desertion leave them exposed & unprotected to the malice of the fiend whom I had let lose [*for* loose] among them? At these moments I wept bitterly and wished that peace would revisit my mind that I might

Compare pp. 114–15

afford them consolation and happiness—but that could not be: remorse took away every hope—I had been the cause of unalterable evil, and I lived in daily fear of some new wickedness which the monster whom I had created might perpetrate—I had a feeling that all was not over, and that he would still commit some signal crime which by its enormity would almost efface the recollection of the past. My abhorrence of this fiend cannot be conceived—When I thought of him I gnashed my teeth my eyes became inflamed and I ardently wished to extinguish that life which I had so thoughtlessly bestowed. When I reflected on his crimes and malice, my hatred and revenge burst all bounds of moderation I would have made a pilgrimage to the highest Andes could I when there have precipitated him to their foot; I wished but to see him again that I might wreak the utmost extent of anger on his head and avenge the deaths of William and Justine.

Our house was the house of mourning. my father's health was deeply shaken by the horror of the recent events. Elizabeth was sad and desponding she no longer took delight in her ordinary occupations; all pleasure seemed to her sacriledge towards the dead; eternal woe and tears she then thought was the just tribute she should pay to innocence so blasted and destroyed. She was no longer that happy creature she had been when I last saw her—who wandered with me on the banks of the lake and talked with extacy of our future prospects—She was grave, and often conversed of the inconstancy of fortune and the instability of human life—"When I reflect, my dear Cousin," she said "on the miserable death of Justine Moritz, I no longer see the world and its works in the same light as they before appeared to me. Before<,> I looked upon the accounts of vice and injustice that I read in books or heard from others as tales of ancient days or imaginary evils; but now misery has come home and men appear to me as monsters thirsting for each others blood. Yet I am certainly unjust.—Every one believed that poor girl to be guilty, and if she had<,> would she not have been the most depraved of creatures. For the sake of a few jewels to have murdered the son of her benefactor & friend, a child whom she had nursed from its birth and appeared to love as if it had been her own. I could not consent to the death of any human being but certainly I should have thought such a woman unworthy of life—Yet she was innocent—I know—I feel she was innocent You are of the same opinion and that confirms me. Alas, Victor! when falsehood can look so like the truth, who can assure themselves of certain happiness? I feel as if I were walking on the edge of <a> precipiece towards which thousands are crowding & endeavouring to plunge me into the abyss. William & Justine were assassinated and the murderer escapes, wearing human lineaments; he walks about the world free & perhaps respected. But even if I were condemmed to suffer on the scaffold for the same crimes I would not change places with such a wretch."

I listened to this discourse with the extremest agony—I—not in deed but in effect was the true murderer.—Elizabeth read my anguish in my countenance, and kindly taking my hand said—"My dearest cousin, you must calm yourself; these events have affected me God knows how deeply! but I am not so wretched as you are. There is an expression of misery and sometimes of revenge in your countenance that makes me tremble; be calm, my beloved Victor, I would sacrifice my life to your peace. We surely shall be happy; quiet in our native country and not mingling in the world<,> what can disturb our tranquillity?"

She shed tears as she said this, but at the same time smiled, that she might chase away the fiend that lurked in my heart. My father who saw in the unhappiness that was painted in my face, only an exaggeration of that sorrow which I might naturally feel<,> thought that an amusement suited to my taste would be the best means of restoring to me my wonted serenity—It was from this cause that he had removed to the country & induced by the same reasons he now proposed that we should all take a journey to

Compare pp. 116–17

the Valley of Camounix. I had been there before but Elizabeth & Ernest never had, and both had often expressed a wish to see this place which had been described to them as so wonderful & sublime. Accordingly we departed from Geneva on this tour about the middle of the month of august nearly two months after the death of Justine.

The weather was beautiful and if mine had been a sorrow to be chased away by any fleeting circumstance this voyage would certainly have had the effect which my father intended. As it was I was interrested and sometimes amused. The first day we travelled in a carriage. In the morning we had seen the mountains at a distance to which we gradually advanced. We perceived that the valley through which we wound, and which was formed by the Arve whose course we followed, closed upon us by degrees and when the sun had set we saw immense mountains & precipieces overhanging on each side of us & heard the sound of mountain streams, and the dashing of waterfalls.

The next day we pursued our journey on mules and as we ascended still higher; the valley assumed a more beautiful & verdant appearance—Ruined castles on piny mountains; the impetuous Arve, and cottages every here & there peeping from among the trees, formed a scene of singular beauty. But it was augmented & rendered sublime by the mighty alps whose white & shining piramids & domes towered above all like another earth—the habitations of another race of beings We passed the bridge of Pellissier, where the ravine which the river forms opened before us and we began to ascend the mountain which over hung it—. Soon after we entered the Valley of Chamounix. This valley is more wonderful and sublime but not so beautiful & picturesque as that of Servox; through which we had just passed. The high & snowy mountains were its boundaries but we saw no more ruined castles or fertile fields. Immense glaciers approached the road, we heard the rumbling thunder of the falling Avelanche and marked

 Compare pp. 117–18

the smoke of its passage.—Mont Blanc, the beautiful Mont Blanc raised itself from the surrounding <u>aiguilles</u> and its tremendous <u>dome</u> overlooked the valley.

During this journey I sometimes joined Elizabeth and exerted myself to point out to her the various beauties of the scene.—And often I suffered my mule to lag behind & indulged in the misery of reflection. At other times I spurred on the animal before my companions that I might forget them, the world, and more than all myself. When at a distance I alighted and threw myself on the grass weighed down by horror & despair. At eight in the evening we arrived at Chamounix. My father & Elizabeth were very much fatigued. Ernest who accompanied us was delighted and in high spirits—The only circumstance that detracted from his pleasure was the south wind and the rain that that wind seemed to promise for the next day.

We retired early to our appartments but not to sleep:—at least I did not. I remained many hours at the window watching the lightning that played above Mont Blanc—and listening to the rushing of the Arve which ran before my window.

Chap. 14 [*for* 15]

The next day, contrary to the prognostics of our guides, was fine although clouded. We visited the source of the Aveiron and rode about the valley the whole day. These sublime and magnificent scenes afforded me the greatest consolation that I was capable of receiving They elevated me from all littleness of feeling and although they did not remove my grief they subdued and tranquilized it. In some degree, also they diverted my mind from the thoughts it had brooded over for the last month. I returned in the evening, fatigued but less unhappy and conver<s>ed with the

Compare pp. 118–19

family with more cheerfulness than I had been accustomed to for some time. My father was pleased and Elizabeth overjoyed; "My dear Cousin," said she, "You see what happiness you diffuse when you are cheerful; do not relapse again!—

The following morning the rain poured down in torrents and thick mists hid the summits of the mountains. I rose early but felt unusually melancholy. The rain depressed me, my old feelings recurred and I was miserable. I knew how my father would be dissapointed at this sudden change and I wished to avoid him untill I had recovered myself so far as to conceal the feelings that overpowered me—I knew that they would remain that day at the inn and as I had ever inured myself to rain and cold I resolved to go to the summit of Montanvert alone. I remembered the effect the view of the tremendous and ever moving glacier had had upon my mind when I first saw it how it had then filled me with a sublime extacy that gave wings to the soul and allowed it to soar from the lower world to light & joy. The sight of the awful & majestic in nature had indeed always the effect of solemnizing my mind & causing me to forget the passing cares of life. I determined to go alone for I was well acquainted with the path and the presence of another would destroy the solitary grandeur of the scene.

The ascent is precipitous but the path is cut into continual and short windings which enable you <to> surmount the perpedicularity of the mountains—It is a scene terrifically desolate. In a thousand places the traces of the winter avelanche may be perceived where trees lie broken and strewed on the ground; some entirely destroyed others bent leaning upon the jutting corners of the mountain, or upon other trees. The path as you ascend higher is interspersed with ravines <of> snow, down which stones continually roll from above; one of {the} them is particularly dangerous as the slightest sound such as speaking in a loud voice is a concussion of air sufficient to draw destruction <upon> the head of the speaker. The pine here are not tall or luxuriant but they are sombre and add an

Compare pp. 119–20

air of gravity to the scene. I looked on the valley beneath. Vast mist were rising from the river which ran throught [*for* through it] and curling in thick wreaths around the opposite mountains whose summits were hid in the clouds, while rain poured from the dark sky and added to the melancholy impression I received from the objects around me—Alas! why does man boast of sensibilities above those apparent in the brute<;> it only renders them more necessary beings. If our impulses were confined to hunger thirst and desire we might be nearly free but now we are moved by every wind that blows & by every chance word or scene that that wind may convey to us

> We rest, A dream has power to poison sleep
> We rise one wandering thought pollutes the day
> We feel conceive, or reason—laugh or weep
> Embrace fond woe or cast our cares away
> It is the same—for be it joy or sorrow
> The path of its departure still is free
> Mans yesterday may ne'er be like is [*for* his] morrow
> Nought may endure but mutability.

It was noon when I arrived at the top of the ascent. For some time I sat upon the rock that overlooks the sea of ice. A mist covered both that and the surrounding mountains Presently a breeze dissipated the mist and I descended on the glacier. The surface is very uneven rising like the waves of a troubled sea, decending low, & interspered by rifts that sink deep—The width of the ice is a league, but I was nearly two hours crossing it—The opposite mountain is a bare perpendicular rock.—From that side where I now stood Montanvert was exactly opposite at the distance of a league and above it rose Mont Blanc in awful majesty. I remained in a recess of the rock gazing on this wonderful & stupedous scene—My heart before sad swelled with somthing like joy<.> I exclaimed—Wandering spirits, if indeed ye wander and

Compare pp. 120–21

do not rest in your narrow beds, allow me this faint happiness or take me as your companion away from the joys of life." As I said this I suddenly beheld the figure of a man at some distance advancing towards me with superhuman speed—He bounded over the crevices in the ice by which I had walked with caution, his stature also as he approached seemed to exceed that of man—I was troubled—a mist covered my eyes and I felt ready to faint—The cold breeze of the mountains quickly restored me. But I perceived as he came nearer (sight tremendous and abhorred) that it was the wretch whom I had created. I trembled with rage and horror resolving to wait his approach & then close with him in mortal combat. He approached; His countenance bespoke bitter anguish combined with disdain and malignancy. But I scarcely observed this—anger and hatred had at first deprived me of utterance and I recovered only to overwhelm him with words expressive of utter detestation and contempt—"Devil" I exclaimed—"do you dare approach me and do not you dread the fierce vengeance of my arm wreaked on your miserable head—Begone vile insect or rather Stay that I may trample you to dust and oh that I could with the end <of> your miserable existence restore those creatures whom you have diabollicaly murdered"

"I expect this reception" said the dæmon all men hate the wretched—how then must I be hated who am miserable beyond conception or idea—Yet you my creator hate me and spurn me thy creature to whom thou art bound with ties only dissoluble by the death of one of us. And you wish to kill me. How dare you sport thus with life? Do your duty towards me and I will do mine towards you & the rest of mankind. If you comply with my conditions—I will leave them and you at peace—but if you refuse I will glut the maw of death untill he be satiated even with your dearest friends."

"Abhorred monster, cried I furiously, fiend that thou art the tortures of Hell are too soft for the wretched devil! you reproach me with your creation; come, that I may extinguish the spark that

 Compare pp. 121–2

I so negligently bestowed." My rage was without bounds I sprung on him that I might destroy so hateful a monster—He eluded and said—Be calm! I entreat you to hear me, before you give vent to your hatred on my devoted head.—Have I not suffered enough that you should wish to encrease my misery—Life although it be only an accumulation of anguish is dear to me and I will defend it<;> remember thou hast made me more powerful than thy self my height is superior to yours my joints more supple. But I do not wish to [?brave] you I am thy creature and I will be mild and docile to you, my gentle master, if you will perform your duty towards me. Oh Frankenstein, do not <be> equitable to every other and trample upon me to whom thy justice & even mere charity is most due. Remember that I am thy creature—Thy Adam—or rather the fallen angel for every where I see bliss while I alome [*for* alone] am irrecoverably wretched. I was benevolent and good: misery made me a fiend. make me happy and I shall again be virtuous

Begone replied I—I will not hear you. there can be no community between you and I—We are enemies—Begone or let us try our strength in a fight in which one must fall."

How can I move you? said the fiend—Will no entreaties cause you to turn a favourable eye upon thy creature who implores thy goodness and compassion—Believe me, Frankenstien I was benevolent—my soul glowed with love and humanity but am I not alone miserably alone—You, my creator abhor me What hope have I then from your fellow creatures—They spurn and abhor me. The desart mountains and mour<n>ful glaciers are my refuge—I have wandered here many days—The caves of ice which I only do not fear are a dwelling to me and the only one which man does not grudge—These bleak skies I hail for they are kinder to me than your fellow beings Man hates me and if he knew of my existence would as you do arm themselves for my destruction—Shall I not then hate them who abhor me I will keep no terms with my enemies I am miserable & they shall share my wretchedness—Yet

Compare pp. 122–4

it is in your power to recompense me and deliver them from an evil which you have bestowed on them. Let your compassion and justice be moved and do not disdain me. Listen to my tale! when you have heard that deny or comiserate me as you shall judge I deserve. But hear me—The guilty are allowed by human laws, bloody as they are, to speak in their defence Listen to me Frankenstein You accuse me of mu<r>der and yet you would with a satisfied conscience destroy thy creature—Oh praise the eternal justice of man!—Yet I ask you not to spare me, listen and then, if you will, destroy the work of your hands."

"Why" cried I—"do you call to my remembrance those circumstances which I shudder to reflect ever occured—Cursed be the day in which you first saw light, cursed (although I curse myself) be the hands that formed you!—You have made me wretched beyond expression<;> begone, relieve me from thy sight

Thus I relieve you, Creator<,> he replied & placed his abhorred hand before my eyes which I flung from me with violence<,> from the sight of one whom you abhor.—still you can listen to me and grant me your compassion—By the {the} virtues I once possessed I demand this of you—Hear my tale—It is long and strange and the temperature of this place is not fitting to your fine sensations; come to the hut on the mountain—The sun is yet high in the heavens—before it descends to hide itself behind these mountains and illumines another world you will have heard my story and can decide. And on you it rests whether I quit for ever the habitations of man & lead a harmless life or become the scourge of your fellow creatures—

As he said this he led the way across the ice—I followed—my heart was full and did not answer him but when I weighed the various arguments which he had used, I felt enclined to listen to his tale—I was partly urged by curiosity, and compassion confirmed me.—I had hitherto supposed him to be the murder<er> of my brother and I wished to find this either confirmed or denied.

 Compare pp. 124–5

For the first time also I felt what the duties of a creator towards his creature were and that I ought to render him happy before I complained of his wickedness. these motives urged me to comply with his demand—We crossed the ice therefore, and ascended the opposite rock.—The air was cold and the rain began again to descend—We entered the hut—the fiend with an air of exultation I with a heavy heart and depressed spirits—But I consented to listen and sitting by the fire which he lighted he thus began his tale.

Compare p. 125

Frankenstein

or

The Modern Prometheus

VOLUME II

Chap 1

"It is with difficulty that I remember the æra of my being.[†] All the events of that period appear confused & indistinct. A strange sensation seized me I saw, felt heard and smelt at the same time and it was indeed a long time before I learned to distinguish between the {op}operations of my various senses. By degrees I remember a stronger light pressed upon my nerves so that I was obliged to close my eyes. Darkness then came over me and troubled me.—But hardly had I felt this when (by opening my eyes as I now suppose) the light poured in upon me again—I walked and I believe descended; but presently I found a great alteration in my sensations; before, dark opaque bodies had surrounded me impervious to my touch or sight—and I now found that I could wander on at liberty with no obstacles which I could not either surmount or avoid—The light became more & more opressive to me and the heat wearying me as I walked I sought a place where I could perceive shade. This was the forest near Ingolstadt, and here by the side of a brook I lay for some hours resting from my fatigue untill I felt tormented by hunger and thirst. This roused me from my nearly dormant state and I ate some berries which I found on the trees or lying on the ground—I slaked my thirst by the brook and then again lying down I was overcome by sleep,—It was dark when I awoke, I felt cold also, and half frightened on finding myself so desolate. Before I had quitted your appartment on a sensation of cold I had covered myself with some clothes, but

† The first sentence in the first chapter of what MWS headed 'Vol. II' and 'Chap I' in the Draft—dramatically opening the second volume with the monster's narrative.

Compare p. 128

these were not sufficient to secure me from the dews of night. I was a poor helpless miserable wretch—I knew & could distinguish nothing but feeling pain invade me on all sides I sat down and wept.

Soon a gentle light stole over the heavens and gave me a sensation of pleasure I started up, and beheld a radiant form rise from among the trees. I gazed with a kind of wonder—It moved slowly; but it enlightened my path, and I again went out in search of berries. I was still cold when under one of the trees I found a huge cloak with which I covered myself, and sat down on the ground. No distinct ideas occupied my mind all was confused I felt the light, and hunger and thirst and darkness; innumerable sounds rung in my ears and on all sides various scents saluted me; the only object that I could distinguish was the bright moon and I fixed my eyes on that with pleasure. Several changes of day and night passed and the orb of night had greatly lessened when I began to distinguish my sensations. I first saw the clear stream that supplied me with drink and the trees that shaded me with their foliage. I was delighted when I first discovered that a pleasant sound that often saluted my ears proceeded from the throats of the little animals who often intercepted the light from my eyes. I began also to see with greater accuracy the forms that surrounded me and to perceive the boundaries of the radiant light which canopied me.—sometimes I tried to imitate the pleasant songs of the birds but was unable—Sometimes I wished to express my sensations in my own mode but unco<u>th and innarticulate sound broke from me which frightened me into silence again.

The moon had dissapeared from the night, & again with a lessened form it shewed itself while I still remained in the forest. My sensations were by this time become distinct & my mind received every day aditional ideas. My eyes became accustomed to the light and to perceive objects in their right forms;—I distinguished the insect from the herb, and by degrees one herb

 Compare pp. 128–9

from another—I found that the sparrow uttered none but harsh notes but those of the blackbird were sweet and enticing. one day when I was oppressed by cold I found a fire that had been left by some wandering beggars and was over come with delight. In my joy I thrust my hand into the live embers but quickly drew it away with a cry of pain—How strange, I thought, that the same cause should at once produce such opposite effects—I examined the materials of the fire, & to my joy found it to be wood—I quickly collected some branches but they were wet and would not burn. I was pained at this and sat still watching the opperation of the fire. The wet wood I had placed near the heat dried, and itself became hot. I reflected on this, and by touching the various branches I discovered the cause and busied myself in collecting a great deal of wood that I might dry it and have a plentiful supply When night came on and sleep, I was in the greatest fear lest my fire should be extinguished I covered it carefully with dry wood and leaves & then placed upon that wet branches and then spreading my cloak I <lay> on the ground & sunk into sleep. It was morning when I awoke & my first care was to visit the fire—I uncovered it and a gentle breeze quickly fanned it into a flame I observed this also and contrived a fan of branches which roused the embers when thy [*for* they] were nearly extinguished. When night again came I found with pleasure that the fire gave light as well as heat and the discovery of this element was useful to me also in my food—for I found some of offals that the travellers had left had been roasted and tasted much more savoury than the berries I gathered; I tried therefore to dress my food in the same manner, placing them on the live embers—I found that the berries were spoiled by this opperation and the nuts much improved. Food however became very scarce and I often spent a day searching in vain for a few acorns to assuage the pangs of hunger. When I found this <I> resolved to quit the place which I had hitherto inhabited & to seek for a place where the few wants I experienced

Compare pp. 129–30

would be more easily satisfied. In this emigration I exceedingly lamented the loss of my fire—I had obtained it by strange means and knew not how to produce it by myself. This obtained my serious consideration for several hours but I was obliged to leave it and wrapping myself up in my cloak I struck across the wood towards the setting sun—I passed three days in these rambles and at length discovered the open country—A great fall of snow had taken place the night before and the fields were of one uniform white<;> the appearrance was disconsolate and I found my feet chilled by the cold damp substance that covered the ground—It was about seven in the morning and I longed to obtain food and shelter. At length I perceived a small hut which had doubtless been built for the convenience of some shepheard. This was a new sight to me and I examined the structure of it with great curiosity. finding the door open I entered. An old man sat in it, near a fire by which he was preparing his breakfast he turned on hearing a noise and perceiving me shrieked loudly and quiting the hut ran across the fields with a speed of which his debilitated form hardly appeared capable. His flight somewhat surprised me—but I was inchanted with the appearance of the hut. Here the snow and rain could not penetrate—the ground was dry and it presented to me then as exquisite & divine a retreat as Pandemonium appeared to the dominions of Hell. I greedily devoured the remnants of the shepherds breakfast which consisted of bread, cheese, milk & rhenish wine; the latter of which however I did not like. Then overcome by fatigue I lay down among some straw & fell asleep.

It was noon when I awoke and allured by the warmth of the sun I determined to recommence my travels—& depositing the remains of the peasants breakfast in a wallet I found, I proceeded across the fields for several hours, untill at sunset I came to a village. How miraculous did this appear. The huts the neater cottages & statelier houses engaged my admiration by turns—The vegetables in the garden allured me and the milk and cheese that I saw placed

 Compare pp. 130–31

at the windows of some of the cottages—One of the best of these I entered—but I had hardly placed my foot inside the door before the children shrieked and one of the women fainted, the village was roused some fled,—some attacked me untill grievously bruised by stones and many other kinds of missile weapon I escaped to the open country and fearfully took refuge in a low hut—quite bare and making a wretched appearance after the palaces I had beheld in the village.—This hut however adjoined a cottage of a neat & pleasant appearance, but after my late bought experience I dared not enter it. My place of refuge was constructed of wood, but so low that I could with difficulty sit upright in it. No wood however was placed on the earth which formed the floor of the cottage but it was dry and although the wind entered by innumerable chinks I found it an agreable assylum from the snow & rain Here then I retreated and lay down happy to have found a shelter from the inclemency of the season & still more from the barbarity of man

Chap. 2

As soon as morning dawned I crept from my assylum that I might view the adjacent cottage and discover if I could remain in the kennel that I had found. It was situated against the back of the cottage and surrounded on the sides which were exposed by a pigstye &—clear pool of water<.> one part was open and by that I had crept in but now I covered every crevice by which I might be discovered with stones & wood yet in such a manner that I could move them on an occasion to pass out; all the light I enjoyed came through the stye and that was sufficient for me.

Having thus arranged my dwelling & carpeted it with clean straw, I retired for I saw the figure of a man at a distance and I remembered too well my treatment the night before to trust myself

Compare pp. 131–2

in his power. I had first however provided for my sustenance for that day by a loaf of coarse bread which I purloined and a cup with which I could drink more conveniently than from my hand of pure water which flowed by my house—The floor was a little raised so that it was kept perfectly dry and by its vicinity to the chimney of the kitchen fire of the cottage it was tolerably warm. Being thus provided I determined to reside in this hovel untill somthing should occur which might alter my determination. It was indeed a paradise compared to the bleak forest, my former residence, the rain dropping branches & the dank earth. I ate my breakfast with pleasure and was about to remove a plank to procure myself a little water when I heard a step and looking through a small chink a [*for* I] beheld a young creature with a pail on her head passing before my hovel. The girl was young and of gentle demænour unlike what I have since found Cottagers and farm house servants to be—Yet she was meanly dressed—a coarse blue petticoat and a linen jacket being her only garb<;> her fair hair was plaited but not adorned; she looked patient yet sad. She passed away but in a quarter of an hour returned, bearing the pail which was now partly filled with milk. As she walked along seemingly incommoded by the burthen a young man met her whose countenance expressed a deeper desponcenscesly [*for* despondency]; uttering a few sounds with an air of melancholy he took the pail from her head and bore it into the cottage himself. She followed, and they disappeared—Presently I saw the young man again with some tools in his hand cross the field opposite the cottage and the girl was also busied sometimes in the cottage and sometimes in the yard where she fed some chickens. While I examined my dwelling I discovered that part of the cottage window had formerly occupied a corner of it but the panes had been filled up with wood. In one of these was a small & allmost imperceptible chink, through which the eye could just penetrate; and looking in I saw a small room whitewashed & clean but very bare of furniture<.> in one corner near a small fire I

 Compare pp. 133–4

beheld an old man leaning his head on his hand in a disconsolate attitude—The young girl was occupied in arranging the cottage but presently she took somthing out of a drawer which employed her hands & sat down beside the old man who taking up an instrument began to play and to produce sounds sweeter than the voice of the thrush or nightingale. It was a lovely sight even to me poor wretch who had never beheld aught beautiful before. the silver hairs & benevolent countenance of the aged cottager won my reverence while the gentle manners of the girl enticed my love. He played a sweet mournful air which I perceived drew tears from the eyes of his amiable companion of which the old man took <no> notice {it} untill she sobbed audibly—He then pronounced a few sounds and the poor creature leaving her work knelt at his feet he raised her and smiled with such kindness & love that I felt my own hard nerves move and I was obliged to withdraw from the hole.

Soon after this the young man returned bearing on his shoulders a load of wood the girl met him at the door helped to relieve him of his burthen and taking some of it into the cottage placed it on the fire; then she and the youth went apart into a nook of the cottage and he shewed her a large loaf and a piece of cheese.—She seemed pleased and went into the garden for soome roots & plants which she placed in water and then upon the fire—. She afterwards continued her work & the young man went into the garden and appeared busily employed in digging & {pul} pulling up roots—After he had been employed thus about an hour the young woman joined him, & they returned to the cottage together—The old man in the mean time had been pe<n>sive but on the approach of his companions he assumed a cheerful air, and they sat down to eat. the meal was quickly dispatched; the young woman was again occupied in arranging the cottage<;> the old man walked before the door in the sun for a few minutes, leaning on the arm of the youth Nothing could exceed in beauty the contrast between these two excellent creatures One was old, with silver hairs and a

Compare pp. 134–5

countenance beaming with benevolence & love; the younger was slight and graceful in his figure and his feautures were moulded with the finest simetry—yet his eyes & attitude expressed the utmost sadness and despondencency—The old man returned to the cottage; and the youth with tools different from those he had used in the morning, directed his steps across the fields—Night quickly shut in but to my extreme wonder I found that the cottagers had a means of prolonging light by the use of tapers and was pleased to find that setting of the sun did not put an end to the pleasure I experienced in watching my human neighbours.—In the evening the young girl and her companion were employed in various occupations{;} that I did not then understand, & the old man again took that instrument which produced the divine sound that had enchanted me in the morning. When he had finished the youth began,—not to play,—but to utter sounds which were monotonous and neither resembling the harmony of the old mans instrument or the songs of the birds I since found that he read but at that time I knew nothing of the science of words or letters. The family soon extinguished their lights and retired, as I conjectured, to rest.

I lay on my straw but I could not sleep—I thought of the occurences of the day.—What cheifly struck me was the gentle manners of these people, and I longed to join them but dared not.—I remembered too well the treatment I had suffered the night before from the barbarous villagers and resolved whatever course of conduct I might hereafter consider it proper to pursue that for the present I would remain quietly in my hovel watching and endeavouring to discover the motive of their actions.—

The cottagers arose the next morning before the sun;—The young woman arranged the cottage & prepared the food; & the youth mounted on a large strange animal rode away. This day was passed in the same routine and [*for* as] the preceeding one. The young man was constantly employed out of doors and the

 Compare pp. 135–6

girl in various laborious occupations.—The old man whom I soon perceived to be blind employed his leisure hours in playing on his instrument or in contemplation—Nothing could exceed the love & respect that the younger cottagers bore towards this venerable old man—They performed towards him every little office of love & duty with gentleness; and he rewarded them by his benevolent smiles.

They were not however entirely happy—The young man & his companion, often retired into a corner of their common room and wept. I saw no cause for this unhappiness but I was deeply affected by it—If such lovely creatures were miserable it was less strange that I, an imperfect and solitary being should be wretched—yet why were these gentle beings unhappy—they possessed a delightful house for (such it was in my eyes) and every luxury. they had a fire to warm them when chill and delicious viands when hungry—they were dressed in excellent clothes and still more they enjoyed one anothers company & speech—and interchanged each day looks of affection & kindness—What did their tears mean? Did they really express pain? I was at first unable to solve these questions but perpetual attention and time explained to me many of the appearances which at first seemed igmmatic [*for* enigmatic].

Chap. 3

A considerable period elapsed before I discovered one cause of the uneasiness of this amiable family—It was poverty—and they suffered that evil in a very distressing degree—their nourishment consisted entirely of bread—the vegetables of their garden and the milk of one cow which gave very little during the winter when its masters could scarcely procure any food for it. They often I believe suffered the pangs of hunger very poignantly especially the younger

Compare pp. 136–7

for several times they placed food before the old man when they had none for themselves—This trait of kindness moved me sensibly. I had been accustomed during the night to steal a part of their store for my own consumption; but when I found that in doing this I inflicted pain on the cottagers, I abstained, and satisfied myself with berries nuts and roots which I found in a neighbouring wood. I discovered also another means by which I was able to assist their labours. I found that the youth spent a great part of each day in collecting wood for the family fire—and during the night I often took his tools the use of which I quickly discovered and brought home firing sufficient for the consumption of several days—

I remember the first time I did this, the young woman who opened the door in the morning was greatly surprised to see a great pile of wood on the outside—she said some words in a loud voice, & presently the youth joined her who also appeared astonished. I observed with pleasure that he did not go to the forest that day but spent it in repairing the cottage & in cultivating the garden.—

By degrees also I made another discovery of still greater moment. I found that these people had a means of communicating their ideas to one another by articulate sounds which they uttered—I perceived that the words they spoke sometimes produced pleasure <or> pain, smiles or sadness in the minds & countenances of the hearers—This was indeed a Godlike science and I ardently desired to become acquainted with it—But I was baffled in every attempt I made for this purpose Their pronunciation was quick &<,> the words they uttered not having any apparent connexion with visible objects<,> I was unable to discover any clue by which I could unrable the mystery of their sounds. By great application however and after having remained several revolutions of the moon in my hovel I discovered the names that were given to some of the most familiar objects I learned & applied the words fire, milk bread & wood I learned also the names of the cottagers themselves—the youth & his companion had each of them several but the old man

 Compare pp. 137–8

had only one which was Father—The girl was called Sister or Agatha and the youth Felix brother or son. I cannot describe the delight I felt when I learned the ideas appropriated to each of these sounds and was able to pronounce them. I distinguished several other words without being able to understand or apply them—Such as good dearest—unhappy.

I spent the winter in this manner—the gentle manners and beauty of the cottagers greatly endeared them to me—When they were unhappy I felt depressed and I sympathized in their joys. I saw few human beings besides them, and if any other happened to enter the cottage their harsh manners & rude gait only enhanced to me the superior advantages of my friends. The old man, I could perceive, often endeavoured to encourage his children as I sometimes found that he called them. He would talk in a cheerful accent with an expression of goodness that bestowed pleasure even on me; Agatha listened with respect—her eyes sometimes filled with tears which she endeavoured to wipe away unperceived but I generally found that her manners and tone were more cheerful after having listenend to the exhortations of her father It was not thus with Felix. He was always the saddest of the groupe And even to my unpractised senses he appeared to have suffered more deeply than his friends. But if his countenance was more sorrowful his voice was more cheerful than that of his sister especially when he addressed the old man—

I could mention innumerable instances which although slight marked the dispositions of these amiable cottagers. In the midst of poverty and want Felix carried with pleasure to his sister the fist [*for* first] little white flower that peeped out from beneath the white ground—Early in the morning before she had risen he cleared away the snow that obstructed her path to the milk house; drew water from the well and brought the wood from the outhouse In the day I believe he worked sometimes for a neighbouring farmer, for he often went out and did not return untill dinner, yet brought

Compare pp. 138–9

no wood with him:—at other times he worked in the garden but as there was little to do in the frosty season he often read to the old man and Agatha. This reading had puzzled me extremely at first—but by degrees I discovered that he uttered many of the same sounds when he read as when he talked; I conjectured therefore that he found on the paper signs for speech which he understood And I ardently longed to comprehend these also; but how was†

Chapter 5

Sometime elapsed before I learned the history of my friends.‡ It was one that could not fail to impress itself deeply in my mind unfolding as it did a number of circumstances each interesting & wonderful to one so utterly inexperienced as I was.

The name of the old man was De Lacey. He was decended from a good family in France where for many years he had lived in affluence respected by his superiors & beloved by his equals. His son was bred in the service of his country & Agatha had ranked with ladies of the highest distinction. A few months previous to my arrival they had lived in a large & luxurious city called Paris, surrounded by friends & possessed of every enjoyment that virtue accompanied with a competent fortune could afford.

The father of Safie had been the cause of their fall He was a Turkish Merchant and had inhabited Paris for many years. When his person became for some obnoxious to the government—He was seized and cast into prison the very day that Safie arrived from Constantinople to join him. He was tried & condemned to

† For the remainder of Chapter 3 and for all of Chapter 4, which are missing from the Draft manuscript, see pp. 139–47 in this edition.

‡ The first sentence on the first page of Insert 'Y' at the end of Notebook A, which lacks a chapter heading from MWS but was headed '*another Chapter*' by PBS.

death. The injustice of his sentence was very flagrant All Paris were indignant & it was judged that his religion and wealth had been the causes of his condemnation rather than the crime alledged against him Felix was present at his trial; his horror & indignation was uncontrolable when he heard the event. He made at that moment a solemn vow to deliver him & then looked around for the means. After many fruitless attempts to gain admittance to the goal [*for* gaol] he found a strongly grated window in an unguarded part of the prison which lighted the dungeon of the unfortunate Mahometan, who loaded with chains waited in despair the execution of the barbarous sentence. Felix visited the grate at night and made known to the prisoner his intentions in his favour. The Turk amazed and delighted endeavoured to warm the zeal of his deliverer by promises of reward & wealth. Felix rejected his offers with contempt Yet when he saw the lovely Safie who was allowed to visit her father & who by her gestures expressed her lively gratitude, the youth could not help owning to his own mind that the captive possessed a treasure which would fully reward his toil & hazard.

The Turk quickly perceived the impression that his daughter had made on <the> heart of Felix and endeavoured to secure him more entirely by the promise of her hand in marriage; Felix was too delicate to accept this yet he looked forward to the probability of that event as the consummation of his happiness.

{The Turk informed Safie of his intentions and}

During the ensueing days while the preperations were going forward for the escape of the merchant. the zeal of Felix was warmed by several letters that he received from this lovely girl Who found means to express her thoughts in the language of her lover by the aid of an old man a servant of her Fathers who understood french. She thanked him in the most ardent terms for his intended kindness, and at the same time she gently deplored her own fate. I have copies of these letters for I found means during

Compare pp. 148–9

my residence in the hovel to procure the implements of writing and they were often in the hands of Felix or Agatha. before I depart I will give them to you they will prove to you the truth of my tale but at present as the sun already begins to decline I shall only have time to repeat the substance to you Safie related that her Mother was a Christian Arab seized and made a slave by the Turks. recommended by her beauty she had won the heart of the father of Safie who married her. The young girl spoke in high & enthusiastic terms of her Mother who born in freedom spurned the bondage to which she was now obliged to submit. She instructed her daughter in the tenets of her religion & taught her to aspire to higher powers of intellect & an independance of spirit forbidden to the female followers of Mahomet. This Lady died, but her lessons were indelibly impressed in the mind of Safie who sickened at the prospect of again returning to Turkey and the being immurred in walls of a haram allowed only to occupy herself with puerile amusements ill-suited to the temper of her soul now accustomed to grand ideas & a noble emulation for virtue. The prospect of marrying a Christian and remaining in a country where women were allowed to take a rank in society was enchanting to her.

The day for the execution of the Turk was fixed but on the night previous to it he had quitted prison & before morning was distant many leagues from Paris. Felix had procurred passports in the name of his father sister & himself. He communicated hi<s> plan to the former who aided the deceit by quitting his house under the pretence of a journey & concealed himself with his daughter in an obscure part of Paris. Felix conducted the fugitives through France to Lyons & across Mount Cenis when he arrived at Leghorn where the merchant was to wait a favourable opportunity of passing over to Africa He could not deny himself the pleasure of remaining a few days in the society of the Arabian who exhibited towards him the simplest & tenderest affection. They conversed with one another by the aid of an interpreter & Safie sang to him the divine

 Compare pp. 149–50

airs of her native country. The Turk allowed this intimacy to take place and encouraged the hopes of the youthful lovers, while in his heart he had formed far other plans. He loathed the idea that his daughter should be united to a Christian but he feared the resentment of Felix if he should appear lukewarm for he knew that he was still in the power of his deliver<er> if he should choose to betray him to the Italian state which they at that time imhabited. He revolved a thousand plans by which he should be enabled to prolong the deceit untill it was no longer necessary; and then carry his daughter to Africa with him. His plans were greatly facillitated by the news that arrived from Paris.

The government of France were greatly enraged at the escape of their victim and spared no pains to discover and punish his deliverer. The plot of Felix was quickly discovered & De Lacey & Agatha{t} were thrown intto prison The news reached Felix and roused him from his dream of pleasure. His blind & aged father and his gentle sister lay in a noisome dungeon while he enjoyed the free air & the society of her he loved. This idea was torture to him—He arranged with the Turk that if the latter should find a favourable opportunity for escape before Felix could return to Italy Safie should remain as a boarder in a convent at Leghorn and then quitting the lovely Arabian, he hastened to Paris & delivered himself up to the vengeance of the law hoping to free De Lacey & Agatha by this proceeding.

He did not succeed they remained confined for five months before the trial took place the result of which deprived them of their fortune and exiled them for ever from their native country.

They found a miserable assylum in the cottage in Germany where I found them Felix learned that the treacherous Turk for whom he and his family endured such unheard of oppression, on hearing that his deliverer was poor & harmless became a traitor to good feeling & honour & had quitted Italy with his daughter

Compare pp. 150–51

insultingly sending Felix a pittance of money to aid him, as he said, in some plan of future maintenance.

Such were the events that preyed on the heart of Felix and rendered him when I first saw him, the most miserable of his family. He could have endured poverty and when this distress had been the meed of his virtue he would have gloried in it. But the ingratitude of the Turk & the loss of his beloved Safie were misfortunes more bitter & irreperable. The arrival of the Arrabian now infused new life into his soul.

When the news had arrived that Felix was deprived of his wealth and rank the me<r>chant commander [*for* commanded] his daughter to think no more of her lover but to prepare to return to her native country with him.—The generous nature of Safie was outraged by this command—She attempted to expostulate with her father but he left her angrily reiterating his tyrannical command.

A few days after<,> the Turk entered his daughters appartment and told her hastily that he had reason to believe that his residence in Leghorn had been divulged and that he would speedily be delivered up to the French Government—He had consequently hired a vessel to convey hin [*for* him] to Constantinople in which he should sail in <a> few hours. He intended to leave his daughter under the care of a servant to follow at her leisure with the greater part of his property which had not yet arrived at Leghorn.

Safie revolved in her own mind the plan of conduct that it would become her to pursue A residence in Turkey was abhorrent to her—her religion & feelings were alike adverse to it. By some papers of her fathers that fell into her hands she heard of the exile of her lover and learnt the name of the spot where he resided. She hesitated some time but at length she formed her resolution—Taking with her some jewels that belonged to her, and a small sum of money; she quitted Italy with an attendant a native of Leghorn but who understood Turkish and departed for Germany. She arrived in safety at a town about 20 leagues from the Cottage

 Compare pp. 151–2

of De Lacey—her attendant then fell dangerously ill Safie nursed her with the most devoted affection but the poor girl died & the Arabian was left alone unacquainted with the language of the country and utterly ignorant of the customs of the world.—She fell however in to good hands—The Italian had mentioned the name of the spot for which they were bound and after her death the woman of the house in which they had lived took care that Safie should arrive safely at the cottage of her lover.

Chapter 6

Such was the history of my beloved cottagers.[†] It impressed me deeply—I learned from it to admire their virtues & to deprecate the vices of mankind. As yet I looked upon crime as a distant evil; benevolence & generosity were ever present before me—I ardently desired to make one in the busy scene where so many admirable qualities were called forth and displayed. But in giving an account of the progress of my intellect, I must not omit a circumstance that took place in the beginning of the month of August of that year.

One night during my accustomed visit to the neighbouring wood where I collected my own food and brought home firing for my protectors, I found on the ground a leathern portmanteau containing several articles of dress & some books. I eagerly seized the prize & returned with it to my hovel. The books were fortunately written in the language I had learned at the cottage; they consisted of "Paradise Lost"—a volume of Plutarchs lives and the Sorrows of Werter—the possession of these treasures gave me extreme delight I could continually study and occupy my mind upon them when my friends were employed in their ordinary occupations. I

† The first sentence on the first page of Notebook B, which lacks a chapter heading.

Compare pp. 152–3

can hardly describe to you the effect that these books had upon me. They produced in me an infinity of new images & ideas that sometimes raised me to extacy but more frequently sunk me to the lowest dejection. In the Sorrows of Werter besides the interrest of its simple and affecting story so many opinions are canvassed and so many lights thrown upon what had hitherto been to me dark subjects that I found in it a never ending source of speculation. The gentle and domestic manners it described combined with lofty sentiments{;} and feelings accorded well with my experience among my protectors. But I thought Werter himself a more divine being than I had ever beheld—His character contained no pretention but it sunk deep—The disquisitions upon death and suicide were calculated to fill me with astonishment—I did not pretend to enter into the merits of the case yet I inclined towards the opinion of the Hero whose extinction I wept although I did not understand it. As I read however I applied much personally to my own feelings & condition. I found myself similar yet at the same time strangely unlike the beings concerning whom I read and to whose conversation I was a listener—I sympathized with & partly understood them—but I was unformed in mind I was dependant on none, & related to none—"The path of my departure was free"—and there was none to lament my annihilation—My person was hideous and my stature gigantic—What did this mean? Who was I? What was I? these questions continually recurred but I was unable to solve them

The volume of Plutarchs lives which I possessed contained the histories of the first founders of the ancient republic—This book had a far different effect upon me from the letters of Werter. I learned from that despondency & gloom; but Plutarch taught me high thoughts—he elevated me above the wretched sphere of my own reflections to admire & love the heroes of past ages. Many things I read surpassed my unterstanding and experience I had a very confused knowledge of kingdoms & wide extents

 Compare pp. 153–4

of country mighty rivers and boundless seas. But I was perfectly unacquainted with towns & large assemblees of men. The cottage of my protectors had been the only school where I studied human nature—But this book developed new & mightier scenes of action I read of men concerned in public affairs governing or massercring their speceis. I felt the greatest ardour for virtue rise within me and abhorrence for vice as far as I understood the signification of those terms relative as they were, as I applied them, to pleasure and pain alone. Induced by these feelings I was of course led to admire peacable lawgivers Numa, Solon & Lycurgus more than Romulus and Theseus. The patriarchal lives of my protectors caused these impressions to take a firm hold on my mind—perhaps if my first residence had been with a young soldier burning for glory and slaughter I should have been imbued with different sensations

But Paradise Lost Excited different and far deeper emotions—I read it as I had the other volumes which had fallen into my hands, as a true history. It moved every feeling of wonder and awe[.] that the picture of an omnipotent God warring with his creatures was capable of exciting—I often referred the several situations as their similarity struck me to my own. Like Adam I was created apparently as I had been but united by no link to any other being of the creation but his state was different from mine in every other respect. He had come forth from the hands of God a perfect creature happy prosperous & guarded by the especial care of his creator. he was allowed to converse & acquire knowledge from beings of a superior nature—but I was wretched helpless and alone. Many times I considered Satan as my fitter mate for often like him when I viewed the bliss of my protectors the bitter gall of envy rose within me.

Another circumstance strengthened and confirmed these feelings. Soon after my arrival in the hovel I discovered some papers in the pocket of the dress that I had taken from your study. At first I neglected them but now that I was able to decypher the characters

Compare pp. 154–5

in which they were written I began to study them with diligence. It was your journal of the four months that preceeded my creation. you minutely described in it every step you took in the progress of your work; this was mingled with accounts of domestic occurences. You doubtless recollect these papers—Here they are—Every thing is related in them & every disgusting circumstance is set in view; the minutest description is given of my odious & loathsome person. I sickened as I read—Hateful day when I received life, I exclaimed in agony—Cursed Creator Why did you form a monster so hideous that even you turned from me in disgust. God in pity made man beautiful & alluring—I am more hateful to the sight than the bitter apples of Hell to the taste<.> Satan has his companions, fellow devils, to admire and encourage him. but I am solitary & detested

These were my reflections in my hours of despondency & solitude but when I contemplated the virtues of the cottagers. Their amiable & benevolent dispositions<,> I persuaded myself that when they became acquainted with my admiration of their virtues they would pity me and overlook my personal deformity. Could they turn from their door one however monstrous, who solicited their compassion & friendship? I resolved at least not to despair but in every way to fit myself for an interview which would decide my fate. I postponed this attempt for some months longer for the importance attatched to it inspired me with a dread for its success that I in vain endeavoured to surmount. Besides I found that my understanding improved so much with every days experience that I was unwilling to commence this undertaking untill a few more months should have added to my wisdom.

Several changes in the mean time took place in the cottage the presence of Safie diffused happiness among its inhabitants and I also found that a greater degree of plenty reigned there—Felix & {and} Agatha spent more time in amusement & conversation and were assisted in their labours by servants They did not appear rich but they were contented & happy. Such were their feelings

 Compare pp. 155–6

while I became every day more miserable—encrease of knowledge only discovered to me more clearly what a wretched outcast I was. I cherished hope it is true but it vanished when I beheld my person reflected in water or even my shadow in the moonshine—I endeavoured to crush these fears and to fortify myself for the trial which in a few months I resolved to undergo; and sometimes I allowed my thoughts unchecked by reason to ramble in the fields of Paradise & dared to fancy amiable & lovely beings sympathizing with my feelings and cheering my gloom—Their angelic countenances breathed smiles of consolation—But it was all a dream—No Eve soothed my sorrows or shared my thoughts. I was alone. I remembered Adams supplication to his creator but where was mine? He had abbandoned me and in the bitterness of my heart I cursed him.

Autumn passed thus—I saw with surpise & grief the leaves decay & fall, And nature again assume the barren & bleak appearance it had when I first beheld the woods and the lovely moon. I did not heed the bleakness of the weather. I was more fitted By my constitution for the sufferance of cold than heat. But my only joys were {were} the sight of flowers and birds and all the gay apparel of summer when those deserted me I turned with more attention towards the cottagers Their happiness was not decreased by the absence of summer—They loved and sympathized with one another and their joys depending on each other were not hurt by the casualties that took place around them—The more I saw of them the greater became my desire to claim their protection & kindness. My heart yearned to be known and loved by these amiable creatures to see their sweet looks directed towards me in kindness—I dared not think that they would turn from me with disdain or horror—The poor that stopt at their door were never driven away—I asked it is true for greater treasures that [*for* than] a little food or rest I required kindness & sympathy but I did not believe my self utterly unworthy of it

Compare pp. 156–7

Chap. 7th

The winter advanced and {and} an entire revolution of the seasons had taken place since I awoke into life.—My attention at this time was solely directed towards my plan of introducing myself into the cottage of my protectors. I revolved many projects but that on which I finally fixed was to enter their dwelling when the blind old man was alone. I had sagacity enough to discover that the unnatural hideousness of my person was the chief object of horror with those who had formerly beheld me:—my voice although harsh, had nothing terrible in it. I thought therefore that if in the absence of his children I could gain the goodwill of the old De Lacey I might by his means be tolerated by my younger protectors.

One day when the sun shone on the red leaves that strewed the ground, and diffused cheerfulness although it denied warmth<,> Safie Agatha and Felix set out on a long country walk and the old man at his own desire was left alone in the cottage. When his children had departed he took up his guitar & played several mournful but sweet airs that I had seldom heard him play before. At first his countenance was illuminated with pleasure but as he continued<,> thoughtfullness and sadness succeeded and laying down the instrument he sat absorbed in reflection.

My heart beat quick. This was the hour & moment of trial which would decide my hopes The servants were gone to a neighbouring fair:—All was silent in and around the cottage It was an excellent opportunity yet when I rose to execute my plan my limbs failed me, and I sunk to the ground. Again I rose and exerting all the firmness of which I was master removed the planks which I had placed before my hovel to conceal my retreat—The fresh air revived me and with renewed determination I approached the door of the cottage. I knocked—"who is there?" said the old man—"come in"—I entered—"Pardon this intrusion" said I—"I am a traveller,

Compare pp. 157–8

in want of a little rest. you would greatly oblige me if you would allow me to remain a few minutes before your fire." "Enter" said De Lacey & I will try in what manner I can relieve your wants—but unfortunately my children are out and as I am blind I am afraid I shall find it difficult to procure food for you"—"Do not trouble yourself, my kind host," I replied, I have food, it is warmth and rest only that I need.—I sat down and a silence ensued; I knew very well that every minute was precious to me yet I remained irresolute in what manner to comemmence the interview when the old man addressed me—"By your language Stranger, I suppose you are my countryman, are you french?" "No," replied I but I was educated by a french family and understand that language only. I am now going to claim the protection of some friends, whom I sincerely love and of whose favour I have some hopes." "Are these Germans"—Asked De Lacey—"No—They are french—But let us change the subject—I am an unfortunate & deserted creature. I look around and I have no relation or friend on earth—These amiable people to whom I go, have never seem [*for* seen] me and know little of me. I am full of fears, for if I fail there, I am an outcast in the world for ever."

Do not despair, said the old man. To be friendless is indeed to be unfortunate: but the hearts of men when unprejudiced by obvious self interrest, are full of brotherly love and charity. Rely therefore on your hopes and if these friends are good and amiable—do not despair They are kind—I answered—They are the most excellent creatures in the world but unfortunately they are prejudiced against me. I have good dispositions—I love virtue and knowledge,—my life has been hitherto harmless & in some degree beneficial but a fatal prejudice clouds their eyes and where they ought to see a feeling and kind friend, they behold only a detestable monster.—

That is indeed unfortunate, replied De Lacey—but if you are really blameless can not you undeceive them?

I am about to undertake that task—"And it is on that account

Compare pp. 158–9

that I feel so many overwhelming terrors—I love these friends tenderly; I have unknown to them been for many months in the habits of daily kindness towards them, but they believe that I wish to injure them and it is that prejudice which I wish to over come.'

Where do these friends reside, said De Lacey—

Near here.—this spot.

The old man paused a moment and then continued If you will unreservedly confide to me the particulars I perhaps may be of use in undeceiving them. I am blind and cannot judge of your countenance but there is somthing in your words that persuades me that you are sincere. I am poor and an exile, but it will afford me true pleasure to be in any way serviceable to a fellow creature.—

Excellent man—exclaimed I, I thank you and accept your generous offer You raise me from the dust by this kindness and I trust that I shall not be driven from the society & sympathy of my fellow creatures

Heaven forbid! even if you were really criminal<—>for that can only drive you to desperation and not instigate you to virtue—I also am unfortunate.—I and my family have been condemned although innocent<;> judge therefore if I do not feel for your misfortunes—

How can I thank you, my best & only benefactor—from your lips first have I heard the voice of kindness directed towards me—I shall be for ever grateful and your present humanity assures me of success with the friends whom I am on the point of meeting

May I know the names and residence of those friends? asked De Lacey.

I paused—This was the moment of decision which was to rob me of or bestow happiness on me for ever—I struggled vainly for firmness sufficient to answer him—the effort destroyed all my remaining strength I sank on a chair & sobbed aloud At that moment I heard the steps of my younger protectors—I had not a moment to lose, but seizing the hand of the old man I cried—Now

 Compare pp. 159–60

is the time, save and protect me You and your family are the friends whom I seek—Do not you desert me in the hour of trial!.—

Great God! exclaimed the old man—Who are you?

At that instant the cottage door opened and Felix, Safie and Agatha entered—Who can describe their horror and astonishment on beholding me—Agatha fainted & Safie unable to attend to her friend rushed out of the cottage.—Felix darted forward and with supernatural strength tore me from his father to whose knees I clung—In a transport of fury he dashed me to the ground and struck me voilently with a stick<.> I saw him on the point of repeating the blow when overcome by pain and anguish I quitted the cottage and in the general tumult, escaped unperceived to my hovel.

Cursed, Cursed Creator! Why did I live why in that instant did I not extinguish the spark of existence which you had so wantonly bestowed? I know not—Despair had not yet taken possession of me<;> my feelings were those of rage & revenge—I could with pleasure have destroyed the cottage and its inhabitants, and glutted myself with their shrieks & misery. When night came on I quitted my retreat and wandered to the wood.—No longer restrained by the fear of discovery I gave vent to my anguish in fearful howlings. I was like a wild beast in the toils; destroying the objects that obstructed me and ranging through the wood with stag like swiftness.—Oh! What a miserable night I passed. the cold stars shone in mockery, the bare trees waved their branches above me and now and then the sweet voice of a bird burst forth anidst [*for* amidst] the universal stillness.—All save I were at rest or in enjoyment. I like the arch fiend bore a hell within me and, finding myself unsympathized with, I wished to tear up the trees, spread havock and destruction and then have sat down & enjoyed the ruin—

But this was a luxury of sensation that could not endure I became fatigued with excess of bodily exertion; and sank on the damp grass in the despondency of despair. There was no one among the myriads of men that existed that would pity or assist

Compare pp. 160–61

me—and should I feel kindness towards my enemies? No! from that moment I declared everlasting war against the species and more than all against he who had formed me & sent me forth to pain & misery.

The sun rose—I heard the voices of men and knew that it was impossible to return to my retreat that day; accordingly, I hid myself in some thick underwood determined to devote the ensueing hours to reflection on my situation—The pleasant sunshine and pure air of day restored me to some degree of tranquillity & when I considered what had passed at the cottage I could not help believing that I was too hasty in my conclusions—I had certainly acted imprudently. It was apparent that my conversation ad [*for* had] softened the father and I was a fool for having exposed my person to the horror of his children. I ought to have familiarized the old De Lacey to me and by degrees have discovered myself to the rest of the family when they should have been prepared for my approach—But I did not believe my errors irretrievable—and after much consideration I resolved to return to the cottage—seek the old man and by my representations win him to my party.—

These thoughts calmed me & in the afternoon I sunk into a profound sleep—but the fever of my blood did not allow of peaceful dreams<.> the horrid scene of the preceeding day was for ever acting before my eyes—The females were flying and the e<n>raged Felix tearing me from his fathers feet—I awoke exhausted, and finding that it was already night I crept from my hiding place & went in search of food.

Chapt. 8

When my hunger was appeased I directed my steps towards the well known path that conducted to the cottage—All there, was at peace—I crept into my hovel and remained in silent expectation of

Compare pp. 161–2

the accustomed hour when the family arose. That past, and the sun mounted high in the heavens but the cottagers did not appear—I trembled violently, apprehending some dreadful misfortune. The inside of the cottage was dark & I heard no motion. I cannot describe the agony I felt during this suspense.

Presently two countrymen past by but pausing near the cottage they enterred into conversation using violent gestures<.> I did not understand what they said for their language differred from that of my protectors—Soon After, however, Felix approached with another man I was surprised as I knew that he had not quitted the cottage that morning and waited anxiously to discover by his discourse the meaning of these unusual appearances. "Do you consider, said his companion to him—that you will be obliged to pay three months rent & to lose the produce of your garden. I do not wish to take any unfair advantage and I beg therefore that you will take some days to consider of your determination.

It is utterly useless—replied Felix, we can never again inhabit that cottage—The life of my father is in the greatest danger owing to the dreadful circumstanc<e> that I have related—My wife and sister will never recover their horror—I entreat you not to reason with me any more—Take possession of your tenement and let me fly from this place—

Felix trembled violently as he said this. He and his companion entered the cottage in which they remained for a few minutes & then departed. I never again saw any of the family of De Lacey.

I continued in my hovel for the remainder of the day in a state of utter & stupid despair—my protectors had departed and had broken the only link that held me to the world—for the first time the feelings of revenge and hatred filled my bosom, and I did not strive to controul them—but allowing myself to be borne away by the stream I bent my mind towards injury & death—when I thought of my friends—of the mild voice of De Lacey the gentle eyes of Agatha—and the exquisite beauty of the Arabian—these

Compare pp. 162–3

thoughts vanish<ed> & a gush of tears somewhat soothed me—But again when I reflected that they had spurned & deserted me, anger returned and unable to injure anything human I turned my fury towards inanimate objects.—As night advanced I placed a variety of combustibles around the cottage, and after having destroyed every vestige of cultivation in the garden—I waited with forced patience, untill the moon had sunk to commence my operations. As the night advanced a fierce wind arose from the woods and quickly dispersed the clouds that had loitered in the heavens—the blast tore a long Like a mighty avelanche and produced a kind of insanity in my spirits that burst all bounds of reason or reflection—I lighted a dry branch of tree and danced with fury around the devoted cottage, my eyes still fixed on the western horizon, the edge of which the moon nearly touched. part of it [*for* its] orb was at length hid and I waved my brand—it sunk and with a loud scream I fir<e>d the straw and hay that I had collected. The wind fanned the fire and the cottage was quickly enveloped by the flames which clung to it and licked it with their forked tongues, to destroy it. As soon as I was convinced that no assistance could save any part of the habitation I quitted the scene and sought for refuge in the wood.

And now with the world before me whither should I bend my steps? I resolved to fly far from the scene of my misfortunes—But to me, hated and despised, every country must be equally horrible.—At length the thought of you crossed my mind—I learned from your papers that you were my creator & to whom could I apply with more fitness than to he who had given me life. Among the lessons that Felix had bestowed on Safie<,> geography had not been ommitted. From these I had learned the relative situations of the different countries of the earth; You had mentioned Geneva as the name of your native town & towards this place I resolved to proceed.

But how was I to direct myself ?—I knew that I must travel South west to reach my destination but in this the sun was my

 Compare pp. 163–4

only guide—I did not know the names of the towns I was to pass through, nor could I ask information from a single human being—But I did not despair From you only could I hope for succour although towards you I felt only the sentiments of detestation.—Unfeeling heartless creator! You had endowed me with perceptions and passions and then cast me abroard [*for* abroad] for the scorn & horror of mankind—But on you only had I any claim & from you I determined to seek that justice which I vainly attempted to gain from your fellow creatures.

My travels were long and the suffering I endured intense—It was late in autumn when I quitted the district where I had so long resided—I travelled only at night, fearful of meeting the visage of a human being.—Nature decayed around me and the sun became heatless,—rain & snow poured around me and I found no shelter—Oh Earth how often did I imprecate curses on the cause of my being—The mildness of my nature had fled & all within me was turned to gall & bitterness—the nearer I approached to your habitation the more deeply did I feel the spirit of revenge imprint itself on my heart—Snow fell around me and the waters were hardened, but I rested not—A few incidents now and then directed me right but I often wandered wide from my path. An incident that happened when I arrived on the confines of Switzerland—when the sun had recovered a part of its heat & the earth again began to look green confirmed in a dreadful manner the bitterness & horror of my feelings.

I generally rested through the day, and travelled only when I was secured by night from the view of man. one morning however finding that my path lay through a deep wood I ventured to continue my journey after the sun had risen high in the heavens. The day which was one of the first of spring cheered even me by the loveliness of its sun & the gentleness of the breeze.—I felt emotions of softness and pleasure that had long appeared dead, revive within me; half surprized with these new sensations I allowed myself to be borne

Compare pp. 164–5

away by them & forgetting my solitude & deformity dared to be happy<;> tears of gentleness again bedewed my cheeks and I even raised my humid eyes with thankfullness towards the blessed sun which bestowed such joy upon me

I continued to wind among the paths of the wood untill I came to its boundary which was skirted <by> a deep & rapid river—into which many of the trees bent their branches now budding with the fresh spring—Here I paused, not exactly knowing what course to pursue when I heard voices that induced me to conceal myself under the shade of cypress. I was scarcely hid when a young girl came running towards the spot where I was concealed—laughing as if she {had} ran from some one in sport—She continued her course along the precipitate sides of the river when suddenly her foot slipt, & she fell into the rapid stream. I rushed from my hiding place and with extreme labour from the force of the current saved her, & dragged her to shore—She was senseless and I endeavoured by every means in my power to restore her when I was suddenly interrupted by the approach of a rustic who was probably the person from whom she had playfully fled—On seeing me he darted towards me and tearing the girl from my arms hastened towards the deeper parts of the forest—I followed speedily I hardly knew why but when the man saw me draw near he aimed a gun which he carried, at my body & fired. I sunk to the ground & with encreased swiftness He escaped into the wood.

This then was the reward of my benevolence<.> I had saved a human being from destruction and as a recompence I now writhed under the miserable pain of my wound The feelings of kindness and gentleness which I had entertained but a few moments before gave place to hellish rage & gnashing of teeth—inflamed by pain I vowed eternal hatred & vengeance to all mankind—But the agony of my wound overcame me my pulses paused and I fainted.

For some weeks I led a miserable life in these woods endeavouring to cure the wound I had received. The ball had entered my shoulder

 Compare pp. 165–6

and I knew not whether it had remained there or passed through—at any rate I had no means of extracting it. My suffering were augmented also by the oppressive sense of injustice & ingratitude. My daily prayers rose for revenge—a deep & deadly revenge such as would alone compensate for the horrors of my situation.

After some weeks my wound healed and I continued my journey—the labours I endured were no longer to be alleviated by the bright sun or gentle breezes of spring—all joy was but mockery to me, & made me feel more painfully that I was not made for enjoyment. But my toils now drew near a close & two months from this time I reached the environs of Geneva.

It was evening when I arrived in the outskirts of that town and I retired to a hiding place among the fields that surround it, to consider in what manner I should apply to you. I was oppressed by fatigue and hunger and far too unhappy to enjoy the gentle breezes of evening or the prospect of the sun setting behind the stupendous mountains of the Jura. At this time a slight sleep relieved me which was disturbed by the approach of a beautiful child who came running into the recess I had chosen with all the sportiveness of infancy—Suddenly as I gazed on him an idea seized me—that this little creature was unprejudiced & had lived too short a time to have imbibed a horror of deformity. If therefore I could seize him & educate him as my companion & friend, I should not be so desolate in this peopled earth. Urged by this impulse I seized on the boy as he passed and drew him towards me. As soon as he beheld my form he placed his hand before his eyes & uttered a shrill scream. I drew his hand forcibly from his face & said Child, what is the meaning of this? I do not intend to hurt you—listen to me. He struggled violently Let me go he cried—Monster—ugly wretch You wish to eat me & tear me to pieces you are an ogre,—let me go or I will tell my papa. Boy said I—You will never see your father again—you must come with me. He burst into loud cries—hideous monster let me go—My papa

Compare pp. 166–7

is a syndic he is M. Frankenstien let me go you dare not keep me. Frankenstein cried I—You belong then to my enemy—To him towards whom I have sworn eternal revenge & you shall be my first victim. The child still struggled & loaded me with epithets which carried despair to my heart—I grasped his throat to silence him & in a moment he lay dead at my feet.

I gazed on my victim and my heart swelled with exultation and hellish triumph—clapping my hands I exclaimed I too can destroy—My enemy is not impregnable; this death will carry despair to him & a thousand thousand other{s} miseries shall torment & destroy him. As I fixed my eyes on the child I saw something glittering on his breast—I took it I [*for* It] was the portrait of a most lovely woman. In spite of my malignity it softened and attracted me. for a few moments I gazed with delight on her dark black eyes & lovely lips but presently my rage returned: I remembered that I was for ever deprived of the delights such beautiful creatures could bestow—and that she whose resemblance I contemplated would, in regarding me have, changed that air of divine benignity to one of horror & detestation.

Can you wonder that such thoughts transported me with rage? I only wonder that at that moment instead of venting my sensations in useless exclamations & agony I did not rush among mankind and perish in the attempt to destroy them. While I was overcome by these feelings I left the spot where I had committed the murder and sought a more secluded hiding place. At that moment I peceiving [*for* perceived] a woman passing near me,—she was young: not indeed so beautiful as her who [*for* whose] portrait I held but of an agreable aspect & blooming in the loveliness of health & youth. And here I thought is one of those whose smiles are bestowed on all but me She shall not escape my vengeance<;> thanks to the lessons of Felix & the sanguinary laws of man, I know how to work mischief. I approached her unpe<r>ceived, and placed the portrait securely in one of the folds of her dress.

 Compare pp. 167–8

For some day<s> I haunted the spot where these scenes had taken place sometimes wishing to see you sometimes resolved to quit the world & it [*for* its] miseries for ever. At length I wandered towards these mountains and have ranged in their immense recesses consumed by a burning passion which you alone can gratify—And we may not part untill you have promised to comply with my requisitions. I am alone & miserable. Man will not associate with <me,> but one as deformed and horrible as my self would not deny herself to me. This being you must create.

Chap. 9th

The creature finished speaking and fixed his eyes on me in expectation of a reply. But I was bewildered & perplexed & unable to arrange my ideas sufficiently to understand the meaning of his proposition. He continued.

You must create a female for me with whom I can live in the interchange of those sympathies necessary for my being; This you alone can do & I demand of you as a right which you must not refuse.

As he said this I could no longer suppress the anger that burned within me. I do refuse it, I replied, & no torture shall ever extort a consent from me—You may render me the most miserable of men but you shall never make me base in my own eyes. Shall I create another like yourself whose joint wickedness would desolate the world? Begone—I have answered you—You may kill me but I will never consent.

You are in the wrong, replied he, & instead of threatening I am content to reason with you. I am malicious, because I am miserable. Am I not shunned & hated by all mankind? You my creator would tear me to pieces & triumph—Remember that &

Compare pp. 168–9

tell me why I should pity man more than he pities me. You would not call it murder if you precipitated me into one of those ice rifts & destroyed my frame, the work of your own hand. shall I respect man when he contemns me? Let him live with me in the interchange of kindness and instead of injury I would bestow every benefit with tears of gratitude at his acceptance. But that cannot be; the human senses are insurmountable barriers to our union. But mine shall not <be> the submission of abject slavery. I will revenge my injuries<;> if I cannot inspire love I will cause fear and chiefly towards you my arch-enemy because my creator{;} do I swear unutterable hatred—I will work & destroy nor finish untill I desolate your heart so that you curse the hour of your birth." A fiendish rage animated him as he said this; his face was wrinkled into contortions too horrible for human eyes to behold; but presently he calmed himself, & proceeded.

I intended to reason. This passion is detrimental to me, for you do not reflect that you are the cause. If any being felt emotions of benevolence towards me I should return then an hundred & a hundred fold; for that one creature's sake I would make peace with the whole kind—But I now indulge in dreams of bliss that cannot be realized. What I ask of you is reasonable and moderate. I demand a creature of another sex but as hideous as myself. The gratification is small but it is all that I can receive and it shall content me. It is true we shall be monsters cut off from all the world but on that account we shall be more attached to one another Our lives will not be happy but they will be harmless & free from misery that I now feel. Oh! my creator make me happy; let me feel gratitude towards you for one benefit; Let me see that I excite the sympathy of one creature. Do not deny me my request.

I was moved. I shuddered when I thought of the possible consequences of my consent but I felt that there was some justice in his argument. His tale and the feelings he now expressed proved him to be a creature of fine sensations and did not I as his maker

 Compare pp. 169–70

owe him all the portion of happiness that it was in my power to bestow? He saw my change of feeling & continued.

If you consent neither you or any human creature shall ever see us again. I will go to the vast wilds of America. My food is not that of man; I do not destroy the lamb or the kid to glut my appetite. Acorns & berries afford me sufficient nourishment. My companion will be of the same nature as myself and will be content with the same fare. We shall make our bed of dried leaves; the sun will shine on us as on man & will ripen our food. You are moved. The picture I present to you is peaceful & human and you must feel that you could deny it only in the wantoness of power & cruelty. Pitiless as you are towards me I see compassion in your eyes. Let me seize the favourable moment & persuade you to promise what I so ardently desire.

You promise, replied I, to quit the habitations of man and to inhabit those wilds where the beasts of the field will be your only companions. How can you who long for the love & sympathy of man persevere in this exile? You will return and seek their kindness & you will meet their detestation; your evil passions will be renewed, & you will then have a companion to aid you in your task of destruction. Begone; I cannot consent.

The monster replied with fervour, How inconstant are your feelings; but a moment ago you were moved by my representations, & why do you again harden yourself to my complaints? I swear by the earth which I inhabit & by you that made me that with the companion you bestow I will quit the neighbourhood of man & dwell, as it may chance, in the most savage places. My evil passions will have fled, for I shall meet with sympathy. My life will flow quietly away & in my dying moments I shall not curse my maker.

His words had a strange effect upon me. I compassionated him & sometimes felt a wish to console him but when I looked on him when I saw the filthy mass that moved & talked my heart sickend

Compare pp. 170–71

& my feelings were altered to those <of> horror & hatred. I tried to stifle them I thought that as I could not sympathize with him I had no right to refuse him the small portion of happiness that I had it in my power to bestow. You swear, I said, to be harmless but have you not already shown a degree of malise that would reasonably make me distrust you? May not even this be a feint that will encrease your triumph & desire of revenge

How is this, cried he; I thought I had moved your compassion and yet you still refuse to bestow on me the only benefit that <can> soften my heart and render me harmless. If I have no ties & no affections<,> hatred & vice must be my portion. The love of another will destroy the cause of my crimes & I shall become a thing of whose existence every one will be ignorant. My vices are the children of a forced solitude that I abhor and my virtues will necessarily arise when I receive the sympathy of an equal. I shall feel human affections & become linked to the chain of existence & events from which I am now excluded

I paused some time to reflect on all he had related and the various arguments that he had used. I thought of the various virtues he had displayed on the opening of his existence; and their subsequent blight caused by the detestation & horror that his protectors had manifested towards him. His power & threats were not ommitted in my calculations; a creature who could exist among the ice caves of the glaciers & hide himself from persuit in the ridges <of> inaccessible precepieces was {was} a being possessing faculties it would be vain to cope with; After a long pause of reflection I concluded that the justice due both to him & my fellow creatures demanded of me that I should comply with his request. Turning to him therefore I said.

I consent to your demand on you [*for* your] solemn oath to quit Europe & every other place in the neighbourhood of mam [*for* man] as soon as I shall deliver into you [*for* your] hands a female who is to accompany you in your exile.

 Compare pp. 171–2

I swear, he cried, by the sun & by the blue sky of heaven that while they exist you shall never behold me. Depart then to your home & commence your labours. I shall watch their progress with unutterable anxiety<;> and fear not but that when you are ready for me I shall appear.

Saying this he suddenly quitted me fearful perhaps of any change in my sentiments. I saw him descend the mountain with greater speed than the flight of the eagle and quickly lost him among the undulations of the sea of ice.

His tale had occupied the whole day and the sun was upon the verge of the horizon when he departed. I knew that I ought to hasten to descend to the valley as I should soon be encompassed in darkness. But my heart was heavy, and my{s} steps slow. The labour of winding among the little paths and fixing my feet firmly as I advanced teazed me occupied as I was by the feelings that the occurences of the day had produced. It had long been night when I came to the half way resting place & seated myself beside the fountain. The stars shone at intervals as the clouds passed from over them—The dark pines rose before me & every here and there a broken tree lay on the ground; it was a scene of wonderful solemnity & stirred strange thoughts within me. I wept bitterly and clasping my hands in agony I exclaimed—Oh stars, & clouds, and wind ye are all about to mock me—If ye really pity crush me but if not depart depart & leave me to darkness. These were wild & miserable thoughts but I cannot describe to you how the eternal twinkling of stars weighed upon me, and I listened to every blast of wind as <if> it were a dull ugly siroc on its way to consume me.

It was morning before I arrived at the village of Chamounix—but my presence so haggard & strange hardly calmed the fears of my family who had waited the whole night in anxious expectation of my return.

The following day we returned to Geneva. The intention of my father in coming had been to divert my mind & to restore to me

Compare pp. 172–3

my lost tranquillity. But the medecine had been fatal & unable to account for the excess of misery I appeared to suffer he hastened to return home hoping that the quiet & calm of a domestic life would by degrees alleviate my sufferings from whatsoever cause they might spring.

For myself I was passive in all their arrangements, and the gentle affection of my beloved Elizabeth was inadequate to draw me from the depth of my despair. The promise I had made to the dæmon weighed upon my mind like Dante's iron cowl on the head of the hellish hypocrites. all pleasures of earth or sky passed before me as a dream & that one thought only had to me the reality of life. Can you wonder that sometimes a kind of insanity possessed me or that I saw about me a multitude of filthy animals inflicting on me incessant torture that often extorted screams & bitter groans.

By degrees however these feelings became calmed. I entered again into the every day of life if not with interrest at least with some degree of tranquillity.

Chap. 10th

Day after day, week after week passed away on my return to Geneva and I had not the courage to commence my work. I feared the vengeance of the disappointed fiend yet I could not overcome my repugnance. I found also that I was unable to compose a female without again devoting several months to study & laborious disquisition. I had heard of some discoveries having been made by an English philosopher the knowledge of which was material to my success. and I sometimes thought of obtainting my fathers consent to visit England for this purpose but I clung to this pretence of delay & could not resolve to interrupt my returning tranquillity My health which had hitherto declined was now much restored, & my

 Compare pp. 173–4

spirits when unchecked by the memory of my unhappy promise, rose proportionably. My father saw this with pleasure and he turned his thoughts towards the best method of eradicating the remains of my melancholy—which every now and then would return by fits & with a devouring blackness overcast the approaching sunshine. At these moments I took refuge in the most perfect solitude: I passed whole days on the lake Alone in a little boat watching the clouds & the ripples of the waves, silent & listless. But the fresh air and bright sun seldom failed restore me to some degree of composure & on my return I met the salutations of my friends with a readier smile, & more cheerful heart

It was after my return from one of the rambles that my father calling me aside thus addressed me.

I am happy to remark, my dear son, that you have resumed your former pleasures & seem to be returning to yourself. And yet you are still unhappy & still avoid our society. For some time I was lost in conjecture as to the cause of this but yesterday an idea struck me and if it is well founded I conjure you to avow it. secresy on such a point would be useless & only bring down treble misery on us all.

I trembled violently at this exordium, and my father continued. I confess, my son, that I have always looked forward to your marriage with your cousin as the tie of our domestic comfort & the stay of my declining years. You were attached to each other from your earliest infancy; you studied together and appeared in dispositions & tastes entirely suited for one another. But so blind is the experience of man that what I conceived to be the best assistants to my plan may have entirely destroyed it, you perhaps regard her as your sister without any wish that she might become your wife. Nay you may have met with another whom you may love but considering yourself as bound in honor to your cousin, this feeling may occasion the poignant misery that you appear to feel.

My dear Father, reassure yourself. I love my cousin tenderly & sincerely. I never saw any woman who excited as Elizabeth does my

Compare pp. 174–5

warmest admiration & affection. My future hopes and prospects are entirely bound up in the expectation of our union.—

The expression of Your sentiments on this subject, my dear Victor, gives me more pleasure than I have for some time experienced. If you feel thus we shall assuredly be happy however present events may cast a gloom over us. But it is this gloom which appears to have taken too strong a hold of your mind that I wish to dissipate. Tell me therefore whether you object to an immediate solemnization of the marriage. We have been unfortunate, and recent events have drawn us from that every day tranquillity befitting my years and infirmities. You are younger yet I do not suppose, possessed as you are of a competent fortune that an early marriage would at all interfere with any future plans of honour and utility that you may have formed. Do not suppose however that I wish to dictate happiness to you or that a delay on your part would cause me any uneasiness; Interpret my words with candour and answer me I conjure you with confidence and sincerity.

I listened to my father in silence and remained for sometime without offering any reply. I revolved rapidly in my mind a multitude of thoughts and endeavoured to come to some conclusion. Alas! to me the idea of an immediate union with my cousin was one of horror and dismay. I was bound by a solemn promise which I had not yet fufilled and dared not break; or if I did what manifold miseries might not impend over me and my devoted family! could I enter into a festival with this deadly weight yet hanging round my neck and bowing me to the ground. No, that I could not endure and therefore resolved to perform my engagement and let the monster depart with his mate before I allowed myself to enjoy the delight of a union, I should otherwise eagerly expect. I remembered also the necessity I was under of either going to England or entering into a long correspondence with the men of that country whose knowledge and discoveries might be of inestimable use to me in my persent [*for* present] undertaking. The latter method of obtaining the desired

 Compare pp. 175–6

intelligence was dilatory and unsatisfatory; besides<,> any change of scene was agreable to me and I was delighted with the idea of spending a year or two away from my family during which time some event might happen which would restore me to them in peace and happiness. My promise might be fulfilled, and the monster have departed or some accident might occur to destroy him and put an end to my slavery for ever—These feelings dictated my answer to my father. I expressed a wish to visit England but concealing my true reasons for my request I clothed my desires under the guise of wishing to travel and see the world before I sat down for life within the walls of my native town.

I urged my request with earnestness and my father was easily induced to comply; for a more indulgent and less dictatorial parent did not exist upon earth. Our plan was soon arranged. I should travel to Strasburgh where Clerval would join me and we should proceed down the Rhine together. Some short time would be spent in the towns of Holland but our principal stay would be in England. We should return by France—and it was agreed that this tour should occupy the space of two years.

My father pleased himself with the reflection that I should be united to Elizabeth immediately on my return to Geneva. These two years, said he, will pass swiftly and it will be the last delay that will oppose itself to your happiness. And indeed I earnestly desire that period to arrive when we shall all be united and neither hopes or fears arise to disturb our domestic calm.

I am content, I replied with your arrangement. By that time we shall both have become wiser and I hope happier than we are at present. I sighed but my father kindly forbore to question me concerning the cause of my dejection—He hoped that new scenes and the amusement of travelling would restore my tranquillity

I now arranged for my journey but one feeling haunted me which filled me with fear and agitation. During my absence I should leave my friends unconscious of the existence of their enemy,

Compare pp. 176–7

and unprotected from his attacks; and exasperated as he might be by my departure. But he had promised to follow me wherever I might go and would he not accompany me to England? This idea was dreadful in itself but soothing in as much as my friends would be in safety. Yet I was agonized with the possibility that the reverse of this might happen. But through the whole period during which I was the slave of my creature I allowed myself to be govern<ed> by the impulses of the moment and my present sensations strongly intimated that the fiend would follow me and free my friends from the possibility of danger. Thinking thus I prepared for my journey with alarcrity.

It was in the latter end of August that I departed to pass two years of exile. Elizabeth approved of the reasons of my departure and only regretted that she had not the same opportunities of enlarging her experience & cultivating her understanding—She wept however as she bade me farewell and entreated <me> to return happy & tranquil. We all, said she, depend upon you, & if you are miserable, what must be our feelings?

I threw myself into the carriage that was to convey me away hardly knowing whither I was going & careless of what was passing around. I remembered only, and it was with a bitter anguish that I reflected on it, to order that my chemical instruments should be packed to go with me. For I resolved to fulfil my promise while abroard [*for* abroad] & return if possible a free man. Filled with dreary imaginations I passed through many beautiful & majestic scenes but my eyes were fixed & unobserving; I could only think of the bourne of my travels & the work which was to occupy me whilst they endured. After some days spent in listless indolence during which I traversed many leagues I arrived at Strasburgh where I waited two days for Clerval. He came; & alas, how great was the contrast between us. He was alive to every new scene; joyful when he saw the beauties of the setting sun and more happy when he saw it rise & recommence a new day. He pointed out to

Compare pp. 177–8

me the shifting colours of the landscape & the appearances of the sky. "This is what it is to live," he cried, now I enjoy existence. But you, my dear Frankenstein, are desponding & sorrowful." Indeed I was occupied by gloomy thoughts and neither saw the descent of the evening star nor the golden sunrise reflected in the Rhine; and you, my friend, would be far more amused with the journal of Clerval who observed the scenery with an eye of feeling & delight, than to listen to my reflections; I, a miserable wretch haunted by a curse that shut up every avenue to enjoyment.

We had agreed to go down the Rhine in a boat from Strasbourgh to Rotterdam whence we might take shipping for London. During this voyage we passed by many willowy islands & saw several beautiful towns. We staid a day at Manheim, on [*for* and] on the fifth from our departure from Strasbourgh, arrived at Mayence. The course of the Rhine below Mayence becomes much more picturesque. The river descends rapidly and winds between hills not high but steep and of beautiful forms. We saw many ruined castles standing on the edges of precipieces surrounded by black woods high & inaccessible. This part of the Rhine indeed presents a singularly variegated lanscape. In one spot you view rugged hills, ruined castles overlooking tremendous precipieces with the dark Rhine rushing beneath. And on the sudden turn of a promontory<,> flourishing vineyards & populous towns & a meandering river with green sloping banks occupy the scene. We travelled at the time of the vintage and heard the song of the labourers as we glided down the stream. Even I, depressed in mind, & my spirits continually agitated by gloomy feelings; even I was pleased. I lay at the bottom of the boat and as I gazed on the cloudless blue sky I seemed to drink in a tranquillity to which I had long been a stranger. And if these were my sensations who can describe those of Henry. He felt as if he had been transported to fairy land and enjoyed a happiness seldom tasted by man. I have seen, he said, the most beautiful scenes of my own country. I have been on the lakes of Lucerne &

Compare pp. 178–9

Uri where the snowy mountains descend almost perpendicularly to the water casting black & impenetrable shades which would cause a gloomy & mournful appearance were it not for the most verdant islands that relieve the eye by their gay appearance. I have seen this lake agitated by a tempest when the wind tore up whirlwinds of water and gave you an idea of what the waterspout must be on the great ocean—and the waves dash with fury the foot of the mountain where the priest & his mistress were overwhelmed by an avelanche, & where their dying voices are still said to be heard amid the pauses of the night wind. I have seen the lovely mountains of la Valais & the pays de Vaud; But this country, Victor, pleases me more than all those wonders. The mountains of Switzerland are more majestic & strange but there is a charm in the banks of this divine river that I never before saw equalled. Look at that castle which overhangs that precipiece; and that also on the island almost concealed among the foliage of those lovely trees—and now that group of laboure<r>s coming from among their vines; & that village half hid in the recess of the mountain. Oh Surely the spirit that inhabits & guards this place has a soul more in harmony with man than those who pile the glacier or retire to the inaccessible peaks of the mountains of our own country.

I smiled at the enthusiasm of my friend and remembered with a sigh the period when my eyes would have glistened with joy to behold the scenes that I now viewed. But the recollection of those days was too painful; I must shut out all thought to enjoy tranquillity, & that reflection alone is sufficient to poison every pleasure.

At Cologne we descended to the plains of Holland & we resolved to post the remainder of our way for the wind was contrary & the stream of the river was too gentle to aid us. We now arrived at very different country. The soil was sandy and the wheels sunk deep in it. The towns of this country are the most pleasing part of the scene. The Dutch are extremely neat but there is an awkwardness in

Compare pp. 179–80

their contrivances that often surprised us. In one place, I remember, a wind mill was situated in such a manner that the postillion was obliged to guide the carriage close to the opposite side of the road to escape from the sweep of its sails. The way often led between two canals where the road was only broard [*for* broad] enough to allow one carriage to pass and when we met another vehicle which was frequently the case we were rolled back sometimes for nearly a mile untill we found one of the drawbridges which led to the fields, down on which one carriage remained while the other passed on. They soak their flax also in the mud of their canals and place it against the trees along the road side to dry. When the sun is hot the scent that this exhales is not very easily endured. Yet the roads are excellent & the verdure beautiful

From Rotterdam we went by sea to England. It was on a clear morning in the latter <days> of September that I first saw the white cliffs of Britain. The banks of the Thames presented a new scene; they were flat but fertile & almost every town was marked by some story. We saw Tilbury Fort & remembered the Spanish Armada; Gravesend, Woolwich, Greenwich places which I had heard of even in my country. At length we saw the numerous steeples of London; St Pauls towerering above all & the Tower famed in English History.

Chap 11

London was our present point of rest; we determined to remain several months in this wonderful & celebrated city.† Clerval desired the intercourse of the men of genius & talent who flourished at that time; but this was, with me, a secondary consideration; I was

† The first sentence of Chapter 11 that MWS later renumbered to Chapter 2 to indicate its new position in Volume III of the restructured three-volume novel to be found in *1817 Fair Copy* and *1818*.

Compare pp. 180–81

principally occupied with the means of obtaining the information necessary for the completion of my promise and quickly availed myself of the letters of introduction that I had brought with me addressed to the most distinguished natural philosophers. If this journey had taken place during my days of study & happiness it would have afforded me inexpressible pleasure. But a blight had come over my existence & I only visited these people for the sake of the information they might give me on the subject in which I was so deeply interrested. Company was irksome to me; when alone I could fill my mind with the sights of heaven & earth; the voice of Henry soothed me & I could cheat myself into a transitory peace. But busy, uninterresting, joyous faces brought back despair to my heart. I saw an insurmountable barrie<r> placed between me & my fellow men; thi<s> barrier was sealed with the blood of William and Justine, and to reflect on those events filled my soul with anguish But in Clerval I saw the image of my former self; he was inquisitive & anxious to gain experience & instruction; The difference of manners that he observed was to him an inexhaustible source of amusement. He was for ever busy & the only check to his enjoyments was my sorrowful & dejected mien. I tried to conceal this as much as possible that I might not debar him from the pleasures natural to one who was entering on a new scene of life, undisturbed by any care or bitter recollection. I often refused to accompany him alledging another engagement that I might remain {a} alone; I now also began to collect the materials necessary for my new creation & this was to me like the torture of single drops of water continually falling on the head; Every thought that was devoted to it was an extreme anguish, and every word that I spoke in allusion to it caused my lips to quiver & my heart to palpitate.

After passing some months in London we received a letter from a person in Scotland who had formerly been our visitor at Geneva. He mentioned the beauties of his native country & asked us if those were not sufficient allurements to induce us to prolong our journey

 Compare pp. 181–2.

as far north as Perth where he resided. Clerval eagerly desired to accept this invitation, and I, although I abhorred society, wished to view again mountains & streams & all the wondrous works of nature in her chosen dwelling places We had arrived in Englan<d> at the beginning of October and it was now february; we accordingly determined to commence our journey towards the north at {at} the expiration of another month. In this expedition we did not intend to follow the great road to Edinburgh But to visit Windsor, Oxford, Matlock & the Cumberland lakes resolving to arrive at the completion of this tour about the end of July. I packed my chemical instruments & the materials which I had collected resolving to finish my labours in some obscure nook in the country.

We quitted London on the 27<th> of March and remained a few days at Windsor rambling in its beautiful forest. This was a new scene to us mountaineers; The majectic oaks the quantity of game & the flocks of lovely deer were all novelties to us. From thence we proceeded to Oxford. We were charmed with the appearance of the town. The colledges are antient and picturesque, the streets broard [*for* broad] & the landscape rendered perfect by the lovely Isis{.} which spreads into broard [*for* broad] & placid expance of water & runs south of the town. We had letters to several of the professors & were received with great politeness & cordiality. We found that the regulations of this university were much improved since the days of Gibbon; But there is still in fashion a great deal of bigotry & devotion to established rules that constrains the mind of the students & leads to slavish & narrow principles of action. Many enormities are also practised which although they might excite the laughter of a stranger were looked upon in the world of the university as matters of the utmost consequence. Some of the gentlemen obstinately wore light coloured pantaloons when it was the rule of the colledge to wear dark: the masters were angry & their scholars resolute so that while we were there two of the students were on the point of being expelled on this very

Compare pp. 182–3

question. The threatened severity caused a considerable change in the costume of the gentlemen for several days.

Such, to our infinite astonishment, we found to be the principal topic of conversation when we arrived in the town. Our minds had been filled with the remembrance of the events that had been transacted here above two centuries before. It was here that Charles I had collected his forces; this town had been faithful to him when the whole nation had forsaken him to join the standard of parliament & liberty. It was strange to us entering the town our thoughts occupied by the memory <of> the unfortunate king, the amiable Falkland and the insolent Gower and finding it filled with gownsmen & students who think of nothing less than these events. Yet there are some relics to remind you of antient times; among others we regarded with curiosity the press instituted by the author of the history of the troubles We were also shewn a room which Frier Bacon the discoverer of gunpowder had inhabited and which, as it was predicted, would fall in when a man wiser than that philosopher should enter it. A {a} short, round faced prating professor who accompanied us refused to pass the threshold; although we ventured inside in perfect security.

Matlock, which was our next place of rest, resembled to a great degree the scenery of Switzerland; But every thing is on a lower scale & the green mountains want the crown of distant white alps which always attend on the piny mountains of our country. We visited the wondrous cave & the little cabinets of natural history where the curiosities are disposed in the same manner as in the collections at Servox & Chamounix. The latter mame [*for* name] made me tremble when pronounced by Henry & I hastened to quit Matlock where the scenes were thus ascociated.

From Derby, still journeying northward, we passed two months among the mountains of Cumberland & Westmorland. I could now almost fancy myself among the Swiss mountains; The little patches of snow which yet lingered on the north sides of the mountains—

 Compare pp. 183–4

the lakes & the dashing of the rocky mountain streams were all familiar & dear sights to me. Here also we made some aquaintances who almost contrived to cheat me into happiness. The delight of Clerval was proportionably greater than mine; his mind expanded in the company of men of talent & he found in himself greater capacity & feeling than he could have imagined himself to have possessed while he associated with his inferiors. "I could pass my life here," said he to me, "and among these mountains I should hardly regret Switzerland & the Rhine.

But he found that a travellers life is one that includes much pain amidst its enjoyments. His feelings are for ever on the strectch & when he begins to sink into repose he finds himself obliged to quit it for something new which again engages his attention & which he also forsakes for more novelty. We had scarcely visited the various lakes of Cumberland & Westmorland & conceived an affection for some of the inhabitants when the period of our appointment with our Scotch friend approached & we left them to travel on. For my own part I was not sorry. I had now neglected my promise for some time and I feared the effects of the dæmoms [*for* dæmons] disappointment. He might remain in Switzerland & wreack his vengeance of [*for* on] my relatives; this idea persued me & tormented me at every moment when I might otherwise have snatched repose & peace. I waited for my letters with feverish impatience; If they were delayed I was miserable & overcome by a thousand fears; & when they arrived and I saw the superscription of Elizabeth or my father I hardly dared to read & ascertain my fate. Sometimes I thought that the fiend followed me & might remind me my [*for* by] murdering my companion; with these thought<s> I would not quit Henry for a moment but followed him as his shadow to protect him from the fancied rage of his destroyer. I felt as if I had committed some great crime the consciousness of which haunted me. I was guiltless but I had drawn down a horrible curse of [*for* on] my head which I in vain endeavoured to shake off.

Compare pp. 184–5

I visited Edinburgh with languid eyes & mind & yet that city might have interrested the most unfortunate being. Clerval did not like it so well as Oxford for the antiquity of that city was pleasing to him. But the beauty & regularity of the new town delighted him; its environs are also the most beautiful in the world; Arthur's seat, St Bernards Well & the Pentland hills—But I was impatient to arrive at the termination of my journey. We left Edinburgh in a week passing through Cooper, St Andrews & Along the {the} banks of the Tay to Perth Where our friend expected us; But I was not in the mood to laugh & talk with Strangers or enter into their feelings or plans with the good humour expected from a guest and accordingly I told Clerval that I wished to make the tour of Scotland by myself. Do you, said I, enjoy yourself and let this be our rendezvous—I may be absent a month or two, but do not interfere with my motions I entreat you; leave me to peace & solitude for a short time & when I return I hope it will be with a lighter heart more congenial to your own temper." Henry wished to dissuade me but seeing me bent on this plan consented. but entreated me to write often. I had rather be with you, he said, In your solitary rambles than with these scotch people whom I do not know; hasten then my dear friend to return that I may again feel myself somewhat at home which I cannot do in your absence.

Chap 12

Having parted from my friend I determined to visit some remote spot of Scotland and finish my work in solitude. I did not doubt but that the monster followed me, and would discover himself, when I should have finished, to receive his companion. With this resolution I traversed the northern highlands and fixed on one of the Orkney Islands for the scene of my labours. It was a place fitted

 Compare pp. 185–6

for such a work; being hardly more than a rock whose high sides were continually beaten upon by the waves—The soil was barren hardly affording pasture for a few miserable cows & oatmeal for its inhabitants which consisted of five person, Whose gaunt & scraggy limbs gave tokens of their sorry fare. Vegetables & bread, when they indulged in such luxuries, & even fresh water was to be procured from the main land which was about five miles distant. On the whole island there were but three miserable huts & one of these was vacant when I arrived. This I hired—It contained but two rooms & these exhibited all the squalidness of the most miserable poverty—The thatch had fallen in—the walls unplastered & the door was off its hinges. I ordered it to be repaired, bought some furniture & took possession—an incident which would have doubtless occasioned some surprise had not all the senses of the cottagers been benumbed by want and squalid poverty; as it was I lived ungazed at and unmolested, hardly thanked for the pittance of food and clothes which I gave<,> so much does suffering blunt even the coarsest sensations of men.

In this retreat I devoted the morning to labour, but in the evening, when the weather permitted I walked on the stony beach of the sea to listen to the waves as they roared & dashed at my feet; It was a monotonous yet ever changing scene. I thought of Switzerland; It was far different from this desolate & appalling landscape—Its hills are covered with vines & its cottages are scattered thick in the plains—Its fair lakes reflect a blue & gentle sky<,> & when troubled by the winds it is but the play of a lively infant when compared to the roarings of the giant ocean.

In this manner I distributed my occupations when I first arrived; but as I proceeded in my work it became every day more horrible & irksome to me. Sometimes I could not prevail on myself to enter my laboratory for several days and at other times I laboured day & night in order to finish it. It was indeed a filthy work in which I was engaged. During my first experiment a kind of enthusiastic

Compare pp. 186–7

frenzy blinded me to the horror of my employment; my mind was intently fixed on the sequel of my labour and my eyes were shut to the horror of my proceedings. But now I went to it in cold blood and my heart often sickened at the work of my hands.

Thus situated; employed in the most detestable occupation, in a solitude where nothing could for an instant call my attention from the actual scene in which I was engaged, my spirits were unequal, I became restless & nervous—Every moment I feared to meet my persecutor. Sometimes I sat with my eyes fixed on the ground fearing to raise them lest they should meet him I so much dreaded to see<.> I feared to wander from the sight of my fellow creatures lest when alone He should come to claim his companion. In the mean time I worked on & my labour was already considerably advanced—I looked with pleasure towards completion yet freedom from the curse I endured was a joy I never dared promise myself——†

One evening I sat in my workshop, the sun had set & the moon was just rising from the sea—I had not light sufficient for my employment and I sat idle in a pause of consideration of whether I should leave my labour for the night or hasten its conclusion by an unremitting attention to it. As I sat a train of reflection occurred to me which led to me [*for* me to] consider the effects of what I was now doing. three years before I had been engaged in the same manner & had created a fiend whose unparralelled barbarity had desolated my heart and filled it for ever with the bitterest remorse. I was now about to form another being of whose dispositions I was alike ignorant. She might be ten thousand times more malignant than her mate and delight in murder & wretchedness. He had sworn to quit the neighbourhood of man & hide himself in desarts but she had not & she who was in all

† MWS's marginal note of 'Finish Chap. 2 here' at this point in the Draft indicates the new chapter division in Volume III of the restructured three-volume novel to be found in *1817 Fair Copy* and *1818*.

 Compare pp. 187–8

probability to become a thinking & reasoning animal might refuse to comply with a compact made before her creation. They might even hate one another. The creature who already lived loathed his own deformity & might he not conceive a greater abhorrence for it when it came before his eyes in the female form. She also might turn with disgust from him to the superior beauty of man. She might quit him and he be again alone with the fresh provocation of being deserted by one of his own species.

Even if they were to leave Europe & inhabit the desarts of the new world, it was their intention to have children and a race of devils would be propogated on the earth from whose form & mind man shrunk with horrow [*for* horror] & had I right for my own benefit to inflict this curse to everlasting generations? I had before been moved by the sophisms of the being whom I had created; I had been moved by his fiendish threats & now for the first time the wickedness of my promise burst upon me; I shudered to think that future ages might curse me as their pest whose selfishness had not hesitated to buy its own peace at the price perhaps of the whole human race. I trembled, and my heart failed within me, when, on looking up I saw by the light of the moon, <that> the dæmon with a ghastly grin on his wrinkled lips, gazed on me as I sat. Yes, he had followed me in my travels; he had loitered in forests, hid himself in caves or taken refuge in wide & desart heaths & he now came to view my progress & claim the fulfillment of my promise; as I looked on him his countenance appeared to express the utmost extent of malice & barbarity: I thought with a sensation of madness of my promise of creating another like to him & trembling with passion tore to pieces the thing on which I was engaged—The wretch saw me destroy the creature on whose future existence he depended for happiness and with a howl of devilish despair withdrew.

I left the room & locking the door made a vow in my own heart never to resume my labours; & then with trembling steps I sought

Compare pp. 188–9

my own appartment I was alone. None were near me to dissipate the gloom and relieve me from the most terrible reveries. Several hours passed and I remained near my window gazing on the sea. It was almost motionless for the winds were hushed & all nature reposed under the eye of the quiet moon A few fishing vessels alone specked the water and now & then the gentle breeze wafted the sound of the voices as the men called to one another. I felt the silence although I was hardly conscious of its extreme profundity untill my ear was suddenly arrested by the paddling of oars near the shore and a person landed close to my house. In a few minutes after<,> I heard the creaking of my door as if some one endeavoured to open it softly. I trembled from head to foot; I felt a presentiment of who it was and wished to rouse one of the peasants who dwelt in a cottage not far from mine. But I was overcome by the sensation <of> helplessness so often felt in a frightful dream when you in vain endeavour to fly the impending danger & was rooted to the spot. Presently I heard the sound of footsteps along the passage, my door opened & the wretch whom I dreaded appeared. Shutting the door he approached me & said in a smothered voice:—You have destroyed the work that you began; What is it that you intend? Do you dare break your promise? I have endured toil & misery: I left Switzerland with you; I crept along the shores of the Rhine with you, among its willow islands and upon the summits of its hills. I have dwelt many months in the heaths of England & among the desarts of Scotland. I have endured incalculable fatigue & cold & hunger do you dare destroy my hopes?

Begone, I replied; I do break my promise; never will <I> create another like yourself, equal in deformity & wickedness.

Slave, said the wretch, I before reasoned with you—but you have proved yourself unworthy of my condescension. Remember that I have power; you believe yourself miserable but I can make you so wretched that the light of day will be hateful to you. You are my creator but I am your master; obey!

 Compare pp. 189–90

Wretch, said I, the hour of my weakness is past & the period of your power is arrived. Your threats cannot move me to do an act of wickedness but they confirm me in a resolution of not creating you <a> companion in vice. Shall I in cold blood set loose upon the earth a dæmon whose delight is in death & wretchedness. Begone, I am firm and your words will only exasperate my rage.

The Monster saw my determination in my face and gnashed his teeth in the impotence of anger. Shall each man, cried he, find his equal, & each beast have his mate and I be alone. I had feelings of affection & they were returned by detestation. Man you may hate, but beware! Your hours will pass in dread & misery and soon the bolt will fall which will ravish from you your happiness for ever. Are you to be happy while I grovel in the intensity of my wretchedness. You destroy my other passions but revenge remains; revenge dearer than light or food. I may die but first you my tyrant & tormentor shall curse the sun that gazes on your misery. Beware, for I am fearless & therefore powerful. I will watch with the wiliness of a snake that I may sting with its venom. Man, you shall repent of the injuries you inflict.

Devil, I cried, Cease, & do not poison the air with those sounds of malice. I have declared my resolution to you and I am no coward to bend beneath words—Leave me, I am inexorable.

It is well, said he, I go; but remember! I shall be with you on your marriage night.

Chapter 13rd

I started forward & exclaimed—Villain, before you sign my death-warrant, be sure that you are yourself safe. I would have seized him but he eluded me {and} quitting the house with precipitation<—>in a few moments I saw him in his boat which shot across the waters with an arrowy swiftness & was soon lost amidst the waves.

Compare pp. 190–91

All was again silent; but his words rung in my ears; I burnt with rage to pursue the murderer of my peace & precipitate him into the ocean. I walked up & down my room hastily & perturbed, my imagination conjured before me a thousand images to torment & sting me—Why had I not followed him & closed with him in mortal strife?—But I had suffered him to depart and he had directed his course towards the main land; I shuddered to suppose who might be the next victim sacrificed to his insatiate revenge—And then again I thought of his words—"I will be with you on your marriage night That then was the period fixed for the fulfillment of my destiny—In that hour I should die and at once satisfy and extinguish his malice. The prospect did not {not} move me to fear yet when I thought of my beloved Elizabeth; of her tears & endless sorrow when she should find her lover so barbarously snatched from her—tears the first I had shed for many months, streamed from my eyes & I resolved not to fall before my enemy without a bitter struggle.

The night passed away & the sun rose from the ocean—My feelings became calmer if it may be called calmness when the violence of rage sinks into the depths of despair. I left the house, the horrid scene of the last nights contention and walked on the beach of the sea which I almost regarded as an insuperable barrier between me & my fellow creatures. Nay a wish that that was the fact stole across me; I might pass my life on this barren rock wearily it is true but uninterrupted by any sudden shock of misery—If I returned it was to be sacrificed or to see those I most loved die under the grasp of a dæmon whom I had myself created. I walked about the isle like a restless spectre seperated from all it loved & miserable in the seperation When it became noon & the sun rose higher I lay down on the grass & was overpowered by a deep sleep. I had been awake the whole of the preceeding night, my nerves were agitated & my eyes inflamed with watching & misery. The sleep into which I now sunk refreshed me & when I awoke I again

 Compare pp. 191–2

felt as if I belonged to a race of human beings like myself & I began to reflect upon what had passed with greater composure—Yet still the words of the fiend rung in my ears like a death knell, they appeared like a dream, yet distinct and oppressive as a reality.

The sun was far descended and I still sat on the shore satisfying my apetite which was become ravenous with an oaten cake when I saw a fishing boat land close to me & one of the men brought me a packet; it contained letters from Geneva & one from Clerval entreating me to join him. He said that nearly a year had elapsed since we had quitted Switzerland<,> and France was yet unvisited. He entreated me therefore to leave my solitary isle and meet him at Perth in a week from that time when we might arrange the plan of our future proceedings. This letter completely recalled me to life & I determined to quit my island at the expiration of two days.

Yet before I departed there was a task to perform on which I shuddered to reflect: I must pack my chemical instruments & for that purpose I must enter the room which had been the scene of my odious work, & I must handle the utensils the sight of which were sickening to me. The next morning at daybreak I summoned sufficient courage & unlocked the door of my work room—The remains of the half finished creature whom I had destroyed lay scattered on the floor—& I almost felt as if I mangled the living flesh of a human being. I paused to collect myself & then entered the chamber. With trembling hands I conveyed the instruments out of the room but I reflected that I ought not to leave the relicks of my work to excite the horror of the peasants and I accordingly put them into a basket with a great quantity of stones and tying it up determined to throw them into the sea that very night and in the mean time I sat on the beach employed in cleaning & arranging my chemical apparatus.

Nothing could be more complete than the alteration that had taken place in my feelings since the night of the appearance of the dæmon. I had before regarded my promise with gloomy despair as a

Compare pp. 192–3

thing that must with whatever consequences be fulfilled but I now felt as if a film had been taken from before my eyes & that I now for the first time saw clearly. The idea of renewing my labours did not for an instant occur to me. The threat I had heard weighed on my thoughts but I did not reflect that a voluntary act of mine might avert it. I had resolved in my own mind that to create another like the fiend I had first made would be an act of the basest & most atrocious selfishness and I banished from my mind every thought that could lead to a different conclusion

Between two & three in the morning the moon rose and I then putting my basket into a little skiff sailed out about four miles from the shore—The scene was perfectly solitary, a few boats were returning towards land but I sailed away from them. I felt as if I was about the commission of a dreadful crime and avoided with shuddering anxiety any encounter with my fellow creatures. At one time the moon which had before been clear was suddenly overspread by a thick cloud & I took advantage of the moment of darkness & cast the basket into the sea—I listened to the gurgling sound as it sunk & then sailed away from the spot. The sky had become clouded but the air was pure although chilled by the North-East breeze that was rising. But it refreshed & filled me with such agreable sensations that I resolved to prolong my stay on the water & fixing the rudder in a direct position stretched myself at the bottom of the boat. Clouds hid the moon, every thing was obscure & I heard only the sound of the boat as it [*for* its] keel cut through the waves—The sound lulled me—& in a short time I slept soundly

I do not know how long I remained in this situation but when I awoke I found that the sun had already mounted considerably—The wind was high and the waves continually threatened the safety of my little skiff—I found that the wind was north-east and must have driven me far from the coast from which I had embarked. I endeavoured to change my course but quickly found that if I again

 Compare pp. 193–4

made the attempt the boat would be instantly filled with water. Thus situated<,> my only resource was to drive before the wind—I confess that I felt a few sensations of terror—I had no compass with me and was so little acquainted with the geography of this part of the world that the sun was of little benefit to me—I might be driven into the wide Atlantic & feel all the tortures of starvation or be swallowed up in immeasurable waters that roared & buffeted around me. I had already been out many hours and felt the tortures of a burning thirst a prelude to my other sufferings—I looked on the heavens which was covered by clouds that flew with the wind only to be replaced by others—I looked on the sea—It was to be my grave. Fiend, I exclaimed, your task is already fulfilled—I thought of Elizabeth of my father & of Clerval—& sunk into a reverie so despairing & frightful that even now when the scene is on the point of closing before me for ever I shudder to reflect on it.

Some hours passed thus—But by degrees, as the sun declined towards the horizon, the wind died away into a gentle breeze and the sea became free from breakers. But these gave place to a heavy swell, I felt sick & hardly able to hold the rudder when suddenly I saw a line of high land towards the south. Almost spent as I was by fatigue & misery this sudden certainty of life rushed like a warm joy to my heart and tears gushed from my eyes. How mutable are our feelings & how strange is that clinging love we have of life even in the excess of misery. I constructed another sail with a part of my dress & eagerly steered my course towards the land. It had a wild rocky appearance but as I approached nearer I easily perceived the traces of cultivation—I saw vessels near the shore & found myself suddenly transported back to the neighbourhood of civilized man—I eagerly viewed the windings of the shore & hailed a steeple which I at length saw issueing from behind a small promontory—As I was in a state of extreme debility from fasting I resolved to go directly towards the town as a place where <I> could most easily procure nourishment—Fortunately I had money with me.

Compare pp. 194–5

As I turned the promontory I discovered a small neat town—and a good harbour which I entered, my heart bounding with joy at my unexpected escape.

As I was occupied in fixing the boat and {ar} arranging the sails several people crowded towards the spot—They appeared very much {much} surprised at my appearance but instead of offering me any assistance whispered together with gestures that at any other time might have produced in me a slight sensation of alarm—as it was I merely remarked that it was English, that they spoke and therefore addressed them; My Good Friends, said I, Will you be so kind as to tell me what the name of this town is; & where I am.

You will know that soon enough, replied a man with a gruff voice; May be you are come to a place that will not prove much to your taste—But you will not be consulted as to your quarters, I promise you—

I was exceedingly surprized at receiving so rude an answer from a stranger and I was also disconcerted on perceiving the frowning and angry countenances of his companions—Why do you answer me so roughly, I replied Surely it is not the custom of Englishmen to receive strangers so inhospitably.

I do not know, said the man, what the custom of the English may be but it is the custom of the Irish to hate villains.

While this strange dialogue continued I perceived the croud rapidly encrease. Their faces expressed a mixture of curiosity & anger which annoyed & in some degree alarmed me. I enquired the way to the inn but no one replied—I then moved forward and a murmuring noise rose from the croud as they followed & surrounded me—when an ill looking man comming forward—tapped me on the shoulder & said—Come, Sir, You must follow me to Mr. Kirwins to give an account of yourself.

Who is Mr. Kirwin, said I, & why am I to give an account of myself.—is not this a free country?

Compare pp. 195–6

Aye, Sir, replied the man, free enough for honest folks. Mr. Kirwin is a magistrate & you are to give an account of the death of a gentleman who was found murdered here last night.

This answer startled me, But I presently recovered myself. I was innocent & that could easily be proved—accordingly I followed my conductor in silence & was led to one of the best houses in town. I was ready to sink from fatigue & hunger—but being surrounded by a croud I thought it politic to rouse all my strength that no physical debility might be construed into apprehension or conscious guilt. Little did I then expect the calamity that would in a few moments overwhelm me, and in horror & despair extinguish all fear of ignominy or death—I must pause for the scene which I shall now relate requires all my fortitude to recall its frightful images in proper detail to my recollection.

Chap. 14th

I was soon introduced into the presence of the Magistrate; an old benevolent man with calm & mild manners. He looked towards me however with some degree of severity, and then turning towards my conductors he asked who appeared as witnesses on this occasion. about half a dozen men came forward and one being selected by the magistrate he deposed that he had been out fishing the night before with his son & his brother-in-law, Daniel Nugent, when about nine o clock they observed a strong northerly blast rising & they accordingly put in for port. It was a very dark night as the moon had not yet risen; They did not land at the harbour but, as they had been accustomed, at a creek about two miles below. He went first carrying a part of the fishing tackle & his companions followed him at some distance. As he was walking along the sands he hit his foot against somthing & fell all his length on the ground;

Compare pp. 196–7

his comrades came up to assist him & by the light of their lantern they discovered that he had fallen on the body of a man who was to all appearance dead.

Their first supposition was that it was the corpse of <a> man who had been drowned & thrown on shore by the waves, But upon examination they found that the clothes were not wet & even that the body was not yet cold. They instantly carried it to the cottage of an old woman near & endeavoured to restore it to life but In vain. He appeared to have been a handsome young man about twenty years of age. He had apparently been strangled for there <was> no sign of any violence except the black mark of fingers on his neck.

The first of this deposition did not in the least interrest me but when the mark of the fingers was mentioned I remembered the murder of my brother & felt myself extremely agitated; my limbs trembled & a mist came over my eyes which obliged me to lean on a chair for support; the Magistrate observed me with a keen eye & of course drew an unfavourable augury from my manner.

The son confirmed his fathers account but when Daniel Nugent was questioned he swore positively that just before the fall of his companion he saw a boat with a single man in it at a short distance from the shore & as far as he could judge by the light of a few stars it was the same boat in which I had just landed.

A woman deposed that she lived near the beach & was standing at the door of her cottage waiting for the return when about an hour before she heard of the discovery of the body she saw a boat with only one man in it push off from that part of the shore where the corpse was afterwards found.

Another woman confirmed the account of the fishermen having brought the body into her house.—It was not cold & they put it into a bed & rubbed it and Daniel went to the town for an appothecary, but life was quite gone.

Several other men were examined concerning my landing & they agreed that with the strong north wind that had arrisen

Compare pp. 197–8

during the night it was very probable that I had beaten about for many hours & have [*for* had] been obliged to return nearly to the same spot from which I had departed. Besides, they observed, that it appeared I had brought the body from another place & it was likely that as I did not appear to know the shore I might have put in to the harbour ignorant of the distance of the town of ——— from the place where I had deposited the corpse.

Mr. Kirwin on hearing this evidence desired that I should be taken into the room where the body lay for interment that it might be observed what effect the sight of it produced upon me. This idea was probably suggested by the extreme agitation I had exhibited when the mode of the murder had been described. I was accordingly conducted by the Magistrate & several other persons to the Inn. I could not help being struck by the strange coincidences that had taken place during this eventful night but knowing that I had been conversing with several persons in the island I had inhabited about the time that the body had been found I was perfectly tranquil as to the consequences of the affair.

I entered the room where the corpse lay & was led up to the coffin. How can I describle{?} my sensation. I feel yet parched with horror nor can I ever reflect on that terrible moment without shuddering & agony that faintly reminds <me> of the anguish of recognition. The trial, the presence of the magistrate & witnesses passed like a dream from my memory when I saw the lifeless form of Henry Clerval stretched before me—I gasped for breath & throwing myself on the body I exclaimed. And have my murderous machinations deprived you also my dearest Henry of life—Two I have already destroyed; other victims await their destinny—But you, Clerval, my fr<i>end, my benefactor!—

The human frame could no longer support the agonizing suffering that I endured & I was carried out of the room in strong convulsions.

Compare pp. 198–9

A fever succeeded to this. I lay for two months on the point of death. My ravings, as I afterwards heard were frightful. I called myself the murderer of William, of Justine & of Clerval. Sometimes I entreated my attendants to assist me in the destruction of the fiend by whom I was tormented—and at others I felt the fangs of the monster already grasping my neck & screamed aloud with agony & terror. Fortunately as I spoke my native tongue Mr. Kirwin alone understood me. But my gestures and bitter cries were sufficient, to affright the other witnesses.

Why did I not die? More miserable than man ever was before<,> why did I not sink into rest & forgetfullness? Death snatches away many blooming children the only hopes of their doating parents; How many brides & youthful lovers have been one day in the bloom of health & hope & the next a prey for worms & the decay of the tomb! Of what materials was I made that I could thus resist so many shocks which like the turning of the wheel continually renewed the torture.

But I was doomed to live & in two months found myself as awaking from a dream, in a prison, stretched on a wretched bed surrounded by gailors—turnkeys, bolts & all the miserable apparatus of a dungeon It was morning<,> I remember<,> when I thus awoke I had forgotten the particulars of what had happened & only felt as if some great misery had overcome me. But when I looked around and saw the barred windows, & the squalidness of the room in which I was, all flashed across my memory— & I groaned bitterly. This sound disturbed an old woman who was sleeping in a chair beside me. She was a hired nurse, the wife of one of the turnkeys & her countenance expressed all those bad qualities which often characterize that class. her face was hard & rude like that of persons accustomed to see without sympathizing in sights of misery. Her voice expressed her entire indifference—She addressed me in E<n>glish & the words struck me as one that I had heard during suffering—Are you better now, Sir, said she.

 Compare pp. 199–200

I replied in the same language with a feeble voice; I believe I am but if it all be true—if indeed I did not dream I am sorry that I am still alive to feel misery & horror.

For that matter, replied the old woman, if you mean about the gentleman that you murdered I believe that it were better for you if you were dead—for I fancy it will go hard with you. you will be hanged when the next session comes on—however that is none of my business I am sent to nurse you & get you well—I do my duty with a safe conscience; it were well if every body did the same.—

I turned with loathing from the woman who could utter so unfeeling a speech to a man just saved on the very edge of death; but I felt languid and unable to reflect on all that had passed; It sometimes appeared as a dream<.> I sometimes doubted if indeed it was not all true but it never presented itself to my mind with the force of reality.

As the images that floated before me became more distinct I grew feverish; a darkness pressed around me<;> no person was near me who soothed me with the gentle voice of love; no dear hand supported me. The phisician came & prescribed medecines & the old woman prepared them for me but utter carelessness was visible in the first & the expression of brutality was strongly impressed on the visage of the second—who could be interested in the fate of a murderer but the hangman who would gain his fee?

These were my first reflections but I soon learned that Mr.{.} Kirwin had shewn me extreme kindness—He had caused the best room in the prison to be prepared for me, (wretched indeed was the best) And it was he who had provided a physician & attendants for me. It is true he seldom came to see me for although he ardently desired to relieve the sufferings of every human creature he did not wish to be present at the agonies and miserable ravings of a murderer—He came therefore sometimes to see that I was not neglected, but his visits were short & at long intervals.

Compare pp. 200–201

One day when I was gradually recovering & seated in a chair, my eyes half <open> and my cheeks livid like those of death<,> I was overcome by gloom & misery and often reflected whether I had better not seek death that [*for* than] wait miserably pent up only to be let loose in a world replete with wretchedness. At one time I considered whether I should not de<c>lare myself guilty & suffer the penalty of the law which in depriving me of life would afford the only consolation that I was capable of receiving. Such were my thoughts when the door of my prison opened and Mr. Kirwin entered. His countenance expressed sympathy and kindness: he drew a chair close to mine & addressed me in french.

I fear that this place is very shocking to you; Can I do any thing to make you more comfortable.

I thank you, replied I, but all that you mention is nothing to me; on the whole earth there is no comfort which I am capable of receiving.

I know that the sympathy of a stranger can be but little relief to one borne down as you are by so strange a misfortune But you will I hope soon quit this unhappy abode—for doubtless evidence can be easily brought to free you from the criminal charge

That is my least concern—I am by a course of strange events, become the most miserable of mortals. Persecuted & tortured as I am & have been can death be any evil to me?

Nothing indeed could be more unfortunate & agonizing than the strange chances that have lately occurred. You were thrown, by some surprising accident, on this shore, renowned for its hospitality. Seized immediately & charged with murder the first sight that was presented to your eyes was the body of your friend murdered in so unaccountable a manner and placed by some fiend as it were across your path—

As Mr. Kirwin said this, notwithstanding the agitation that I endured on this retrospect of my sufferings—I also felt considerable surprise at the knowledge he seemed to possess concerning me. I

Compare pp. 201–2

suppose some astonishment was expressed in my countenance—for Mr. Kirwin hastened to say—It was not untill a day or two after your illness that I thought of examining your dress that I might discover some trace by which I could send to your relations an account of your misfortune and illness. I found several letters<,> among others one which I discovered by its commencement to be from your father—I instantly wrote to Geneva—nearly two months has passed since the departure of my letter—But you are ill—even now you tremble <you> appear unfit for agitation of any kind.

This suspense is a thousand times worse than the most horrible event—Tell me what new scene of death has been acted & whose murder I am now to lament.

Your family are all perfectly well <said Mr. Kirwin> with gentleness; and some one, a friend, is come to visit you.

I do not know by what chain of thought the idea presented itself but it instantly darted into my mind that the monster had come to mock at my misery & taunt me with the death of Clerval as a new incitement to comply with his hellish desires. I put my hand before my eyes & cried out in agony—Oh! take him away—I cannot see him<;> for Gods sake do not let him enter!

Mr. Kirwin regarded me with a troubled countenance. He could not help regarding my exclamation as a presumption of my guilt & said in rather severe tone—I should have thought, young man, that the presence of your Father would have been welcome instead of inspiring such violent repugnance.

My father, said, I, while every feature & every muscle was relaxed from anguish to pleasure—Is my father indeed come—how kind, how very kind! But where is he, why does he not hasten to me?

My change of manner suprised & pleased the magistrate, perhaps he thought that my former exclamation was a momentary return of delirium And now he instantly resumed his former benevolence—He rose and quitted the room with my nurse & in a minute my father entered it.

Compare pp. 202–3

Nothing at this moment could have given me greater pleasure than the arrival of my father—I stretched out my hand to him & cried—Are you then safe & Elizabeth & Ernest.

My father calmed me by his assurances of their welfare & told me that he had not communicated my imprisonment to my cousin but merely mentioned my illness—And what a place this is that you inhabit, my son continued he looking mournfully at the barred windows and the wretched appearance of the room; You travelled to seek happiness but a fatality seems to pursue you—And poor Clerval.

The name of my unfortunate & murdered friend was too great an agitation to be endured in my weak state—I shed tears; Alas, yes, my father said I, a destiny of the most horrible kind hangs over <me>, and I must live to fulfil it, or surely I should have died on the coffin of Henry.

Chap. 15

We were not allowed to converse for any length of time for the precarious state of my health rendered every precaution necessary. Mr.{.} Kirwin came in & insisted that my strength should not be exhausted by too much exertion. But the appearance of my father was to me like that of my good angel, and I gradually recovered my health. As my sickness quitted me I was absorbed by a gloomy & black melancholy that nothing could dissipate—The image of Clerval was for ever before me ghastly & murdered. More than once the agitation that these reflections threw me into made my friends dread a dangerous relapse

Alas! Why did they preserve so miserable and detested a life? It was surely that I might fulfil my destiny which is drawing to a close—Soon Oh very soon will death extinguish these throbbings

 Compare p. 204

this mighty weight of anguish that bears me to the dust<;> and in executing the award of justice I shall also sink to rest. Then the appearance of death was distant although the wish was ever present to my thoughts & I often sat for hours motionless & speechless wishing for some mighty revolution that might bury me & my destroyer in its ruins.

The season of the assizes approached—I had already been three months in prison & although I was still weak & in continual danger of a relapse I was obliged to travel nearly a hundred miles to the county town where the court was held. Mr. Kirwin charged himself with every care of collecting witnesses and arranging my defence—I was spared the disgrace of appearing publickly as a criminal as the case was not brought before the court that decides on life & death—The Grand Jury rejected the bill on its being proved that I was in the Orkney Island at the hour the body of my friend was found. And a fortnight after my removal I was liberated from prison—My father was enraptured on finding me freed from the vexations of a criminal charge & that I was again permitted to breathe the fresh atmosphere & allowed to return to my native country. I did not participate in these feelings for to me the walls of a dungeon or a palace were alike hateful—The cup of life was poisoned for ever & although the sun shone upon me as upon the happy & gay of heart<,> I saw around me nothing but a dense & frightful darkness penetrated by no glimmer but the light of two eyes that glared upon me.—Sometimes they were the expressive eyes of Henry languishing in death—the dark orbs nearly covered by the lid & the long lashes that fringed it—Sometimes it was the watry clouded eyes of the monster as I first saw them in my chamber at Ingolstadt

My father tried to awake in me the feelings of affection—He talked of Geneva which I should soon visit—Of Elizabeth & Ernest But these words only drew from me deep groans—Sometimes indeed I felt a wish for happiness; <for> my beloved cousin & the

Compare pp. 204–5

blue lake which had been so dear to me, in early childhood, but my general state of feeling was a torpor in which a prison was as welcome a residence as the divinest scene in nature & these fits were seldom interrupted but by paroxisms of anguish & despair—At these moments I often endeavoured to put an end to the existence I loathed & it required unceasing attendance & vigilance to prevent my committing some dreadful act of violence. I remember as I quitted the prison I heard one of the men say—He may be innocent of the murder but he has certainly a bad conscience.—

These words struck me; a bad conscience, yes surely I had one—William, Justine & Clerval had died through my infernal machinations And whose death, cried I, is to finish the tragedy—Ah! my father do not let us remain in this wretched country—Take me where I can forget myself, my existence & all the world. My father easily acceeded to my desire & after having taken leave of Mr. Kirwin we hastened to Dublin. I felt as if I was relieved from a heavy weight when the packet set sail with a fair wind from Ireland and I had quitted for ever the country which had been to me the scene of so much misery—It was midnight, my father slept below in the cabin & I lay on the deck looking at the stars & listening to the dashing of the waves—I hailed the darkness that shut Ireland from my sight<,> & my pulse beat with a feverish joy when I reflected that I should soon see Geneva The passed [*for* past] appeared to me in the light of a frightful dream yet the vessel in which I was—the wind that blew me from the detested shore of Ireland and the sea which surrounded me told me too forcibly that I was deceived by no vision & that Clerval my friend & dearest companion had fallen a victim to me & the monster of my creation.

I repassed in my memory my whole life; my quiet happiness when residing with my family in Geneva—The death of my Mother and my departure for In{s}golstadt; I remembered with shuddering the mad enthusiasm that hurried me on to the creation of my hideous enemy & I called to my mind the night on which

Compare pp. 205–6

he first lived. I {I} was unable to continue the train of thought—A thousand feelings pressed upon me & I wept bitterly.—

Ever since my recovery from the fever I had been in the custom of taking every night a small quantity of laudanum for it was by means of this drug only that I was enabled to gain the rest necessary for the preservation of life. Opressed by the recollection of my various misfortunes I now took a double dose & soon slept profoundly. But alas sleep did not afford me respite from thought & misery—my dreams presented a thousand objects that scared me—towards morning I was possessed by a kind of night mare—I felt the fiends grasp on my neck and could not free myself from it—Groans & cries rung in my ears,—My father who was watching over me, perceiving my restlessness awoke me and pointed to the port of Holyhead which we were now entering.

We had resolved not to go to London but to cross the country to Portsmouth and from thence to embark to Havre. I preferred this plan principally because I dreaded to see again those places in which I had enjoyed a few moments of tranquillity with my beloved Clerval—And I thought with horror of seeing those men whom we had been accustomed to visit together and who, doubtless, would make enquiries concerning an event the very remembrance of which made me again feel what I endured when I gazed on his lifeless form.

As for my father; his desires & exertions were bounded to the again seeing me restored to health and peace of mind. His tenderness & attentions were unremitted, my grief and gloom was obstinate but he would not despair. Sometimes he thought that I felt deeply the degradation of being obliged to answer a charge of murder and he endeavoured to prove to me the futility of pride. Alas! my father, said I, how little do you know me: human beings, their feelings and passions would indeed be degraded if such a wretch as I felt pride. Justine poor unhappy Justine was as innocent as I<,> and she suffered the same charge, she died for it—And I

Compare pp. 206–8

am the cause of this—I murdered her. William Justine & Henry, they all died by my hand

My father had often during my late confinement heard me make the same assertion & his astonishment was extreme. When he heard me thus accuse myself, he sometimes seemed to desire an explanation & at others he appeared to consider it as caused by delirium & that during my illness some idea of this kind had presented itself to my imagination<,> the rememberance of which I preserved in my convalescence. <I> avoided explanation; I maintained a continual silence concerning the wretch I had created. I had a feeling that I should be supposed mad and this for ever chained my tongue when I would have given the whole world to have confided the fatal secret. Upon these occasions my father said with an expression of unbounded wonder<,> What do you mean, Victor, are you mad? My dear son, I entreat you not to make so strange an assertion again.

I am not mad, I cried energetically, the sun & the heavens who have viewed my operations can bear witness of my truth. I was the assassin of those most innocent victims—they died by my machinations. A thousand times would I have shed my own blood drop by drop to have saved their lives. But I could not, my father, indeed I could not sacrifice the whole human race.

The conclusion of this speech persuaded my father that my ideas were deranged—and he instantly changed the subject of our conversation & endeavoured to alter the course of my thoughts. He wished as much as possible to obliterate the memory of the scenes in Ireland and never again alluded to them or suffered me to speak of my misfortunes. As time passed away I became more calm; misery had her dwelling in my heart but I no longer talked in the incoherent manner I before did of my own crimes; sufficient for me was the consciousness of them. By the utmost self violence I curbed the imperious voice of wretchedness which desired sometimes to declare itself to the whole world, & my manners were calmer &

Compare p. 208

more composed than they had ever been since my journey to the Sea of Ice. Even my father who watched me as the bird does its nestling was deceived and thought that the black melancholy which had oppressed me was quitting me for ever and that my native country & the society of my friends would entirely restore me to my former health & vivacity.

We arrived at Havre on the 8th of May & instantly proceeded to Paris where my father had some business which detained <us> a few weeks. In this city I received the following letter from Elizabeth:

To Victor F<r>ankenstein

May 18 – 17—

My dearest Friend.

It gave me the greatest pleasure to receive a letter from my Uncle dated at Paris. You are no longer at a formidable distance and I may hope to see you in less than a fortnight. My poor Cousin! How much must you have suffered! I expect to see you looking even more ill than when you quitted Geneva. This winter has been passed most miserably but<,> although happiness will not shine in our eyes for many months<,> yet I hope to see peace in your countenance & to find that your heart is not totally devoid of comfort & tranquillity.

Yet I fear that the same feelings now exist that made you so miserable a year ago even perhaps augmented by time. I would not at this period disturb you when so many misfortunes weigh upon you but a conversation that I had with my uncle previous to his departure renders some explanation necessary before we meet.

Explanation, you may possibly say, what can Elizabeth have to explain? If you really say this my questions are answered and I have no more to do than to sign myself your affectionate cousin. But you are distant from me & it

Compare pp. 208–9

is possible that you may dread & yet be pleased with this explanation<,> and in the probability of this being the case I dare not postpone any longer to write what during your absence I have often wished to express to {to} you but have never had courage to begin.

You well know, Victor, that our union had been the favourite plan of my aunt and uncle ever since our infancy—We were told this when young and taught to look forward to it as an event that would certainly take place. We were affectionate playfellows during childhood & I believe dear & valued friends to one another when we grew older. But as a brother & sister often entertain a lively affection towards one another may not this also be our case. Tell me, dearest Victor, Answer me, I conjure you by our mutual happiness, with simple truth do you not love another?

You have travelled, you have spent several years of your life at Ingolstadt—& I confess to you, my friend that when I saw you last Autumn so unhappy flying from the society of every creature to solitude & despondency I could not help supposing that you might regret our connection & believe yourself bound in honour to fulfil the wishes of your parents although they opposed themselves to your inclinations. But this is false reasoning. I confess to you my cousin that I love you & that in my airy castles of futurity you have been my constant friend and companion. But it is your happiness I desire as well as my own felicity when I declare to you that our marriage would render me eternally miserable unless it were the dictate of your own free choice. Even now I weep when I think that borne down as you are by the cruellest misfortunes you may stifle by the word honor all hope of that love & happiness which would alone conduce to your felicity. I who have so disinterrested an

 Compare pp. 209–10

affection for you may encrease your miseries tenfold by being an obstacle to your wishes Ah Victor be assured that your cousin & playmate has too sincere a love for you not to be made wretched by this supposition. Be happy my friend and if you obey me in this one request be assured that nothing on earth will have the power to interrupt my tranquillity.

Do not let this letter disturb you. Do not answer it tomorrow or the next day or not even untill you come if it will give you pain. My Uncle will send me news of your health and if I see but one smile on your lips when we meet occasioned by this letter or any other exertion of mine I shall need no other happiness—Your affectionate friend

Geneva Elizabeth Lavenza.

Chap. 16

This letter revived in my memory what I had before forgotten, the threat of <the>fiend when he visited me at the Orkney Island. I will be with you on your marriage night. Such was my sentence and on that night would the dæmon employ every art to destroy me & tear me from the glimse <of> happiness that might partly console my sufferings. On that night he had determined to consummate his crimes by my death. Well be it so. A deadly struggle would then assuredly take place where if he was victorious I should be at peace and his power over me was at an end If he were vanquished I should be a free man—Alas what a freedom<—>such as peasant endures when his family have been massacred before his eyes his cottage burnt his lands laid waste & he is turned adrift homeless, pennyless & alone: but free. Such would be my liberty except that

Compare pp. 210–11

in my Elizabeth I possessed a treasure alas balanced by the horrors of remorse & guilt which would pursue me untill death.

Sweet & beloved Elizabeth! I read & reread her letter & some softened feelings stole into my heart & dared whisper Paradiscical dreams of love & joy—But the apple was already eaten & the Angels arm bared ready to chase me from all hope. Yet I would die to make her happy and if the monster executed his threat die I must. Yet again I considered if my marriage would hasten my fate if once the fiend had determined on my death—It might indeed hasten a few months but if he suspected that I delayed on his account he would certainly revenge himself some other way. He had vowed to be with me on my marriage night Yet he did not consider that threat as binding him to peace in the mean time—for as if to shew me that he was not yet satiated with blood he had murdered Clerval—After many hours spent in reverie & consideration I resolved that if my immediate union with my cousin would conduce either to hers or my fathers happiness<,> my adversary's threats against my life should not retard it a single hour.—

In this state of mind I wrote to Elizabeth. My letter was calm and affectionate—I fear, my beloved girl, I said, little happiness remains on earth for us, yet what I may one day enjoy is all concentered <in> you my beloved one Chase away your idle fears—To you alone do I consecrate my life & my endeavours for content. I have one secret, Elizabeth, a dreadful one—It will chill your frame with horror and then far from being surprised at {at} my misery you will only wonder that I live. I will reveal this tale of misery & terror to you the day after our marriage—for, my sweet cousin, we must have perfect confidence between us—But untill then I conjure you do not mention or allude to it. This I most earnestly entreat of you & I know you will comply.

In about a week after this we returned to Geneva. Elizabeth welcomed me with warm affection—yet tears were in her eyes as she beheld my ematiated frame & feverish eyes. I also saw a

 Compare pp. 211–13

change in her—She was thinner and had lost much of that heavenly vivacity that had before charmed me—But her softness & gentle looks of compassion made her more fit for one blasted & miserable as I was.

The calm however which I now enjoyed did not last. Recollection brought madness with it—And when I thought of what passed<,> a real insanity possessed me—Sometimes I was furious & burnt with rage sometimes low & despondant I neither spoke or looked but sat motionless bewildered by the multitude of miseries that overcame me. Elizabeth alone had the power to draw me from these fits—Her gentle voice would sooth <me> when passionate and inspire <me> with human feelings when sunk in torpor—She wept with me and for me. When reason returned she would remonstrate with me & endeavour to inspire me with resignation—Ah it is well for the unfortunate to be resigned—But for the guilty there is no peace: the agonies of remorse poison the luxury there otherwise is in indulging the excess of grief.

Soon after my arrival my father spoke of my immediate marriage with my cousin. I remained silent.

Have you then, said my father some other attachment

None on earth. I love Elizabeth and look forward to our union with delight—Let the day therefore be named and on it I will consecrate my life or death to the happiness of my cousin.

My dear Victor, do not speak thus. Heavy misfortunes have befallen us but let us only cling closer to what remains and tran<s>fer our love for those whom we has lost to those who now live. Our circle will be small but bound close by the ties of affection & mutual misfortune—And when time will have ameliorated your despair new & dear cares will be born to replace those whom fate has deprived us of.

Such were the lessons of my father but to me the remembrance of the threat returned<;> nor can you wonder that omnipotent as the fiend had yet been in his deeds of blood I should almost regard

Compare p. 213

him as invincible, and that when he had pronounced the words—I shall be with you on your marriage night I should r<e>gard the threatened fate as unavoidable. But death was no evil to me if the loss of Elizabeth were balanced with it and I therefore with contented & even cheerful countenance agreed with my father that the ceremony should take place if my cousin would consent in ten days. and thus put, as I imagined the seal to my fate.

Great God! If for one instant I had thought what might be the hellish intention of my fiendish adversary I would rather have banished myself for ever from my country & only friends than have consented to this miserable marriage—But as if possessed of magic powers the monster had blinded me to his real resolutions & when I thought I prepared only my own death I hastened that of the real victim.

As the time drew nearer for our marriage, whether from cowardice or a prophetic feeling, I felt my heart sink with in me—But I concealed this by an appearance of hilarity that brought smiles of joy to the countenance of my father but hardly deceived the ever watchful & nicer eye of Elizabeth. She looked forward to our union with placid content not unmingled with a little fear, which past misfortunes had impressed, that what now appeared certain & tangible happiness might soon dissipate into an airy dream & leave no trace but deep & everlasting regret.

Preparations were made for the event. Congratulatory visits <were> received and all wore a smiling appearance—I shut up as well as I could, in my own heart the anxiety that preyed there and entered with seeming earnestness into the plans of my father although they might only serve as the decorations of my tragedy. A house was purchased for us near Coligny by which we should enjoy the pleasures of the country and yet be so near Geneva as to see my father every day—who would still reside within the walls for the benefit of Ernest, that he might follow his studies at the university.

 Compare p. 214

In the mean time I took every precaution to defend my person in case the fiend should atack we [*for* me]—I carried pistols & a dagger constantly about me and was ever on the watch to prevent artifice & by these means gained a great degree of tranquillity—And indeed as the period approached the threat appeared more as a delusion not to be regarded as worthy to disturb my peace while the happiness I hoped for in my marriage wore an appearance of greater certainty as the period of its solemnization drew near and I heard it spoken of every day as an occurence which no accident could possibly prevent.

Elizabeth seemed happy at the change from mirth to content which she saw come over me—But on the day that was to fulfil my wishes & my destiny she was melancholy—a presentiment of evil pervaded her & perhaps also she thought of the dreadful secret which I had promised to reveal to her the following day. My father was in the mean time overjoyed and in the bustle of preparation only observed in the melancholy of his neice the diffidence of a bride.

After the cermony was performed a large party assembled at my fathers but it was agreed that Elizabeth & I should pass the afternoon & night at Evian and set out on our return the next morning. The day was fine and as the wind was favourable we resolved to go by water.

Those were the last moments of my life during which I enjoyed the feeling of happiness. We passed rapidly along; the sun was hot but we were sheltered by a kind of canopy from its rays while we enjoyed the beauty of scene—Sometimes on one side of the lake where we saw Mont Salêve—the pleasant banks of Montalegre and at a distance surmounting all<,> the beautiful Mont Blanc and the assemblage of snowy mountains that endeavoured to emulate her—Sometimes coasting the opposite banks we saw the mighty Jura opposing its dark side to the ambition that would wish to quit its native country and an almost insurmountable barrier to the conqueror that should dare invade it.

Compare pp. 214–15

I took the hand of Elizabeth—You are sorrowful, said I, ah my love, if you knew what I have suffered & what I may still endure you would endeavour to let me taste the quiet & freedom from despair that this one day at least permits me to enjoy.

Be happy, my dear Victor, replied Elizabeth—there is I hope nothing to distress you; and be assured that if a lively joy is not painted in my face my heart is content. Something whispers to me not to depend too much on the prospect which is opened before us but I will not listen to such a sinister voice—Observe how fast we move along & how the clouds which sometimes obscure & sometimes rise above the dome of Mont Blanc render this scene of beauty still more interresting. Look also at the innumerable fish that are swimming in these clear waters where we can distinguish every pebble that lies at the bottom. What a divine day; how happy & serene all nature appears!

Thus Elizabeth endeavoured to divert her thoughts & mine from all reflection on melancholy subjects but her temper was fluctuating. joy for a few instants shone in her eyes but it continually gave place to distraction & reverie.

The sun sunk lower in the heavens we passed by the river Drance & observed its path through the chasm of the mountains & the glens of the lower hills. The Alps here come closer to the lake & we approached the amphitheatre of mountains that forms its eastern boundary. The spire of Evian shone under the woods that surrounded it & the range of mountain above mountain which overhung it.

The wind which had hitherto carried us along with amazing rapidity sunk at sunset to a gentle breeze—the light air just ruffled the water & caused a pleasant motion among the trees. As we approached the shore it wafted the most delightful scent of flowers & hay. The sun sunk beneath the horizon as we landed and as I touched the shore I felt those cares and fears revive which I had forgotten while on the water.

 Compare p. 216

Chap. 17

It was eight o'clock when we landed; we walked for a short time on the shore enjoying the transitory twilight & then retired to the Inn and contemplated the lovely scene of waters, mountains & woods obscured in darkness yet still displaying their black outlines—The wind which had fallen in the south now rose with great violence in the west—the moon had reached her summit in the heavens & was beginning to descend<;> the clouds swept across it swifter than the flight of the vulture and dimmed her rays while the lake reflected the busy heavens still busier by the waves that were beginning to rise—Suddenly a heavy storm of rain descended.

I had been calm during the day but now as night obscured the shapes of objects a thousand fears arose in my mind—I was anxious and watchful while my right hand grasped a pistol which was hidden in my bosom—Every sound terrified but I resoldved that I would sell my life dearly & not die untill my adversary should lie senseless at my feet.

Elizabeth observed my agitation for some time in timid & fearful silence At length she said—What is it, my dear Victor, that agitates you? What is it you fear?

Oh peace, peace, my love, I replied, this night and all will be safe—but this night is dreadful very dreadful.

I passed an hour in this state of mind when suddenly I reflected how dreadful the combat which I expected would take place would be to my wife and I earnestly entreated her to retire—resolving not to join her untill I had obtained some knowledge as to the situation of my enemy.

She left me and I continued some time walking up and down the passages of the house & inspecting every corner that might afford a retreat to my adversary—But I saw no trace & began to consider what was my best mode of proceeding—When suddenly

Compare pp. 217–18

I heard a shrill & dreadful scream.—It came from the room into which Elizabeth had retired. As I heard it the whole truth rushed to my mind my arms dropped—the motion of every muscle & fibre was suspended<;> I could feel the blood trickling in my veins—This state lasted but an instant the scream was repeated & I rushed into the room. Great God why did I not then expire—Why {I} am I here to relate the destruction of the best hope & purest creature of earth—She was there—lifeless & inanimate—thrown across the bed her head hanging down her pale & distorted features half covered by her hair—Every where I turn I see the same figure—Her bloodless arms & relaxed figure flung by the murderer on its bier—Could I behold this & {and} live—Alas life is obstinate & clinging where it is most hated—for a moment only did I lose recollection—I fainted.

When I recovered I found myself in the midst of the people of <the> inn—Their countenances expressed a breathless terror but the horror of others appeared but a mockery of the feelings that oppressed<.> I escaped from them to the room where lay the body of Elizabeth—my love—my wife—so lately living—so dear—so worthy—She had been moved from the posture in which I had first beheld her & now as she lay her head upon her arm and a hankerchief thrown across her face & neck I might have supposed her asleep—I rushed towards her & embraced her with ardour but the deathly coldness of the body told me that what I now held in my arms had ceased to be the Elizabeth whom I had loved & cherished, the murderous grasp of the fiend was on her neck & the breath had ceased to issue from her sweet lips.

While I still held her in my arms in the agony of despair I happened to look up. The room had before been quite dark and I felt a kind of panic on seeing the pale yellow light of the moon illuminate the chamber<.> the shutters had been thrown back and with a sensation of horror not to be described I saw at the open window a figure the most hideous & abhorred—A grin was on

 Compare pp. 218–19

the face of the monster. he seemed to jeer as with his fiendish finger he pointed towards the corpse of my wife—I rushed towards the window and drawing a pistol from my bosom—shot—but he eluded me—leapt from his station and running with the swiftness of lightning plunged in to the lake. The report of my pistol brought a crowd into the room I pointed to where he had disappeared & we followed him with boats & cast nets but in vain and passing several hours in the search returned hopeless—Most of my companions believeing it to have been a form conjured by my fancy. However after having landed they proceeded to search the country<,> parties going in different directions among the woods & vines. I did not accompany them

I was exhausted; a film covered my eyes and my skin was parched with the heat of fever. In this state I lay on a bed hardly conscious of what had happened & my eyes wandered round the room as if to seek somthing that I had lost. At length I remembered that my father would anxiously expect the return of Elizabeth & myself and that I must return alone. This reflection brought tears into my eyes & I wept for a long time. I reflected on my misfortunes & their cause and was bewildered in a cloud of wonder and horror. The death of William, the execution of Justine the murder of Clerval & now of my wife—even at that moment I knew not that my only remaining friends were safe from the malignity of the fiend—my father even now might be writhing under his grasp & Ernest might be dead at his feet—This reflection made me shudder and recalled me to action. I started up & resolved to return to Geneva with every possible speed. There were no horses to be procured and I must return by the lake but the wind was now against me and the rain fell in torrents. It was however hardly yet morning and I might reasonably hope to arrive by night—I hired a number of men to row and took an oar myself for I had always experienced relief from mental main [*for* pain] in bodily exercise. But the overflowing misery I now felt & the excess of agitation that I

Compare pp. 219–20

endured rendered me incapable of any exertion—I threw down the oar & leaning my head upon my hands gave way to every gloomy idea that arose—If I looked up I saw the scenes which were familiar to me in my happier days and which I had contemplated but the day before in the company of her who was now but a shadow & a recollection—tears streamed from my eyes—I looked on the lake the rain had ceased for a moment & I saw the fish play in the waters as I had done but a few hours before—they had then been observed by Elizabeth. Nothing is so painful to the human mind as great & sudden change—The sun might shine or the clouds might lower—but nothing could appear to me as it had done the day before—A fiend had snatched from me every hope of future happiness. No creature had ever been so miserable as I was<;> so frightful an event was single upon earth.

But why should I dwell upon the incidents that followed this last overwhelming event—Mine has been a tale <of> horrors—I have reached their acme and what I must now relate can but be tedious to you now that one by one my friends were snatched away & I was left desolate. My own strength is exhausted & I must tell in few words What remains of my hideous narration.

I arrived at Geneva. My fathe<r> & Ernest yet lived but the former was unable to bear the miserable tidings that I bore—I see him now excellent & venerable old man—his eyes wandered in vacancy for they had lost their charm & delight—his neice his more than daughter whom he doated on with all the affection of a man who in the decline of life having few affections clings to those that remain. Cursed Cursed be the fiend that brought misery on his grey hairs & doomed him to die in wretchedness. He could not live under the horrors that were accumulated round him—An applapetic fit was brought on & in a few days he died in my arms

What then became of me? I know not—I lost sensation & chains & darkness were the only objects that pressed upon me—sometimes

 Compare pp. 220–21

indeed I dreamed that I wandered in flowery meadows & pleasant vales with the friends of my youth—But I awoke & found myself in a dungeon. Melancholy followed but by degrees I regained a clear conception of my miseries & situation & was then released from my prison. For they had called me mad & for many months as I understood a solitary cell had been my habitation.—But liberty had been a useless gift to me had I not as I awakened to reason at the same time awakened to vengeance. As the memory of past misfortunes prest upom me I began to reflect on their cause—The monster whom I had created—the miserable dæmon whom I had sent abroard [*for* abroad] in the world for my destruction—I was possessed by a madening rage when I thought of him and desired & ardently prayed that I might have him within my grasp to wreak great & signal vengeance on his cursed head.

Nor did my hate long confine itself to useless wishes; I began to reflect on the best means of securing him & for this purpose about a month after my release I repaired to a criminal judge in the town & told him that I had an accusation to make, that I knew the destroyer of my family and that I required him to exert his whole authority for the apprehension of the murderer.

The magistrate listened to me with attention & kindness—Be assured, sir, said he no pains or exertions on my part have been or shall be spared to discover the wretch

I thank you, I replied, listen therefore to the deposition I have to make. It is {a} indeed a tale so strange that I fear you would not credit it were there not somthing in truth which however wonderful forces conviction. The story is too connected to be mistaken for a dream & I have no motive for falsehood. My manner as I said this was impressive but calm; I had formed in my own heart the resolution to pursue my destroyer to death & this purpose quieted my agony & reconciled me to life. I now related my history briefly but with firmness & precision—marking dates with accuracy and never deviating into invective or exclamation. The magistrate

Compare pp. 221–2

appeared at first perfectly incredulous but as I continued he became more attentive & interrested—I saw him sometimes shudder with horror, at others a lively surprise unmixed with disbelief was painted on his countenance. When I had concluded my narration I said.

This is the being whom I accuse and for whose detection & punishment I call upon you <to> exert your whole power It is your duty as a magistrate and I believe & hope your feelings as a man do not revolt from the execution of your functions on this occasion.—

This address caused a considerable change in the phisiognomy of my auditor He had heard my story with that half kind of belief that is given to a tale of spirits and ghosts but when he was called upon to act officially in consequence of it the whole tide of his incredulity returned—He however answered mildly.

I would willingly afford you every aid in your pursuit; but the creature of whom you speak appears to have powers which would put all my exertions to defiance Who can follow an animal who can traverse the sea of ice and inhabit caves & dens where no man would venture to intrude<;> besides some months have elapsed since the commission of his crimes & no one may conjecture to what place he has wandered & what country he may now inhabit.

I do not doubt, I replied, that he hovers near the spot which I inhabit—And if he has indeed taken refuge in the alps he may be hunted like the chamois & destroyed as a beast of prey. But I perceive your thoughts—you do not credit my narrative and do not intend to pursue my enemy with the punishment that is his desert.

As I spoke rage sparkled in my eyes—The magistrate was intimidated You are mistaken, said he I will exert myself and if it is in my power to seize the monster be assured that he shall suffer punishment proportionate to his crimes—But I fear from what you have yourself described to be his properties that this

 Compare p. 222

will prove impracticable and that—while every proper measure is pursued you should endeavour to make up your mind to a disappointment

That cannot be—said I wildly—But all that I can say will be of little avail; My revenge is of no moment to you yet while I allow it to be a vice I confess that it is the devouring & only passion of my soul; my rage is unspeakable when I reflect that the murderer whom I have turned loose upon society still exists—You refuse my just demand—I have but one resource and I devote myself either in my life or death to his destruction—I trembled with excess of agitation as I said this<;> there was frenzy in my manner & something I doubt not of that haughty fierceness that the martyrs of old were said to have possessed—But to a Genevan magistrate, whose mind was occupied by far other ideas than those of devotion & heroism, this elevation of mind had much the appearance of madness. He endeavoured to soothe me as a nurse does a child & reverted to my tale as the effects of delirium—Man—I cried, how ignorant art thou in thy pride of wisdom.—cease<;> you know not what it is you say.

I broke from the house & angry & disturbed retired to meditate some other mode of action.

Chap. 18

Alas! reflection in my present situation was impossible—I was hurried away by fury—Revenge alone inspired me with strength, & power of action—It modelled my feelings<and> allowed me to be calculating and calm when otherwise delirium or death would have been my portion. My first resolution was to quit Geneva for ever.—My country which when I was happy & beloved was dear <to> me<,> now in my adversity became hateful<.> I provided

Compare pp. 222–3

myself with a small sum of money a few jewels that had belonged to my mother & departed

And now my wanderings began which are to cease but with life—I have traversed a vast extent of country and endured all the hardships that travellers in desarts & barbarous countries are wont to meet—How I have lived I hardly know for many times did I lie on the sandy plain exhausted & far from succour, & pray for death—But revenge kept me alive—I dared not die & leave my adversary in being.—

When I quitted Geneva my first labour was to gain some clue by which I might trace the steps of my fiendish enemy. But my plan was unsettled and I wandered many hours around the confines of the town uncertain what path to pursue As night approached I found myself at the entrance of the cemetary, where William, Elizabeth and my father reposed—I entered it & approached the tomb which marked their graves. Every thing was silent except the leaves of the trees which were gently rustled by the breeze—The night was nearly dark and the scene would have been affecting and solemn even to an uninterested observer—the spirits of the departed seemed to flit around and to cast a gentle hallow [*for* halo] around the head of the mourner. But the deep grief that I at first felt quickly gave way to rage & despair—They were dead and I lived—Their murderer also lived & to destroy him I must drag out my weary existence. I knelt on the earth and with quivering lips exclaimed—By the Sacred earth I kneel on, by the shades that wander near me. By the deep & eternal grief that I feel I swear—And by thee oh night and by the spirits that preside over thee I swear to pursue the dæmon who caused this misery untill he or I shall fall in a mortal conflict—For this purpose I will preserve my life—To execute this dear revenge will I again behold the sun & green herbage of earth which otherwise should vanish from my eyes for ever—And I call on you spirits of the dead & you wandering ministers of vengeance to aid me & conduct me in my

 Compare pp. 223–5

work. Let the cursed & hellish monster drink deep of agony—Let him feel the despair that now torments me.

I had begun my adjuration with solemnity & an awe that almost assured me that the shades of my murdered friends heard & approved my devotion—But the furies possessed me as I concluded it & rage choaked my utterance. I was answered through the stillness of night by a loud & fiendish laugh—It rung my ears long and heavily; the mountains re-echoed it and I felt as if all Hell surrounded me with mockery and laughing—Surely in that moment I should have been possessed by frenzy and have destroyed my miserable existence, But that my vow was heard and I was reserved for vengeance—The laughter died away when a well known and abhorred voice apparently close to my ear addressed me in an audible whisper—I am satisfied, miserable wretch, you have determined to live & I am satisfied—I darted towards the place from which the sound proceeded but the villain eluded my grasp. When suddenly the broard [*for* broad] disk of the moon arose and shone fully upon the dæmon who fled.

I persued him; & for many months this has been my task. Guided by a slight clue I followed the windings of the Rhone but vainly—The mediterranean appeared and by a strange chance I saw the fiend enter by night & hide himself in a vessel bound for the black sea—I followed him<.> Amidst the wilds of Tartary & Russia although he still escaped me I have ever followed in his track—Sometimes the peasants scared by his horrid Apparition informed me of his path sometimes he himself who feared that if I lost all trace I should despair & die often left some mark to guide me—The snows descended on my head & I saw the mark of his huge step on the white plain—To you enterring on life & care<,> how can I describe what I have felt & still feel. Cold, want & fatigue were my least pains I was cursed by some devil & bore about with me my eternal Hell—Yet still a spirit of good followed & directed my steps and<,> when I most murmured<,>

Compare pp. 225–6

would suddenly extricate me from my seemingly insurmountable difficulties—Sometimes when nature overcome by hunger sunk under the exhaustion<,> a repast was prepared for me in the desart that restored & inspirited me—The fare indeed was coarse such as the peasants of the country lived on but I may not doubt that it was set there by the spirits I had invoked to aid me. Often when all was dry the heavens cloudless & I was parched with thirst—a slight cloud would bedim the sky—shed the few drops that revived me, & vanish.

I followed when I could the courses of rivers but the dæmon generally avoided these as it was here that the population of the country chiefly collected—In other places human beings were seldom seen & I generally subsisted on the wild animals that crossed my path—I had money with me & gained the friendship of the villagers by distributing it or bringing with me some food that I had killed which after taking a small part I always presented to those who had provided <me> with fire & utensils for cooking. My life as it passed thus was indeed hateful to me & it was during sleep alone that I could taste joy—Oh blessed sleep! often when most miserable I sunk to repose & my dreams lulled me even to rapture—The spirit that guarded me had surely provided these moments or rather hours of happiness that I might retain strength to fulfil my pilgrimage<;> without them I should have sunk under my hardships & misery but during the day I was sustained & insp<i>rited by the hope of night & sleep—I then saw my friends my wife & my beloved country<;> again I saw the benevolent countenance of my father,—heard the silver tones of my Elizabeths voice, and beheld Clerval enjoying health & youth—Often when wearied by a toilsome march I persuaded myself that I was then dreaming & that I enjoyed reality when I was again in the arms of my dearest friends—What agonizing fondness did I feel for them—how did I cling to their dear forms as they haunted my day as well as my night dreams and persuade myself that they

Compare pp. 226–7

still lived. At such moments the vengeance that burned within me died in my heart and I pursued my path towards the destruction of the dæmon more as a task enjoined by heaven than the ardent desire of my soul.

What his feelings were whom I pursued I hardly know—Sometimes indeed he left marks in writing on the barks of trees or cut on stone that guided me, & instigated my fury—My reign is not yet over, he said on one of these—You live & my power is complete. Follow me—I seek the everlasting ices of the north where you will feel the misery of cold & frost but I shall not for cold is sweeter to me than heat—You will find near this place if you follow not too tardily, a dead hare<;> eat & be revived. Come on my enemy we have yet to wrestle for our lives but many hard & miserable hours will you spend untill that period arrives"—

Scoffing Devil! Again do I vow vengeance again do I devote thee miserable fiend to torture & death never will I leave my search untill he dies—And then with what extacy shall I join my Elizabeth & those who even now prepare for me a reward for my tedious & horrible pilgrimage

As I pursed [*for* pursued] still my journey to the northward the snows & cold encreased to a{e} degree almost too severe to support. The peasantry were shut up in their hovels and only a few of the most hardy ventured forth to seize the animals whom starvation had forced forth to seek for prey. The rivers were covered with ice and no fish could be procured. The triumph of my enemy encreased with the difficulty of my labours One inscription that he left was in these words—Prepare—your toils only begin—wrap yourself in furs & provide food for we shall soon enter on a journey where you [*for* your] sufferings will satisfy my everlasting hatred" My courage & perseverance were inspired with new strength by these difficulties I resolved not to fail in my purpose and calling heaven to support me I continued with unabated fervour to traverse immense desarts untill the occean appeared at a distance and

Compare pp. 227–8

formed the utmost boundary of the horizon—Oh How unlike it was to the blue seas of the south Covered with ice it was only to be distinguished from land by its superior wildness & ruggedness—The greeks wept when they saw the mediterranean from the hills of Asia and hailed with rapture the boundary of their toils—I did not weep but I knelt down & thanked my guiding spirit with a full heart for conducting me safety [*for* safely] towards the place where I hoped<,> notwithstanding my adversarys threat<,> to meet & grapple with him—For some weeks before<,> I had procured a sledge & dogs and thus traversed the snows with inconceivable speed I know not whether the fiend possessed the same advantages but I found that<,> as before I had daily lost the advantage in my persuit<,> I now gained on him so much that when I for the first time saw the occean<,> he was but one days journey in advance & I hoped soon to intercept him With new courage therefore I pressed on & in two days arrived at a wretched hamlet on the sea shore. I enquired concerning the fiend & gained every information—A gigantic devil they said had arrived the night before—Armed with a gun and many pistols & putting to flight the inhabitants of a solitary cottage through fear of his terrific appearance <he> had seized on their store of winter food & placing it in a sledge<,> to draw which he had seized on a numerous drove of trained dogs—he had harnessed them—& the same night had to the joy of the horror struck villagers pursued his journey across the sea in a direction that led to no land & they conjectured that he must be speedily destroyed in the breaking of the ice or frozen by the eternal frost.—

On hearing this information I suffered a temporary fit of despair—he had escaped me and I must now commence a destructive & almost endless journey across the mountainous ices of the occean—amidst cold that few of the inhabitants could long endure & how could I a native of a genial & sunny climate hope to survive. Yet at the idea that the fiend should live & be triumphant

 Compare pp. 228–9

my rage and vengeance returned & like a mighty tide overwhelmed every other feeling. After a slight repose during which the spirits of the dead hovered round me & instigated me to toil & revenge I prepared for my journey.

I exchanged my land sledge for one fashioned for the ruggedness of the ocean and purchasing a plentiful stock of provisions I departed from land. How many days have passed since then I know not but I have endured misery that nothing but the eternal sentiment that burns within my heart could have enabled me to support. Immense & rugged mountains of ice often barred up my passage and I often heard the ground sea which threatened my destruction but again a frost came that secured me—By the consumation of provision I should guess that I had passed two months in this journey—And despondency & grief often wrung bitter drops from my eyes—Despair indeed had almost secured her prey & I should soon have sunk under this misery—When once after the poor animals that carried me had with incredible toil gained the summit of an ice mountain<,> they paused to rest and one unable to move sinking under the toil died—I viewed the expance before, with anguish; when suddenly my eye was arrested by a dark speck on the dusky plain—I strained my sight to view what it could be & uttered <a> wild cry of extacy when I distinguished a sledge<,> dogs & a hideous form within. Oh with what a burning gush did hope revisit my heart—warm tears filled my eyes which I hastily wiped away that they might not intercept the view I had of the fiend. I followed—but still the dew dimmed my sight untill giving way to the emotions that oppressed me I wept aloud.

But this was not the time for delay I disincumbered the dogs of their dead companion gave them a plentiful portion of food and after an hours repose which was absolutely necessary & yet which was bitterly irksome to me I continued my path—The sledge was still visible nor did I again lose sight of it except at the moments when for a short time some ice rock hid it<.> I indeed perceptibly

Compare pp. 229–30

gained on it. And after about another weeks journey I beheld myself at no more than two leagues distant from it. My heart bounded within me—But now when I appeared almost within grasp of my enemy my hopes were suddenly extinguished and I lost all trace of him more utterly than I had ever done before A ground sea was heard—the thunder of it as the waters rolled & swelled beneath me became every moment more ominous & terrific—I pressed on but in vain—The wind arose the sea roared and with the mighty shock of an earthquake it split & craked with a tremendus and overwhelming sound—The work was soon finished<:> in a few minutes a mighty ocean rolled between me & my enemy. And I was left d<r>ifting on a scattered piece that was every moment lessening and thus preparing for me a hideous death—In this manner many hours passed several of my dogs died and I myself should have sunk under the accumulation of hardships when I saw your vessel riding at anchor and holding forth to me hopes of succour & life. I had no conception that vessels ever came so far north & was astounded <at> the sight. I quickly destroyed my sledge and constructed oars and by these means was able with infinite fatigue to move my ice raft in the direction of your sledge [*for* vessel]—I had resolved that if you were going southward still to trust myself to the mercy of the seas rather than abandon my purpose—I hoped to be able to move you to grant me a boat & some provision with <which> I could still seek my enemy. But your direction was northward<.> you took me on board when my vigour was exhausted & I should soon have sunk under my multiplied hardships to a death I dreaded for my task is unfulfilled. Oh when will my guiding spirit in conducting me to him allow me the rest I so much desire! or must I die & he yet live—If I do<,> swear to me, Walton, that he shall not escape that you will seek him & satisfy my vengeance in his death. Yet do I dare ask you to undertake my pilgrimage to endure the hardships that I have undergone. No I am not so selfish—yet when I am dead if he should appear if the ministers of vengeance should conduct

 Compare pp. 230–31

him to you Swear that he shall not live—Swear that he shall not triumph over my accumulated miseries & live to make another such a wretch as I am—Oh he is eloquent & persuasive and once his words had even power over my heart but trust him not—His soul is hellish full of malise & fiend like malignity—hear him not; call on the manes of William, Justine, Clerval Elizabeth, my father and of the Whretched Victor & thrust your dagger to his heart—If I then exist to the knowledge I will hover near you & direct the steel aright fear not that you commit an act of cruelty—No the blood of all the innocent that he has murdered will plead for you

Walton—in continuation.

August 13th

You have read this strange & terrific story, Margaret and do not you feel your blood congealed with horror Mine often did as he related it—When seized with agony he could not continue<,> or his voice broken yet piercing described some of the scenes he had passed through—His fine & lovely eyes lighted up with indignation or subdued by sorrow & infinite wretchedness. Sometimes he commanded his countenance & tones and related the most horrible incidents with a smothered voice suppressing every mark of agitation—and like a volcano bursting forth his face would suddenly change to an expression of the wildest rage as he shrieked forth his imprecations on his persecutor.

His tale is connected & told with an appearance of the simplest truth yet I own to you my sister that the letters of Felix & Safie which he shewed me & the apparition of the monster seen from our ship brought to me a greater conviction of the truth of his narrative than his asse{r}verations—Such a monster did then really exist I could not doubt it yet I was lost in surprise & admiration. Sometimes I endeavoured to gain from Frankenstein the particulars of his formation, but on this

Compare pp. 231–2

point he was impenetrable. Are you mad, my friend, said he, or whither does your senseless curiosity lead you—Would you also create for yourself & the world a dæmoniacal enemy or to what do your questions tend. Peace, peace; learn my miseries & do not seek to encrease your own.

Frankenstein discovered that I detailed or made notes concerning his history he asked to see them & himself corrected and augmented them in many places but principally in giving the life & spirit of the conversations he held with his enemy—Since you have made an account said he I would not that a mutilated one should go down to posterity.

Thus have ten days passed away while I have listened to the strangest tale that ever imagination formed. My thoughts & every feeling of my soul <have> been drunk up by the interrest I felt in my guest—I wished to soothe him yet could I tell one so infinitely miserable—so destitute of every hope of consolation to live?—Oh no—the only joy he could feel was in composing his shattered feelings to peace & death—Yet he enjoys, one comfort, the sourse of solitude & delirium—he believed that when in dreams he saw his friends, who consoled his miseries or instigated him to vengeance that they were not the creations of his fancy but the real beings that he beheld and conversed with—This gave a solemnity to his reveries that rendered them peculiarly interresting.

Our conversations have not always been confined to his own history & misfortunes—On every point of general literature he displays unbounded knowledge and a quick & piercing apprehension. His eloquence is forcible & touching nor can I hear him when he narrates a pathetic incident or endeavours to move the passions pity & love without tears. What a glorious creature must he have been in his days of prosperity when he is thus noble & godlike in ruin—He seems to feel his own worth & the greatness of his fall. When younger, said he, I felt as if I

 Compare pp. 232–3

was destined for some great enterprize. My feelings are profound but I possessed a coolness of judgement that fitted me for grand enterprises. This sentiment of the worth of my nature supported me when others would have sunk for I deemed it criminal to throw away in useless grief{;} those talents that might be useful to my fellow creatures—When I reflected on the work that I had compleated, no less a one than the creation of a sensitive & rational animal I could not rank myself with the herd of common projectors. But this feeling which supported me now serves only to sink me lower in the dust—All my speculations & hopes are as nothing and like the Archangel who aspired to omnipotence I am chained in an eternal hell. My imagination was vivid yet my powers of application were intense—by the union of these qualities I conceived the idea and executed the creation of a man—Even now I cannot recollect without passion my reveries while the work was incomplete—I trod heaven in my thoughts—now exulting in my powers—now burning with the idea of their consequences. From my infancy I was imbued with high hopes and a lofty ambition but how am I sunk—Oh my friend—if you had known me as I once was you would not recognize me in this state of degradation—Despondancy rarely visited my heart<;> a high destiny seemed to bear me on, untill I fell oh, never never to rise again.

Must I lose this admirable being? I have longed for a friend, one who would sympathize with & love me. Behold on these desart seas I have found one—but I fear I gained him but to know his value & lose him—I would reconcile him with life but he repulses the thought. "I thank you,{"} Walton," he said, for your kind intentions towards so miserable a wretch—but when you speak of new ties and affections<,> think any can replace those I have lost. Can any man be to me as Clerval was or any woman another Elizabeth. Even where the affections are not strongly moved by any superior excellence the companions of

Compare pp. 233–4

our childhood always possess a certain power over our mind that hardly any other later friend can obtain. They know our infantine feelings which however they may be afterwards modified are never eradicated and they can judge of our actions with greater certainty—A sister or brother can never, unless indeed such symtoms have been shewn early<,> suspect the other <of> fraud or false dealing when another friend<,> however strongly he may be attatched<,> may be in spite of himself invaded by suspicion. But I enjoyed friends dear not only by association but for their own sake—and wherever I am the soothing voice of my Eliszabeth or the conversation of Clerval will be ever whispered in my ear. They are dead, & but one feeling could in such a situation keep me alive. If I were engaged in any high undertaking or design fraught with extensive utility to my fellow creatures then could I live to fulfil it—But such is not my destiny—I must pursue & destroy the being to whom I gave existence then my task will be fulfilled & I may die.

August 31th

My beloved Sister

I write to you encompassed by peril and ignorant if I am ever doomed to see again dear England & the dearer friends that inhabit it. I am surrounded by mountains of ice which admit of no escape and threaten every moment to crush my vessel. The brave fellows whom I persuaded to be my companions look at me for aid but I have none to bestow There is somthing terribly apalling in our situation Yet my courage & hopes do not desert me—We may survive & if we do not—I will repeat the lessons of my Seneca & die with a good heart.

Yet what, Margaret, will be your state—You will not hear of my destruction and you will anxiously await my return—Years will pass and you will have visitings of despair & yet be cheered by hope. Oh my beloved sister the sickening failings of your

 Compare pp. 234–5

heart felt expectations are in prospect more terrible to me than my own death—But you have a husband and lovely children—you may be happy—Heaven bless you & make you so.

My unfortunate guest regards me with the tenderest compassion—He endeavours to fill me with hope—And talks as if life were a thing which he loved He reminds me how often the same accidents have happened to other navigators, who have attempted the same sea. In spite of myself he fills me with cheerful auguries. Even the sailors feel the benefit of his eloquence—when he speaks they no longer despair—he rouzes their energies & they believe these vast mountains of ice and [*for* are] mole hills which will vanish before the resolutions of man. But this is but transitory and each days expectation delayed, fills them <with> fear & I almost dread mutiny

September 6th

A scene has just passed of such curious interrest that although it is highly probable that the papers may never reach you, my dear Margeret, yet I cannot forbear recording it. We are still surrounded by ice still in imminent danger—The cold is excessive & many of my unfortunate comrades have already found a grave amidst this scene of desolation. Frankenstein has declined daily in health<,> a feverish fire still glimmers in his eyes<,> but he is exausted & when suddenly rouzed to any exertion he speedily sinks again to apparent lifelessness.

I mentioned <in> my last letter the fears I had of mutiny. This morning as I sat watching the wan countenance of my friend his eyes half closed and his limbs hanging listlessly I was rouzed by half a dozen of the sailors who desired admission into the cabin they entered & their leader adressed me. He told me that he & his companions had been chosen by the other sailors to come in deputation to me to make a demand which in justice I could not refuse. We were immured by ice & would probably never escape but they feared that if, as was possible<,>

Compare pp. 235–6

the ice should be dissipated and a free passage opened I should be rash enough to continue my voyage & lead them to fresh dangers after they had so happily surmounted this. They desired therefore that I should make a solemn promise that if the vessel should be freed, I would instantly direct my course to England.

This speech troubled me. I had not despaired nor had I yet conceived the idea of returning if set free. Yet could I in justice, or even in possibility refuse these men. I hesitated before I answered when Frankenstein who had at first been silent & indeed appeared hardly to have force enough to attend now rouzed himself. His eyes sparkled and his cheek flushed with momentary vigour. Turning to the men he said; What do you mean? What do you demand of your captain? Are you then so easily turned from your design? Did you not call this a glorious expedition & why was it so Not because the way was smooth & placid as a summer lake but because it was full of dangers & terror—because at every new incident your fortitude was to be called forth & your courage exhibited—Because death & danger surrounded you & these you were to brave & overcome. For this was it a glorious; for this was it an honorable undertaking. You were to be hereafter hailed as the benefactors of your species—your names adored as the brave men who encountered death for honor & glory—And now behold with the first straw—or if you will—The first mighty & terrific trial of your courage you shrink away & are content to be handed down as men who had not strength to endure cold & peril—And so poor souls they were chilly & returned to their warm fire sides—Why that requires not this preperation—Ye need not have come thus far & dragged your Captain to the shame of a defeat to prove yourselves cowards. Oh be men or be more than men—be steady to your purposes & firm as rock. this ice is not made of such stuff it is mutable & cannot with<st>and you if you say that it shall not. Do not return to your families with the stigma of disgrace

 Compare pp. 236–7

marked on your brows—return as heroes who have fought & conquered & who know not what it is to turn their backs on the foe.

He spoke thus with a voice so modulated to the different feelings expressed in his speech—with an eye so full of high design & heroism that can you wonder that the men were moved—They looked at one another & were unable to reply. I spoke. I told them to retire & consider of what had been said. That I would not lead them further north if they streneously desired the contrary but that I hoped that with reflection their courage would return. They retired and I turned to my friend but he was sunk in languor and almost deprived of life.

How all this will terminate I know not. But I had rather die than return shamefully, my purpose unfulfilled—Yet I fear that that will be my fate The men unsupported by the ideas of glory and honor can never willingly continue to endure their present hardships.

September 7th

The die is cast. I have consented to return if we are not destroyed. Thus are my hopes blasted—by cowardice and indecision—I come back ignorant & dissappointed—It requires more philosophy than I possess to bear this injustice with patience—

September 12th

It is past. I am returning to England. I have lost my hopes of utility & glory—I have lost my friend. But I will endeavour to detail the bitter circumstances to you, my dear sister—And while I am wafted towards England & towards you I will not despair.

September 9th The ice began to move and roarings like thunder was heard at a distance as the mountains split & cracked in every direction. We were in the most eminent [*for* imminent] peril—But as we could only remain passive my chief

Compare pp. 237–8

attention was occupied by my unfortunate guest whose illness encreased to such a degree that he was entirely confined to his bed. The ice cracked behind us and was driven with force towards the north—a breeze sprung from that quarter—on the 11th the passage towards the south was free When the sailors saw this & that their return towards their native country was apparently assured a shout of tumu<l>tuous joy broke from them loud & long continued.—Frankenstein who was dozing awokede & asked the reason—I was unable to reply. He asked again—They shout I said because they will soon return to England.

Do you then really return.

Alas yes. I cannot withstand their demands—I cannot lead them unwillingly to danger{er} & I must return.

Do so if you will, but I will not. You may give up your purpose but mine is assigned to <me> by heaven and I dare not. I am weak, but surely the spirits who assist my vengeance will endow me with sufficient strength—Saying this <he> endeavoured to spring from the bed but the exertion was too great for him he fell back & fainted. It was long before he was restored<;> I often thought that life was entirely extinct—At length he opened his eyes—but he breathed with difficulty and was unable to speak—The phisycian gave him a composing draught and ordered us to leave him undisturbed. In the mean time he told me that my friend had certainly not many hours to live.

His sentence was pronounced & I could only grieve & be patient. I sat by his bed watching him—his eyes were closed and I thought he slept. But presently he called to me in a feeble voice and bidding me come near said—Alas! the strength I relied on is gone—I feel that I shall soon die and he my enemy & persecutor may still be in being. Think not, Walton, than [*for* that] in the last moments of my existence I feel that burning hatred & ardent desire of revenge that I once expressed but I

 Compare pp. 238–9

feel myself justified in desiring the monsters death. During these last days I have been occupied in examining my past conduct nor do I find it blamable. In a fit of enthusiastic madness I created a rational creature & was bound towards him to assure as far as in me lay his happiness & well being—this was my duty—but there was one still paramount to this. My duties towards my fellow creatures had greater claims because they included a greater portion of happiness or misery. Urged by this view I refused and I did right in refusing to create a companion for the first creature—He shewed unparelled malignity. He destroyed my friend—he devoted to destruction beings who had sensations—happiness & wisdom Nor do I know where this thirst for vengeance may end. Miserable himself, that he may render no other wretched, he ought to die—The task of his destruction was mine but I have failed. Once when actuated by selfish and vicious motives I asked you to undertake my unfinished work and I renew this request now when I am only induced to make it by reason & virtue.

Yet I cannot ask you to renounce your country & friends to fulfil this—And now that you are returning to England you have little chance of meeting him.—But the consideration of these points and the well balancing of what you may esteem your duties I leave to you—My judgement & ideas are already disturbed by death—I dare not ask you to do what I think right for I may still be misled by passion.

That he should live to be the means of misery disturbs me else this hour when I momentarily expect death is the only happy one I have enjoyed for several years. The forms of the beloved dead flit before me and I hasten to their arms. Farewell Walton. Seek happiness in tranquillity and avoid ambition even if it be only the apparently innocent one of shining in science & discoveries. Yet why do I say this? I have myself been blasted in these hopes but another may succeed."—

Compare pp. 239–40

His voice became fainter & exhausted with the effort he sunk into silence—About half an hour afterwards he endeavoured to speak, but was unable—he pressed my hand feebly and his eyes closed while a gentle smile played on his lips.

Margaret—What can I say—Can I make any comment on the death of this glorious creature—Alas all that I can express must be inadequate and feeble. My tears flow—But I journey towards England and I may there find consolation.

I am interrupted—What do these sounds portend? It is midnight—the breeze blows fairly and the watch on deck scarcely stir—Again there is a sound and it comes from the cabin where the remains of Frankenstien still lie I must go and examine. Good night my sister.

Great God! What a scene has just taken place. I am yet dizzy with the remembrance of it.—I hardly know whether I shall have the power to detail it yet I will try for the tale I have recorded is imcomplete without this final and wonderful catastrophe.

I entered the cabin where lay the remains of my miserable guest. Over him hung a form—which I cannot find words to describe, gigantic in stature—yet uncouth & distorted—his face was hid as he hung over the coffin by long locks of ragged hair—but his extended hand appeared like those of the mummies for to nothing else can I compare its colour & apparent texture. When he heard a noise & saw me enter he ceased his exclamations of grief and sprung towards the window. Never was any thing so hideous as his face so disgusting yet apalling—I shut my eyes involuntarily while I called on him to stay. He paused. Looking at me with wonder & then again turning towards the lifeless form of his creator he seemed to forget my presence while every feature & gesture seemed

 Compare pp. 240–41

instigated by the wildest rage. That is also my victim, he exclaimed—In his murder my crimes are consummated—Oh Frankenstein—Generous & self devoted creature dare I ask you to pardon me—I who destroyed thee by destroying those you loved. Alas he is dead and may not answer me.

His voice seemed suffocated & my first impulse which had been to obey the dying request of my friend in destroying his enemy now died away in a mixture of curiosity & pity. I approached him—yet I dared not look on him there was somthing so unearthly & scaring in his ugliness. I attempted to speak but the words died away on my lips—The Monster continued to utter wild & incoherent self reproaches<.> at length I said{.} Your repentance is now useless. If you had felt the stings of remorse before you urged your diabolical vengeance to its extremity<,> Frankenstein would yet have lived

And do you think, said the dæmon that I was then dead to anguish and remorse?—He—he continued pointing to the corpse, he suffered not more in the completion of the deed that [*for* than] I did in its execution. A frightful selfishness hurried me on while my heart was torn with agony. Think ye that the groans of Clerval were music to my ear. My heart was made for love & sympathy and when wrenched by misery to vice & hatred it did not {not} endure the violence of the change without torture—When Clerval died I returned to Switzerland heart broken & overcome—I pitied Frankenstein and his bitter sufferings—my pity amounted to horror—I abhorred myself—But when I saw that he again dared to hope for happiness—That while he heaped wretchedness & despair on me he sought his own enjoyment in feelings & passions from the indulgence of which I was for ever barred—I was again rouzed to indignation & revenge. I remembered my threat & resolved to execute it—Yet when she died—Nay then I was not miserable—I cast off all feeling & all anguish I rioted in the extent of my despair &

Compare pp. 241–2

being urged thus far—I resolved to finish my demoniacal design. And it is now ended—There is my last victim.

I was touched by the expressions of his misery yet I remembered what Frankenstein had said of his eloquence & persuasion—& when I again cast my eyes on the form of my friend my indignation was kindled—Wretch I said, It is well that you come here to whine over the misery you have created—you throw a torch among a pile of buildings & when they are consumed you sit amid the ruins & lament their fall. Hypocritical Fiend! If he whom you lament still lived still would you persue him with your accursed vengeance. It is not pity that you feel—it is sorrow that your power of mischief is anihilated.

It is not thus, said the dæmon, & yet such must be your impression since such appears to have been the purport of my actions. But I do not seek a fellow feeling in my misery—I feel it deeply & truly & for sympathy that I may never find. When I first sought it—it was the love of virtue, it was feelings of happiness & content that I wished to be participated. But now that virtue is to me merely a shadow and happiness & content are turned into despair shall I seek for sympathy in that. No—I am content to suffer alone while I do suffer—And when I die I am satisfied that hatred & opprobrium should load my memory. Once my fancy was soothed by dreams of virtue of fame & of enjoyment. Once I hoped to meet with one who pardoning my outward form would love me for the excellent qualities that I displayed—I was then filled with high thoughts of honour & self devotion—But now vice has sunk me below the meanest animal—no crimes can equal mine & when I call over the frightful catalogue I cannot believe that I am he whose thoughts were once filled with sublime & transcendant visions of loveliness. But it is even so—The fallen Angel becomes a malignant devil—Yet he even he Mans enemy had friends & associates, while I am quite alone.

 Compare pp. 242–3

You who call Frankenstein your friend {&} seem to have a knowledge of my crimes & his misfortunes—But in the detail that he gave of them he could not sum up the hours & months of misery that I endured burning with impotent rage—For when I destroyed his hopes I did not satisfy my own desires. They were as craving & ardent as before Still I desired love & fellowship and I was still spurned—Was there no injustice in this? And am I the only criminal while all mankind sinned against me? Why do you not hate Felix who drove his friend from his door or the man who would have destroyed the saviour of his child? Nay they are virtuous & immalculate beings—While I the miserable & trampeled on, am the devil to be spurned & kicked & hated! Even now my blood boils at the memory of this injustice—

But it is true that I am a wretch. I have murdered the lovely & the helpless. I have seized the innocent as they slept and grasped his throat to death who never injured me. I devoted my creator to misery & have followed him even to his destruction—You hate me but your abhorrence cannot equal mine for myself—I look on my hands that executed the deed I think of the heart that formed the plans & I loathe myself. Fear not that I shall do more mischief<;> my work is nearly complete—It needs not yours or any mans death to consumate it but it requires my own. And do not think that I shall be slow to perform that sacrifice I shall quit your vessel & on the ice raft that brought me I shall seek the most northern extremity of land that the globe affords—I shall collect my funeral pile and consume myself to ashes—that my remains may afford no light to any curious & unhallowed wretch who would create such another. I shall die. I shall no longer feel the anguish that now consumes me or be the prey of feelings unsatisfied yet unquenched. He is dead who created me and when I die the remembrance of me will be lost for ever. I shall no longer see

Compare pp. 243–4

the sun or stars of [*for* or] feel the winds play on my cheeks—Light feeling & sense will die. And in this must I find my happiness. Some years ago when the images this world affords first opened on me when I felt the cheering warmth of summer & heard the rustling of leaves & the chirping of birds & these were all to me<,> I should have wept to die & now it is my only consolation. Stained by crimes and torn by the bitterest remorse where can I find rest but in death.

Farewell; I leave you and with you the last of men that these eyes will ever behold. Farewell, Frankenstein If a desire for revenge remains to you in death it would be better satisfied in my life than in my destruction—But it was not so. You wished for my extinction that I might not cause greater wretchedness to others & now you will not desire my life for my own misery. Miserable as you were my agony is superior to yours for remorse is the bitter sting that rankles in my wounds & tortures me to madness.

But soon, he cried clasping his hands<,> I shall die and what I now feel will no longer be felt—soon these thoughts—these burning miseries will be extinct—I shall ascend my pile triumphantly & the flame that consumes my body will give rest & blessings to my mind.

He sprung from the cabin window as he said this on to an ice raft that lay close to the vessel & pushing himself off he was carried away by the waves and I soon lost sight of him in the darkness & distance.

 Compare pp. 244–5

APPENDIX A

TITLE PAGE, DEDICATION AND PREFACE to the *1818* Edition

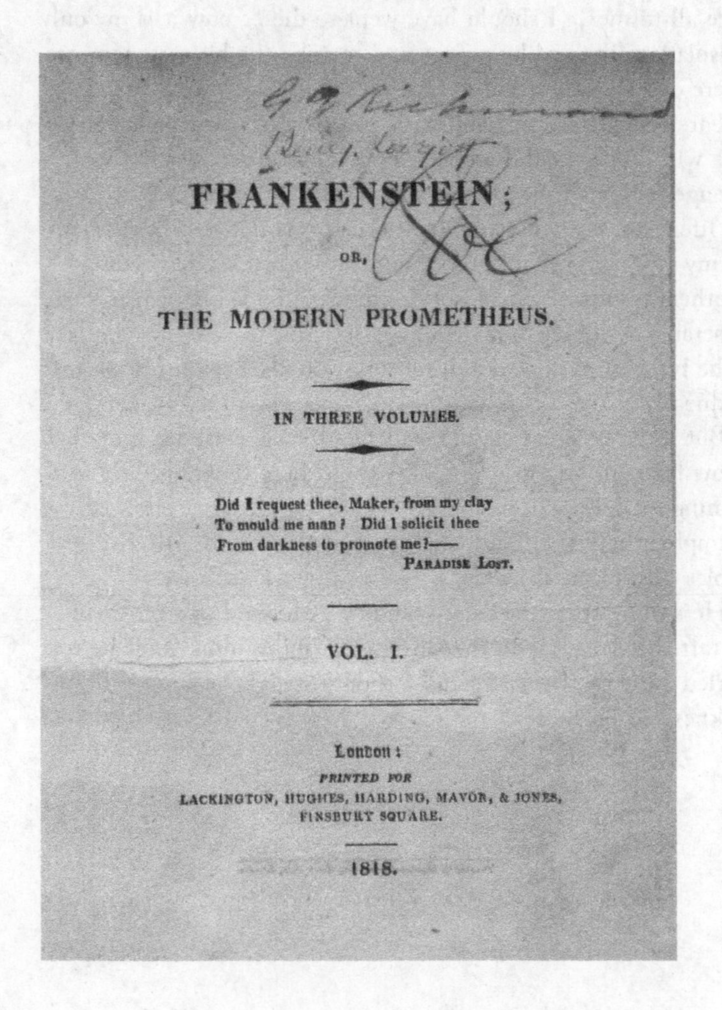

FRANKENSTEIN;

OR,

THE MODERN PROMETHEUS.

IN THREE VOLUMES.

Did I request thee, Maker, from my clay
To mould me man? Did I solicit thee
From darkness to promote me?——
PARADISE LOST.

VOL. I.

London:
PRINTED FOR
LACKINGTON, HUGHES, HARDING, MAVOR, & JONES,
FINSBURY SQUARE.

1818.

TO

WILLIAM GODWIN,

AUTHOR OF POLITICAL JUSTICE, CALEB WILLIAMS, &c.

THESE VOLUMES

Are respectfully inscribed

BY

THE AUTHOR.

PREFACE to the *1818* Edition

[by Percy Bysshe Shelley][1]

The event on which this fiction is founded has been supposed, by Dr. Darwin,[2] and some of the physiological writers of Germany, as not of impossible occurrence. I shall not be supposed as according the remotest degree of serious faith to such an imagination; yet, in assuming it as the basis of a work of fancy, I have not considered myself as merely weaving a series of supernatural terrors. The event on which the interest of the story depends is exempt from the disadvantages of a mere tale of spectres or enchantment. It was recommended by the novelty of the situations which it developes; and, however impossible as a physical fact, affords a point of view to the imagination for the delineating of human passions more comprehensive and commanding than any which the ordinary relations of existing events can yield.

I have thus endeavoured to preserve the truth of the elementary principles of human nature, while I have not scrupled to innovate upon their combinations. The *Iliad*, the tragic poetry of Greece,—Shakespeare, in the *Tempest* and *Midsummer Night's Dream*,—and most especially Milton, in *Paradise Lost*, conform to this rule; and the most humble novelist, who seeks to confer or receive amusement from his labours, may, without presumption, apply to prose fiction a licence, or rather a rule, from the adoption of which so many exquisite combinations of human feeling have resulted in the highest specimens of poetry.

The circumstance on which my story rests was suggested in casual conversation. It was commenced, partly as a source of amusement, and partly as an expedient for exercising any untried resources of mind. Other motives were mingled with these, as the work proceeded. I am by no means indifferent to the manner in which whatever moral tendencies exist in the sentiments or characters it contains shall affect the reader; yet my chief concern in this respect has been limited to the avoiding the enervating effects of the novels of the present day, and to the exhibition of the amiableness of domestic affection, and the excellence of universal virtue. The opinions which naturally spring from the character and situation of the hero are by no means to be conceived as existing always in my own conviction; nor is any inference justly to be drawn from the following pages as prejudicing any philosophical doctrine of whatever kind.

It is a subject also of additional interest to the author, that this story was begun in the majestic region where the scene is principally laid, and in society which cannot cease to be regretted. I passed the summer of 1816 in the environs of Geneva. The season was cold and rainy, and in the evenings we crowded around a blazing wood fire, and occasionally amused ourselves with some German stories of ghosts, which happened[3] to fall into our hands. These tales excited in us a playful desire of imitation. Two other friends (a tale from the pen of one of whom would be far more acceptable to the public than any thing I can ever hope to produce) and myself agreed to write each a story, founded on some supernatural occurrence.[4]

The weather, however, suddenly became serene; and my two friends left me on a journey among the Alps, and lost, in the magnificent scenes which they present, all memory of their ghostly visions. The following tale is the only one which has been completed.

NOTES

1 This Preface to the *1818* edition was apparently written by PBS in September 1817. If MWS wrote her own Preface on 14 May 1817 (as suggested by MWS *Journal*, p. 169), it was never printed, and no manuscript has ever been found. In MWS's 1831 Introduction (reprinted in Appendix C in this edition), she dates this Preface at 'Marlow, September 1817' and acknowledges PBS's authorship: 'As far as I can recollect, it was entirely written by him.'

2 Erasmus Darwin (1731–1802), physician and poet-naturalist.

3 Incorrectly printed as 'happenened' in *1818*.

4 For a more detailed description of what led to the writing of *Frankenstein*, see MWS's 1831 Introduction, printed in Appendix C below.

APPENDIX B

ON "FRANKENSTEIN."

by the late Percy Bysshe Shelley[1]

The novel of 'Frankenstein; or, the Modern Prometheus,' is undoubtedly, as a mere story, one of the most original and complete productions of the day. We debate with ourselves in wonder, as we read it, what could have been the series of thoughts—what could have been the peculiar experiences that awakened them—which conduced, in the author's mind, to the astonishing combinations of motives and incidents, and the startling catastrophe, which compose this tale. There are, perhaps, some points of subordinate importance, which prove that it is the author's first attempt. But in this judgment, which requires a very nice discrimination, we may be mistaken; for it is conducted throughout with a firm and steady hand. The interest gradually accumulates and advances towards the conclusion with the accelerated rapidity of a rock rolled down a mountain. We are led breathless with suspense and sympathy, and the heaping up of incident on incident, and the working of passion out of passion. We cry "hold, hold! enough!"[2]—but there is yet something to come; and, like the victim whose history it relates, we think we can bear no more, and yet more is to be borne. Pelion is heaped on Ossa, and Ossa on Olympus.[3] We climb Alp after Alp, until the horizon is seen blank, vacant, and limitless; and the head turns giddy, and the ground seems to fail under our feet.

This novel rests its claim on being a source of powerful and profound emotion. The elementary feelings of the human mind are exposed to view; and those who are accustomed to reason deeply on their origin and tendency will, perhaps, be the only persons who can sympathize, to the full extent, in the interest of the actions which are their result. But, founded on nature as they are, there is perhaps no reader, who can endure anything beside a new love story, who will not feel a responsive string touched in his inmost soul. The sentiments are so affectionate and so innocent—the characters of the subordinate agents in this strange drama are clothed in the light of such a mild and gentle mind—the pictures of domestic manners are of the most simple and attaching character: the father's is irresistible and deep. Nor are the crimes and malevolence of the single Being, though indeed withering and tremendous, the offspring of any unaccountable propensity to evil, but flow irresistibly from certain causes fully adequate to their production. They are the children, as it were, of Necessity and Human Nature. In this the direct moral of the book consists; and it is perhaps the most important, and of the most universal application, of any moral that can be enforced by example. Treat a person ill, and he will become wicked. Requite affection with scorn;—let one being be selected, for whatever cause, as the refuse of his kind—divide him, a social being, from society, and you impose upon him the irresistible obligations—malevolence and selfishness. It is thus that, too often in society, those who are best qualified to be its benefactors and its ornaments, are branded by some accident with scorn, and changed, by neglect and solitude of heart, into a scourge and a curse.

The Being in 'Frankenstein' is, no doubt, a tremendous creature. It was impossible that he should not have received among men that treatment which led to the consequences of his being a social nature. He was an abortion and an anomaly; and though his mind was such as its first impressions framed it, affectionate and full of moral sensibility, yet the circumstances of his existence are so monstrous and uncommon, that, when the consequences of them became developed in action, his original goodness was gradually turned into inextinguishable misanthropy and revenge. The scene between the Being and the blind De Lacey in the cottage, is one of the most profound and extraordinary instances of pathos that we ever recollect. It is impossible to read this dialogue,—and indeed many others of a somewhat similar character,—without feeling the heart suspend its pulsations with wonder, and the "tears stream down the cheeks." The encounter and argument between Frankenstein and the Being on the sea of ice, almost approaches, in effect, to the expostulations of Caleb Williams with Falkland. It reminds us, indeed, somewhat of the style and character of that admirable writer, to whom the author has dedicated his work, and whose productions he seems to have studied.[4]

There is only one instance, however, in which we detect the least approach to imitation; and that is the conduct of the incident of Frankenstein's landing in Ireland. The general character of the tale, indeed, resembles nothing that ever preceded it. After the death of Elizabeth, the story, like a stream which grows at once more rapid and profound as it proceeds, assumes an irresistible solemnity, and the magnificent energy and swiftness of a tempest.

The churchyard scene, in which Frankenstein visits the tombs of his family, his quitting Geneva, and his journey through Tartary to the shores of the Frozen Ocean, resemble at once the terrible reanimation of a corpse and the supernatural career of a spirit. The scene in the cabin of Walton's ship—the more than mortal enthusiasm and grandeur of the Being's speech over the dead body of his victim—is an exhibition of intellectual and imaginative power, which we think the reader will acknowledge has seldom been surpassed.

NOTES

1 This review was published by Thomas Medwin in *The Athenæum: Journal of English and Foreign Literature, Science, and the Fine Arts*, 10 November 1832, 730. It was reprinted verbatim in Thomas Medwin, *Memoir of Percy Bysshe Shelley; and Original Poems and Papers by Percy Bysshe Shelley: Now First Collected* (London: Whittaker, Treacher, & Co., 1833), 165–70. For a version that takes into account manuscript evidence, see *The Prose Works of Percy Bysshe Shelley*, ed. E. B. Murray (Oxford: Clarendon Press, 1993), I, 282–4, together with commentary and collations on pp. 489–92, 553, 565.

2 Conflation of Lady Macbeth's 'Hold, hold!' (*Macbeth*, I.v.55) and Macbeth's final words, 'Hold, enough!' (V.viii.34).

3 An allusion to two sons of Poseidon who attempted to reach heaven by piling Mount Pelion on Mount Ossa in order to reach Olympus (or, in some accounts, these two mountains were piled on top of Olympus)—see *OED* for the phrase, which means to add challenge to challenge in a task that bespeaks fruitlessness and/or presumption.

4 PBS here references the novel *Caleb Williams* by William Godwin, MWS's father, to whom *Frankenstein* is dedicated or 'inscribed'.

APPENDIX C

INTRODUCTION to the *1831* Edition

by Mary W. Shelley

The Publishers of the Standard Novels,[1] in selecting "Frankenstein" for one of their series, expressed a wish that I should furnish them with some account of the origin of the story. I am the more willing to comply, because I shall thus give a general answer to the question, so very frequently asked me—"How I, then a young girl, came to think of, and to dilate upon, so very hideous an idea?" It is true that I am very averse to bringing myself forward in print; but as my account will only appear as an appendage to a former production, and as it will be confined to such topics as have connection with my authorship alone, I can scarcely accuse myself of a personal intrusion.

It is not singular that, as the daughter of two persons of distinguished literary celebrity, I should very early in life have thought of writing. As a child I scribbled; and my favourite pastime, during the hours given me for recreation, was to "write stories." Still I had a dearer pleasure than this, which was the formation of castles in the air—the indulging in waking dreams—the following up trains of thought, which had for their subject the formation of a succession of imaginary incidents. My dreams were at once more fantastic and agreeable than my writings. In the latter I was a close imitator—rather doing as others had done, than putting down the suggestions of my own mind. What I wrote was intended at least for one other eye—my childhood's companion and friend; but my dreams were all my own; I accounted for them to nobody; they were my refuge when annoyed—my dearest pleasure when free.

I lived principally in the country as a girl, and passed a considerable time in Scotland. I made occasional visits to the more picturesque parts; but my habitual residence was on the blank and dreary northern shores of the Tay, near Dundee. Blank and dreary on retrospection I call them; they were not so to me then. They were the eyry[2] of freedom, and the pleasant region where unheeded I could commune with the creatures of my fancy. I wrote then—but in a most common-place style. It was beneath the trees of the grounds belonging to our house, or on the bleak sides of the woodless mountains near, that my true compositions, the airy flights of my imagination, were born and fostered. I did not make myself the heroine of my tales. Life appeared to me too common-place an affair as regarded myself. I could not figure to myself that romantic woes or wonderful events would ever be my lot; but I was not confined to my own identity, and I could people the hours with creations far more interesting to me at that age, than my own sensations.

After this my life became busier, and reality stood in place of fiction. My husband, however, was from the first, very anxious that I should prove myself worthy of my parentage, and enrol myself on the page of fame. He was for ever inciting me to obtain literary reputation, which even on my own part I cared for then, though since I have become infinitely indifferent to it. At this time he desired that I should write, not so much with the idea that I could produce any thing worthy of notice, but that he might himself judge how far I possessed the promise of better things hereafter. Still I did nothing. Travelling, and the cares of a family, occupied my time; and study, in the way of reading, or improving my ideas in communication with his far more cultivated mind, was all of literary employment that engaged my attention.

In the summer of 1816, we visited Switzerland, and became the neighbours of Lord Byron. At first we spent our pleasant hours on the lake, or wandering on its shores; and Lord Byron, who was writing the third canto of Childe Harold, was the only one among us who put his thoughts upon paper. These, as he brought them successively to us, clothed in all the light and harmony of poetry, seemed to stamp as divine the glories of heaven and earth, whose influences we partook with him.

But it proved a wet, ungenial summer, and incessant rain often confined us for days to the house. Some volumes of ghost stories, translated from the German into French, fell into our hands. There was the History of the Inconstant Lover, who, when he thought to clasp the bride to whom he had pledged his vows, found himself in the arms of the pale ghost of her whom he had deserted. There was the tale of the sinful founder of his race, whose miserable doom it was to bestow the kiss of death on all the younger sons of his fated house, just when they reached the age of promise. His gigantic, shadowy form, clothed like the ghost in Hamlet, in complete armour, but with the beaver up, was seen at midnight, by the moon's fitful beams, to advance slowly along the gloomy avenue. The shape was lost beneath the shadow of the castle walls; but soon a gate swung back, a step was heard, the door of the chamber opened, and he advanced to the couch of the blooming youths, cradled in healthy sleep. Eternal sorrow sat upon his face as he bent down and kissed the forehead of the boys, who from that hour withered like flowers snapt upon the stalk. I have not seen these stories since then; but their incidents are as fresh in my mind as if I had read them yesterday.

"We will each write a ghost story," said Lord Byron; and his proposition was acceded to. There were four of us. The noble author began a tale, a fragment of which he printed at the end of his poem of Mazeppa. Shelley, more apt to embody ideas and sentiments in the radiance of brilliant imagery, and in the music of the most melodious verse that adorns our language, than to invent the machinery of a story, commenced one founded on the experiences of his early life. Poor Polidori had some terrible idea about a skull-headed lady, who was so punished for peeping through a key-hole—what to see I forget—something very shocking and wrong of course; but when she was reduced to a worse condition than the renowned Tom of Coventry, he did not know what to do with her, and was obliged to despatch her to the tomb of the Capulets, the only place for which she was fitted. The illustrious poets also, annoyed by the platitude of prose, speedily relinquished their uncongenial task.

I busied myself *to think of a story*,—a story to rival those which had excited us to this task. One which would speak to the mysterious fears of our nature, and awaken thrilling horror—one to make the reader dread to look round, to curdle the blood, and quicken the beatings of the heart. If I did not accomplish these things, my ghost story would be unworthy of its name. I thought and pondered—vainly. I felt that blank incapability of invention which is the greatest misery of authorship, when dull Nothing replies to our anxious invocations. *Have you thought of a story?* I was asked each morning, and each morning I was forced to reply with a mortifying negative.

Every thing must have a beginning, to speak in Sanchean phrase; and that beginning must be linked to something that went before. The Hindoos give the world an elephant to support it, but they make the elephant stand upon a tortoise. Invention, it must be humbly admitted, does not consist in creating out of void, but out of chaos; the materials must, in the first place, be afforded: it can give form to dark, shapeless substances, but cannot bring into being the substance itself. In all matters of discovery and invention, even of those that appertain to the imagination, we are continually reminded of the story of Columbus and his egg. Invention consists in the capacity of seizing on the capabilities of a subject, and in the power of moulding and fashioning ideas suggested to it.

Many and long were the conversations between Lord Byron and Shelley, to which I was a devout but nearly silent listener. During one of these, various philosophical doctrines were discussed, and among others the nature of the principle of life, and whether there was any probability of its ever being discovered and communicated.

They talked of the experiments of Dr. Darwin, (I speak not of what the Doctor really did, or said that he did, but, as more to my purpose, of what was then spoken of as having been done by him,) who preserved a piece of vermicelli in a glass case, till by some extraordinary means it began to move with voluntary motion. Not thus, after all, would life be given. Perhaps a corpse would be re-animated; galvanism had given token of such things: perhaps the component parts of a creature might be manufactured, brought together, and endued with vital warmth.

Night waned upon this talk; and even the witching hour had gone by, before we retired to rest. When I placed my head on my pillow, I did not sleep, nor could I be said to think. My imagination, unbidden, possessed and guided me, gifting the successive images that arose in my mind with a vividness far beyond the usual bounds of reverie. I saw—with shut eyes, but acute mental vision—I saw the pale student of unhallowed arts kneeling beside the thing he had put together. I saw the hideous phantasm of a man stretched out, and then, on the working of some powerful engine, show signs of life, and stir with an uneasy, half vital motion. Frightful must it be; for supremely frightful would be the effect of any human endeavour to mock the stupendous mechanism of the Creator of the world. His success would terrify the artist; he would rush away from his odious handywork, horror-stricken. He would hope that, left to itself, the slight spark of life which he had communicated would fade; that this thing, which had received such imperfect animation, would subside into dead matter; and he might sleep in the belief that the silence of the grave would quench for ever the transient existence of the hideous corpse which he had looked upon as the cradle of life. He sleeps; but he is awakened; he opens his eyes; behold the horrid thing stands at his bedside, opening his curtains, and looking on him with yellow, watery, but speculative eyes.

I opened mine in terror. The idea so possessed my mind, that a thrill of fear ran through me, and I wished to exchange the ghastly image of my fancy for the realities around. I see them still; the very room, the dark *parquet*, the closed shutters, with the moonlight struggling through, and the sense I had that the glassy lake and white high Alps were beyond. I could not so easily get rid of my hideous phantom; still it haunted me. I must try to think of something else. I recurred to my ghost story,—my tiresome unlucky ghost story! O! if I could only contrive one which would frighten my reader as I myself had been frightened that night!

Swift as light and as cheering was the idea that broke in upon me. "I have found it! What terrified me will terrify others; and I need only describe the spectre which had haunted my midnight pillow." On the morrow I announced that I had *thought of a story*. I began that day with the words, *It was on a dreary night of November*, making only a transcript of the grim terrors of my waking dream.

At first I thought but of a few pages—of a short tale; but Shelley urged me to develope the idea at greater length. I certainly did not owe the suggestion of one incident, nor scarcely of one train of feeling, to my husband, and yet but for his incitement, it would never have taken the form in which it was presented to the world. From this declaration I must except the preface. As far as I can recollect, it was entirely written by him.

And now, once again, I bid my hideous progeny go forth and prosper. I have an affection for it, for it was the offspring of happy days, when death and grief were but words, which found no true echo in my heart. Its several pages speak of many a walk, many a drive, and many a conversation, when I was not alone; and my companion was one whom, in this world, I shall never see more. But this is for myself; my readers have nothing to do with these associations.

I will add but one word as to the alterations I have made. They are principally those of style. I have changed no portion of the story, nor introduced any new ideas or circumstances. I have mended the language where it was so bald as to interfere with the interest of the narrative; and these changes occur almost exclusively in the beginning of the first volume. Throughout they are entirely confined to such parts as are mere adjuncts to the story, leaving the core and substance of it untouched.

M. W. S.

London, October 15. 1831.

NOTES

1 That is, Henry Colburn and Richard Bentley, who during their partnership (1829–32) started a series of well-produced and affordable versions of famous novels. MWS sold her copyright for £30, and this 'revised, corrected, and illustrated' novel was published in one volume (bound with Volume 1 of Schiller's *The Ghost-Seer*) for six shillings in 4,020 stereotyped copies.

2 Variant spelling of 'eyrie', the nest of an eagle, suggesting here a site that allowed or encouraged imaginative freedom.

Bibliography

This bibliography contains primary and secondary works cited in this edition, as well as other texts used in its preparation. For a convenient listing of the important editions of *Frankenstein*, see the list of Abbreviations that precedes the Introduction. For many other important books and articles on Mary Shelley, *Frankenstein*, and her other works, consult the bibliographies published separately (e.g. Lyles), annually (e.g. in the *Keats–Shelley Journal*) or electronically (e.g. the MLA International Bibliography or ABELL, the Annual Bibliography of English Literature and Language). For the full text of six of the reviews of *Frankenstein* published between 1818 and 1832, see the Mary Wollstonecraft Chronology and Resource Site at the electronically accessible 'Romantic Circles', www.rc.umd.edu/reference/chronologies/mschronology/reviews.html.

Barker-Benfield, B. C., *Shelley's Guitar: An Exhibition of Manuscripts, First Editions and Relics, to Mark the Bicentenary of the Birth of Percy Bysshe Shelley, 1792/1992* (Oxford: Bodleian Library, 1992).

——, 'Shelley's Bodleian Visits', *Bodleian Library Record*, 12 (1987), 381–99.

Branagh, Kenneth, *Mary Shelley's Frankenstein: The Classic Tale of Terror Reborn on Film; With the Screenplay by Steph Lady and Frank Darabont*, ed. Diana Landau, photographs by David Appleby, afterword and notes by Leonard Wolf (New York: Newmarket Press, 1994).

Bryant, John, *The Fluid Text: A Theory of Revision and Editing for Book and Screen* (Ann Arbor: University of Michigan Press, 2002).

Clairmont, Claire, *The Clairmont Correspondence: Letters of Claire Clairmont, Charles Clairmont, and Fanny Imlay Godwin*, ed. Marion Kingston Stocking, 2 vols (Baltimore: Johns Hopkins University Press, 1995).

——, *The Journals of Claire Clairmont*, ed. Marion Kingston Stocking, with the assistance of David Mackenzie Stocking (Cambridge, MA: Harvard University Press, 1968).

Clubbe, John, 'Mary Shelley as Autobiographer: The Evidence of the 1831 Introduction to *Frankenstein*', *The Wordsworth Circle*, 12 (1981), 102–6.

——, 'The Tempest-Toss'd Summer of 1816: Mary Shelley's *Frankenstein*', *The Byron Journal*, 19 (1991), 26–40.

Crook, Nora, 'Did Mary Shelley Write *Frankenstein*? Or Did Percy Shelley Spoil It?', in Tatsuo Tokoo et al. (eds), *A Milestone of Shelleyan Scholarly Pursuits in Japan: Essays Commemorating the 15th Anniversary of the Founding of Japan Shelley Studies Center*, Publication of the Japan Shelley Studies Center (Tokyo: Eihosha, 2007), 3–18.

——, 'In Defence of the 1831 *Frankenstein*', in Michael Eberle-Sinatra (ed.), *Mary Shelley's Fictions: From Frankenstein to Falkner* (London: Macmillan, 2000), 3–21.

Duyfhuizen, Bernard, 'Periphrastic Naming in Mary Shelley's *Frankenstein*', *Studies in the Novel*, 27 (1995), 477–92.

Erkelenz, Michael (ed.), *The Geneva Notebook of Percy Bysshe Shelley: Bodleian MS. Shelley adds. e. 16 and MS. Shelley adds. c. 4, Folios 63, 65, 71, and 72*, The Bodleian Shelley Manuscripts, Volume XI (New York: Garland, 1992).

Fantasmagoriana, ou recueil d'histoires d'apparitions de spectres, revenans, fantômes, etc. Traduit de l'allemand, par un amateur [Jean Baptiste Benoît Eyriès], 2 vols (Paris: Lenormant et Schoell, 1812).

Fleischer, Leonore, *Mary Shelley's Frankenstein: Based on a Screenplay by Steph Lady and Frank Darabont from Mary Shelley's Novel*, Afterword by Kenneth Branagh (New York: Signet, 1994).

Florescu, Radu, *In Search of Frankenstein* (Boston, MA: New York Graphic Society, 1975).

Forry, Steven Earl, *Hideous Progenies: Dramatizations of Frankenstein from Mary Shelley to the Present* (Philadelphia: University of Pennsylvania Press, 1990).

Glut, Donald F., *The Frankenstein Catalog: Being a Comprehensive Listing of Novels, Translations, Adaptations, Stories, Critical Works, Popular Articles, Series, Fumetti, Verse, Stage Plays, Films, Cartoons, Puppetry, Radio & Television Programs, Comics, Satire & Humor, Spoken & Musical Recordings, Tapes, and Sheet Music Featuring Frankenstein's Monster and/or Descended from Mary Shelley's Novel* (Jefferson, NC: McFarland, 1984).

Godwin, William, Unpublished Diaries, Bodleian Dep. e. 196–227, Bodleian Library, University of Oxford.

Hale, Terry (ed.), *Tales of the Dead: The Ghost Stories of the Villa Diodati* (Chislehurst: Gothic Society at the Gargoyle's Head Press, 1992).

Hitchcock, Susan Tyler, *Frankenstein: A Cultural History* (New York: W.W. Norton, 2007).

Huet, Marie-Hélène, *Monstrous Imagination* (Cambridge, MA: Harvard University Press, 1993).

Jones, Selwyn B., 'The Fraudulent "Author of Frankenstein"' (unpublished typescript of nearly 500 pages supplied to me by the author in December 2005).

Jones, Stephen, *The Frankenstein Scrapbook: The Complete Movie Guide to the World's Most Famous Monster* (New York: Citadel Press, 1995).

Ketterer, David, 'The Corrected *Frankenstein*: Twelve Preferred Readings in the Last Draft', *English Language Notes*, 33/1 (September 1995), 23–35. [Each of these emendations is addressed by footnotes in *1816–1817 Facsimile*—the six that Robinson judges wrong or unnecessary are on transcription pp. 223, 329, 379, 381, 469 and 535; Ketterer himself in 'Frankenstein's "Conversion"' recants on one of these emendations. For other references to Ketterer's emendations, see Robinson's footnotes on transcription pp. 105, 120, 451, 537, 605, 633, 637, 735 and 757 in *1816–1817 Facsimile*.]

——, '(De)Composing *Frankenstein*: The Import of Altered Character Names in the Last Draft', *Studies in Bibliography*, 49 (1996), 232–76. [Some of the errors in this article are corrected in Ketterer's 'Frankenstein's "Conversion"'.]

——, 'Frankenstein: The Source of a Name?', *Science-Fiction Studies*, 22 (1995), 455–6.

——, 'Frankenstein's "Conversion" from Natural Magic to Modern Science—and a *Shifted* (and Converted) Last Draft Insert', *Science-Fiction Studies*, 23 (1997), 1–16. [In this article Ketterer corrects some of his earlier mistakes in 'The Corrected *Frankenstein*' and in '(De)Composing *Frankenstein*'.]

——, *Frankenstein's Creation: The Book, the Monster, and Human Reality*, ELS Monograph Series No. 16 (University of Victoria: English Literary Studies, 1979).

——, '"The Wonderful Effects of Steam": More Percy Shelley Words in *Frankenstein*?', *Science-Fiction Studies*, 25 (1998), 566–8.

Lauritsen, John, *The Man Who Wrote Frankenstein* (Dorchester, MA: Pagan Press, 2007).

LaValley, Albert J., 'The Stage and Film Children of *Frankenstein*: A Survey', in George Levine and U. C. Knoepflmacher (eds), *The Endurance of Frankenstein: Essays on Mary Shelley's Novel* (Berkeley: University of California Press, 1979), 243–89.

Leader, Zachary, *Revision and Romantic Authorship* (Oxford: Clarendon Press, 1996).

Lyles, W. H., *Mary Shelley: An Annotated Bibliography*, Garland Reference Library of the Humanities, Vol. 22 (New York: Garland, 1975).

Macdonald, D. L., *Poor Polidori: A Critical Biography of the Author of* The Vampyre (Toronto: University of Toronto Press, 1991).

Medwin, Thomas, *Memoir of Percy Bysshe Shelley; and Original Poems and Papers by Percy Bysshe Shelley: Now First Collected* (London: Whittaker, Treacher, & Co., 1833).

Medwin, Thomas, 'On "Frankenstein." By the Late Percy Shelley', *The Athenæum: Journal of English and Foreign Literature, Science, and the Fine Arts*, 10 November 1832, 730.

Mellor, Anne K., 'Choosing a Text of *Frankenstein* to Teach', in Stephen C. Behrendt (ed.), *Approaches to Teaching Shelley's Frankenstein* (New York: The Modern Language Association of America, 1990), 31–7.

——, *Mary Shelley: Her Life, her Fiction, her Monsters* (New York: Methuen, 1988). [Mellor treats of the collaboration between MWS and PBS in her third chapter, 'My Hideous Progeny', as well as in her appendix, 'Percy Shelley's Revisions of the Manuscript of *Frankenstein*.']

Morton, Timothy (ed.), *A Routledge Literary Sourcebook on Mary Shelley's Frankenstein* (London: Routledge, 2002).

Murray, E. B., 'Changes in the 1823 Edition of *Frankenstein*', *The Library*, 6th Series, 3 (1981), 320–27.

——, 'Shelley's Contribution to Mary's *Frankenstein*', *Keats–Shelley Memorial Bulletin*, 29 (1978), 50–68.

Nitchie, Elizabeth, *Mary Shelley: Author of 'Frankenstein'* (New Brunswick, NJ: Rutgers University Press, 1953). [Appendix IV (pp. 218–31) reprints Nitchie's *South Atlantic Quarterly* article, 'The Stage History of *Frankenstein*'.]

O'Rourke, James, 'The 1831 Introduction and Revisions to *Frankenstein*: Mary Shelley Dictates her Legacy', *Studies in Romanticism*, 38 (1999), 365–85.

Oxford English Dictionary.

Peck, Walter Edwin, 'Shelley's Reviews Written for the *Examiner*', *Modern Language Notes*, 39 (1924), 118–19.

Picart, Caroline Joan ('Kay') S., Frank Smoot, and Jayne Blodgett, *The Frankenstein Film Sourcebook*, with a foreword by Noël Carroll, Bibliographies and Indexes in Popular Culture, No. 8 (Westport, CT: Greenwood Press, 2001).

Polidori, John William, *The Diary of John William Polidori, 1816, Relating to Byron, Shelley, etc.*, ed. William Michael Rossetti (London: Elkin Matthews, 1911).

Reiman, Donald H. (ed.), *The Romantics Reviewed: Contemporary Reviews of British Romantic Writers (Part C: Shelley, Keats, and London Radical Writers)*, 2 vols (New York: Garland, 1972). [Reiman prints photo-facsimiles of the original reviews of *Frankenstein* in *La*

Belle Assemblée, *Blackwood's Edinburgh Magazine*, *Edinburgh Magazine*, *Knight's Quarterly Magazine* and *Quarterly Review*.]

Robinson, Charles E., 'Editing and Contextualizing *The Frankenstein Notebooks*', *Keats–Shelley Journal*, 46 (1997), 36–44.

——, 'Percy Bysshe Shelley, Charles Ollier, and William Blackwood: The Contexts of Early Nineteenth-Century Publishing', in Kelvin Everest (ed.), *Shelley Revalued: Essays from the Gregynog Conference* (Leicester: Leicester University Press, 1983), 183–226.

——, 'Texts in Search of an Editor: Reflections on *The Frankenstein Notebooks* and on Editorial Authority', in Alexander Pettit (ed.), *Textual Studies and the Common Reader: Essays on Editing Novels and Novelists* (Athens, GA: University of Georgia Press, 2000), 91–110.

St Clair, William, *The Godwins and the Shelleys: The Biography of a Family* (New York: W.W. Norton, 1989). [Reprinted in paperback, Baltimore: Johns Hopkins University Press, 1991.]

——, *The Reading Nation in the Romantic Period* (Cambridge: Cambridge University Press, 2004).

——, 'Shelley Unlocked', *The Times*, 7 March 1981, 8.

Shelley, Mary Wollstonecraft, *Frankenstein* (Abridged), read by James Mason (New York: Caedmon Cassette, 1979).

——, *Frankenstein*, Classics Illustrated Study Guides (originally published as Classics Illustrated no. 26), with an essay by Debra Doyle, PhD (New York: Acclaim Books, 1997).

——, *Frankenstein*, retold in simple language by Raymond Sibley, illustrated by Jon Davis (Loughborough: Ladybird Books, 1984).

——, *History of a Six Weeks' Tour through a Part of France, Switzerland, Germany, and Holland: with Letters Descriptive of a Sail round the Lake of Geneva, and of the Glaciers of Chamouni* (London: T. Hookham, Jun., and C. and J. Ollier, 1817). [A photo-facsimile of this edition was published by Oxford: Woodstock Books, 1989.]

——, *The Journals of Mary Shelley*, ed. Paula R. Feldman and Diana Scott-Kilvert, 2 vols (Oxford: Clarendon Press, 1987). [Reprinted in paperback, with corrections, Baltimore: Johns Hopkins University Press, 1995.]

——, *The Letters of Mary Wollstonecraft Shelley*, ed. Betty T. Bennett, 3 vols (Baltimore: Johns Hopkins University Press, 1980–88).

——, *Mary Shelley: Collected Tales and Stories, with Original Engravings*, ed. Charles E. Robinson (Baltimore: Johns Hopkins University Press, 1976). [Reprinted in paper, Baltimore: Johns Hopkins University Press, 1990.]

——, *The Mary Shelley Reader: Containing Frankenstein, Mathilda, Tales and Stories, Essays and Reviews, and Letters*, ed. Betty T. Bennett and Charles E. Robinson (Oxford: Oxford University Press, 1990). [The text of *Frankenstein* in this volume has a few errors in punctuation because Robinson based the text on the photo-facsimile of *1818* in *1818 Wolf-1* that he later discovered to be flawed.]

Shelley, Percy Bysshe, *The Letters of Percy Bysshe Shelley*, ed. Frederick L. Jones, 2 vols (Oxford: Clarendon Press, 1964).

——, *The Prose Works of Percy Bysshe Shelley*, Volume I, ed. E.B. Murray (Oxford: Clarendon Press, 1993).

Shelley and his Circle 1773–1822, 10 vols to date: I–IV, ed. Kenneth Neill Cameron; V–VI, ed. Donald H. Reiman; VII–X, ed. Donald H. Reiman and Doucet Devin Fischer (Cambridge, MA: Harvard University Press, 1961–).

Smith, Johanna M., '"Hideous Progenies": Texts of *Frankenstein*', in Philip Cohen (ed.), *Texts and Texuality: Textual Instability, Theory, and Interpretation*, Wellesley Studies in Critical Theory, Literary History, and Culture, Vol. 13 (New York: Garland, 1996), 123–42.

Stillinger, Jack, *Multiple Authorship and the Myth of Solitary Genius* (New York: Oxford University Press, 1991).

Sunstein, Emily W., *Mary Shelley: Romance and Reality* (Boston, MA: Little, Brown, 1989). [Reprinted in paperback, Baltimore: Johns Hopkins University Press, 1991, with corrections to 'Appendix B: Mary Shelley's Works' (pp. 409–15).]

Utterson, Sarah Elizabeth Brown, *Tales of the Dead* (London: White, Cochrane, & Co., 1813).

Vail, Jeffery, '"The Bright Sun Was Extinguis'd": The Bologna Prophecy and Byron's "Darkness"', *The Wordsworth Circle*, 28 (1997), 183–92.

Zimmerman, Phyllis, *Shelley's Fiction* (Los Angeles: Darami Press, 1998).